# BLOOD RAGE

# Praise for *Both Ways*

"[T]his sleek paranormal romance introduces Danika Karson, the best vampire hunter on the city's payroll... High points of this fast-paced novel include Danika's relationships with her mother and sister, the smoldering attraction that starts between Danika and Rayne, and detailed worldbuilding. This captivating story draws readers in immediately and keeps them hooked."
—*Publishers Weekly*

"This book was nothing like I imagined and completely outdid my expectations. *Both Ways* is a wonderful read that spikes your heart rate and possibly makes your eyes well up. It is exciting and I cannot wait to see what the future entails for the characters."—*Hsinju's Lit Log*

"Honestly, if you're a fan of the genre, and enjoy pure escapist fun, get this book. You'll enjoy the story, root for all the good guys, cheer the downfall of the bad guys, and look on with interest what happens to those in the moral middle of ambiguity. The action leads you from one thing to the next and you won't want to put the book down. At the end, you'll have had a good time, and will want to see what happens next."—*Lesbian Review*

## By the Author

**SPEAR Mission Files**

Both Ways

Moon Fever

Blood Rage

Visit us at www.boldstrokesbooks.com

# BLOOD RAGE

*by*

Ileandra Young

2024

**BLOOD RAGE**
© 2024 By Ileandra Young. All Rights Reserved.

ISBN 13: 978-1-63679-539-3

This Trade Paperback Original Is Published By
Bold Strokes Books, Inc.
P.O. Box 249
Valley Falls, NY 12185

First Edition: February 2024

---

**CREDITS**
Editor: Ruth Sternglantz
Production Design: Stacia Seaman
Cover Design by Jeanine Henning

Hey Boithing1, Boithing2…
maybe the next one Mummy writes you'll be allowed to read. ;-)

# Chapter One

"...leave your message after the tone, and I'll get back to you as soon as I can."

I can't help but roll my eyes at the pre-recorded voice. But then, what choice do I have? Once more I wait for the tone, then begin to speak.

"Mum? Hi. It's me, again. Danika." Ugh. It hasn't been long enough that she would forget my voice. Has it? "Um. I know you're still upset but...but...please talk to me. Please?"

Voices swirl around me, soft but excited. Something warm and soft, though oddly scaly, drops into my lap. I chance a glance around the room and find several pairs of eyes staring at me expectantly.

Crap, is it my turn?

The coffee table in front of me is covered in an array of cards, one of the piles with two more than when I last looked. The stack of brightly coloured matchsticks serving as currency is also larger.

"Um, yeah, that was it, Mum. Bye, I guess."

I squish the end call button and shove it into a pocket low on the thigh of my trousers.

The tiny, cheerful, and incredibly affectionate chittarik in my lap purrs softly, a rumble of sound that turns slowly into an utterance of my name. "Daaaan. Danika?" she murmurs. "Kar-kar. Karson."

I hug the talkative pest to my chest and nuzzle my chin into the space between her thin, gossamer wings. Cuddling her resembles getting close to a lizard, mixed with a cat, bred with a dragonfly, but I don't care. She's my baby and I adore her. "Thanks, Norma."

From across the table comes an impatient grunt. "Chica, you make us wait? Match or fold? Your hand, it can't be so good. I know so, your bluff is terrible."

"Yeah? Well, Noel, your face is terrible." I shoot back the angry retort without thinking.

Thankfully, both he and the woman at his side snort with laughter rather than offence.

Noel slaps a hand to his mouth, feigning distress. "Aah, so cruel, so cruel. Jadz, my love, she hates me so. She hates me." He stretches tall, then slumps dramatically across his girlfriend. Once there, he murmurs happily and nuzzles his face deeper into her lap.

She smacks him over the top of the head. "Oi. Later, boy. I have a bet to win."

"You will not win."

"I damn well will. And you'll eat those words."

He surfaces long enough to smirk. "I would rather eat *other* things."

"Pig," she murmurs.

"Bitch," he fires back.

Their banter makes me laugh, almost enough to put aside the gnawing sense of loss and pain growing in my chest.

Another week, another phone message.

I've lost count of how many messages I've left for my mother by this point. How many voicemails and handwritten letters, and emails too. I even sent Norma to her house at one point, though in hindsight, that probably wasn't my smartest move.

Mum never did enjoy my choice of pets.

But I can't give up. For one thing, it has never been in my nature, and for another, neither my sister nor my girlfriend will let me. Even if I wanted to.

As Norma claws her way up my shoulder, using all twenty of her damn claws in the process, I glance at the fan of cards I'm holding.

A ten, a three, and a six. All clubs. Hmm.

On the table, a nine, seven, and an eight. In diamonds. Of course. Then beside them, a king and a two, heart and spade respectively.

I force a smile to my lips and push six of my matchsticks into the centre. "I'll see that, and raise. You two are going down."

Jadz drags Noel's head off her lap and shoves him into a sitting position. With her gaze pinned hard on me, she shoves the rest of her matches into the centre. "All in." Her grin is wide and feral, showing off teeth slightly too sharp to be entirely natural. A long wing of dark hair falls across one half of her face, throwing shadows. The blue-black tattoos on the other side of her head, shaved bald, seem to stand out in sharp relief.

I hold the smile, confident. Screw them. Of course I can bluff. I've been a SPEAR for years—this stuff is my bread and butter.

After tutting at his hand, Noel dumps the cards on the table and sits back against the soft cushions of the sofa. "Fold, ladies. I want no fight with you. I know I'll lose, sí?"

I tighten my fingers on the cards. A small motion, but these two will probably notice it. Damn. Well, no choice left now, right?

I push my matchsticks towards hers. "Oh, it's like that, is it?"

"Hell yeah, Queen B."

That makes me laugh. Sure, it might sound like a wonderful compliment in some circles, but *I* know what the *B* stands for.

Norma screeches like a harpy and digs her claws into the side of my neck. Not viciously, of course, but apparently because she knows something I don't. She bends close to my face and rubs the side of her beak against my cheek. "Dan, dan, dan." She seems to sigh.

"What?"

Jadzia Ramachandra, werewolf, poker master, and all-round badass, squeals and claps her hands together like a child. "Why do you do this, Agent? Are you so off your game?" She fans her cards across the table, still grinning.

Well, shit.

A ten and a seven of diamonds nestle among the rest of the selection.

I arch an eyebrow. "Fuck."

She bounces up and down on the sofa, still clapping, before putting out both hands to scoop the matchsticks towards her. "Game, set, match," she says.

"That's tennis."

"Who cares? I win."

Another little sofa bounce, then she turns and hurls herself at Noel. Her lips meet his with crushing force, and the pair of them fall heavily over the arm of the sofa. "I win," she growls. The pair then spend a few seconds whispering into each other's mouths and swapping spit before remembering themselves.

Noel fights his lips free long enough to call out, "Thanks for the game, Dee-Dee." He returns to kissing Jadz with renewed ferocity.

I roll my eyes at the pair of them, not that they can see, and leave my cards on the table when I stand.

The kitchen, when I reach it, is dark and gloomy. I would snap on the light, but the dimness reminds me of the passing time, and a sudden thrill buzzes through me. Norma seems to feel it too, because she chitters low in the back of her throat and taps lightly against my shoulder with her barbed tail.

Yup. Nearly sundown. Time to go home.

On the sideboard lie my car keys and utility belt. The first go into my pocket, the second around my hips, and then I'm striding for the back door. "Thanks for putting up with me, you two. You can go back to shagging now."

A giggle floats through the air but not much else.

Fine. Let them have their fun.

Assuming I can get home with no trouble, I'm about to enjoy plenty of my own.

❖

Back home, Norma flies ahead of me towards the double-reinforced doors. Since sunset has only just arrived, the security system takes an extra few seconds to let us through. To either side, and across the front of the house, blackout shutters rise from the windows on the ground and first floors.

She swoops in, glides back and forth in front of the opening, crooning that throaty cackle I love so much. She's through before they open fully and cuts to the right and out of sight.

I know where she's going. That's where our kitchen is, and my sentiment no doubt matches hers. Food sounds like a great idea.

Inside, the rooms are light and bright, compensating for a lack of natural sunshine with carefully curated fake illumination. Even the windows rotate through beautiful outdoor scenes, including a park at midday, a snowy mountaintop, ocean views, and glittering cities by night.

Rayne's idea. Not my taste exactly, but I can't clearly remember the last time I was able to say no to her. Pippa doesn't seem to mind either, so I let them do what they want with the indoor decor.

Seems only fair when they're the ones who can't go out by day.

As if to think of her is to call her to me, my sister pops her head through the doorway of the room she has taken for her study. She sleeps there too sometimes, and by the fact that she steps out wearing a creased and rumpled trouser suit, I know this was one of those days.

"Another late morning?"

She grunts and drags a hand back through her hair. With effort. It's tangled all over the place. "I lost track of time."

"Don't you have a built-in timer?"

Pip eyes me coolly. "I'm a vampire, not an alarm clock."

"Look who woke up on the wrong side of the coffin today."

"Oh, shut up." She yawns loud and long, and for a second I catch a flash of her fangs. "Do we have any B-pos in?"

I shrug. "We have apple and blackcurrant."

Her eyes briefly flash silver. "Why are you like this?"

"My mama never loved me?"

"Drama queen." She yawns again, stretches, then pads ahead of me towards the kitchen on light, bare feet.

I can't help but giggle. Maybe I should be over it by now—I'm old enough, after all. But messing with my baby sister is too much fun. Especially when she's barely woken up.

Norma sits on her perch near the fridge. There is already food up there for her, or at least I assume there is, because she seems to be eating happily.

I catch sight of a wisp of fur flying through the air and the skinny strand of something that might once have been a tail.

Oh. At least we don't have to worry about mice in this house.

At the large silver fridge, Pip roots through the various neatly labelled medical bags stacked on shelves within. With a triumphant cry, she drags one from the very back of the fridge. "Aha. I knew we had some. Goody, goody."

Pip simply bites through the plastic and sucks from the pack. The redness within oozes and bubbles as it slides into her greedy mouth.

"Animal," I mutter.

The other fridge, smaller and black, houses all the *actual* food in the house. From it I pull a tub of butter and the last two crumpets in a rumpled pack. I shove the latter in the toaster and lean against the sideboard to watch my sister finish her breakfast.

I cock my head. "You know, that's equivalent to just drinking milk straight out of the bottle?"

"So?" She burps. "Not like I plan to share it. Do you think Rayne wants my leftovers?"

I shake my head. "She prefers O-neg."

Pippa drains the blood bag and dumps the carcass in the bio-waste container near the oven. "She's showering, by the way. No doubt she'll be down soon."

Another little thrill hums through me at the thought of my super sexy, naked girlfriend in the shower. "I hope not."

A smirk. Then, "So what did you do all day?"

"Noel and Jadz entertained me for a bit. Poker. Movies. Bitching about Maury." I pull a plate from the cupboard and lay it on the table, ready for my toasted treat.

"Ah, classic workday."

Soft but persistent crunching sounds drift from the top of the fridge. Norma mutters to herself, soft and contented. Mangled bone fragments fall from the sides of her beak.

I really am living with a bunch of monsters. Wonderful, lovable, kind ones...but monsters, just the same.

"I just want to get back to *actual* work."

"Dani—"

I raise my hand. "Please don't. I don't need the lecture from you too. I get it. But I'm allowed to be bored, aren't I?"

"Bored is better than dead."

As if to add weight to the sentiment, the skin on my back abruptly begins to prickle. I twitch my shoulders, a weak attempt to get some friction from my clothing. "But I'm fine. Look at me—you can see that well enough."

"We'll all be able to see later."

I shoot her a questioning look.

Eye roll. "You forgot again, didn't you?" When I continue to stare blankly, she sighs. "You've more tests today. We're running them at Clear Blood after your desk shift."

Ah. Of course.

Another three hours wearing half a gown, exposing my butt to a bunch of scientists, so they can study the marks spanning my back and shoulders. Another three hours being poked and prodded, scraped and jabbed, weighed and measured.

"Pip, I can't—"

"You can. And you will." Her voice becomes stern. "I don't make the rules, but to be honest, I would probably have made this one myself if I had the option. We don't know what that creature did to you and—"

"And he's dead," I cry out. "Dead. Doornail dead. Rayne saw to that."

"Flint Liddell is dead"—she nods—"but the *thing* that came out of him isn't. Come on, Dani, you know this. We've talked about this. We don't know what it is."

She's right. Of course she is. But frustration bubbles through me like lava.

"Well, all these tests aren't helping, are they? We're no closer to learning more than we were weeks ago. Meanwhile I'm wasting away. I'm...I'm losing my mind."

Before I see her move, Pip is in front of me. Her smile is kind and gentle, and her arms, when she wraps them around me, are strong and full of love. I allow her to hold me, to hug me, to let me vent into the huge mass of tangled curls that make up her hair.

"It's going to be okay," she murmurs. "It will. Just give us more time."

"How much longer?" I know I must sound like a child, but I can't help it. "I just want it to be over."

After a moment, I realise she is stroking my back through the layers of clothing.

Though I can't see them, I know her fingers are tracing the lines of the strange marks that absolute creep Flint Liddell carved into my back. Or rather, the thing living inside him.

The thing that still gives me nightmares.

Tall, skinny, black as ichor, and wispy like smoke. The thing with huge yellow eyes and a harsh, grating voice like stones grinding over chunks of shattered glass. The thing that literally crawled out of Flint Liddell's mouth. Tried to crawl into mine.

"Go see Rayne," she says at last. "I know she'll want to see you."

I pull back from the embrace, startled to find faint pink streaks on her cheeks. "Pip…"

She shakes her head. "I'm fine. I'm just…I'm fine."

She's not. Obviously. But I won't push her.

Instead I give her one last squeeze and leave the kitchen.

Behind me, I hear her sniffling, followed by the cooing sounds she always uses when talking to Norma.

And Norma, of course, responds in her usual, gravelly way: "Dan-dan? Nika, kar, kar, dan…"

# CHAPTER TWO

I trudge upstairs with my head bowed, counting each step as I go. The floorboards, though recently buffed, still show scuff marks and signs of heavy use. At the top, on the landing, a long line of framed photographs meets me.

As always, I scan the pictures of myself and Pippa, through varied stages of childhood. My parents. But with them now are shots of myself and Rayne.

The myth about vampires not showing in photographs or mirrors is one I've always enjoyed, but unlike some others, I'm really glad they're not true. I love being able to see Rayne and me like this. Pippa too. The most recent one shows the three of us gathered close around a table in some fancy restaurant. They each hold a spoon above icy goblets of authentic blood sorbet, while I hold my own spoon like a dagger, angled down at a melting lump of rum and raisin ice cream.

Not least is it amusing to note that blood sorbet is even a thing, but I find comfort in recognising that despite our differences, we're still able to experience full and enjoyable lives together.

If only Mum could understand that.

Another picture shows Rayne and me sitting on a checkered blanket in our back garden, gazing at the stars. Pip had been sneaky in taking that one, somehow managing to do so without either of us noticing. That was the only reason she caught the tender moment, the pair of us looking up, with our fingers gently entwined.

But Mum wouldn't understand that either.

Sometimes I can't tell if she's more offended about the vampire part, or the lesbian part. Sometimes I don't dare to think about it overmuch.

Soft singing floats through the air. Light, lilting, and a higher pitch than I could ever hope to reach without a good punch to the tits.

It's some ancient pop song about pieces of love on a Monday or something like that. Cute and peppy.

I love it.

I find myself following the voice towards the closed bathroom door. Soft curls of steam float beneath the tiny strip of space at its base where door meets frame, and the singing now comes with an accompaniment of splashes and water drips.

I lean my forehead to the wood and just listen.

Rayne finishes her last verse with a stunning verbal trill and falls silent.

I imagine her standing beneath the jets, head upturned, soft, choppy hair plastered flat to her head. I see her skin in my mind's eye, so pale compared to mine, soft and smooth. My mind then turns to other parts of her body—slender arms, subtly muscled, meeting at strong shoulders and chest with the most beautiful set of brea—

"Instead of lusting through the door, why not join me?" Rayne's voice is soft but clear, edged with amusement.

Busted.

"How long have you known?"

A giggle. "Since you reached the stairs."

Vampire hearing. How unfair.

I open the door, slip through, then shut it firmly behind me. I'm sure neither of us wants distractions for what is about to follow.

The room, as I suspected, is filled with steam. I like a warm shower, for sure, but Rayne clearly prefers to dance in the fiery depths of hell itself, complete with lava and the oil of a half dozen Carolina Reapers.

Sweat erupts across my skin, while my locs flop limp and weary around my face as they absorb the moisture in the air.

I fan my tee against my chest. "Rayne, for real?"

She giggles and opens the door to the shower compartment. "What? I like to be warm."

"So do I, but isn't sitting in a hydrothermal vent a bit much?"

"Ooh," she murmurs, "been watching the Discovery Channel again?"

I glare.

She crooks her finger in a beckoning gesture.

Well…it would be rude not to.

In record time my clothes are off and on the floor. Soon after, my locs are up and off my neck in the self-secured knot I learned as a child. Then I'm in the shower, yelping as the stinging jets pepper my flesh.

"Please, Rayne?"

She shakes her head but reaches around me to pull the glass door shut before spinning the dial on the temperature controls.

Much better. Merely oven hot, as opposed to solar flare hot.

There's no time to appreciate it, though. Rayne already has her arms around me, her hands slick with sweet smelling body wash. She starts at my neck and shoulders and rubs gently, forming foamy bubbles across my skin.

I lick my lips.

She groans softly. "So, what did you do today?"

Does she really expect me to answer? To form a clear thought while her hands are toying with the underside of my breasts? Circling my nipples?

"I"—cough—"I went"—whimper—"poker..."

A slow smile. "Noel's house?" Her stroking turns to gentle pinching.

"Ye—no. Jadz—"

Back to stroking.

How can she do this to me? So easily? So instantly?

I know my eyes are glazed, I know my mouth is hanging open, but I can't help it. I try to lick my lips again, but my mouth is dry, despite the shower and heat.

"What's wrong, Danika?"

Fuck, when she says my name like that...

"I—"

She's not stroking or pinching any more. She's rubbing shower gel into my body again, carefully soaping my sides and hips with her fingers splayed. My tail bone. The base of my stomach. My thighs.

I barely realise I've parted my legs until her forehead bumps against my pubic bone. When did she get to her knees?

Oh, right. My eyes are closed.

When I pry them open, I find Rayne crouched low in the shower, balanced perfectly on the balls of her feet. Her hands are on the outsides of my thighs, her mouth oh-so close to the place I've dreamed of all fucking day. But her eyes are on me, steady and intense.

If I had thought the shower was hot, I now know how wrong I was. That was nothing. This? Her gaze on mine? *That* is real heat.

Never once breaking eye contact, she leans closer, closer still, until her lips brush the damp curls between my thighs.

My legs tremble.

She grips tighter.

"Danika?"

"Yes?" The cracks in my voice turn a single syllable word into three.

"Hold on to something."

I barely have time to brace my hands against the shower walls before her tongue is on me, a slow, languid dance against the very core of me that forces my head back and my eyes open wide.

I'm gasping, keening, trembling, whimpering, and Rayne is silent but for the slow, skilful lap of her tongue and the low needy growl growing in the back of her throat.

Somewhere in the lost depths of rational thought, I think *vampire hearing* and *Pippa downstairs*, but when Rayne's forefinger and thumb move to join her tongue, all thoughts flee my mind on a fizzing bolt of pleasure.

Soon my pleasured cries fill the small space, barely dampened by the heavy steam, while my body jerks back and forth on the skilled surface of Rayne's lashing tongue.

❖

When next I open my eyes, I realise I'm sitting down. My legs must have given out ages ago. Rayne cradles me against her, somehow managing to support and envelop me with her smaller, delicate frame.

The pounding of the shower has slowed to a more reasonable trickle, and the steam has given way just enough to see more features of the room.

She's stroking my hair, whispering something against the side of my neck. Once or twice she nips at my ear, playful and harmless, while her other hand fondles my breasts.

At last, my pleasured brain fog clears enough for me to hear what the hell she's saying. Something about food and messages. Work.

Great.

I nuzzle deeper into her embrace. "Give me a minute."

"Another? We've been here forty minutes."

"Seriously?"

"Mmm. Pippa even checked on us at one point."

Embarrassment snaps my head up. "She came in?"

"No, no. She called from the bottom of the stairs."

Ah. Vampire hearing.

"Fuck." I raise my voice a little. "Sorry, sis."

Rayne cocks her head, as if listening. A moment later, she chuckles. "She said don't worry about it, but that maybe telling your mother how often you pray to God would get her to speak to you again."

I have no need to see my sister to know she must be giggling her head off. Rayne is too, and I lean away from her warmth and her hands to finally take my feet.

Ah. Better. Now I can actually think without being led by my libido.

I stretch a few kinks and tensions out of my legs and arms, then step out of the shower. The mirror above the sink is entirely fogged up, so I wipe it clear with my hands.

There. My face, soft with relaxation and leftover pleasure, flushed too, just like the rest of me. I can feel the sensitivity of it as the air finally begins to cool around me.

I sigh.

"Better?" Rayne hasn't left the shower. Instead she stands on the tiles with an ice scraper in hand, quickly running the rubber blade down the glass panels to clean them.

Funny, but I never thought about how much easier it is to clean a bathroom when doing it each day. Without fail, after each shower, she will use the scraper to scoot the water down towards the plughole, leaving the shower glass sparkling. She usually does the mirror while cleaning her teeth.

Just one of those small domestic touches that mark her as a real-ass grown-up. Unlike me.

"Much, thanks. But what about you?"

She shakes her head. Water droplets fly. "I want some time to chill before work. Plus, if you're going to pass out after every orgasm, we need a hell of a lot more time to get to me. You know I prefer to leave you well-satisfied."

"Hey, it wasn't just one."

"My point remains."

I take the ice scraper as she holds it towards me and dutifully clean off the mirror. I have been well-trained.

"Well, if *you* can still function after six back to back, then you're a stronger woman than me."

She arches an eyebrow. "Six? Pretty sure I counted nine."

This time I know damn well I'm flushed all over. I can tell because Rayne starts laughing maniacally.

"You counted?"

"Actually, *you* did. But somewhere between seven and eight you started to lose coherent speech."

I leave the ice scraper on its dedicated hook—*very* well-trained—and snag a pair of towels from the drying rack. "Well I...I..."

"Yes?"

"Oh, shut up."

I toss her a towel, then wrap the second around myself and flounce out of the bathroom. I'm not upset, of course not, but I think us living together has made Rayne far more of a tease than ever she was. Maybe I've been doing some training of my own.

I head to my room first to quickly dry off, moisturise, and try to do something with my locs. They're heavy with moisture, so I bind the whole lot in the towel and help myself into a set of pyjamas. I'm not going to bed immediately, but there's no point getting dressed again. It's not like I have a night shift to head out for.

When Rayne joins me, she is already dressed and ready for her day—night—carrying my discarded clothes and utility belt. She leaves the lot on my bed, then stops in front of me for a gentle, tender kiss. "Breakfast?"

"We have some O-neg in, and I've got...oh. Bugger."

She looks the question at me.

"I had crumpets. I left them in the toaster."

"Oops."

One more kiss, then she hurries me down the stairs towards the kitchen. On the way past the living room, I spy Pip, her attention focused on a tall, old, and worn looking book. The leather cover is cracked and flaking, the pages delicate and crispy in their yellowness. She handles it like spun glass, barely using her fingertips to turn the pages.

"What's that?"

"Research," she calls, without looking up. "And Norma is helping with breakfast."

Norma is? The chittarik with more gusto and bravery than common sense?

I follow Rayne into the kitchen and, sure enough, find Norma perched on the side of the toaster. She is digging in one of the slots with her claws, fighting to reach the savoury treat within. Fascinated, I watch her lever it up high enough to grab in her powerful, hooked beak. Then, with a satisfied cackle, she flies her prize across the room and drops it on the plate I took out earlier.

Rayne grins as she opens the silver fridge. "Good girl, Norma. Aren't you? Yes, you are. You are. Such a good girl, so, so good."

"Nika, dan, kar-kar," she yells back.

I'm not so sure. Considering what I saw Norma munching earlier, in all its raw, gory glory, I don't know that I want to eat anything that she's carried with her mouth. Still, the sentiment is well-meaning and adorable.

"Thanks, Norma. I'll get the other one."

But my pet is having none of it. She returns to the toaster and perches again, using the same jabbing trick to reach the second crumpet. This time, her weight lands on the depressing arm of the toaster, and a soft red glow fills the slots.

"*Dan,*" Norma bellows, seemingly enraged at the hindrance to her plan. Again she tries to shove her beak into the slot.

"Whoa, you bloody moron, come here." I snatch her bristling, struggling form off the toaster, just as smoke starts to curl from the barbs on the end of her tail.

"Nika-nika-nika-nika-nika-ni—"

I trap her beak closed with my thumb and forefinger. "Oi. I get it, but don't burn yourself, you daft thing."

A low groan from under my fingers. I release her beak. Slowly.

"Nika-nika-nika-nika-nika-nika-nika-ni—"

Rayne looks up from her own meal, chilled O-neg blood poured neatly into a mug, to consume like the sophisticated lady she is. "I think she wants to help."

"*I* think she needs to get a grip before she kills herself. Freaking pest."

One hand secure on Norma's wriggling body, I use the other to pop the toaster slot and fish the now burned crumpet out myself. "There. Happy?"

"Nika." Her gravelly voice is sad and soft. "Dan, kar, dan-dan."

"I know, baby, I know." I stroke her head. "But you don't hurt yourself, all right? Never, ever do that."

She turns her head to give me the full weight of her beady-eyed stare. She seems to gaze right into my soul. "Danika Karson," she intones solemnly.

I roll my eyes and bump her up to her true favourite perch, the top of my head. "Thank you."

Rayne sits across from me, smirking into her mug. Her gaze flicks towards my plate.

The unburned crumpet is mangled and torn, with a tuft of soft, brown fur sticking out of one of the many holes. A tiny chip of bone sits on top, gleaming white and slightly bloody. The second crumpet is a holey lump of blackened carbon, a true trypophobic nightmare.

"Bon appétit?" Rayne murmurs.

I sigh.

# CHAPTER THREE

One bacon sandwich later finds Rayne and me cuddled together on the sofa. Norma lies beside us, curled into a tight, sleepy ball, with her wings waving gently at each soft breath.

We still have a little time before Rayne has to head to HQ, so we use it to watch TV, chat gently about nonsense, and occasionally snog like teenagers. Even now she has one hand tucked into the neck of my pyjama top, while my hands play gently over her thighs. The TV is set to local news, with more coverage on the ongoing efforts of SPEAR to recover from the Werewolf Wars.

Such a gross way to describe the colossal fuck-up of a few weeks prior, but then we humans have always had this burning need to lay names to things, as though that might make them less awful.

It doesn't, though. Because every time some newsreader in a suit stands in the wreckage of The Bowl, I see some signs of the fallout. Sure, it was a mess before, with people sleeping in doorways and burned-out cars lining the streets, but now? The people are changed. Now they walk stoop-backed and shuffling, or quick and sneaky, with frightened glances over their shoulders. At least before, the inhabitants of the area felt safe and secure. Now, if anybody is on the streets at all, they aren't there for long, moving quickly towards their destination with the aim of creating as few ripples as possible.

Though the screen doesn't show it, I know that the newsreader, with her perfectly styled hair and fancy microphone, is standing in a circle of at least seven police officers. Maybe even a SPEAR agent or two, with their gazes turned outward, hands on weapons, poised to tackle any threat.

Rayne squeezes me gently. "Stop it."

"What?"

"You're grinding your teeth. And I feel you getting tense. Stop it."

I stretch my mouth open to wriggle my bottom jaw. Damn it, she's right. "Sorry."

"Don't be sorry—just, take a breath."

I do, but it doesn't help. Instead my gaze picks out more detail on-screen, more specifically, the carcass of an abandoned kids' play area, with a gutted swing set and broken roundabout.

My gut tightens.

"Danika—"

"Do they have to do it there?" I splutter. "Right there? In that spot? Where Wendy and I used to—"

She grips me tighter, as tears threaten to fill my eyes. Her body is soft, warm too after the meal and blistering shower, a comfort that I abruptly need more than I have all day. She doesn't speak, just holds me, waiting for me to breathe it all out.

The newsreader turns to indicate something behind her, but I don't even hear her at this point.

Instead I hear howls—loud, haunting, animalistic calls of rage and pain. I hear the crack of gunfire and the wet squelch of flesh shredded by huge, angry claws. Cries. Sobs. The pained wails of a young soul mourning their father figure.

"Rayne, I—"

"No, you didn't." She cuts across me firmly. "It's not your fault."

I bite my lip over the automatic objection already brimming on my tongue.

Not my fault.

Sure, not my fault that my actions led the much-respected, longest standing alpha of the Dire Wolf pack to his death at the hands of a cruel and brutal enemy. Not my fault that his young second in command is now crippled for life, both as a wolf and a human. Can't be my fault that the entire pack is now led by a monster who, if given half the chance, would eat my face, heart, and guts without a second thought.

Nope. Not my fault.

"Danika." Rayne's voice has a bite in it now. "Look at me."

When I finally lift my gaze to hers, a small ripple of peace washes over me.

Her eyes, always so beautiful, seem more so in this moment. All the colours of autumn meet in her eyes and swirl into a brown so deep, so stunning that it near steals my breath. But more than that is the love there. The quiet, but obvious desire to see me well.

"Wensleydale Gordan was a strong, powerful man," she murmurs, "and an intelligent, ferocious werewolf. Even without the drug, you had no control over his actions."

I look away. "He was bound to me. I could have forced him to stay home."

"And in so doing, destroyed any love or respect he ever had for you. The battle was his choice. Don't take that on to yourself."

I've heard this so many times, from Rayne, from Pippa, from the SPEAR therapist Maury insists I see once a week, on top of all the other nonsense he's using to keep me away from active duty.

Maybe one day I'll believe it. But not today.

"I miss him." My voice cracks.

"I know you do." Rayne doesn't apologise or try to fill the silence that follows with platitudes or feel-goods. Instead, she holds me, just holds me, while the voices on the TV continue to murmur through their local news.

We're still sitting like that when the scene on-screen shifts to the news studio in which two more newsreaders sit in high-backed chairs before a projected photo of an old church.

"And in other news, an abandoned church in the small village of Moarwell has finally been restored. Six years of crowdfunding and volunteer work by members of the community have restored the building to its once former glory."

The picture changes to show the interior of a church with large stained-glass windows in all the outer walls. Lower down, beneath the vaulted ceiling, the stations of the cross are picked out in finely detailed wooden carvings all around the back of the nave.

"The first incarnation of Saint Peter's Church dates back to the early 1400s and is said to look very much as it does now. The chief project leaders, Kimberly and Bruce Dixon, paid particular attention to old images of the building in order to recreate it as closely and authentically as possible. In most cases, where stone required replacement, materials were excavated from old quarries and caves in the local area, much as they would have been hundreds of years ago."

Rayne jerks bolt upright.

The sharp motion dislodges me from her lap and causes Norma to wake with a shriek. She darts around the room like a crazy thing before landing on the rim of a tall lamp near the window. Her expression is one of cool distaste and disappointment.

"Rayne, what—"

She jerks a hand up to silence me and stares intently at the screen.

Baffled, I follow her gaze and listen to the article continue. Back in the field, yet another reporter stands in front of the church, speaking to a man and woman, with soft, gentle expressions and greying hair. The woman is short, round, and dimpled, while the man is tall, thick in the shoulders, and as hairy as a grizzly, with hands sized to match.

The pair speak brightly, occasionally pausing to indicate some detail about the church and the restorations.

Eventually, the woman claps her hands together and speaks in a voice soft, excited and oddly familiar. "*And to celebrate, we've been given special permission to hold a function on the premises. Our oldest daughter, Viola, will be getting married here. It's going to be beautiful.*"

Rayne chokes. On what I've no idea, but her body is so stiff and still now, that if not for that sound, I could be forgiven for thinking she had disappeared entirely.

"Rayne—"

Again she stops me without even looking, still focused on the screen.

The man grins at the reporter. "*Our small community came together to build something beautiful, so it's only right that we all celebrate it together. So the after-party is open to all locals, though the service itself will be restricted to friends and family.*"

The three strangers continue to speak, now gushing over specific features of the church and how many of them were handmade by craftsmen of the village.

The feature ends with another shot of the exterior of the church, this time with the man and the woman—presumably Bruce and Kimberly Dixon—standing outside it, with two others I've not yet seen.

The news programme returns to the studio, but the voices are cut short when Norma, still angry at being woken, flits across the room and lands hard on the remote control. Whatever button she presses with her heavy backside turns off the TV entirely, leaving it to stare back at us like a blank glass eye.

Rayne slumps against the sofa, her gaze wide and distant.

"Rayne, for crying out loud, what? You look like you've seen the rising sun."

Slowly, she turns to me, soft brown eyes filled with an emotion I can't quite place. "Mama and Bubi," she murmurs.

"What?"

"My parents…that's them. Bubi. Mama." She continues to stare at the black screen.

I scramble to catch up. "I thought your parents were jailed drug addicts."

"My foster parents." She stands, sending me half flying as she darts across the room to begin pacing back and forth. "Bruce and Kimberly Dixon, my parents."

"Oh."

I want to say more, but I've no idea how. So I don't. Instead, I watch as she strides back and forth in front of me, tangling her hands in her still-damp hair.

"They fixed the church. I wasn't sure they'd ever finish. It's beautiful."

I'm still behind. "I thought your name was Friedman."

"My birth name. I didn't take theirs when I lived with them." She's moving faster now, her bare feet slamming hard against the rug.

"But what's wrong? Why are you so...?" The words die on my lips as she finally turns to look at me.

The odd expression lifts and is replaced instead by one of wonderment and joy. "Viola. Little baby Viola...My sister is getting married."

## Chapter Four

I risk a smile. "But…that's good, right? The marriage, I mean. That means she—Viola?—is happy and has found someone she really loves. Doesn't it?"

Rayne nibbles on her bottom lip. Her eyes take on the smallest edge of silver that pulses once before ebbing away. "I can't believe it. I didn't think she ever would."

"Okay, Rayne, calm down for a moment. You're going to need to give me more detail. Sit with me?"

She does at last, but I can feel how excited she is. Her body is animated and lively in a way it rarely is and her smile keeps growing. "When I…left home, Viola was so young. I mean, nineteen isn't *young* exactly, but she felt young, if you understand me. She was so innocent and sweet. And her paramour Harlow was just the same. They were so good for each other."

Her smile is infectious. "That's great. And they have the full support of your parents too, from the looks of things."

"And the village too." Rayne leans back into the sofa, staring at her fingers. "That church restoration has been a project for as long as I remember. Maybe even before I arrived there. Mama would always talk about how beautiful it would be when done."

"It looked pretty enough."

"I wish I could see it. Even I did some work in there, cutting wood planks for floorboards in the lower levels."

I cock my head at her. "So go visit. I bet they'd be pleased to see you."

"Danika…"

"What?"

She faces me, lips slightly parted. A quick blink of her eyes fills them with silver yet again, and her lips draw back further to showcase neat little fangs. "I'm unsure I'll be welcome there."

"But—"

Rayne places a hand on my knee. "Moarwell is not like Angbec, Danika. They'll accept Viola and Harlow, perhaps, but more than that is asking them for too much."

"So they don't know? Your parents, I mean?"

The hand on my knee flexes hard, squeezing. I don't think she even notices.

"Rayne—"

"When I left, it was because Vixen…" She struggles to finish, and I know exactly why. I wouldn't want to dwell overmuch on the evil vampire who tore me from my life for her own evil schemes.

"I know." I keep my voice low and gentle.

"She brought me to Angbec so quickly. It was a blur. I had no time to say goodbye, and even if I had, what could I possibly say?"

Though she phrases it as a question, I know full well I'm not supposed to answer. So I keep my mouth shut. Eventually she goes on.

"I was afraid. And it was so new. And Vixen made such broad and expansive plans to find our place in the human world that I simply couldn't…" She sniffs. "I wrote them a short, cowardly, and deeply dishonest letter."

More silence.

As if sensing the turn in mood, Norma inches over to crawl into Rayne's lap. She tucks her scaly head beneath her chin and curls her barbed tail in to stroke Rayne's limp arm.

I want to do the same. But I wait.

"I told them I had found a job with the police force that required me to go undercover. I said they wouldn't be able to contact me for a long time, but that I was safe and happy. That I would contact them if and when I could."

"How long ago was that?"

She can barely look at me.

"Rayne?"

"Six months."

I exhale a heavy breath. "Shit."

She nods.

"Well, it's not that long, right?" I try to rationalise it out. "It could easily have been an undercover sting? I don't know how civvie bashers do these things, but that's surely a reasonable length of time."

"But they don't know about Vixen."

She says Vixen, but I know that's not what she truly means. Head of a fast-growing, and cruel nest of vampires, Vixen had once planned to stage a coup in Angbec in an attempt to put vampires on top. Her plan had been to convert humans in positions of power and use them as her new vampire minions to extend her reach across the city. At one point, she even held a stranglehold on Jackson Cobé by funding his campaign to become mayor.

It was all going well for her too, until she found Rayne. Rayne, who had quickly realised the dangerous nature of her maker's plans and joined forces with me to stop her. Which we did.

Or rather, *I* did. When I cut off her head with a battleaxe.

"They don't know what she did to you? What you are?"

Rayne shakes her head. "I told them it was drugs. Neither of them are fond of drugs, and given my history, I knew they wouldn't ask questions."

It made sense. I had learned much earlier that Rayne's birth mother had been a prostitute and her father some random cocaine dealer her mother had the major misfortune of owing a favour. The poor woman had paid her debt, using her body as currency, and nine months later…Well.

I shake my head, as if to knock the thoughts out of them.

"But your dad—Bruce, was it? You said he's a Rancher. He's used to dealing with *edanes*."

She gives a distressed little cry. "It has never been about that. Vampires, werewolves, goblins, sprites, he's met them all." A long, pained pause. "They think I'm dead."

Words die on my tongue. My lips part into a soft, silent O of surprise.

She buries her head in her hands. "I didn't know what to do. I didn't want them looking for me, not with Vixen so hateful towards humans. I didn't want to hurt them either—you remember what I was like back then." A single red tear slides down her cheek. "If they believed for even one moment that I needed their help, they would have looked for me. And Vixen would have…"

I grip her hands as the words fail. I know all too well what Vixen would have done. Old and powerful, prideful and violent, she would have had them killed in an instant. Or fed them to her followers as a live snack. Hell, she tried to do it to me once. And to Pippa.

"It's okay," I whisper. "It's all right."

"I forged a letter. Convinced another of the vampires in the nest to play a role on the phone. We told them I died in the field and that there were no remains."

"Holy shit."

She sniffs. "They couldn't even mourn me with a proper funeral. But I saw them when they received the news. My Bubi…I'd never seen him cry before. Ever. And Mama couldn't speak for hours afterwards. She collapsed and sobbed on the ground until my sisters carried her out. It was awful."

An understatement if ever I heard one.

Gently, I curl my arms around her and let her body sink down against mine. She's shaking now, misery and guilt blending to make her seem frail and pitiful.

"You've never told me this before."

She wipes the back of her hand across her nose. "I didn't want to relive it. I'm sure you understand that better than most."

I sure do. The memory of my father's death haunts me to this very day, and even with fresh perspective, it's hard to ignore the effect it had on the course of my life.

"Viola took it so much worse than anybody else. We had always been the closest, though there were several years between us. We had been with the Dixons together the longest." Her words crack. "And now, she's getting married, and I can't be there."

Her words dissolve into sad little sniffles, and I just hold her. I stroke her still-damp hair, croon the most comforting nonsense I can think of, while letting her work through it all. And in the middle of it, Norma sits between us, her fine, glittering wings beating gently against our faces.

❖

Several minutes pass before either of us moves again, Rayne first, gathering herself together with two sharp coughs and a businesslike swipe of her tear-streaked face.

"Sorry," she murmurs, "that's unlike me."

I wave aside the apology. "It's okay to feel, Rayne. Good grief, you're only human."

She pins me with a dry look.

I wince and rush on. "But maybe it's not so bad. After all, you were right."

Confusion fills her eyes.

"Think about it. You *did* die." I speak faster now, suddenly caught up with the best idea I've ever had in the history of all my marvellous ideas. "Vixen changed you, and if Clear Blood studies are to be believed, it is a type of death."

"Perhaps but—"

"And it was in the line of work. You told me—Vixen first found you when you were acting as additional security. More than that, it makes sense when you say there were no remains, because…well…there aren't. You're right here. You're still living, existing, being awesome, and protecting the people who can't protect themselves."

Rayne sits straight. "What are you saying?"

"You should go. To the wedding, I mean."

Her eyes widen. "I couldn't—"

"Of course you could." I can't stop now—the idea is too exciting, too perfect. "You go back there and explain what happened. You can even tell them that it was for their own safety. Not a lie, right? And you can explain that you needed time to adjust to your new life-state before going back. I'm sure they'd understand."

"Danika—"

"Your father is a Rancher. Your mother is married to one. They get it. They'll understand. Imagine how happy they'll be to see you well."

"You don't even know them. How can you say that?"

"No, but I know you. And they're the ones who raised you, right? So I have a good sense of the type of people they are. Imagine the joy you could bring them by telling them the truth."

Rayne stares at her fingers. Dainty and slender, they match the rest of her perfectly, but for the faint red smears from where she wiped away earlier bloody tears.

"It's not that simple. Bubi might be a Rancher, but that wasn't *in* the family. His work with *edanes* was always so distant and detached. It's different when it's family."

"You think they'd reject you?"

"No…" She says it slowly, as though thinking it through.

"Then what's the problem?"

"There is no problem. Or rather, my family isn't the problem. But they live in Moarwell."

She stops and I wait. When no further information is forthcoming I nudge her with my elbow.

"So?"

"Moarwell isn't like Angbec. In fact I don't think there's *anywhere* like Angbec. It's not about my family but the people of the village. If they learn my family have any connection to *edanes*, beyond professional ones, they could be ostracised. Shunned. They might even lose their license to foster."

"What?" This nonsense slaps hard, like a smack to the face. "That's stupid, I—"

"Have you ever left Angbec?" Rayne murmurs.

I have to pause at that. The question gives me sudden verbal whiplash, and I struggle to pull myself into this new conversation.

"Yeah, of course I have. Why?"

"But have you ever *lived* outside Angbec? Or visited any smaller towns?"

I shrug. "Sure. In fact, we did it together before Wendy...I mean before. Remember, we went to that small town down south to clear chittarik hatchlings from a storm drain?"

She smiles. "Oh, they were so cute."

"They were pests. But at least Norma was able to make herself useful for once."

My pet lifts her head in my direction, chittering softly at the back of her throat, before settling in closer to Rayne again. The pocket flap of skin beneath her chin flares slightly as she breathes.

"She made a great surrogate dam. Those hatchlings survived purely because of her."

And indeed they had. Norma took in the clutch with no prompting at all, cleaning them, feeding them, teaching them as though they were her own. Despite myself it had been a little sad to see them go.

"But that's not what I'm talking about." Rayne pins me with a firm look. "We only *visited* that village for a short time, we didn't stay. We didn't even have much of an opportunity to speak with the locals. We arrived, we picked up the hatchlings, and we left."

"So?"

"So you've no experience of what it is truly like living outside of a city like this." Rayne's voice takes on a frustrated edge. "Of visiting a place where some people still don't believe *edanes* are real."

I snort. "Oh, come on, don't they watch the news? Have they opened their eyes?"

"Danika, I'm serious. Moarwell is one of those places. *Edanes* are a weird and wonderful fairy tale for children or inpatients. Bubi might have been a Rancher, but it was never comfortable for him. It was a fight. Every day."

"So you can't go back home because some idiots in your hometown can't get with the times? The Interspecies Relations Act passed more than five years ago. Did they miss the memo?"

Serious and unblinking, Rayne stares me down. "If the locals of Moarwell learn of my family's connection to me, they could be run out of town."

I nod decisively. "Guess that means we'll have to be subtle when we go over there."

"What?" Rayne's eyebrows shoot towards her hairline. Even

Norma gives a grumpy little snort and glares at me with her head cocked to one side. "You can't be serious."

I stand. "Of course I am. Why should you have to miss your sister's wedding just because a bunch of middle-aged idiots haven't noticed the world changing around them?"

"But—"

"But nothing. You should visit them. You should see your little sister before her wedding, and you should get the chance to see your parents again."

"I can't."

"Of course you can. We'll go tomorrow, stop in for a day or two, give you some time to be with them and reconnect. No one will even know we're there."

"We?" Rayne's voice becomes a high squeak. "You're coming too?"

"Of course. As if I'd let you do something like that without any emotional support. Who do you think I am?"

As if I'd pass up the opportunity to get away from SPEAR and tests and the pitying looks of my old team, for a couple of days. But I keep that part to myself.

"Think about it. We'll just book into a B & B somewhere on the edges and go into Moarwell to visit. I could even contact them beforehand to warn them we're coming, rather than just showing up." I snap my fingers. "In fact, yeah, I think that's better. I'll tell them who I am and that I have some information about Emily Friedman. And then we can meet them together and give you a chance to reintroduce yourself as who you really are."

Rayne goes very quiet. And still. It's that creepy, spooky stillness that only *edanes* are capable of. The sudden cessation of every sign that the woman before me is a living creature and not a beautiful, lifelike statue.

Her lips part, and I watch a small string of saliva stretch between them before breaking. She's nervous.

"I don't know."

"I do." The idea is firmly rooted now. I can't stop myself from grinning and pacing back and forth across the rug in front of her.

Norma leaves Rayne's side and hops to the ground beside me, matching each of my steps with five of her own, trotting back and forth in the wake of my pacing.

"Don't you want to see them again?"

"Of course I do, but—"

"And don't you want to go to Viola's wedding?"

"Danika," she snaps.

The words die on my lips.

She unfurls gracefully from the sofa and walks up to meet me. Her skin is soft and warm against mine as she grips my hands in hers.

"Stop. Calm down."

"But—"

"No"—her voice takes on the tiniest growl—"I'm speaking now."

I slap my lips shut with a meek *mm-hmm* sound.

She stares up at me for long, thoughtful seconds. Her gaze is deep and piercing, her expression pensive. At last she shifts her grip on my fingers to lift my hands to her lips. She kisses the back of each one in turn. "Thank you. Truly. I know you mean well and that the idea excites you, but it isn't as simple as all that. There is so much for me to consider."

My lips tremble with the effort to keep them closed.

"I have to go to work now. Maury wants me to look over a few new files from the Fire Fangs, and even the Dire Wolves have a meet with us."

All thoughts of family, weddings, and small rural villages fly from my mind.

"The Dire Wolves? You mean Aleksandar?"

Rayne's hands tighten on mine, as though she senses my flare of anger.

"He's still under the terms of his community service agreement with City Hall. He's required to check in with us three times a week."

"He and I need a quiet word."

"The pair of you need to stay away from each other for the foreseeable. That's another of the terms he's operating under."

"I'll break his neck."

"He'll eat your face," she says simply.

I laugh. Can't help it. It's so very odd to hear her talk like me, even for a moment.

And just like that, the growing tension and distress bubbles to its head and breaks.

Her hands loosen on mine, and at their loss I jab my fingers into the warmth of my underarms. "I hate this."

"I know," she murmurs. "But those files are for you, so I need you rested before your day shift. So will you try to get some rest?"

I wag a finger at her. "That was slick, Rayne, but don't think we're done. I think seeing your family would be good for you and—"

"And rest is good for you. You'll need some sleep before the next round of tests."

Eye roll. Ugh. I'd almost forgotten about those.

She steps away then and smiles a small half-smile. "Will you at least try?"

"I guess. If I can't even win a game of poker, then maybe I really am tired."

Rayne has already found her coat and shrugged into it. A moment later, she's feeding her feet into ankle high boots with a zip up the side. "You can't play poker."

I follow her into the hallway and lean against the wall. "Of course I can. We play all the time."

"Perhaps." She taps her bottom lip with the tip of her finger. "But you were playing with Noel and Jadzia, I assume?"

"Of course." I toss my head. "Who the hell else isn't at work right now?"

Rayne nods as though confirming a long considered thought. "Well…Noel has known you for years, and Jadzia is a Grey Tail, so it's a little unfair, wouldn't you say?"

What the ever-loving hell is she talking about?

Spying my expression, Rayne grins and slings a bag over her shoulder. "Wow, you really are tired. Rest. Please. I'll see you before sunup." She darts over and pushes up on tiptoe to press a dainty kiss to the side of my cheek.

"Um, yeah, I guess."

I watch her leave, trying to figure out exactly what she's talking about. Only when she has walked fully out of sight does the truth hit me.

I gasp. Frown. Stamp my foot.

"Fuck's sake, Noel!"

Fuming, I march back into the kitchen to snag my phone from the table where I left it earlier. I open up the messaging app and fire off a quick text: *Oi, dickface. I want my matchsticks back.*

Only a minute or two passes before the response arrives: *Oh, sore loser, chica. Jadz and I will happily play again for you to make back your little sticks.*

I grit my teeth. *Screw you. Jadz is a Grey Tail. She can smell when I'm lying, you sneaky little shit.*

A few more minutes. The next response to hit my phone is a long line of cry-laugh emoji.

Ugh. Maybe I *am* tired.

The phone trills again, with a second, even longer line of cry-laugh emoji. And a pointing finger.

I leave the phone on the table and stomp towards my bedroom. Halfway there, Norma catches up with me and flies up to my shoulder to rub her face against my cheek in what she probably hopes is a comforting way.

"Yeah, you're right," I murmur to the faithful pest. "Sleep it is. At least for a couple hours."

"Dan, dan, nika, dan," says Norma in her most helpful tone.

# Chapter Five

Cold again. Like always. The only windows funnel frigid air through the entire house. It lifts tablecloths, rustles curtains, and jerks framed photos from their wall hooks. In the middle of it stands a tall, broad-shouldered figure with locs just like mine, though longer and streaked with grey. A figure in the familiar colours of store security.

"Daddy?"

Oh. That voice doesn't sound like mine. It's smaller, almost dainty. In fact, everything about me is petite and childlike, from my hands to my pretty toes, locked into patent leather sandals. And my locs aren't even locs yet, just a wild tangle of dense curls unsuccessfully tamed into cornrows.

Then I'm flying, swept into the air by the big man and his strong, fatherly arms.

"Bean," he cries.

I laugh and cling to him, playing my fingers through the long lengths of his hair. "Daddy, where did you go? I've not seen you in forever and evers."

"Forever and evers?" A laugh. "That's a very long time."

"I know. I missed you."

He strokes my cheek gently. "I know, Bean. I missed you too. But..." The stroking stops. Becomes a rough prodding. Then a scratching. "But it's your fault."

"Daddy?"

But he's holding tighter now, pinning me to him with one great bear arm, while the other hand pries my mouth open.

"Your fault." His words are a rattling hiss, like gravel rolling through the inside of empty tin cans. "I'm gone now. Because of you. You did it. You did."

"Da—" But he chokes my words with his fingers. Shoves the huge digits between my lips and holds them open.

"Your fault, Danika." His mouth hangs open, and dark smoke begins to billow out. Small threads at first, which grow quickly into longer and thicker threads like snakes. Snakes that curl and wind their way towards my open mouth.

I try to scream. The sound is stuck.

I wriggle. Kick at empty air.

The smoke snakes glide between my parted lips and straight down, filling me, choking me.

More smoke billows in inky-black clouds, thick and sooty and heavy with the scent of death and decay.

Through it all, my father's eyes gleam sunshine yellow, each cut in half by the long, narrow slit of a reptilian pupil.

"Be still, Bean. My bird. Bean bird. Little bird."

Screams claw from my gut, forced up and through the billowing smoke, but the more air leaves my body, the more of that awful stuff goes in. More and more, filling me, tainting me, corrupting me.

The skin across my back erupts with white hot pain.

I can't see. Can't think. Can't breathe. Can't move.

"Your fault, little bird. And I'm coming for you. For you, little bird. I'm coming. I'm coming."

My last scream morphs into terrified whimpers of agony and terror and a single, plaintive cry.

"No—!"

❖

I grab at the smoke, the tendrils, the source of my pain. My hands close on something warm and scaly. My entire body shudders with revulsion.

Shoulders tense, I tighten my grip and prepare to throw.

"Dan, dan, dan, dan, dan dan—"

An instant later my fingers flex. Release. Norma lands hard on my face, shrieking and batting her tiny claws against my cheeks.

I have just the presence of mind not to shove her away before I finally come to my senses. I'm awake. There is no smoke. Or yellow eyes. Or forced ingestion of some strange, otherworldly force.

There are tears, though. And sweat. I'm caked in both, and my body shudders with it. The pyjamas I elected to wear to bed are drenched, my hair dripping. My duvet lies on the floor at the other end of the room while the lamp to my side table lies in pieces on the ground.

Norma settles beside me at last, her yells reduced to a concerned growling.

I see this, because the curtains are, for some reason, wide open, and moonlight streams in unabated, cool and silver.

"Fuck…"

"Karson!"

"Norma, baby—" Before I can finish, she dives at me, straight into my arms, wedging her entire body into the space beneath my chin. She clings like I've never known her to, wings rigid, tail tense and locked.

"Nika, dan, kar, dan. Son, son."

Who even needs the comfort right now? Me? Her? Both?

No idea. So I hold her. Hold her while my heart rate begins to slow and my skin prickles with goosebumps from the chilling sweat.

We sit like that for a long time.

The house around us is silent. I've no idea of the time, but both Rayne and Pippa are out. They must be, because neither of them is hammering at my door right now.

I know I must have been crying. Screaming, even. Thrashing around the bed like a woman possessed, all in my sleep. The tears on my face dry crusty and stiff on my cheeks, which are sore and stinging.

Did Norma scratch me? Did I scratch myself?

I return to myself in that time, holding my pest of a pet, gazing sightlessly at the opposite wall.

I would close my eyes, but it doesn't matter. Each time I do, I see my father and his safe, warm eyes taken over by those horrible, frightening yellow ones. I hear his voice change. Feel the vile clench of his hands on my weak, frail child's body. Smell the decay of the smoke pouring from his mouth.

"Fuck…"

Yeah. Maybe I *am* tired. But at least I know why.

An abrupt burst of hip-hop music jolts me off the bed and Norma out of my arms. She starts yelling again, and I lower my face to my hands.

My mobile phone is still downstairs, right where I tossed it after yelling at Noel. If I can hear it from here, that means it has rung several times already, with the notification sounds increasing in volume each time.

Surely it's not Rayne. She wouldn't call me during the sleep portion of my day unless she really had to. And none of the house warning systems have alerted me to the coming sunrise. It must still be pretty late.

Norma darts up and across the room, dumping her entire body on the knob to open the door. Unfortunately my bedroom door isn't a handle like others in the house, so she succeeds only in sliding off it with a graceless splat.

"Son, daaaan?"

"Yeah, yeah." I stand to let her go, and she shoots out of the room, leaving me to retrieve the duvet and shattered pieces of my lamp. It's ugly, thankfully, with garish swirl designs in gold and silver around a stylised scene of the Garden of Gethsemane.

Oh well. Another reason for Mum to avoid talking to me.

"Fuck…"

A nightmare. Again. The same one, in fact. Four nights in a row.

For the fourth night in a row I strip down the soaked bed and cart the sheets down to the laundry room. If I'm quick, I can rinse them out and get them through the dryer before Rayne comes home.

Harder to explain will be my fatigue, though. That isn't as simple as a quick wash and dry.

My eyes feel grainy when I rub them, my cheeks dry and gross.

Like the yellow-eyed creature.

A shudder ripples down my body.

Why? Why now after so long has this *thing* started to invade my dreams? And is it an invasion? Am I being possessed like Flint Liddell was?

Not for the first time do I reconsider my decision to keep the dreams to myself. Four nights in a row, perhaps, but more before that. Nights filled with dreams of loved ones hunting me down over empty fields of inky black, the only colour the yellow of their eyes. Rayne, Jack, Pippa, Mum, even Quinn at one point, attacking from a darkness that swirls like clouds of midnight smoke.

And now, Dad.

I dump a cup of laundry liquid into the machine drum, then fill the insert tray with softener.

Dad. Daddy. Charles Karson. Deceased.

I had thought that my encounter with the weird demon creature brought me peace, that the new perspective offered on my father's passing made more sense and didn't require more mental self-flagellation. Apparently I was wrong.

A fresh burst of that hip-hop tune. Closer this time and approaching. A moment later, Norma enters dragging my phone awkwardly across the ground.

I pick her up, snag the machine from her grip, and wipe it against my top before glancing at the screen.

*Shit Bag* flashes the display.

Oh. What the hell does *he* want?

I hold the phone to my ear. "Shakka, it's my night off, whatever it is can—"

"Why the hell don't you answer your phone, woman? How many times do I have to call you?"

"It's the middle of the night. I was asleep."

A grunt. "I'm calling in my favour."

Fresh sweat prickles across my skin.

Sure, at the time, promising a favour to get what I needed was fine and dandy, but now, quite suddenly, I remember how dangerous it can be to owe a goblin a favour. Particularly this goblin.

I imagine him now, standing at his control panel in *edane* lock-up, chewing something red, sticky, and raw. I envision him with a long-nailed finger in his ear, or up his nostrils, digging for treasures I don't dare think about. I picture the bent hook of his nose, with the horrendous scarred hole across it that characterises the entirety of his warty face.

"What do you need?" I make my question and tone as easy and non-committal as I can manage.

"Get over here. I can't tell you on the phone."

"Shakka—"

"Your word, Karson," he snaps. "You gave me your word. Doesn't that mean anything?"

The fight to stop my hands clenching is short, but intense. "Never ask me that again."

"Then get over here. Now."

"Can you at least tell me what's going on? Do I need gear? Are you in trouble? Will I want backup?"

A pause.

The fact that he seems to be thinking about it makes me nervous as hell. I can hear him pacing, the heavy slap of his long feet, brisk against the floor.

"Maybe. I don't know."

I sigh. "Can I at least shower first?"

"Why? Weren't you sleeping?"

My mouth opens, but there's no point in telling him about my dreams. Hell, there's no point lying either—he won't care either way.

"Don't worry about it. I'm on my way."

"Hurry up. I need to get some rest."

"*You* need some rest? I—"

The phone beeps against my ear. He's gone.

What a dick.

Norma looks a question at me, and I pause long enough to give her a loving pat on the head. "Stay here, baby. I've got to visit a mean, grumpy goblin man."

"Dan, nika. Son kar, dan?"

"No idea. But whatever it is, I'm sure it will be just great." The last two words fall off my lips as a weary drawl as I make my way back upstairs to find my clothing.

# CHAPTER SIX

I park outside the lock-up and allow my forehead to touch the steering wheel. Even the dim light from my dashboard is too bright for me, and I find myself scrunching both eyes shut to combat it.

To my side, on the passenger seat, my phone beeps twice.

Text message. *Another* text message. By my count that's six on the short drive over. Does Shakka expect me to read while driving?

When I exit the car, a chill rush of night air lifts my locs and tosses them.

The street is dark and quiet, and the subtle, nondescript staff door takes effort to find. I give the scanners a moment to assess my ID, then push.

A hiss, a click, and the mechanical door whispers back to let me through.

Inside, a narrow tunnel with a high ceiling is lit by small, white lights that grow gradually brighter as I walk.

Last time I came this way, I had been forced to negotiate my way past armed military soldiers. It seems so long ago now that Colonel Benedict Addington and his arm of the British Army—the graciously named Extra Mundane Control Unit—came and took over. And now, though gone, signs of their presence remain in the form of additional unmanned checkpoints. Each time I show my ID, and each time the little LEDs flick from red to green to accept my credentials.

The last checkpoint is a pair of huge metal doors with a keypad. In front of it stands a short, warty-looking figure with mean, black eyes and a twisted mouth.

He glares. "You took your time."

"It's the middle of the night, Shakka, give me a break."

"Excuses. Get in here. I have other things to be doing tonight."

I close my lips over the urge to argue. After all, what's the point? Instead I follow his slap-slapping, barefoot steps across the threshold and to another set of doors. These lead to a raised mezzanine around the edge of a huge collection of cells.

They seem to be empty right now. Unusual, but not surprising. Most *edanes* seem to be on their best behaviour after the Army's intervention. Even the werewolves have taken to solving their disagreements and conflicts with words rather than dominance battles. Apparently Wendy's death has shaken more than just me.

As we round the mezzanine I notice one occupied cell: a childlike pale brown figure with twig-thin fingers, arms, and legs. It has brightly coloured wings, rather like a butterfly, that fold neatly down towards the ground like a stiff cloak. Both eyes are huge and black, no visible whites or iris, while the mouth is small and filled with teeth like daggers.

It stands straight as we enter, dashing to the door of the cell and shaking the bars with tiny fists. "Hey." The voice is small and shrill, like a doll. "Hey. No keep here. Release. Release now. Hey. Hey."

I frown. "Why is there a cave sprite here?"

The empty black gaze follows me as I walk. "You help? Hooman lady? Release? Not keep. Release. Hey. Hey."

"Shakka…?"

He grunts in answer and shoves open the door to his office. A sharp sweeping gesture indicates that I should enter quickly.

I risk one look back at the distraught sprite, then step through, gagging immediately at the powerful scent of slightly too old raw meat. A ripple of revulsion shivers up and down my spine that I'm too slow to disguise.

"Rude," Shakka mutters.

"Says you." With effort, I inhale long and deep through my nose, hold it, then let it go. By now I should be used to the odd smells around Shakka, but apparently a lack of sleep has made me weak. I repeat the long breath several more times to force speedier acclimation to the smell.

"Better?"

"Just tell me why I'm here. And why that sprite is here. We don't have any facilities for them—they could barely hurt a fly."

With narrowed eyes, Shakka helps himself to the stool in front of a huge console of buttons and brightly coloured lights. I know this station controls most aspects of the lock-up, including the cells, the lighting, the weapon store, and even the defence measures. He inspects a row of white dots on the upper right side before flicking a switch beneath the centremost LED. A faint hiss reaches my ears, and a glance through the observation window shows me that a shutter has slipped down over the main door of the cave sprite's cell.

I wait.

He grunts again. "I need you to fetch something for me."

"You *what* now?"

A cough this time. I wonder if he has a cold. Is that something goblins can even get?

"That sprite came from some half-forgotten village up north. Stumbled into that new bar—Bloody Mary's, in the West End. Drunk off their face, and wrecking the place—biting customers, throwing bottles, generally being an ass. So civvie bashers brought them here for processing."

A yawn stretches my lips. I don't try to hide it. "What does that have to do with me?"

"You're a SPEAR, aren't you? Thought you'd be interested. I am." The grumpy goblin settles himself more comfortably on the stool. His narrow eyes turn towards the cell outside before darting back to me. If anything, they are narrower still. "Even more interested when they started talking about some great treasure. You know I love treasure."

I do. A goblin's love for fine riches is second only to their love for food. More than once I've compared them to magpies, given their desire for glittery and shiny things.

"But an hour with this sprite and I know they really do have something valuable. And I need you to go get it."

I rub my fingertips across my eyelids. "I'm not a delivery service, Shakka. Is this really what you pulled me out of bed for?"

"You owe me a favour."

"Yeah, but this? I'm not a postman or courier. If this is really what you dragged me out here for, you're more of a dick than I thought. You couldn't tell me this on the phone? You couldn't explain this nonsense then, so I could tell you to shove it up your arse?"

Shakka leaps to his feet, and for the first time I realise that his eyes are narrowed not in confusion or curiosity but anger. No, rage.

"That damn sprite and their nest have an artifact of my kind. They said it was goblin made, and there is one thing, *one thing*, that could possibly be. You need to get it back. Right now. I want it returned to my people and those sprites punished for stealing what was never, ever theirs."

My fatigue billows away at the strength of his fury. Never before have I seen him so animated, so loud, so passionate. He stomps back and forth in front of me, pounding one fist into his palm and then the other, over and over. His flat feet slap hard against the ground, legs trembling with every step. Even his nose seems to pulse with the passion of it all.

"You need to—"

"No, *you* need to fulfil your favour. Get it back. Go there now, tonight, get it back. Bring it to me."

"I don't even know what *it* is, I—"

"The Blade, Karson, don't you know anything?"

"What blade—"

"The Blade of Glal," he bellows, actually stamping his foot. "You humans are all the same. Every damn one of you. No care at all for the artifacts or history of anybody other than yourselves. Queen this, king that, who cares? But when *true* history is in question, when the real roots of this country come about, not one of you knows anything."

I raise my hands, palm out. "Glal? The goblin king of lower Mercia?"

Shakka whips round to face me so fast that a cascade of spittle flies from his mouth. "What?"

"King Glal. King in south Mercia? Tried to invade north into Northumbria but got steamrollered before making it halfway?"

"You…I…When…?"

"There was a medieval history show on the Discovery Channel." I try not to wince when I think about the sheer number of hours I've spent watching that damn channel. "It didn't say much, but it did mention a couple of notable *edanes* forgotten by human history. One of them was Glal."

A strange, misty look creeps into Shakka's eyes. He breathes deep, then sags, visibly deflating as the righteous rage ebbs. "He was on television?"

"Kinda? Just a mention, but I thought it was cool—this goblin history alongside mine. Made me annoyed that we never learned about it in school."

"When you were in school, humans barely knew we existed." His voice is softer now, almost sad. But that's certainly better than angry. "Back then, people knew, but as the population shifted, we got fewer and fewer. Became less than. Servants. Enslaved."

I nod. "Humans have a bad habit of that. Apparently it started way earlier than most might think." I risk a step forward. "Shakka, are you saying Glal's sword is real?"

"Sword? No, Karson, it's a spear. An iron spearhead decorated in silver on a shaft of ash wood. It was supposed to be buried with Glal, but grave robbers stole it long ago. All we have is the shaft. Goblins all over the country have been looking for the head ever since. We've been scouring historical accounts and journals and notes to get a rough idea of where it was, but nothing concrete. Until now. Now we know for sure where it is because *that* little fucker told me so." He jabs a finger down towards the cells. "They confirmed it."

"Now hold on—"

"They stole it." The rage is back, and now Shakka is on me, long, knobbly finger extended, jabbing upward towards my face. "It has to be. You are going to look for it. You're going to get it back and bring it to me, do you understand?"

Slow, careful, I nudge his finger out of my face. I've never enjoyed being pointed at, but the old-meat smell seems to be clinging under his fingernails and making it still more unpleasant.

"No."

He blinks at me. "What do you mean, no?"

"I mean no." I fold my arms. "I'm not an errand woman, running off to serve the whims of her master. This is stupid. If there *is* an *edane* artifact out there, you should be speaking with the Angbec Museum, not a grounded SPEAR agent."

"Why the hell would I go to the museum?"

"Because that's where a historical artifact belongs."

His cheeks swell and redden beneath the warty skin. "It belongs to goblins. Goblin made, goblin used, goblin owned. The *hell* I'm going to some human warehouse where they'll tuck it away in a box with all the other junk they don't care about."

"But—"

"No. *You* get it. This is my favour. I'm calling it in. I can tell you where to go and what to look for—all you have to do is bring it back."

I roll my eyes. "So you want me to steal it?"

"Retrieve it."

"Don't split hairs. It's stealing. So, no. My favour was coming out to you in the middle of the night when I've got better things to be getting on with. There's no way I'm doing this."

"Karson—"

But I've heard enough. As if the day hasn't been hard enough, now I'm supposed to fetch and carry some ancient weapon that may or may not even exist? Not a chance.

I scoot around Shakka and bull my way out the door, back along the mezzanine. From down below, I can still hear the little squeaks coming from the only occupied cell.

"Hey? Release, please? Not keep. Not here. Release. Release?"

I reach the exit doors and present my ID. Nothing happens.

"Release? Hooman lady?"

Shakka's voice follows me from the office. "I've stuck my neck out for you time and time again, Karson." He steps into view slowly, arms folded, expression fierce. "You take, take, and take without ever giving back, and I'm sick of it."

"Hey? Release?"

My fingers clench.

"I have never asked anything of you before. Not ever. And yet every time I see you, it's to do something that damn near risks my job or my life. Every time."

I glare at the door, willing it to open.

"You gave me your word, Karson. Your word."

"Unlock the door."

He sniffs. "So your word doesn't mean a thing. You're just like every other human I've had the displeasure to know. So keen, so eager, so sweet, until you need to step up. You disgust me."

"I'm tired. Unlock the door."

I can feel his gaze on my back, boring in. It makes my skin prickle and writhe, but I refuse to look back. Not for this.

After long seconds, I hear his feet against the floor, the soft whoosh of his door. Then a click comes from the numerical panel to the left of the door and the lights flash through a sequence of red and orange.

Again I hold up my card, and this time, the door slides open.

Just as I step through, I catch Shakka speak again.

"Is this what happened to Wensleydale?"

I freeze, one foot over the threshold. "What?"

"He trusted your word too. And now he's dead. Just what exactly did you do when you took him away from here? When *I let you* take him from here? How did you fail him?"

I turn, but Shakka is already gone, stomping back into his office. The door slams shut, then clicks with a finality I feel right down in my bones.

My skin seems to burn, prickling all over. I clench one fist, then the other, then the first again, then the second, and with each movement my knuckles crackle and pop like BubbleWrap.

Several seconds pass before I can bring myself to take another step, but when I do, it's slow and halting.

Shakka's words haunt me all the way out of the building and back to my car.

# CHAPTER SEVEN

I drive for hours, or so it feels. Aimlessly east, then west. South, back towards home, more south, then north. The whole time the radio plays songs I barely hear while the moon makes its silent journey across the sky.

The roads are empty at this time of night, which is perhaps the only reason I don't end up in some form of collision because I'm certainly not concentrating.

Shakka's words form a loop in my head, cruel, sharp, and accusatory.

And each time I hear them, each time my mind brings back the conversation, I can't help but wonder if he's right.

Wensleydale *is* dead, and no matter what anybody says, I know my actions brought him to that fate. My decisions. My choices. My needs. He might have made the decision to fight, but it might not have been necessary at all without my input.

I slam my feet down, missing the clutch by a mile, so the car grinds to an uneasy halt and immediately stalls in the middle of the road.

I don't care. I can't see anyway, too many tears in my eyes.

Even as I wipe them up, more seem to come, but between the blurry intervals, I catch glimpses of a barren, abandoned playground, complete with swing set, broken roundabout, and listlessly leaning slide.

I'm in The Bowl.

The understanding brings me back to myself with a startled jolt, and my right hand strays towards my left underarm before I remember that I didn't bother bringing a gun tonight.

Steering wheel, then.

I grip it with both hands and notice each one is shaking.

I haven't been back here in weeks. Not since...

I clear my throat and reach down to put the car back into gear.

My eyes leave the road for a split second, but that's enough. Enough for a figure to tap on my window and draw a strangled yelp of surprise from the depths of my throat.

"I'm so sorry, Agent," a muffled voice comes through the glass. "Did I startle you?"

Agent?

I peer through the glass, foggy with condensation, before finally winding it down.

Outside stands Pete Dunn, a tall, wispy figure almost as pale as I am dark. Their hair remains wild and nestlike, their eyes the faintest shade of red. I stare, taking in their stooped stance, twisted spine, and clawlike grip on the cane in their right hand.

More guilt clutches at me.

"Hi."

They offer me a weak smile. "I'd say good to see you, like, but…"

That's fair. The last time we met was when they were injured enough to need that cane for the rest of their life.

"I'm sorry. I didn't mean to come here."

"I'd hope not. Like, I'm pretty sure you're not supposed to come anywhere near the Dire Wolves. Particularly Aleksandar."

Just hearing that man's name makes my skin crawl. "He's not here, is he?" I'm already preparing to drive away.

"No, no. He's at Clear Blood."

Ah. Of course. Clear Blood is neutral enough territory that the meeting Rayne described earlier was sure to be there. I allow myself to relax, but not much.

Outside the tension and high stakes of our last meeting, Pete is soft-spoken, gentle, and…older. There's an age in their voice that was never present before, and though hints of their old speech remain, it's nowhere near as prominent.

"How are you doing?"

They arch a pale, wispy eyebrow. "Walking is easier. I've had a lot of physio. There's even a chance I might, like, be able to walk without the cane one day. My body is healing."

"And when you shift?"

An uneasy silence stretches between us.

"I won't get my tail back, if that's what you mean."

I stare at my hands. "I'm so sorry, Pete."

"You should be."

Ouch. But fair.

"I am. And if I could make it up to you in any way—"

"You can't. Like, how?" They drum their fingers against the

head of the cane, and even from within the car, I can see the darkness creeping over their fingernails. "But it's over. It's done. We are what we are, and this is what it is. No changing it."

I want to leave the car. I want to step out and wrap my arms around them, giving them the biggest hug that I can manage.

As if sensing my thoughts, Pete backs up. "You should go. Aleksandar might not be here, but this place isn't safe for you...any more."

Damn. This wolf is flaying me with every single word. Guilt bubbles up and threatens to spill over into more tears, but I force it back down.

"Can I visit the memorial before I go?"

Pete shrugs. "Your call. I won't tell you what to do, Agent. Like, it never worked before, did it?" And with that, Pete limps away, leaning heavily on the cane.

I sit in the car for several seconds, letting that sink in.

For some reason, after the kindness of the likes of Rayne, Pip, and even Noel, it's almost comforting to find someone willing to tell me to my face that I fucked up. It supports the gnawing guilt I've been working through with my therapist and reminds me that even though my life is kinda back to normal, dozens of others can't say the same.

The Dire Wolves, though a small pack, were once the most respected werewolves in Angbec. They were strong, secure, and loyal and a perfect example of how *good little wolves* should act when humans were around. Much, if not all, of that came from Wensleydale Gordon's guidance, wisdom, and patience.

Aleksandar Rhodes has none of those skills. He rules the pack through force and fear and bolsters their numbers to match his overinflated ego. In the space of weeks, the Dire Wolf werewolves have become nothing more than thugs and playground bullies, flexing their physical strength and size over other packs, while neglecting the very real needs of those beneath them.

Though officially named Misona, The Bowl has become a far more accurate name for the territory run by the Dire Wolves—a figurative hole, a scooped-out section of Angbec into which the homeless, ill, and rejected members of society fall to be forgotten. Many of them are werewolves, but not all.

Once, the humans of the area knew they were safe, not only from the wolves but from those outside The Bowl, because Wendy considered every resident a member of his pack, wolf or not. Now, the few humans brave enough to remain sleep with one eye open, and perhaps one hand resting on the handle of a silver knife.

Slowly, I climb out of the car and let the door swing shut.

I should leave, I know it, but there's one last thing I want to do. I *need* to do.

I lock the car—for the good it does—and walk through the abandoned playground out to the other side, where a single wooden bench sits beneath the skeletal remains of a young birch tree.

The glint of brass catches my eye, and I allow myself a sigh of relief to recognise that the memorial plaque on the bench has not been removed or damaged, even if the bench is missing a slat or two.

*In memoriam:*
*Wensleydale Gordan, Alpha of the Dire Wolves*
*Nunc et in perpetuum*

So small. The plaque is almost invisible unless one knows to look for it, but this is all that remains of the incredibly large and powerful being that was the friend I loved. In my own way.

More tears. More blurriness.

I dash them away with the heel of my palm and use the salty moisture to wipe streaks of dirt off the plaque.

"You big, ugly mongrel," I whisper. "I'm sorry. This idiotic meat sack screwed it all up."

No answer, of course not, just a soft gust of wind that skids a pile of scrunched-up paper and plastic bags across the pavement.

"I know you'd tell me I'm a fool. A moron. I'm pretty sure you might even tell me it's not my fault. But...but I miss you. I never thought I would, but I do, you miserable old bastard."

Again I touch the smooth, shiny brass. It's cold beneath my fingers, the engraved writing far shallower than it should be. But if Pete and I are going to keep replacing the damn thing each time it's vandalised or stolen, we need to keep it cheap. Until we can find somewhere else to put it, at least.

I want to stay longer. Hell, I'd happily sit on the bench in the cool, dark night and guard the damn thing until morning, but trilling from my phone calls me back.

There's only one person in my phone with that particular ringtone, and if she's calling now, I've been out far too long.

I answer and press the small device to my ear. "Rayne?"

She sighs in audible relief. "Where are you? I thought you were going to get some rest."

"Shakka called. He wants to call in his favour."

Startled silence from the other end of the line. And then, "Are we going to need backup?"

I laugh as I explain the details. Can't help it.

Oh, Rayne. Beautiful, funny, intelligent, and understanding Rayne. I love her too.

"I hope you told him no." Rayne's voice is firm over the line as I walk back to the car. "You aren't permitted to leave the city until we know what's wrong with your back."

Odd, but I hadn't even considered that when rejecting the miserable goblin. It probably wouldn't have made much difference either way, but at least I could blame my answer on someone else.

"I did say no," I say carefully, "but not because of that."

"You weren't mean about it, were you?"

"I was honest."

"So you *were* mean. Danika, why? From what you describe, he was obviously upset."

I roll my eyes. "So?"

She tuts at me. "Imagine how you would feel if someone had something of yours that you valued. I shouldn't have to explain empathy to you."

With a grunt I slide back into my car and slam the door. "It's different. I'm not an errand maid or a servant. He just wants to see me jump to the click of his fingers."

"What makes you say that?"

"It's Shakka."

A soft sigh. "While I'm glad you're not going, I think you should be more sympathetic towards him. Think of it like someone holding on to your watch."

Reflexively, my left hand snaps shut around my right wrist, clutching at the bulky men's watch wrapped there. One of the few remaining physical memories of my father, I remember well my panic the last few times someone tried to take it from me, much less succeeded.

"Is this why you called?" Not a graceful subject change, but it works.

Rayne briskly clears her throat. In my mind's eye I see her flick her hair in that sharp, this-means-business sort of way she has. "No. You weren't home, so I was worried. It's nearly sunup."

Only now that she mentions it do I notice the faint paling of the sky. Dawn is long enough away that the air is dark, but as a vampire, Rayne is far more attuned to these things than I. At this rate, she will likely be down for the day before I can make it home.

Pity. I was hoping for a cuddle.

"Kappa wants to debrief before your appointment at Clear Blood. We have some reports, so they decided to wait for you."

Talk of work brightens my mood a little. "Debriefs on what?"

"Mostly Blood Moon and witness accounts from the few pack members we've managed to find. Most of them are gone, though."

"It's so weird that Liddell going down had such an effect on the pack. Have you ever heard anything like that?"

"Never."

"Right? Maybe I'll ask Pete before I leave." The words are barely free of my mouth before I realise the mistake. Too late, though.

Rayne inhales sharply and I wince against the tirade I know is coming.

"Pete? Pete *Dunn*? Are you in Misona?"

Now, Rayne is no Grey Tail, but I don't think I've ever been able to successfully lie to her. So I don't try. "Yes…"

"Danika"—her voice becomes shrill—"what are you doing there? You know it's not safe—"

"I didn't mean to—"

"—and Aleksandar wants you dead—"

"I was just driving, and—"

"You really do go looking for trouble, don't you?"

That one stings. "I wanted to talk to Wendy."

"That is specifically the one place in the entire city wholly unsafe for you to go. Do I need to come get you?"

I start the car at once. "No. It's too close to sunrise, it's not safe for you, and—"

"Its not safe for *you*." Her voice reaches alarming levels of shrill. "Danika, please. Get away from there. Head to SPEAR if you don't want to come home, but don't stay out surrounded by enemies. If Maury knew where you were, he would lose his mind."

"Are you going to tell him?"

"Danika!"

"Fine, fine." I pull off from my unofficial parking spot in the centre of the street and start to navigate my way out. Rayne remains silent the entire time, as if waiting to hear that I have left the area. When I circle the roundabout that marks the westernmost edge of their territory, I hear her sigh of relief.

"How did you know?"

She sniffs. "Engine sounds. I can estimate your speed by listening to gear changes, and if you did what I guessed and went to the memorial, there was only one way to exit the area quickly. And it's a mile and a half away from the bench."

My lips part a little. "You knew exactly where I was?"

"I guessed. Suppose that means I was right."

I nod, realise she can't see it, then answer to the positive.

"Wonderful. Now promise me you won't go driving around there any more. Even if Pete is around, there's no way they would be able to do anything to help you if Aleksandar arranged a convenient accident for you."

Good point. Well made.

"I didn't mean to worry you."

"There's a lot you don't mean, Danika. Please just head to SPEAR HQ. Hawk was on night shift and will probably want some sleep. So was Erkyan. The others will meet you there too."

A smile captures my lips as I think about my teammates. It will be good to see their faces again if only for a short while.

"Was Maury around?"

"No, but he might be later. So maybe be sure to finish up before he arrives."

She's right. Not that it would be unpleasant to see him, but bizarrely, my direct lead has taken to hovering over me, watching me, questioning everything I say and do. I know it comes from a place of concern, but the mother-hen nature of it all lost its charm long ago.

Maurice Cruush is a round-bellied, weary-faced sort of man who has gathered enough greys since we first met that he now shaves his head clean. That doesn't help the whiskers around his mouth and chin, but since he doesn't speak about them, I've chosen not to either.

"Danika?"

Only then do I realise I've been thinking quietly, my thoughts all wrapped up close in my own mind. The traffic lights before me switch from amber to green, and I coast through without slowing as the final traces of The Bowl give way to cleaner, richer, more pleasant parts of the city.

"What? Sorry, I'm here."

A pause. "I'll see you tonight. Will you at least get some rest during the day?"

"Yeah. Of course."

Again I catch a glimpse of her in my mind's eye, the dubious look on her face and a slight twist to the corner of her mouth. She doesn't say anything, but the silence is loud.

"I will."

"Fine. And please remember your Clear Blood appointment. Those tests are important."

I catch the sarcastic response behind my teeth, swallow it down, and say instead, "See you later."

"Have a good day."

"Have a good sleep."

# CHAPTER EIGHT

It feels good to walk into SPEAR's large headquarters once more. The building spans several floors, including an expansive underground area where some of the more nocturnal employees work. There are even sleeping areas there for those *edane* staff, or even human ones, who prefer not to go home.

From field agents, to medics, to trainers, to researchers, everybody has a home in this swift-moving place. A handful of chittarik fly high to the ceilings, some carrying memos, most being a loud, cackling nuisance.

From the corner of my eye I catch sight of one of the newer combat training suites. It's empty but for one woman, tall and slender, who hammers hard at a training dummy with a heavy, spiky mace.

I love combat training, and I love using weapons like those. Always have. Sure, a gun is usually more practical, but there is something infinitely more exciting about swinging a sword, or an axe, or a flail. Most of my use of those things happens in this building, if only to keep up the practise.

Briefly I wonder what it might be like to fight with a spear. Especially since we're named for one.

As I think it, Shakka's angry face swims across my memory.

But his anger is not my problem. I can't make it my problem, either. When I promised him a favour, it was supposed to be for something important and worthy, not a pickup mission like a courier company.

The powerful beating of wings is the only warning I receive before a huge figure drops from above to land directly in front of me, knees well bent, arms outflung. The massive gargoyle gathers me into his arms, squeezing tight until my elbows creak.

"Danika." His skin is rough and firm, his grip firmer still. Both wings curl tight around us both as he hugs me.

I wrestle my mouth free of his chest, where he's squished my face. "Hi, Hawk."

He grins. "It's too quiet around here without you. I've no one around to tease, either."

"Surely Duo is a good target for that."

"Not if I want to keep my teeth in my mouth."

That makes me grin. Duo is a quiet, gentle sort, but his twin brother, Solo, is unlikely to stand for that sort of nonsense.

When Hawk finally lets me go, I smooth the hug wrinkles out of my clothes the best I can.

"Are we all here?"

"Willow is downstairs and Erkyan went to get a drink. I think the matched buttheads are on their way in too."

I wag my finger at him. "Don't let Solo hear you say that."

Hawk flexes his right arm. Huge muscles bulge across his bicep, and I'm reminded again of just how big he really is. Though small for a gargoyle, Hawk stands at a respectable seven feet when on his toes.

He follows me now, wings folded down, occasionally ducking to escape a collision with a low-flying chittarik. His tail waves behind him, creating the occasional batting sound as it taps the floor to regulate his balance.

"Did Rayne tell you about the Blood Moon wolves?"

"Only that you had some information."

Hawk's grin widens. "We found two more. After all this time I didn't think there would be any, but there were two men who hadn't experienced their first full moon before Flint Liddell died. We think that's maybe why they weren't at the church and why they don't seem to have the same symptoms as everybody else."

That is excellent news.

After the Blood Moon pack visited Loup Garou territory with intent to force the female-only pack to join with them, most experienced memory loss, extended confusion, and heart problems when their alpha died.

Though Liddell himself couldn't be saved when the strange, yellow-eyed, smoky black creature fled his body, the rest recovered slowly and gradually returned to whatever counted for normal life. They elected an alpha to lead them and retreated to a neighbouring village with a total population of no more than two hundred. The quiet seemed to suit most of them, but a small handful returned to Angbec in an attempt to reclaim what remained of their human lives.

Every one of those wolves had been turned within weeks of the showdown at the church. Whatever Liddell and that creature had been doing, they worked fast.

SPEAR and Clear Blood did what they could to help those displaced, but with so much memory loss and accompanying anxiety, there was little to be learned from them.

But now…

"I need to speak to them. As soon as possible."

Hawk eyes me warily. "You're on leave."

"But I can still talk to them, right?"

He hesitates and heaves a sigh of relief when he spots Erkyan approaching through the main doors. He abandons my question to wave wildly at the sleepy looking goblin, who flicks a finger at him in return.

"Please, no loudness today," she murmurs. "I tired."

"Been drinking?" Hawk seems amused at the idea.

"No. You know not." A wide yawn briefly exposes the sharpness of her teeth. "Research. Many books. Hard to translate."

I want to ask what she's researching, but before I can, Hawk draws me closer with a wing hooked around my shoulders.

"She's been researching for days now." The sarcastic stress he puts on *researching* makes me stare up at him in surprise.

"You don't sound happy about it."

"She won't let me help. All she's done is complain about how hard it is to translate from English to Goblin. But apparently it's none of my business."

"Maybe it's not."

He grunts. "Maybe. But she's so cross all the time now. She's no fun."

"What happened?"

"No idea. We had a call out to Veranna about a disturbance at a bar. We brought the troublemakers back, and she stayed to handle the paperwork. Day after"—he waves his big hands around—"ghastly grumpy goblin gal."

I smile. "No one likes paperwork."

"Maybe, but she's never snapped at me for trying to help before. She's never snapped at me ever. You know how gentle she is."

Actually, he's right. That *is* unlike her.

I slip away from the grip of Hawk's wing and approach Erkyan, who now seems to be fumbling with a cup of coffee, a notepad almost the size of her head, and several pens.

"Need a hand?"

"Not need," she says, barely looking my way. "Just table."

I follow as she struggles her way across the open plan office to dump the entire lot on her desk, which is also dotted with papers, still more pens, and a tarnished length of linked metal chains. Her desk, like mine and many other agents', resembles a scattered bomb site.

"What are you researching?"

"History." Her answers are less forthcoming than usual, and I begin to understand why Hawk is so frustrated.

"History of what?"

"Many things. Findings."

I have no idea what she means by that. "Are you coming to the debrief?"

Erkyan pauses her study of the desk to flick her gaze my way. "Of the wolves? Yes. I come. But after. This first." And with that, she sits on her stool, cranks violently at the handle to raise the seat level, and buries her face in the untidy stack of papers.

Across the room, Hawk throws me an *I told you so* sort of look.

I back away from the clearly preoccupied goblin and head for my own desk.

In my absence, the messy space has become something still worse to behold. Clearly my desk is now a dumping ground for the small tasks, jobs, and objectives SPEAR has decided are best suited to Kappa.

I get it, my team is the only wholly *edane* team within the organisation—except for me—but surely this can't all be for us? And what about the Blood Moon survivors? Don't they get some form of priority?

I lift a couple of the pages with wary fingers, very aware that I shouldn't be working. I've barely lifted one sheet of paper before I spy Willow rushing towards me.

Willow is a willow sprite, tall, flexible, and slender just like the tree she is named for. She moves like branches gusted by the wind and seems to make the same sounds as she moves. It's all the sound she makes, though, because Willow is unable to speak.

Some sprites, like the cave sprite at lock-up, are more than able to utilise their throats to form human or at least humanlike sounds, but Willow is not one of those. She communicates with sign instead and approaches now with her long hands moving swiftly through what I think is a sound scolding for trying to work while on leave.

I yank my hands away. "I wasn't, I promise. I just wanted to see."

*"But you're not allowed. You know that. You're supposed to be resting."* Her signs are big and faster than usual, meaning she's more upset than her facial expressions give away.

"You sound like Rayne."

"*I sound like someone who cares*," she claps back. "*No touching. Listen, but that's all.*"

"Yes, ma'am."

I can tell she doesn't like that, but instead of fighting, she simply threads her arm through mine and steers me away. And still she signs.

"*Rayne said you would come, but I didn't know it would be so soon. I saw you only an hour ago.*"

"Hour? Did you say hour?"

"*Is that the wrong word? More than that?*"

"It's been weeks, Willow."

She taps the side of her head. "*Maybe. I remember I ate something then. Maybe that's why I'm hungry now.*"

I shake my head with an amused sigh. I know time and its passage must be strange to her, given that she's almost, well, a tree. But her forgetfulness and confusion around hours and minutes is actually quite funny.

"You've not eaten since we last met?"

"*I can't remember. It doesn't matter. I've been busy with all the little rubber rings.*"

I blink. "You might need to sign that again."

She does. Slowly.

"Wolves. The wolves? Not rubber rings?"

"*Yes. Good, Danika, you're learning. Well done.*"

I smile, and she treats me to a gentle kiss on the forehead.

Willow sprites are so strange. Gentle, but flighty. Kind but forgetful. Honest, but careless. Her sign for my name is a huge gesture, one that requires both hands to be near her chin and cheeks. When I asked her how she decided on such a sign, she told me, through much silent laughter, that it represented my big and powerful personality.

So nice of her to phrase it that way, when my mother might have said *overbearing* or *aggressive*.

By the time we get back to Hawk, Solo and Duo have also arrived.

The werewolf twins look more alike than ever before, with the same calm, steady expressions, same slight builds and stride. The one difference this time, which throws me off entirely, is their hair.

Still short, still neat, but that's where the similarity ends.

Solo's hair is red. Like bright, diablo red.

Beside him, Duo's hair is coloured a clown-bright orange.

The pair come to a stop in front of me and draw their lips back in huge playful grins. This close I can see that they've even dyed their eyebrows in tones to match their hair.

I raise my hands. "Why?"

"Why not?" they shoot back in unison.

Hawk snorts.

Willow's shoulders buck with silent laughter.

I nod. "If I had the balls, I'd go purple."

The twins share a glance. "It would suit you."

This time, I can't help but laugh myself. This...I've missed this. Banter with my colleagues who have become so much more since our team of misfits was formed.

Solo slaps me on the shoulder by way of greeting, while Duo curls me into a gentle hug. Then they lead the way to one of the meeting rooms with Willow and Hawk in tow, while I try, without success, to rub the lingering sting out of my arm.

# CHAPTER NINE

"...but I think we should investigate further with more interviews. Maury has already given us the go-ahead, so we can start today. Or at least, Solo and I will." Duo finishes his rundown of Blood Moon activity by decisively clicking the lid onto his whiteboard marker.

The board in question is covered with his neat, precise handwriting, giving bullet points of each topic and subtopic of the last hour.

I press the back of my hand to my mouth to hide the yawn brewing there. "That's a good plan—I like it. But what about the wolves you've already spoken to?"

Duo shoots a glance at his brother.

Like always, they seem to have a quick conversation without ever saying a word, and once more I struggle to decide if that's a by-product of their identical genetics or the near hive-mind nature of their telepathic Fire Fang wolf pack. One, both, neither, it doesn't matter—each time they do it, I feel a little weird.

Solo peers at me from behind the toes of his shoes, which are mounted on the table in front of him. "They don't want to talk much. Still in shock or some shit."

"But Hawk mentioned"—I peer at the board—"fear essence. Is that what they have?"

Hawk sniffs and shifts his glasses to rest more comfortably on his face. It's always so weird to see him wearing them, even if he only does to read. I would have loved to be a fly on the wall during that optometrist session. His head is significantly wider than that of the average human. And he has horns.

"We don't know what else to call it, but all of them seem to have it. The wolves we've spoken to, anyway." He scratches the tip of his nose, making the glasses wobble. "They all have the memories, like what you had at the church, but now that the *thing* is gone, there's a leftover unease and fear in their day-to-day lives."

"Like an anxiety disorder?"

"Maybe?" Duo frowns at his notes. "But it's not so much a mental health issue, but a direct result of what the yellow-eyed creature did to them. They seem to think that thing left a stain on them."

"How is that possible?"

Solo shrugs. "How did it carve a sign into your back that healed like a tattoo but feels like a curse?"

"Curse?" I fight the urge to reach around behind me.

"Maybe you can't feel it, but I can. It's like a smell. Never had anything like that in my nose before. But it's only when you're around."

"But I had a shower..."

"No." He yanks his feet down to lean over the table at me. "It's like leftovers. Or a...a..."

"Stain," says Duo. He refuses to look at me as he says it.

I know my mouth is hanging open, but I can't help it. I stare at him, then Solo, then Hawk. Then Willow. None of them seems willing to give me their gaze.

"Do you all feel it?"

Hawk clears his throat.

Duo stares at his fingers.

Solo grunts. "Sometimes. Not always. Not now, but there is a hint of *something* not quite right. And what else can it be but that mark?"

"But is it just you? Nobody has said anything to me. Not Rayne, not Pip."

Willow thumps her fist against the table and, when she has our attention, begins to sign. "*Do you really think they would? Besides, they live with you, they are close. More than us. Maybe they don't feel it?*"

I want to know more. Hell, I'm desperate for more, but Erkyan chooses that moment to make an appearance, slinking through the meeting room door like a small, timid mouse. One hand tightly clutches a small mug of what is probably coffee, which she holds close to her chest as she moves.

She starts when she notices that we're all watching, slopping her beverage all over the carpet. She clears her throat. "Is meeting finished?"

I shake my head. "No, I—"

"Yeah." Solo cuts across me and grabs his brother by the scruff. It's not a rough gesture, exactly, but he clearly means for Duo to follow, which he does, at once. The pair of them scoot around the table towards the door, calling over their shoulders as they go.

"We'll get started with the first batch of interviews." Duo scrambles to keep hold of his pen and papers.

"The rest of you get some rest." Solo opens the door. "I know you were working all night."

With that, they're gone, vanished like puffs of red and orange smoke.

Hawk and Willow eye Erkyan uncertainly.

"You okay?" Hawk speaks softly.

She nods, gnawing on her bottom lip. "Sorry I missed meeting."

I smile in as reassuring a way as I can manage. "The notes are all on the board, so don't worry about it. Willow, Hawk, those two had the right idea. Why don't you get some rest?"

Hawk opens his mouth as if to protest, but Willow jabs him hard in the ribs. Her eyes are wide and filled with warning.

"But—"

She jabs him again and quickly herds him towards the door, signing expansively as if to mask his protests.

Good. She was always quick off the mark.

Erkyan looks a little worried as the door closes, leaving the pair of us alone, but I widen my smile and gesture to the nearest seat.

"It's okay. I just wanted to check on you."

"Check how? Check what?" She doesn't sit but instead grips tighter at her mug.

Okay. Gently, gently does it.

"Hawk mentioned you're in the middle of some research…"

"Private," she says at once. "Favour for friend. But doesn't take from SPEAR work."

I lift my hands, palm out. "It's okay, honestly. I just wanted to know if I could help."

Her eyes narrow. Never before have I seen such a caged expression on her small, warty face. "Help how?"

"Hawk mentioned translations. My Goblin isn't great, but my English is. Perhaps between us we could figure out what you're reading."

"Not hard. Only diaries for missing thing."

"You're not going to tell me, are you?"

She winces.

"That's fine," I assure her. "Honestly, but we're a team. If we can help each other, don't you think we should?"

"Not for team. Goblins only."

My fingers stiffen in mid-air. I stare at her more keenly, but now she refuses to meet my gaze. If anything, she seems more uncomfortable than before, as though she's said too much.

Goblins only. History.

I think again of Hawk and his brief mention of a disturbance in Veranna. Veranna, otherwise known as the West End. Where Bloody Mary's bar is located.

There's no way, is there? Really?

I lower my hands. Look her dead in the eye. "The Blade of Glal."

Erkyan drops her mug. It shatters. Her drink—definitely coffee—slops everywhere, drenching the table legs, the chairs, and my boots. "How do you know this?"

Well, if I doubted it before, I no longer do. "I—" The words die on my tongue. Erkyan has been deliberately cagey with me to this point. Did Shakka not want anybody else to know? But then, why would he tell me? And why is Erkyan looking?

I lick my lips. "Shakka told me."

Her eyes grow wide and round. "Shakka? Our Enk'mal?"

I blink at her. "Your *what*?"

She recovers fast, stooping to gather the broken mug fragments. "Nothing. No thing. Don't worry of it."

"No, no, I *will* worry about it. My Goblin isn't great, but I know *that* word. Your leader?"

Erkyan mutters something, too quick and too low for me to catch it. When she next looks at me, her expression is calmer, though her fingers shake ever so slightly on the fragments of her mug. "If he told you, then I can say. Is fine. Yes. Glal's Blade. We found it."

"The cave sprite?"

She nods. "You saw?"

"Shakka called me to lock-up last night. That's why I'm here so early. He wants me to go find it."

For the first time all morning, her eyes brighten. She smiles, showing off her tiny pointed teeth. "So glad you go. Our history returned for first time in many years. Thank you, Danika. Thank you very—"

"Wait, wait, I'm not actually going."

A frown. A stutter. "You not?"

"Of course not. He's trying to send me out into the hillbilly villages of the country like some slave who jumps at the snap of his fingers."

"But…" She bites her lip. "He told you."

"He called me out of bed at stupid o'clock, yeah, he did."

"Enk'mal tells no one. It is secret."

I gently pluck the broken mug fragments from her hands and

begin to overhand toss them into the bin by the door. "He told me. And you really need to stop calling him that. It's weird."

"Not weird, true." She stares at me as if a second head has sprouted from my shoulders. "You not know?"

I shrug.

"Enk'mal. Not lord, like your lord. Enk'mal is distant king."

My last throw struggles and the chipped mug handle lands several inches short of the bin. "King?"

"Not king now, but children of king." She frowns. "Have not the word. Child of child of child of old king. What that is?"

"Descendant?"

"Yes. Enk'mal Shakka is descendant of Glal. Many children in between. He is last."

"You've got to be kidding me."

The words touch me but don't quite penetrate. Because how can they? Shakka? Miserable, foul-mouthed, constantly complaining, raw-meat munching Shakka is descended from kings? It has to be a joke.

"No kid. Only truth. You not know?"

I lift my hands skyward. "How the hell would I know that? He works in lock-up. He gets paid minimum wage—barely. He dresses like a hobo and eats almost rotten meat from recycled takeaway boxes."

Erkyan glares at me. "Not rotten. Delicacy."

"It smells like trash."

"Gifts from followers. Your word is maybe *vassal*." She shakes her head. Her large ears flap from side to side. "You know so little. Sad. I thought more for you."

Okay, ouch. The words flay me like fillet knives. "Erkyan, I—"

"No worries. Humans are like children. Ignorant? You not know."

Double ouch.

I can't help but stare at her now, trying to take it in. But then, the more I think about it, the more I find that I could believe it.

Shakka has always been haughty and overbearing. Autocratic, almost, even if nobody else around him seemed to care. Could this be why? I would certainly be angry and grumpy around the clock if no one acknowledged my history. After all, to be related to Glal in any way would make him almost royalty, right?

But then, why is he working for SPEAR in a position barely above a grade two Delta agent?

I open my mouth to ask, but Erkyan is much faster.

"He asked you find Blade?"

A small nod.

"And you say no?"

"I—"

"Disappointed. Is not errand or slave task, Danika. Is honour. He would ask you, human, to find his property? Allow you to touch? Hold? No higher glory for human. And you say no."

My skin crawls with discomfort and shame. Holy crap. "I didn't know."

"Now know. What say?" Her gaze is calm and steady. Hot and intense.

"But I'm grounded. I'm not even supposed to leave Angbec—"

Erkyan sighs. Her disgust is palpable. "Rules. When, before now, did you ever care for rules?" With a last glare, she turns away. At the bin, she kicks her toes beneath the broken mug handle and hikes it into the bin. Then she's gone, through the door and out of sight.

I stare at the empty space she just left, my mind whirling several hundred miles per hour.

# CHAPTER TEN

I don't have time to follow or even question Erkyan. An absent glance at my watch reminds me I'm supposed to be at Clear Blood in fifteen minutes.

The journey is thirty by car.

By the time I reach the fancy research facility, I'm twenty minutes late for the appointment, a problem made still worse by the fact that parking is a nightmare.

After much searching, I find a space at the far end of the underground car park, wedged between a pillar and a wall. It might not even be a true parking space because I'm forced to wriggle my way out the window to escape the narrow space.

Inside, after showing off my ID, climbing several sets of steps at a run, and diving into the research labs, I'm sweating buckets. My clothes stick to my back and thighs, and my locs have tumbled free of their pony.

Two figures in lab coats wait for me, one clutching a clipboard, the other gnawing on the end of a pen.

"I'm sorry, I'm sorry." The words tumble out on the back of my loud panting. "I got held up."

The pen gobbler frowns at me. "After last time, we didn't think you were coming."

Last time? Oh, but of course. Now I remember him. This is the guy who insisted on standing behind me the entire time I stood in front of the scanners wearing a chilly, backless gown. To this day, I'm unsure if he intended to protect my modesty or take advantage of my lack of it. Can't remember his name, but it doesn't matter all that much. The biro he chews on is chipped and broken, and I can't think of any more appropriate name than Pen Gobbler.

Clipboardina, on the other hand, is new. Or at least, I don't recognise her. She moves with the smooth, near boneless glide of an *edane*, but I've no idea what flavour. When I begin to shrug off my clothes, she raises a hand to stop me.

"Not this time, Agent. Given how low we are on time today, we'll be doing some different studies. You won't need to change."

Thank fuck. Last thing I want to be doing now is pulling off all my gear. While I don't have my gun, I still have everything else I tend to carry on my hips and in my pockets, including several knives and all my throwing stars. Those are new.

She leads me along a light, bright corridor lined with several doors while Pen Gobbler brings up the rear.

Yup. He definitely likes being behind me.

Somewhere towards the middle of the corridor, Clipboardina stops and glances at her namesake. "Today we've brought in several different *edane* volunteers to sit with you in controlled conditions for a total of ten minutes each. You are to converse with them calmly and naturally, though we ask that you don't touch anybody. They are instructed to treat you kindly and respectfully on the understanding that they are taking part in a social experiment on humans and *edanes* in tight spaces."

I open my mouth, thinking she might pause to take a breath, but no. She ploughs on again, this time, faster still.

"You will spend time with werewolves, sprites, trolls, various fae, goblins—and humans as a control. Some will be known to you, others not. Of course we can't get any vampires today, but maybe later when the sun sets."

"Sunset? But it's barely midday now. How long do you want me to be here?"

Clipboardina glances away from her notes to eye me over the top of her narrow glasses. "As long as it takes, Agent. I'm sure you understand how serious your condition is."

I fight the urge to reach behind me. "It isn't hurting anybody."

"Nor is it something we understand. Those markings may be the sign of an illness, possession, a calling sign, or even a death message, we don't know. And we also don't know if it isn't hurting people."

"I haven't spat up any black goo if that's what you're worried about."

She actually looks alarmed. Even takes a step back.

"Sorry, poor taste."

Pen Gobbler clears his throat. "Have you experienced any

discomfort since your last visit? Any unusual physical symptoms we don't know about?"

I shrug. "My periods stopped again. But I expected that."

A nod from Clipboardina. "Lupine immunity shots often disrupt that cycle. That's fine. But have there been any mood swings or emotional changes?"

This time I eye them both. "*No.*" The word is slow off my tongue. "Are you two leading somewhere with this?"

No answer. Instead Clipboardina opens the door before us and gestures me inside. "We'll be observing from behind the glass. If you have any questions, there will be a button on the table in front of you. If you need anything, use that same button. There should be a bottle of water and a cup there too, as well as a few snacks."

"Goody." I step through and wince as the door snaps shut behind me with a firm, final click.

It's going to be a long day.

❖

"Are we done yet?" I manage to wait for my latest visitor to step away before I complain. She's an excitable and cheerful werewolf child from the deeply reclusive Long Tooth pack. Barely more than six, her glee at being invited to Clear Blood is a sight to behold.

She asked me questions non-stop for the entire ten minutes, her eyes and voice lively with joy. Apparently she loved the idea of speaking with a SPEAR agent and had all sorts of questions about becoming one herself. Chatting to her had been a much needed breath of fresh air following several conversations with an assortment of bored, confused, weary, or downright agitated others.

And Clipboardina hadn't exaggerated at all—several fae visited me in that room, including a gnome, an oak sprite, and even a spriggan, though I've no idea what they expected from *that* encounter. The tiny thing simply bounced off the walls for ten minutes, screeching and scratching, before settling into a corner to glare at me from behind several rude hand gestures.

Watching them extricate the creature had been fun, though.

I followed my instructions closely and refused to touch it, even when it somehow got hold of a spoon and gnawed the end to make a sharp, deadly point.

On top of them, I'd spoken with several human civilians including a banker, a teacher, a nomad, and an exotic dancer. I have no idea where

Clear Blood found these people, but all of them were normal and boring. Well, compared to the life of a SPEAR.

In between all the strangers came a handful of people I knew— various Deltas or Omegas from within SPEAR. Even a Beta or two, a mixture of humans and *edane*. But now, several hours on…

"That must be the last one, right?"

"One more, Agent." Pen Gobbler's voice crackles through the speakers set into the upper corners of the room. "Then we're done. A goblin colleague of yours."

That sits me a little straighter. Most of the goblins on staff that I know are in Delta or Psi teams, so I'm unlikely to know them well. But it's always interesting to learn what's happening in training and research or even on the switchboard, where a lot of Delta agents work.

I sip the last dregs from my third bottle of water and turn my attention to the door. It opens.

Shakka walks through.

I spit my water.

"What the hell are you doing here?"

He glares back just as hard. "Dealing with you during work hours isn't enough. Seems I have to sit here for a chin-wag during my off time too."

"Great." I stab the button on the desk. "Hey, guys, can we cut this one short?"

"Why?" Clipboardina this time.

Shakka sits and folds his thick arms across his chest. "Because the little SPEAR agent is no good at holding to her word, that's why. She agreed to stay for the whole trial? Bet she's been trying to weasel her way out of it the whole time."

I lower my face to the table, forehead first. "I'm not in the mood, Shakka. I'm tired, I'm hungry, I desperately need a piss, and your miserable face is the last thing I feel like staring at for the next ten minutes."

"Back at you, Karson." He spits, actually spits, on the ground near my feet.

"You two have an antagonistic history?" Clipboardina's voice is high with interest.

I sigh. "You could say that."

"No. I just don't like liars."

"I'm not a liar."

"Breakers of their word, then."

"I'm not that, either."

Shakka slaps his hands on the table and leans forward. He doesn't come close to touching me, but he's certainly in danger of reaching my personal space. "You. Owe. Me." His voice is a low snarl. "If only you understood what this means. What's at stake—"

"Why not send one of your little minions out after it?" Almost the very second I say it, I want the words back. Part of me hopes he doesn't notice, but this is Shakka, after all. He notices everything.

"Minions?"

I sigh. "I spoke to Erkyan today. She"—I glance warily at the speakers above and the cameras mounted in opposite corners—"told me some things."

The goblin becomes very still. "She shouldn't have done that."

"Perhaps not. But I think she did it because she cares for you. Hell if I know why, though."

He smiles, actually smiles. The difference is startling. Abruptly, Shakka is no longer a grouchy, grumbling, ugly old thing, but a bright-eyed, almost coy little figure. His busted up nose and mangled ears do nothing to take from his obvious surprise and joy.

"What did she say?"

"She called me ignorant for one thing—"

"And she's right." The smile is gone in an instant. "You surprised me by even knowing who Glal is, but you're just like the rest."

"I—"

"That blade is mine. Mine. It doesn't belong with any cave sprite or in some human museum—it belongs with *me*. And I want it back. You're the only person who can get it."

"What, no minions available right now?"

He glares. "Do you think I'd ask *you* if I had any other choice? Do you really think I haven't already tried? That sprite is from a tiny town several miles north that barely even recognises the Supernatural Creatures Act. They act like it's still 2001, and no one has a clue who we are. I *need* a human to head out there, and damn it, the only one even remotely competent is you."

I lean back in my seat, alarmed. "That…that was a compliment."

"The hell it was."

"I know what I heard." And for the first time, I look at him. Really look at him.

Shakka looks old. Sure, he's warty, pockmarked, and scarred, but I've never seen the fine lines across his forehead before. Or the darker rim of colour beneath his lower eyelids. His lip corners are stretched and turned down, his long, mangled ears, droopy.

I hesitate. "Erkyan said it's an honour. That you wouldn't have asked me unless you truly trusted me."

Well, that's a slight exaggeration, but no one will know.

He snorts. "At least you know that much. A human laying hands on our treasures without losing several fingers is no small thing. Why do you think Glal decided to march across Mercia in the first place?"

I've no idea, but I keep my mouth well closed, in case my lack of knowledge is enough to set him off again.

"You owe me a favour, Karson, but you…" He winces. "You're also good at what you do. You're stupid, rash, impulsive, and a huge pain in my arse, but you get the job done. This is a job that *needs* to be done."

"Thanks. I think."

We sit in silence for several seconds, him glaring at his balled-up fists, me staring at the top of his head, trying to imagine a crown on it.

Moments later, the door opens, and Pen Gobbler looks through. "That's it, Agent. We're done. Sir, if you'd like to step out, we'll escort you to your next appointment. And you, stay here a moment longer—my colleague will tell you what's next."

Shakka sighs and shoves back from the table. He has to hop to reach the ground, then slap-slaps his barefooted path towards the door.

"Wait." The word is out of my mouth before I can catch it.

Pen Gobbler stares at me expectantly, but Shakka looks bored, waiting for his turn to be through the door.

Deep breath. "*I'll see what I can do, Enk'mal. I keep my word.*" My spoken Goblin is terrible, clunky at best, but I know immediately that Shakka has understood me.

He smiles the smallest of smiles. "*That's more like it, Karson,*" he replies in kind, flawless and fluent, of course. "*I'll get you anything you need. Be ready tonight.*"

And he's gone.

Alarmed, Pen Gobbler treats me to a questioning look.

I shrug, waving off his concern with a smile of my own. "Goblins, am I right?"

❖

I'm barely back in my car—through the window again—and on the move before my phone trills with an incoming message.

This time I have to pull over to slip my Bluetooth headset into place. "Hello?"

"Danika." Maury's voice is clipped and fast. "Are you done at Clear Blood?"

"*Yes.*" I stretch the word into several syllables. "What's wrong?"

"We have a lead. Finally. You need to come back in, right now."

"But—"

"Now, Karson. We can't waste any time on this. How soon can you get here?"

I glance at the road signs ahead of me, particularly the one indicating that SPEAR HQ is a mere half mile away.

"Soon."

"Good. Do it. Trust me, you *want* to hear about this." He hangs up.

I drum my fingers against the steering wheel, thinking.

A lead. Out of nowhere? What on earth. And who? When? How?

I think of this morning's briefing and my team's glumness as they discussed the distinct lack of anything concrete. It seems just a little bit too perfect for something to come up now. Right now.

Back inside after the trial of identifying myself, I weave my way through the office to reach Maury's corner.

And there he is. Maurice Cruush, his chunky, round-bellied self wedged between his chair and desk. He shoves back as I approach, and the wheels on his seat squeal in protest.

"Danika."

"Maury."

He grins.

I wait.

"Crack a smile, Karson, good grief. I thought you'd be pleased."

"I just spent over three hours chatting nonsense with a bunch of strangers inside Clear Blood. I'm tired. I'm fed up. I still haven't slept all that well, and I'm hungry too."

He gestures to a stool hastily pulled up on the other side of his desk. "I won't keep you. Sit. We'll go through it."

The stool is wobbly and uneven. I perch on the end of it and engage my core while trying to feel relaxed and comfortable.

It doesn't work.

"Erkyan brought in a lead not too long ago. We've checked it as best we can, but there's no more we can do without sending you out there."

The reading on my internal-suspicion radar flickers upward. "Me? Why me? And a lead on what?"

"The marks on your back." Maury's eyes are shiny, his voice low but excited. "She found an old scholar in some village called Moarwell who specialises in ancient writings. This woman is old and skilled, but she can't travel."

A cool prickle of alarm washes over my skin. Moarwell. As in Rayne's hometown?

I lean back, trying to make my body as relaxed and unconcerned as I hope my voice sounds. "So…?"

"So you need to go there so she can study your back."

I hesitate. "I'm supposed to be grounded. Why can't we just send this woman pictures?"

Maury shakes his head. "Believe me, I'd prefer that. But according to Erkyan, this woman is something of a savant or a psychic. She needs to physically see you and touch you."

"And *Erkyan* found her?"

He nods.

*Riiiiight.*

"And you're happy with me going?"

A snort. "Of course not. You're supposed to stay here until we figure out what's going on, but no one is making any progress. We have to do something."

"So you're sending me to…?"

"Moarwell. I doubt you'll know it."

Ha. He can doubt whatever he likes, but yes, I know the name. Well enough to know that there may be some complications on the way. "How soon do I need to leave?"

"As soon as Rayne wakes up."

Oof. Yup. There it is.

As if sensing the tonal shift, Maury wags a finger at me. "I'm sending her because of the pair of you, she's the one with the common sense. She can watch over you."

"Only at night-time."

He eyes me. "True. That's why I'm also sending Solo and Duo with you. I think between the three of them, they'll be able to stop you doing anything stupid."

I would fight that remark, but I think Maury has earned his slight distrust and reluctance. I've not had the best track record since he took over from Quinn. But at least he doesn't hate me the way she did.

"Fine. Is there anything else I need to know?"

He fishes a thin folder off his desk and hands it over. "Everything is in there. Make sure you're well informed before you arrive."

"Sure." I turn to leave.

"Oh, and Karson?"

Pause.

"Don't piss anybody off this time. Please?"

"I don't do it on purpose."

"No, but you *do* do it. Stay close to Rayne or the wolf twins. Get in, get out, come home. Clear?"

"Crystal." I tuck the folder under my arm and walk away.

Partway back to my desk, Erkyan intercepts with a shy, almost embarrassed look on her face.

She pats my hip. "*Thank you*," she murmurs. In Goblin, no less.

And with that it comes together in a rush.

This is nothing to do with the black smoke creature or the mark on my back. This is Shakka's doing. I've no idea how, but his last words to me ring loud in my memory.

Be ready tonight.

While I stare at her, gobsmacked and stunned, she presses a USB flash drive into my hand and holds her fingers to her lips. "*All the information is in here*," she murmurs. Again in Goblin. "*If you need help, call. But call me, not SPEAR. Do you understand?*"

I nod wordlessly.

How? How has he done this so very quickly?

Erkyan's smile is bright and broad. "*You're a good person, Danika.*" And with another pat against my hip, she's gone.

I hide a bemused snort behind the back of my hand. Clearly I've underestimated Shakka. Sure, there's more to him than I could ever have known, but all this?

In that moment, I promise myself that I'll do everything in my power to avoid ever getting on his wrong side.

# CHAPTER ELEVEN

I hate packing. There's something so stressful about trying to decide what clothes one might need. And I don't even know how long this journey will take.

Maury instructed that I go in, investigate, and leave, but the true purpose of this mission might not be as simple. Hell, I'm not even sure there *is* a psychic to see. And what about the cave sprites holding the Blade in the first place?

Skimming through the folder of notes barely helps. Neither does reading it in full.

Typed neatly and annotated with Maury's bold hand, the notes indicate a human woman who goes by Fiona Bristow. Apparently she is able to read and see things by way of touch and mystic sight and offered her services to SPEAR in exchange for leniency on a charge of possession of faerie dust, with intent to sell. The charge is signed off by a huge, elaborate scrawl I recognise to be Jack's signature, so I can only assume that she is real. Maybe it's another of Shakka's favours. I get the feeling he has them all over the place.

Beneath that is an address and a headshot from her criminal record, so at least I know who to look for. Fiona appears to be around sixty, with thick, curly hair in an untidy braid over one shoulder. In the photo she wears glasses with achingly thin frames and a sparkling chain that loops about her neck, with the ends attached to each arm. Her expression is calm and sombre, her lips pressed tight into a thin, unimpressed line.

With all that is the receipt for a booking at a small B & B for two twin rooms and the notation of a fuel allowance to make the drive.

Standard stuff.

Nowhere does the file mention Shakka or Glal or cave sprites, but

I should expect that. If Shakka was going to go through all this trouble, there's no way he would risk it by being overt.

I toss a few more pieces of underwear into my holdall and dump a pile of T-shirts on top. Next, two pairs of jeans, joggers, and a jacket. That should do it, right? Then I can worry about things like toothpaste, shampoo, and shower gel.

Nestled inside the bag, seemingly unconcerned at the stacks of clothes lying on top of her, is Norma. She's been calm since my return home but clearly recognised the bag to mean *Danika is going away forever and never coming back*. I assume she intends to sneak along with me, hoping I've not noticed her in the bag. She can't come, of course, but there's no point in upsetting her yet, so I leave her in place and pack around her, occasionally whispering a soothing word her way.

She sleepily coos a few *Nika-nika*s and *Dan, dan, kar*s for me but nothing more.

I decide against packing on Rayne's behalf. Not only is she more likely to want her own choices, but I'd probably have to do it in the dark. Her room is calm, cool, and dark during the day, and though I could turn on the overhead light, it seems, I don't know, rude almost.

Even if she rests like the dead, she's not *actually* dead. So to root about in her room feels intrusive.

Instead, I make my way to the living room and pull out my mobile, ready for yet another phone call.

As I swipe my finger over the screen to reach my mother's details, I wonder once more if there's any point to my continued efforts.

The phone rings and rings and rings some more. *Click.*

"This is Teresa Karson." Her answering message is short and professional. "I'm unavailable right now, so please leave your name and number, and I'll get back to you. Thank you." *Beep.*

I sigh. "Mum. Danika, again. I get the feeling you're not even listening to these any more, but Pip won't let me stop, given she's scared to call herself. Even Rayne wants me to keep it up. So here I am again. My number is the same, my address is the same. Please talk to me. Please? Don't you think this has gone on long enough?" I bite my bottom lip. "I know you're angry, and I know you're scared, but Pip and I, we're still who we always were. We just live differently. Please...I miss you."

Even as I speak the words, I'm stunned to realise they're true. I *do* miss her. I miss the endless chatter about her Bible groups. I miss the occasional psalm or verse she would quote my way when I did something particularly nuts or stupid. I miss the chatter about her

Spanish classes and her fascination with vampire businesses. I even miss her well-meaning but invariably annoying attempts to set me up on blind dates.

That last one is probably the hardest now.

I have Rayne, but now I don't know if Mum will, or can, ever accept that. And not just the vampire part either. The idea of me falling for a woman seems harder to swallow than the fact that Rayne stopped being human long ago. But then, Mum's idea of family has always been something traditional.

Couple that with the fact that Rayne was the one to turn my sister into a vampire, it's no wonder Mum is having a hard time. But surely she'd feel better if she spoke to us, rather than letting her own mind spin tales.

"Mum, I'm not going to keep doing this," I murmur. "I love you, truly I do, but this is hurting me. I need to live my life, and even though I want you in it, I can't force you." I hadn't intended to say that, but now that the words are out, I realise how true they are. "It's up to you now, okay? I'm here. I always will be, but I need to live. I love you."

I swipe my thumb to end the call and let the phone drop into my lap.

Wow. That was harder than I thought it might be.

But I do feel better for it.

I lean my head back and close my eyes. Just for a moment. I allow myself to go through a quick mental inventory of the task ahead and how to balance seeing this Fiona woman on top of visiting the cave sprites. I don't know much about cave sprites beyond the fact that they, well, live in caves. I know they are small, social creatures who tend to be reclusive and skittish. The fact that one came to Angbec at all is strange in and of itself because they tend to travel in packs, but this one must have been deeply troubled to leave the nest and come out alone.

Why did it do that? And how?

A cave sprite alone is vulnerable at best, a walking snack pot at most.

Super freaking weird.

❖

I wake to the gentle press of Rayne's lips against mine.

Hadn't even realised I'd been asleep.

I flutter my eyes open and find the most beautiful of sights above me—short, sweet, delicate Rayne in her underwear, leaning over me, with her hair tumbling down towards her eyes.

"Good morning," I manage.

She smiles. "Good evening. So you did need some extra sleep after all."

"It's been busy."

Rayne settles into my lap, her knees to either side of my hips, and peers into my face. "You've packed a bag. Why? You know you're supposed to stay in Angbec."

For the smallest of moments I think about keeping Shakka's mission to myself. Not because I don't trust Rayne, of course, but because Shakka has revealed himself to be very much a private person.

But the thought is fleeting, barely a second, before I understand how stupid and impossible it would be to try. Besides, I don't like keeping things from Rayne.

"Remember I told you about Shakka and that knife thing?"

"The Blade of Glal," she corrects.

"We need to go get it."

She studies me closely, head tilted slightly to one side. "What changed your mind?"

"All sorts, but mostly there's more to Shakka than either of us ever knew. And he's somehow managed to pull together a psychic to check my back too. It's all cleared by Maury."

"How soon do we leave?"

"When you're packed."

Her study of my face intensifies. "Are you sure about this? Where is it we're going?"

I bite my lip. I don't mean to, of course, but I'm not looking forward to this.

Of course she catches my hesitation instantly and fixes me with a narrow, suspicious stare. "Danika?"

"Moarwell."

Rayne jerks hard. Her entire body stiffens like a lead rod as she stares deep into my face. "Moarwell?" She's so still, that creepy *edane* stillness that I both hate and find fascination in.

"Y-yeah."

"Mama…and Bubi…"

"I know. But maybe it's a different one. Maybe there are two…?"

"I don't know of any other Moarwells that we could reach in one night." The stiffness leaks away, leaving her limp and weary. "It must be the same." She sags against me, her head resting against my shoulder, hair sticking up my nose.

I pat her back gently. "You don't have to come. I'm sure Maury will understand if—"

"No. I don't want him to know. I don't want anyone to know."

"But—"

"It's fine, Danika." Her voice firms up. Slowly she leans back to give me her gaze again. "I can handle it. Just because I'm there doesn't mean…" A soft sniff. "We'll be there for the cave sprites and for the psychic, that's all. Everything else is to the side."

She says that, but I can't quite believe it.

"Rayne." I grip her hands gently. "You don't have to pretend. You were so excited yesterday when you talked about your sister. Surely, now that you have the chance, you want to speak to her?"

"We have a job."

"No, *I* have a job. You're on babysitting duty. But if I promise not to do anything stupid, you'll be free to go visit them. And the twins will be there."

Rayne pulls the smallest of smiles. "Maury really has you on tight reins."

"No kidding. But I don't care. If it gets me out the city or even out the house for a day or two, I'll take it. I'll be on my best behaviour."

"But—"

"Come on, I'm getting cabin fever. And this is the closest I've been to actual work for weeks. Besides, you really think Shakka will let it go? He's the one who arranged all this."

She lifts her eyebrow at me.

"The psychic was *found* by Erkyan." I make the air quotes with my fingers. "And Shakka told me to be ready tonight. Too many coincidences all at once to be anything but his work."

"How does he have that level of power? How many favours does he have?"

I grin. "Oh, I've some stories to tell you. Let's go pack, and I'll fill you in."

And so I do.

Rayne fills a bag while I tell her everything, from my conversations with Erkyan and Shakka, to our encounter during my Clear Blood testing. I explain how I learned about Glal in the first place and Erkyan's revelation about Shakka's heritage.

She seems far less surprised than I was, but then Rayne has always been an accepting sort. Or maybe she just never had to watch Shakka chow down on dripping chunks of raw meat before. I'm pretty sure if she had, she'd have the same trouble as me believing him to be descended from goblin royalty.

In return, she tells me about Moarwell.

It seems the idea has settled in her mind and she is becoming used to the idea of potentially being close to her lost family. But with every word she speaks, the more my confusion grows.

"You're telling me they don't believe in *edanes*? You said it yesterday, but it still doesn't make sense."

She zips the top of her holdall and swings it onto her back along with mine and a third containing the tools from what we've playfully dubbed our travelling spy kit. Holy water, varied bullets and wires, steel cutters, pressed flowers, small phials of coloured liquids, communion wafers, steel knives, silver knives, gold knives, crystal knives…a lot of knives. Sensible, mundane things too, like matches, torches, batteries, water purifiers, a first aid kit, ropes. We might even be going on a camping trip. Oh, and the narrow, light-proof pod designed for Rayne to safely spend the daylight hours.

I was never a Scout or Girl Guide in my youth, but the idea of *be prepared* is a strong backbone to most activities a SPEAR agent does.

"It's not that they don't believe but that the village is small. They don't *have* to acknowledge *edanes* because the entire population is human. And any non-human there stays out of the way. It's hard to explain."

"You make them sound like some lost tribe cut off from civilisation."

Rayne frowns. "They're not the ones cut off. *We* are. *We're* the weird ones, the extraordinary ones, the unusual ones. Angbec isn't like anywhere else. I imagine you'll see it clearly soon enough."

As we walk down the stairs, Norma, now freed of my bag, waits for us at the bottom. She has her wings spread, her tail held high, her head cocked to one side. Though she briefly glances at Rayne, her attention is all for me as we approach.

"Hi, little baby," I coo.

"Karson," she snaps, clearly agitated. "Dan, dan, kar, dan?"

"You can't come. Stay here with Pippa. You'll have a great time together."

I mean, I hope so. Pippa isn't even here, having shot off for Clear Blood as soon as the sun dipped low enough to allow it.

"Son, da-kar, son, son, dan."

No idea what that means, but she sounds as though she means it.

"I can't. Please, Norma, don't make a fuss."

The pesky creature stands fully and weaves herself in and out of my legs. She is more catlike than ever in this moment, rubbing her head against my ankle, butting my shins with her wings. Her tail curls tightly up around my leg, barbs laid flat so as not to hurt.

She's so gentle, even when being a colossal pain.

I glance at Rayne, who immediately shakes her head.

"We can't."

"But look at her." I scoop the spiky chittarik into my arms and hold her out, like a child with a stuffed bear. "We can't leave her, look how sad she is. She's barely been apart from me more than a few hours since she imprinted on me."

Sigh. "If I say no we're going to end up discussing it, aren't we?" The sigh deepens when I nod at her. "Maybe this time we can just take the shortcut?"

No idea what she means, so I just continue holding up my pet, fixing my face into the most pleading and cute expression I can manage. I can't see it, but I feel like an idiot. "*Pleeeeease?*"

"Fine. But only if you keep her with you. And don't tell Maury."

As if sensing the decision, Norma throws out both wings and cackles happily. She wriggles out of my hands and along my arm to reach my shoulder where she drapes herself comfortably, forelegs towards my chest, rear legs down my back. Her tail wraps delicately about the back of my neck.

"Not a word," I promise.

Rayne rolls her eyes and heads towards the kitchen.

I hear the fridge open and know she's loading up a cool box to take some blood supplies for the trip, so I take the chance to cuddle Norma close.

"Best behaviour, okay, baby?"

"Nika?"

"We're on an important mission, and I won't take you to the cave sprites, but you have to sit in the back of the van."

"Ka, dan. Son, da."

"Fine with me. But you have to sit in my lap."

"Nik-ika."

Oh. I've not heard that one before. I pet her scaly head slowly, scratching that area beneath her chin where the pocket flap rests.

She croons and chitters at me, before resting, lowering her head to her front legs.

While it isn't strange for Norma to join me on car journeys, one as long as this is going to be rough on her. Part of me reconsiders the idea of bringing her at all, but the rest has noticed how very clingy she has become over the past few weeks.

While the imprint has always left my pet keen to be near my side, just lately she has been underfoot so much more. Or pulling at my bedsheets, fussing with my hair, sleeping in my dirty clothes. I've no idea why, but maybe with so much else going on this isn't the time to figure it out.

I leave her comfortably on my shoulder and make a quick call to Pippa to let her know we'll be gone for a few days.

She is absent on the phone, barely listening. I have to repeat myself several times just so I can be sure she understands. By the time the call is done, Rayne has packed up her supplies and we're good to go.

I can't help smiling as we head out to the van where Duo and Solo are already waiting. The vehicle is SPEAR issue, meaning it has a safe space for Rayne should we get caught out by sunrise, as well as communication lines that will serve us and allow us to report back to SPEAR. The windows are shatter- and scratch-proof, the engine far more powerful than anything required for casual day-to-day driving. Beneath the seats in the back are secure storage for weapons and survival gear, including a tent and several sleeping bags. There's a lidded cabinet with a chilled interior between the two seats in the front.

Perfect.

The twins seem to be in the middle of some hand-based guessing game rather like rock paper scissors. There are other gestures I don't recognise, though, which means it takes me a moment not only to figure out who has won but what they are playing for.

Duo leaps into the driver's seat with a triumphant grin, while Solo schlumps his way to the passenger side with his head bowed.

Seeing them like this, I'm struck by how young they are, despite their maturity and power.

Without asking, Rayne and I take the back, securing both our bags and ourselves in place. The journey is a long one for us, about two hours, maybe three, so I take the chance to lean and rest my head in Rayne's lap. No, *she* doesn't need sleep, but *I* sure would appreciate it.

The general lack of sleep, coupled with the nightmares, has left its mark on me, that's for sure.

Norma settles herself into the space between my arm and chest, making a small, comfy resting spot.

"All aboard, ladies." Duo grins. "We're off. Keep your hands and arms inside the vehicle at all times unless an angry—"

"Werewolf," Solo cuts in.

"I was going to say troll."

"Werewolf is better. We're far more dangerous than a troll."

"No way. Trolls are so big and powerful…"

"So are we, when we shift."

"*When* we shift." Duo nods sagely. "But until then, we—the pair of us, I mean—are little weaklings with better hair than common sense."

Solo dashes his fingers through the vibrant red of his hair. "It *is* pretty good. But it's fine—if you're worried, I'll protect you."

"Aren't I the one more likely to take care of you?"

As the brothers continue to bicker, Rayne flicks a glance down at me. Though she says nothing, I agree entirely with the sentiment building in her eyes. It's going to be a long drive.

❖

The twins don't stop for the entire journey. Not once. From bickering to singing to reminiscing to play-fighting and back to bickering again, the werewolves in the front seat chatter non-stop.

Once or twice I might have fallen asleep, but I wake swiftly each time when a loud bark of laughter or grunt of annoyance pierces the still of the car. Norma doesn't budge, tucked up against my chest, gently snoring, her tiny chest billowing with each breath.

Beneath me, Rayne has helped herself to Shakka's flash drive and studies the contents via a small handheld device. Each time I wake, she relays a little more information to me, including sketches of what Shakka believes the Blade to look like.

Most of it is history, rather than anything I can use. Shakka has clearly been investigating this artifact for many years, and his notes include plenty of eyewitness accounts, speculation, and supposed sightings.

From what he writes, this area of the country is probably about right for where the Blade might be now. But the world has changed so much since the time when the likes of Glal walked freely.

What if there's nothing to be found?

We talk about it quietly, but Rayne has no comfort for me. Aside from reassurance that we'll do our best, there really isn't more we can do.

So she allows me to rest. But the drive isn't particularly restful. Not least Duo and Solo's constant chatter is a distraction, but each time I do manage to close my eyes, I see flashes of black smoke and twin spots of Day-Glo yellow, gleaming through the darkness. I can't rest. I can't settle, and I can't stop seeing that *thing* crawl out of my father's body.

I do my best to hold it in, or at least be subtle about the nightmarish visions, but I know Rayne will have some questions for me once we leave the van. Her free hand rests lightly on my back, at first as somewhere easy to rest, but gradually as a comforting presence. She rubs gently at my spine each time I wake, not speaking, just being there.

I'm grateful. The last thing I want to do is explain all this to the young wolves, but I don't especially want to explain it to her either. So much for keeping it secret. I should have known better.

Somehow Duo turns the three hour drive into one and a half. I know at this time of night traffic must be lighter and the roads freer, but they're still narrow country lanes designed for lower speeds. So the only conclusion I come to is that he's crazy. Instead of dwelling on how fast we must have been travelling, I sit up and stretch to work some of the knots out of my back.

Norma yawns and wakes enough to follow, crawling up my body so she can curl up on my head.

The sky is still dark as Duo guides the van towards a tall, white sign, lit from beneath with several spotlights. It reads *Welcome to Moarwell, Please Drive Safely* in clear, bold letters of blue, red, and green. Beneath the sign are several clusters of flowers, all closed for the night.

Beyond the sign, the village spreads out before us like something from the back of a Christmas card or chocolate box.

The single road winds down the middle of a double line of houses which would likely be described as cosy or quaint. To me, they're simply tiny. Several metres on, the road branches into two to surround a wide green area with a tall tree in the centre. On the other side, the road joins again only to split shortly after into three. One leads further on our current path and presumably out of the village, and the other two, to the left and right, where they appear to loop around the back of the houses.

Only as we reach the other side do I realise that not all the buildings are houses. At least one of them is a pub, while another is clearly a church. I recognise it from the news reports of the day before, from the stained-glass windows, now dim and gloomy in the darkness, and the lines of scaffolding all over the front. Some have already been removed, from what I can tell, but on the far side, some of the structure remains.

A handful more are probably shops, though that's more difficult to distinguish in this light.

The rest I can't see clearly because the few street lamps lighting the area are dim, if lit at all.

A small cat watches us from atop a wall near the pub, and more than once I spy curtains twitching. There is no one on the streets at all, but for an owl I hear hooting in a tree some distance away.

Past the green, the centremost road crosses a small river by way of a low bridge, and then, more buildings continue. These ones are set further back from the road with cute gardens bursting with flowers, ceramic gnomes, and wind chimes.

This place truly is tiny.

And yet, I'm excited.

Now that we're here, I'm sure Rayne's worry is unfounded. It's not as though I've *never* been to a small village before. During my childhood, we would often take camping trips and caravan holidays to small, picturesque places like this. Once Pippa had been invited to the birthday party of one of her pen friends that took place on a village green very much like the one in the centre of the split roads.

Frankly, after the heaps of tests and the noise of Angbec, part of me grows excited that this might feel more like a holiday than work.

Duo slows the van to a crawl and begins scanning the buildings up ahead. I know he's searching for numbers, but my eyesight isn't good enough to lend a hand. Not in this darkness anyway.

After a moment, Rayne points ahead to a slightly wider, taller building on the right. The street lights there are much brighter, enough for me to see the words *Kidson Bed and Breakfast* in fine, elegant lettering on a narrow sign waving gently in the breeze.

The tiniest of slip roads leads around the side of the building towards an abandoned parking area. In it are several piles of wooden logs, a dilapidated shed, and a fenced-off garden with gaudy plastic furniture turned down for the night. When Duo turns off the engine, the silence of it all is a little daunting.

I'm first out of the van, eager to stretch my legs.

Norma immediately takes off from my head and flies a few quick laps around the small space. She stays close but seems fascinated by the area, gently chittering her interest as she goes.

When Rayne follows, she carries all the bags, with especial care given to the travel pod she will spend her days in. Though I can't see her well, her shoulders are high and her hands twitching. I grasp at them, holding tight with my own.

"You're okay," I whisper.

She doesn't look at me. Instead her gaze is focused on the garden beyond the fence and, maybe, the tree on the far side of it. "I used to play in there." Her voice is haunted. "There used to be a tree house in the old oak back there. Gone now, though."

I squeeze her fingers. "Are you going to be all right?"

"I have to be."

# Chapter Twelve

A door creaks open behind us. A bright spill of warm yellow light lands on the ground and fills the air with the welcome brightness. "Are you the soldiers?" a small voice murmurs.

Solo slides gracefully from the van and bumps his door closed with his hip. "We're the party of four you're expecting if that's what you mean." His voice is low and cool.

"Oh." The owner of the voice continues to hesitate inside the door, just out of sight. "Yes, yes, I'm so sorry. Yes, *visitors*."

"Tourists," Duo adds, taking care to emphasise the explicit term we instructed them to use. He locks the van, and it gives a little bleep of confirmation. Two more bags dangle easily from his grip.

"Oh, of course. Yes. Tourists. Very hush-hush and secret and all that, isn't it? Well, do come in. I've already prepared your rooms. You should be able to settle in for a day of, uh, touring tomorrow."

As I guide Rayne towards the door, at last I'm able to see the figure half hidden on the other side of it.

A woman, sixty if she's a day, with the wildest, curliest grey hair I've ever seen. It forms a huge cloud around her face and shoulders and reaches as far as her elbows. The thick mass is studded with dozens of little charms, sea shells, and crystals, and seems to be winding free of what might have been a braid. A pair of glasses dangle and rest awkwardly on top of the dozens upon dozens of beaded necklaces clattering against her chest. She even wears gloves, long, white ones that reach past her elbows. Ah. Of course.

Rayne finally releases my hand and steps forward. "Mrs. Bristow?"

She flaps a hand around. "Please, call me Fiona. That *Mrs.* nonsense makes me feel so old."

"Fiona, then." I step fully into the light and through the door. "Nice to meet you."

"No, no, nice to meet *you*. I'm too old for jail, child, so a chance to help you is exactly what I needed. Imagine, nine months for carrying faerie dust. Whoever heard of such a thing?"

A little cough from Rayne. "Well, it *is* illegal."

"Not the way I use it. I wasn't hurting anybody."

I step across Rayne's attempt to argue. Given her police background before becoming a SPEAR, I know exactly how she feels about drugs of any sort. "Well, we're grateful. Did you say the rooms were ready?"

"Yes." Suitably distracted, Fiona steps further back to allow us fully into the rear of the building.

With the five of us all crowded near the door, it is cramped and uncomfortable and nothing exciting to look at. Just a kitchen. A large one, with lots of counters and appliances cramped into it. Ahead of us is another door, leading deeper into the house, and to the right a secure door with a large padlock dangling beneath the handle.

A moment later, Norma dives through the open door and crash-lands on the back of my neck, yelling hoarsely.

I grab her and her beak, to trap it shut, while Fiona takes a startled step back.

"Good heavens, what's that?"

"Nika—"

I pinch harder. "This is Norma. She's a pet."

"Fine, but what *is* she?"

Solo snorts. "A pest."

Clearly that doesn't help.

"Norma is a Class A minibeast known as a chittarik." Rayne speaks as though rattling off a script. "They're mostly harmless with an intelligence level said to match that of intelligent dogs."

"Will she bite?"

I hold Norma a little tighter. Just in case. "No. She doesn't like men all that much, but generally she's friendly. Protective, but friendly."

As if knowing we're speaking about her, Norma stills her wriggling and regards Fiona carefully through one beady black eye. After a moment of cool study, she relaxes entirely in my arms, even folding her wings down.

I risk releasing her beak.

"Kar, son-son?"

"This is Fiona," I tell her. "A friend. Be nice."

"Son. Da."

Fair enough. That's probably the best we're going to get right now.

Fiona stares at Norma for a few more moments before visibly shaking herself back to her task. Though she speaks clearly, I see her, more than once, glance back at the winged, scaly creature nestled in my arms.

"You lads"—she points at the wolves—"have a space upstairs. If you walk straight up and follow the landing to the right, you'll find a room that looks out over the back." She points over her shoulder towards the parking area. "The bathroom will be through the opposite door on the left."

Duo looks a question at me.

I nod and he leads Solo through the door and up the stairs just visible beyond. Their footfalls are light and quick, and by the time they are out of sight, I can barely hear them moving across the upper floor. Werewolf stealth is certainly something to behold. Or not, as the case may be.

"As for you, ladies, your, uh, captain said I should house you somewhere with no windows."

Rayne nods. "That's right."

Fiona looks offended. "Well I don't know why anybody would want that—Moarwell is so pretty at this time of year—but I don't have rooms like that."

Rayne grips more tightly at her travelling pod.

"You'll have to use my scrying space, which is down in the basement. So do excuse all my equipment, child, but it was rather last minute, you understand."

"I'm sure it's fine." I address my words to Fiona, but I mean them mostly for Rayne, who looks more horrified than ever.

Fiona frees her glasses from the clutches of her many necklaces and plants them daintily on her face. They make her pale eyes abruptly huge and owl-like, showing off little clumps of poorly applied mascara across her lashes. That done, she pulls a huge bunch of keys from somewhere on her dress and begins to count them out.

"Garden, front door, pantry, car, shed, safe, side door, office?…no, not office, that's the other shed. Bike lock, back door, guest room—oh, this one is the office—second guest room…"

I sigh. This is going to take a while.

❖

After several false starts, Fiona finds the correct key to fit the padlock on the door to her side. She whisks it open with a flourish and points down a narrow set of wooden stairs lined with twinkling lights.

A dreamcatcher hangs on the inside of the door, as well as a clear crystal on a long chain. She spies me looking and draws her shoulders back.

"I know what you must think of me, but sometimes a woman must put on a show to be taken seriously. I'm sure you understand the world is different to what it used to be, but not everybody does." She frowns. "If I have to wear this ridiculous nonsense in my hair and dress my workroom like some medieval fortune teller, I'll do it, child. I do what must be done."

"So you run your *other* business from the basement of the B & B?" Rayne peers down into the darkness of the stairwell. Her nostrils flare slightly, and she wrinkles her nose.

Fiona frowns. "No, child, this place *is* the other business. Nobody wants to accept the fact that I know things. That I see things. It scares them. So I hide it. A bed and breakfast is friendly and kind and respectful. And my mother left it to me, so I couldn't just leave it. Besides, it's a good cover for folk like you, so I use the upper rooms for that. These lower rooms are for my real work."

And she isn't wrong.

As we step down the stairs, I understand what she means. The walls are draped with colourful throws of Celtic knotwork and nonsense mystical symbols. Every other foot of the ceiling drips with crystals, feathers, or sprigs of dried herbs. Along each wall are shelves lined with books, glass pots, jars, and bottles in various sizes. Each of them has a curling, yellowing label, reading essence of this or blessed waters of that. Even the floor is covered in part by a vast black rug dotted with silver runes, which spell out nothing but nonsense.

Rayne wrinkles her nose again, and this time, I smell it too—the thick, sticky scent of far too much incense. Probably sandalwood.

To the right, a small table covered with a purple cloth serves as an altar. A pestle and mortar take centre stage, while around them, artfully arranged, are several gauzy packages of dust or leaves.

Norma slips free of my grip to walk around slowly, sniffing here, tapping there.

I pick up one of the little bags and sniff it. "Is this—?"

"Earl Grey, child," Fiona says, watching Norma warily. "The one next to it is some other black tea, and that long, blue one is edible glitter. The small, grey one is pepper, the white one is chalk dust, and that larger one at the back is washing powder, slug repellent, and ant killer." She points to each in turn. "Oh, and the stuff in the mortar is matcha, table salt, and chilli flakes." A shrug. "Doesn't matter what it is, so long as it looks good, right?"

The more Fiona speaks, the more I begin to like her. Sure, I don't believe too heavily in what she claims to be able to do, but for a tourist-trap side hustle, she's certainly done her homework. One must respect the grind.

I replace the bag and duck to make my way to the next door. Unlike the others, this one is heavy and solid, with three different keyholes.

Fiona finds these three keys with no trouble and pushes the door inward to reveal the space within.

Bare grey walls, stone floor, windowless and cold. But for a small heater on the left and a low, single bed on the right, the room is entirely unfurnished.

Norma immediately bulls her way through and hops up onto the bed to watch us.

"Not so fancy for the tourists," I muse.

She sighs. "I work better without distractions. You're going to be seeing a lot of this room over the next few days."

Rayne winces. "Excuse me, days?"

"Of course." Fiona widens her eyes at us. "You didn't think this was a fast process, did you, child? If I'm going to read and see everything there is to read and see, I need time to prepare."

"I thought you worked by touch." Already I can see problems with staying in this room for too long. If I had cabin fever before, it's sure to be worse in this tiny space. Norma will likely lose her mind. "I'm right here—can't you just hold my arm or something?"

"I could, but then I'd have no protection against whatever it is you're projecting. It's strong, child. You must know that."

Silence.

"There's darkness around you. I could feel it coming." Fiona pulls off one of her gloves and holds her hand near my shoulder. Her fingers flex towards my back, as if feeling the air. She shudders.

"There…do you really believe I stayed up to this obscene hour just waiting for you? No, child, I fell asleep waiting. The darkness woke me. I felt *it* and I felt *you*. So until I can secure myself against whatever you're carrying, you'll need to wait."

More silence.

Then the faint scraping of my boots as I shift from foot to foot. "What's wrong with me?"

"No idea." Fiona pulls her hand away and carefully feeds it back into the long glove. "But that's my real job. We're going to find out. As soon as possible." For the first time, her expression becomes sympathetic. "You did the right thing coming to me, child. If I can figure out what's wrong, I will, don't you worry about that. Why not try to relax and get some sleep."

I nod, but I barely know what I'm agreeing to.

Fiona backs off and slips through the door, pausing only briefly to glide the three keys off the massive bunch and leave them on the bed beside Norma. "I'll see you in the morning."

And she's gone.

Rayne looks at me with wide startled eyes. I know my expression must match.

"During debrief"—I cast my gaze down to the ground—"Solo said he could smell me. Like I was tainted or cursed. Stained." I know she's still staring at me, but I can't look at her. I keep my gaze on the toes of my boots. "Then Willow said she could feel it too. They all could. Now Fiona too? What's going on? Am I...Do you...Am I tainted?"

Rayne drops the bags and her travel pod with a soft thump.

I feel her fingers beneath my chin. I try to fight it, but her touch is strong, and slowly she tilts my face until we're eye to eye again.

"You're not tainted. You're Danika Karson."

"But—"

"Something happened to you that nobody can explain. It left a mark. But we're here to fix it."

My face grows hot. The backs of my eyes start to tingle. "You feel it too, don't you?" The reality of it aches like a punch to the gut. "You and Pip? Why didn't you tell me?"

"I can't feel anything but how much I care for you. I promise."

"But the rest of the team—"

Her fingers shift to rest on my lips. "They're worried for you. We all are. But we're all still here."

I fight hard against the urge to cry. I can feel it there, but I won't. I just won't. "Is this why you've all been so worried about me? Pushing me? Keeping me back?"

"We're worried about you because we love and care for you. Everything else we can deal with."

Can't help but notice that she hasn't answered my question.

"Rayne..."

"Let's go for a walk." She scoops the keys off the bed and shoves them into her pocket. "We have plenty of time before sunrise, so we should use it to get acquainted with the village. Remember, I won't be able to help you after that."

She's done it again, that thing where she distracts me beautifully and swiftly from my worries and fears.

"According to Shakka's information, there's a set of old caves in the hills beyond the village. I know them—every adult around would tell us to stay far away from them because they were dangerous."

"Were they?"

"Definitely. They were accessed via a repurposed quarry. Years ago the local council turned that pit into a gorgeous green space with a pond, plenty of trees, and greenery. Quite beautiful. But the caves down there collected run-off whenever it rained and flooded."

I tense up. "Did anybody get hurt?"

"No, no. But everybody learned how to swim very quickly. And if Shakka's right, then those caves lead further down than any of us ever dared to go."

"You can take me there."

She nods. "And doing it now is probably best. I don't know how accessible they are to tourists these days. Last I heard they were blocked off as a protected site."

"Because of the sprites?"

A shrug. "Back then, I doubt it. Let's have a look." She roots through our travelling bag and pulls out a pair of torches which she shoves into her pockets. "It shouldn't take long." With that, she gently guides me out of the room.

Seeing us leave, Norma immediately springs into action and claims her usual place on my head. She's no longer sleepy but very much alert, her occasional shifting weight telling me how much she is studying the area around her.

Guess she's as fascinated as I am.

Together, the three of us walk back through the tourist space with its heavy incense smells and silly little bags of nonsense and then into the kitchen, out the back door, and once more into the night air, where the moon rides high in the sky, several days from full.

At least that's one thing we don't have to worry about while in this tiny town. The last thing we want is a pair of young werewolves cavorting under the full moon.

A glance back shows the upper floors and two sets of windows, equally spaced. One of these must be the room the twins are sharing, and even as I think it, I spot a dull flash of orange in one of the corners.

The window creaks open. "What are you doing?" Duo calls down to us.

"Quick recon," Rayne assures him. "Figured it's a good plan while the sun is down."

"You on comms?"

I call back quickly, "No need. You've been driving all night, get some rest. We won't be long."

"Sure thing, boss." And then, "Hey, butthead. Are you done in the bathroom yet? I need to..." His words fade off as he shuts the window and we start walking out of the rear parking space.

Rayne slips her arm through mine and guides me to the right, back the way we came along the main village road.

The gesture could be mistaken for the start of a romantic midnight stroll, but I know better.

There is a tension between us now. An urgency and readiness that comes right before the start of a field mission.

Which makes sense.

After all, getting a sense of the village is sensible, but we also have a job to do. One that neither Fiona, Solo, nor Duo can know about.

❖

We walk for several minutes, until we reach the church.

Up close it is a large and beautiful structure that the news report failed to do justice. The stones are thick and tall, roughly hewn and fresh in places. All the windows and doorways are constructed with large arches made with strong, dark wood, lining the decorated stone. Behind the remaining portions of scaffolding, the eight foot stained glass windows shine in the dim light.

Rayne stops in front of it all with her head tilted back. I follow her gaze and find a bell tower, currently empty but surrounded by several stone gargoyles and plenty of arches and layers.

"We worked on this for years," she murmurs. "This building was as much a part of my life as food or water. So much of *my* history is in these stones." Hesitant, almost fearful, she reaches out her hand. Before I can stop her, before I can open my mouth to warn her, Rayne allows her fingers to touch against the corner of the nearest stone.

I wince. Wait for the fizzle, or the burn, or the smoke.

Nothing.

"It's not consecrated yet?"

She nods. "They need that signed off by a high ranking holy figure. I doubt they've been able to do that yet."

"So we could go in, if you wanted."

"No, I—" Rayne's head jerks up. Her nostrils flare. With a little gasp she darts away around the back of the building, a flash of movement so fast I barely see it.

I stand frozen, feet locked to the ground in confusion. What the hell is she doing?

My mouth opens with my intent to call, but at that moment Norma unfurls from her position on my head and darts down to the ground. She zips after Rayne at a speedy pace, the flick of her tail the last to vanish around the corner.

Then I hear it.

Footsteps. Slow, cautious ones, heavy on the stony ground.

I drop my weight to the balls of my feet.

An instant later, a beam of artificial light arcs across the ground, then up towards my face.

Ow.

"Hey." I raise my hands to protect my eyes. "Watch it. You trying to blind me?"

"You're trespassing," gruffs a sullen voice. "Who are you? What do you want? What are you doing here?"

"Mind your business. Nothing. Walking," I clap back.

The torchlight streaks away from my face and back to the ground. Behind it, I can finally see the tall bear of a man holding it, along with a walking cane and a sour expression.

"We already did a bunch of interviews. What are you back here in the middle of the night for?"

Oh. Oh, shit.

I don't bother correcting him. In fact, I suddenly don't want to talk to him at all because, now that I can see his face and his massive, hairy hands, I'm abruptly aware of who I'm speaking to.

No wonder Rayne bolted so fast.

"I'm so sorry, Mr. Dixon is it? I—"

"You're trespassing, I said." Bruce Dixon, Rayne's foster father, is easily six feet and another five inches on top. I'm not short by any stretch, but his height, combined with his overall size, puts me on edge.

"I'm sorry. I-I…just wanted to see."

Silence. Then, very softly, "It is beautiful, isn't it?"

"Sure is. You've done incredible work."

"Not just me. The whole village. We worked on this together."

"It's something to be proud of."

He peers at me through the beam of his torch. I carefully angle my face to give him the tiniest slither of my profile.

"You staying here?"

Lie, Danika, lie. Fast.

"Just a couple of days. I came with the initial news team, but it's so beautiful here. I thought I'd stay a little longer. See the sights. Enjoy the village."

Bruce softens visibly. He even clicks the torch to a less aggressive setting and takes a step or two backward. "Well, don't make a nuisance of yourself. Wandering around at night, you'll likely scare someone, and some folk have dogs."

I press my hands together. "I'm sorry. I really didn't want to bother anyone. I'll just go. Goodnight."

And I flee. Not a run exactly, but certainly a brisk walk further along the road and away, way, way away from the church.

As I go, I can feel Bruce's gaze on me, watching.

Though I've no idea where I'm going, I keep moving quickly along the street until it curves ever so slightly to shield me from view. Only then do I stop and chance looking back.

The street is empty.

By the time I look back again, Rayne is in front of me, with Norma cuddled against her chest. Her mouth is turned down at the corners, her eyes sparkling.

"You okay?"

She shakes her head. "He looks so old. And his voice…there's a tiredness that never used to be there. What happened out here?"

I touch her arm. "I don't know." A soft sigh. "Are you sure you're up to this?"

Rayne shakes herself, visibly bringing herself out of some thoughts I'll never truly know. "Yes. I…yes, I'm fine. Let's head out. If I remember well enough, I've a good idea of where the cave sprites might be."

She moves quickly, one hand not quite in mine but around my wrist. I don't fight it.

The near-miss encounter with Bruce came out of nowhere, and neither of us had discussed what to do if any of the family happened to find us.

Perhaps Rayne thought we could avoid them entirely. Maybe she even hoped for that. But the size of this place even at a glance tells me that it would be very hard to walk from one side of the village to another without running into people.

We can't avoid the Dixons, no matter how hard we try.

And now, as we walk, I think Rayne has finally come to realise that for herself.

# Chapter Thirteen

The walk to the filled-in quarry is quicker than I anticipated, only a half hour at a brisk pace. I find myself wondering how any parent would let their child stray so far from home unattended, the way Rayne seems to claim she would.

But then, village life is very different to city life.

As she described, the spot is beautiful—clearly man-made, but very green and lush. I can only imagine the volume of earth and stone moved to make such a thing possible. The pond in the centre is roughly hewn into the rocky ground once past the initial area of grass and trees. Vaguely round it is dotted with all manner of lilies, weird ferns, and other green things I have no name for. Several ducks swim easily on the surface too, though for the most part the area is quiet and still.

Norma clearly loves it, leaving Rayne's arms to investigate on foot. She hops around the plants and lower stones, scratching, snuffling, cackling. This must be a huge adventure for her, all the new smells and sights.

I leave her to follow at her own pace and allow Rayne to lead me around the nearest edge to the far end, which takes another fifteen minutes. Away from the bank and into the front of some low hills is a fenced area with a tall, steel security gate across the front, easily twelve feet high.

Great.

The padlock is old but secure, and the signs across the front read *DANGER, KEEP OUT.*

"Homey. What was so appealing about this place, anyway?"

She eyes me wearily. "I stopped coming here when I was sixteen, maybe a little older, but other young people would still come. The gate is new. Most of us could easily climb over the first one."

"So long as *we* can get over this one, it's fine."

Rayne grins, bends her legs, and vaults into the air. She clears the gate with room to spare and lands smoothly on the other side with barely a sign of exertion.

"Show-off."

A wider grin. "Can you make it?"

I square my shoulders. "Of course I can. Just give me a minute."

Significantly longer than a minute later, I manage to get up and over.

Rayne has left me because her giggling is far too much of a distraction. Instead she is further ahead, scouting into the entrance of the cave.

She returns just as I reach the bottom, shaking a cramp out of my aching fingers.

"It's smaller than I remember. Or maybe I'm taller. But you'll have to duck once we pass this little area here."

The cave walls are uneven, but smooth—clearly they have been exposed for some time. As I run my hand across them, I feel small pockets of moss, the occasional root, and even some thin scratches. Rayne describes them as messages from visitors long past, mostly insults, crude jokes, and promises to get down and dirty. Who knew such a small village homed so many horny teenagers?

Ha.

After my third stumble on the uneven ground, I remember that Rayne and I are not at all the same. "Can I get one of the torches? I'm going to break my ankle in here."

She actually sounds embarrassed as she pulls one from her pocket. "Sorry. Habit."

At last, with a little light I can see, not only the walls but the ground and a little way ahead.

And she's right—the ceiling does get lower, forcing me to hunch low into my shoulders as I walk. It narrows too, not uncomfortably so, but enough that walking side by side is no longer possible.

Rayne takes the lead, insisting it makes sense because she's familiar with the location. I would complain, but somehow the sight of her retreating back—and backside—makes it enjoyable enough a position that I don't.

Occasionally we pass little divots or gaps in the walls where the cave and its tunnels have made some odd shapes. I walk past them without stopping, though Rayne does often stop to assess them, peering into the darkness beyond. "These are new."

I shrug. "Natural structures change all the time."

"Maybe. But there's air coming through them. Like there's space on the other side."

I swing the torch her way, wary of her frown.

"Does it—"

Her hand flies out, a fast, sharp move in front of my face like snatching at air.

My words die as she turns her wrist, exposing the small shard of wood—I think—trapped between her fingers. It has tiny bristles on one end and a sharp tip.

"What the hell is that?"

She studies it, even bringing it close to her face to sniff. "A dart of some kind, maybe? I heard something move and—Get down!"

I obey, hurling myself flat to the ground with the torch wedged beneath me.

The sudden darkness swells like a cloud, almost palpable in the enclosed space.

Rayne moves around me, her feet slamming close to my hands and face but never touching.

Then, nothing.

I wait.

Still nothing.

She's doing that still thing, waiting out whatever is lurking in the darkness. I know it. Rationally I know it, but the longer I lie flat to the hard ground, dampness seeping into my clothing, the more I feel nerves begin to bubble inside me, slow at first, just on the edges of my senses, then building, rising inside me like steam in a plugged kettle. It will explode if I don't let it go, I know it.

And then, in the gloom, I see two spots of yellow.

"Rayne…"

She shushes me, from somewhere behind. How the hell did she get back there?

The yellow brightens, grows larger. Eyes. Just like my dreams.

Tightness fans across my chest. My fingers grip uselessly at the ground.

"Rayne?"

"Wait," she snaps.

But I can't. If I don't say something, see something, do *something*, I'm going to scream. The fear will boil over and consume me until nothing remains but the burned, dried remains of what was once my sanity.

I lean off the torch, flash it ahead of me towards the eyes.

They vanish at once, showing instead the wall of the cave and nothing more.

Rayne is behind me, her back turned to me, crouched low to the ground near my feet. Her entire body sings with tension, and her head is cocked to one side. I've no idea what she can hear, but an instant later, she spins on her heel and darts out her hand again, up, left, down, left.

With each movement I can see she has caught another of those weird darts. She drops them fast, and I see dozens of them now, dotted on the ground around us.

Fuck. Oh fuck, fuck. Are they poisoned?

"Kill the light," she cries.

But I can't. I just can't. Those eyes only ever appear in darkness, and now, trapped beneath tonnes of earth in some strange village, I can't bear the thought of seeing them again.

"I—"

"Danika!"

She's next to me now, and her hand hovers near my shoulder. Three of the weird little darts stick out the back of her wrist.

"Move," she yells.

That I *can* do.

Scrambling, stumbling, I reach my feet and begin to run. Or try to. My legs don't want to work. In fact, nothing wants to work at all. My fingers tremble, and the torch tumbles out of my hand. As the powerful spear of light careens downward, I catch glimpses of movement around us. Then the torch hits the ground and dies.

Darkness again.

Good thing, really, because my vision is swimming, a problem somehow eased by the all-enveloping blackness.

What the hell are we going to do?

❖

I take another step and fall to my knees. The jolt of pain dances up my joints, pausing in my hips and pelvis before racing back down again.

Fuck, it hurts.

Something scratches my ankle, another something on the side of my neck. Tiny, like pinpricks, but abruptly noticeable.

"Danika, get up."

"I can't," I say. Or I think I do. My tongue is large and awkward on my lips, my teeth itchy. Everything is itchy, actually. No, hot.

Everything is hot. A line of sweat glides down the side of my face. I try to touch my lips, but my hands are too big, like massive, puffy pillows against my cheeks.

How weird is that?

"Please, we're leaving," Rayne calls out in the darkness. "Stop, please. Just let us leave—we're not here to hurt you."

Now who on earth is she talking to? There's no one in this cave but us, right?

Oh, and the yellow eyes.

I look for them again, but I can't see anything now. Only feel.

Rayne's hands are on me—I've always loved that—and she's pulling me.

We're moving. Flying. Gliding through the air like birds on warm air currents.

Wow, flying feels great. I laugh and spread my arms, beating them down against the air to gain some height. I've always wanted to fly. Who knew I could actually do that?

The wind is cool on my face, stinging but fresh.

I'm moving so fast now, and the darkness falls back to reveal sky, clouds, and stars.

So shiny.

Have they always been so shiny? And bright.

Maybe because I'm so much closer to them now? I flap again, and something beneath me cries out. A familiar sound, from a long time ago, but it's far enough away that I'm pretty sure I don't need to worry about it.

There's a bird too. It's so big, but still cute. And it talks. It calls my name as I fly alongside it, yelling over and over and over.

"I'm right here," I tell the bird.

It calls again, winging along beside me like a faithful pet.

Cute. Maybe if I get close enough, I'll be able to pet it.

I want to reach out, but I know if I do, if I stop flapping, I'll fall. People can't fly on their own, right? They need to flap, they need to help. Flying is an exercise, like running or jumping.

Oh, but it's hard to fly now. I'm tired. In fact I'm very tired.

The clouds close in around me, cool and fluffy, and I fight the urge to close my eyes. Can't fly if I can't see, after all. Maybe if I can hold on a tiny bit longer, I'll be able to fly all the way home.

But I *am* tired. And it's hard to breathe now. I'm too high. The air is thin, and my chest is tighter than ever before.

Why is everything silver and grey? What are all those sparkles?

Another voice calls my name, but it's not the bird now, it's something else. Familiar.

But I really don't understand why anybody is calling me right now. Can't they see I'm busy? Can't they see I'm flying? Then again, a safe place to land is a good idea, right? That way I can do it carefully without hurting anyone. And then I can figure out why my chest hurts so much. Why my legs don't work. Why my wings don't work.

Did I always have wings, though?

Surely that's not right.

I close my eyes. It's just a blink, really, the smallest wink, but when I open them next, the sky is gone. So is the other little bird calling my name. Instead is a rush of blurry colours like sketched out streaks on black craft paper. More air fans my face, and my skin crawls with pain.

So. Much. Pain.

I cry out, I think. Hard to know. But my hands and my feet, my joints—all of them—why does everything hurt so much? My stomach and chest burn from the inside out. Fuck, it hurts.

Nausea claws through my insides, and I vomit, hot streams of it sliding down my chin and neck.

Someone moans in disgust. Calls my name.

Why can't I answer back?

I catch the scent of my own insides and then warm ooze of *something* down my arms.

For the first time I wonder if I should be worried about all this. The flying was nice, but the vomit? The pain? Those are bad things, I know they are. They have to be.

A fresh sharp pain jabs into my thigh, along with pressure, firm and steady. From that point comes a coolness, like an ice pack, gentle cold that spreads out further and further.

Someone calls my name again. Several someones, actually, many voices all joined together to make a chorus of familiar sounds. Kinda pretty.

"Please, Danika." That's the voice from before. It's desperate now, though. Insistent and frantic. "Danika, you have to open your eyes. Danika. Wake up."

Oh. My eyes are closed? For real? And what are they talking about, of course I'm awake. I have been for ages. Haven't I? People can't fly with their eyes closed after all.

I frown. I feel my brow furrow. People can't fly. *I can't fly.*

"There. She's trying. See her forehead? Danika?"

I turn, but I can't see. Why am I alone in the darkness again? I hate it here. It's frightening. And so lonely. I don't care about the flying—I don't want to be here any more. This place is dark and scary, and I don't want to be in it.

"*H-help*—" Fuck, my lips feel like lead weights. "Help me."

"We're trying, but you have to open your eyes. Can you move your arms? Your legs? Can you move anything?"

I try. Damn it, but I try. Everything is heavy, though, from my arms, to even the tip of my pinkie finger. My eyelids are hardest of all. I fight, push, breathe through the combined pain and cold flooding my body, and then, at last, they open.

Rayne. It's Rayne. She's above me, staring into my eyes, bloodied tears streaking down her cheeks.

This isn't the cave. As soon as my eyes are open, I'm sure of that. This place is indoors, with gentle artificial light and ceiling tiles and painted walls and a carpet and a bed and—I'm in a bed.

I sit up.

Agony pierces my skull, like thousands of tiny needles pricking at my brain.

My stomach roars in fury, and more vomit claws its way into my throat. It doesn't hit my clothes this time. Someone is holding a bucket in front of me to catch the disgusting flow, which stinks worse than anything else I've scented in months. More violent convulsions from my midsection, then a reprieve.

The bucket is whisked away, and Rayne is back, her hands on my shoulders pushing me down.

I let her. Confusion is starting to catch up to the pain. "Where are we? What happened?"

"Relax. We're safe. We need to make sure you have enough of the antidote."

"Antidote?"

I know I must sound like a frightened child, but I don't care. What the hell happened? Why do I need an antidote? How did we get out of the cave? Where are we? Why are my clothes gone?

I notice that last part when I realise that Rayne's hands are against my bare shoulders. A glance shows that my top and jacket are gone, and everything below my lower half is covered with a thin off-white sheet. I don't think I have my jeans or my shoes on, but I can't be sure.

"Rayne—"

"I'll explain everything, I promise. You just need to be still for a few more moments. Can you do that?"

"Everything hurts."

"You need to let the antidote work. You had a shot in the thigh, that should help. Can you drink this?" She holds a small white mug close to my lips.

The liquid inside is thick, brown, and bubbling. I can't think of anything less appealing, but if Rayne wants me to drink it...

I open my mouth and she tips the disgusting mixture in.

It oozes over my lips and tongue like mud, but far worse to taste, like slightly too old milk and stale coffee, on a base of overboiled Brussels sprouts. And it's icy cold, despite the bubbles. What the hell is it?

But Rayne keeps pouring, so I keep drinking.

"Holy hell," I mutter.

Rayne smiles. Actually smiles. "That sounds far more like you. Keep your eyes open if you can. You need to stay awake."

Fine. There's no way I'm sleeping now, anyway. I'm far too confused and nervous about what the hell has happened. "Please, what's going on?"

"Poison, Agent Karson. A pretty hefty dose from what I can tell. You're lucky you got here when you did."

I whip my head around and notice the door for the first time. It's open, and in it stands a figure in protective rubber covers, including gloves, an apron, and booties over their shoes. Their face is mostly lost behind a mask that covers everything from chin to lower eyelids, but it doesn't matter. Even through the gloves I can see the coarse curls of dark hair on those truly massive hands. The rest is just a bonus.

My fingers clench on the sheets. I close my eyes for the briefest moments before remembering that Rayne wants me to keep them open. Then I look at her.

Still beside me, still concerned, still wary. But now I see her clothes are covered in mud and grass stains. In fact, the only clean—well, cleanish—parts of her are her hands and face, though they are stained red from her tears of blood. She looks down at the ground, hands clasped in her lap.

I look again at the figure in the doorway. Back to Rayne. To the door. To Rayne. Door. Rayne.

Oh, balls.

Bruce Dixon moves fully into the room.

# CHAPTER FOURTEEN

In the brighter light and close up, Bruce looks far less intimidating than he had outside. His is broad, yes, but rather more like a cuddly bear than a wrestler. His eyes are narrowed but with concern more than anything else, and his large hands move slowly on the plastic tray he carries.

It's draped with several tablecloths and laid out with two bowls, a saucer, two cups, and a spoon. I can't see the contents, but they look normal enough.

Slowly he sets the tray down and begins to pull off his rubbers, balling them tightly before underhanding them into a basket near the door. The lid twirls once, then slams flat, trapping the contents within.

Only then do I notice where my clothes are, in a small heaped pile near that same bin, with the few items I keep on my person at all times resting on top. My watch, though, that is still on my wrist.

My thoughts are still fuzzy—very fuzzy—but this is a sharp enough slap to the senses to help wake me.

Once more I sit up, and the pain is considerably less, though once more my head swims with uncomfortable dizziness.

Rayne rests her hand on my shoulder again. "Slowly."

Of course.

Inch by inch I work my way up the pillows stacked against the headrest. Rayne helps me by fluffing them up, with intense focus. I suppose that must be far better than meeting her father's gaze.

Bruce approaches the side of the bed. He doesn't look at Rayne either. Instead he gently takes my wrists and positions his fingers to read my pulse. His gaze is on his watch as he counts out the beats of my heart, and I can see the mental note he makes when done. Next, he uses both hands to check the skin under my chin and to the sides of my neck.

He presses in, feeling for...I don't even know what, before shining a tiny penlight into my eyes.

My last GP appointment hadn't been this thorough.

The last thing he does is lift the sheets lower down and inspect my feet.

I cry out. "What the hell is that on my leg?"

He arches an eyebrow. "I assume where the poisoned dart hit you, Agent." He says that last word with slow, deliberate stress. "The site will be inflamed and tender for several more days. You have one on your neck too."

Something about those two areas touches my memory. A brief flash of pain. Short but intense, like a bug bite or blunt pinprick.

"Darts?"

"Those sprites don't like visitors much. They aren't usually hostile, far from it, but lately they have been pretty skittish. The excavation work must have encroached on their territory. Some of them are leaving the area entirely—others are turning up in very odd places."

I'm still fighting to catch up. I shift the sheets myself, and yes, my jeans and boots are gone. Probably for the best because the huge swelling above my ankle would probably hurt a good deal more if wedged into the top of my boot.

Instead the lurid purple lump is free and exposed, the size of a small egg and solid to the touch. I find the one on my neck, relieved to note that it is somewhat smaller. Good luck wearing high-necked tops for the next couple of days, though.

"Sprites? The cave sprites?"

Bruce nods. "I would have told you if I'd known that's where you were going."

He's upset with me. I suppose he has a right to be. I straight-up lied to his face. But then, what would he really have done? What *could* he have done?

I want to look at Rayne, I want to ask her questions, but she refuses to look at anyone. Her shoulders are hunched up, her head lowered. Not sure I've ever seen her look so much like a scolded child.

The door bursts open. Through it darts a young girl, possibly in her early twenties. Her face is drawn and pale, her clothing flapping as she runs—pyjamas beneath a long denim jacket. Did she just get out of bed? Who is she?

She scans the room fast, then lights on Rayne. Her eyes grow wide, her mouth wider. "Emily? Em, is that you?"

Rayne winces.

The girl squeals, a shrill yelp of shock and delight. "Em, I don't believe it. It's you, it really is you." She throws herself at Rayne and clings, hugging with such a grip I'd worry if I didn't know Rayne could take it. "How?" she gushes. "I thought you were dead. We all did. We had a funeral. How can you be here?"

The silence that follows crawls over my skin like dozens of insect legs. I roll my shoulders against it, but the feeling persists. And so too does the stillness.

Several seconds pass before the newcomer seems to realise something is wrong. She pulls back from Rayne slowly, wide eyes relaxing from delight to concern. "Em? Sis?"

Bruce clears his throat. "You need to wait outside."

"But—"

"Viola, no. Emily will be out to you shortly. I have a patient right now."

For the first time, she looks at me. Viola. This is the sister Rayne had been talking about. She's the one getting married.

"Who are you?"

I risk a glance at Bruce. Somehow I don't want to get into the middle of this.

She looks me over again, more keenly this time. "Oh, poison." A nod. "Don't worry, Pa will have you right as rain, just you wait." Again she looks at Rayne. "I'm so glad you're back. I've missed you so much." With that, she leaves, pulling the door closed behind her.

Wow.

❖

I would rather be *anywhere* else in the world right now. On a daft blind date arranged by Mum, working with Quinn, sitting with Shakka, anything. Anything at all.

Bruce sighs. "The poison on those darts is pretty powerful, but I've seen it enough times. The medication isn't hard to come by if you know what to look for, so you had a liquid version and then an additional shot in your thigh. You'll be fine—just take it easy for a day or two and try not to aggravate the areas the darts hit you." He counts across his fingers as though ticking off items on a list. "You may experience a little nausea, possibly memory loss too, though that's rare. Look out for fatigue, and if there's any sort of relapse, or if those lumps start to ooze or bleed, you'll need to let me know."

"I…um…thank you, sir."

He looks surprised at that. "Of course. Least I can do. Any child of mine comes to my home looking for help, then they get help. No questions asked." He addresses that last part towards Rayne, and I know full well he has *many* questions he would love to ask. But he doesn't.

Instead he gestures to the tray, which I can now see holds several varieties of broken up chocolate pieces, soup, ice cream, some orange juice, and some water.

"You'll need to eat as much of that as you can manage. It's a lot, but it will help."

"Thank you." What more can I say?

I look to Rayne, but she still has her head down, refusing to speak.

Bruce waits a moment longer, as though waiting, hoping for something more. When nothing happens, he gathers himself together and heads towards the door.

No. No way. Now that we're here, she has to say something, right?

I clear my throat. Hard.

Rayne twitches but doesn't look up. It doesn't matter—I know she understands.

I twitch my hands on the bed sheets, making small, subtle signs that I hope she can read from upside down.

"*Don't you dare. Talk to him.*"

I hear her inhale. She must truly be stressed if she's falling back into the human habit of breathing.

"*Quick,*" I sign.

She stands. "Bubi?"

Time freezes.

I sit between the pair of them like some spectator at a tennis match, waiting to see if the serve will be returned.

Bruce stiffens. "You still…?"

"Always." Rayne's voice is soft, tiny, childlike, and hesitant. "Always, always."

I hold my breath.

He opens the door and holds it open. "We should talk."

Without another word Rayne stands. She pauses only long enough to give me a fearful look, kiss my cheek, then she's out the door.

Her usual *edane* grace is gone. She moves with the slow, ponderous plod of the condemned. But she does move.

At the door she stops to look back at me. "I'll see you before sundown."

I nod.

The pair leave. The door shuts. I'm alone.

# Chapter Fifteen

What. The. Hell.

I still have no idea what happened out in the cave, though now I can guess at bits of it.

The sprites must have attacked us from the darkness. Rayne did her best, catching as many of the darts as she could, but when I freaked out, she had no choice but to get us out.

She must have carried me.

Not only that but she must have carried me out and all the way back here—through the cave, over the security gate, around the pond, and back along the tiny roads we used to get out there in the first place.

I can't be sure—my sense of time is wrecked—but what else could it have been?

Since Duo and Solo aren't already at my bedside, I have to assume that they don't know. No force on earth could have stopped them otherwise. Norma too.

A little thrill of fear flutters through my chest as I think about my ridiculous pet. I hope she's okay.

In fact, I'm halfway out of the bed with intent to look for her, when the door opens yet again.

A new woman walks in. Not a girl, definitely a woman, with an hourglass figure beneath her jeans and way-too-tight T-shirt. Her hair is blond and shiny, her make-up immaculate. I've no idea why anybody would be wearing a full face of paint at this time of night, but here she is. Even her hair is perfect, slicked back into a mid-height pony. Holy fuck, she looks like a catwalk model, but a decently fed one, which still makes her slimmer than me.

She glares at me, hard enough that I recoil against the pillows.

"Where is Emily?" she snaps.

Right. I've no idea who this woman is, but I dislike her at once.

"Who are you?"

"That's not your concern. I'm looking for Emily."

I grit my teeth. "She's busy. You got me instead. Who are you?"

A cool stare, first up, then down.

I'm abruptly aware that I'm halfway out of bed, in nothing but my underwear and two ugly, lumpy protrusions. My locs must be a mess too.

As gracefully as I can in this bizarre situation, I return to a more reasonable sitting position and pull the sheets up to my chest, where I tuck the edges beneath my underarms.

"Linda Halidon," she says, with a faint tilt to her chin and an edge of expectancy in her voice.

I stare back. Am I supposed to know who she is?

A hiss of frustration. "Where is Emily? Is she here? I want to see her. Where is she?"

Damn.

While I *know* her name was Emily Friedman, I'll never get used to hearing people refer to Rayne that way.

I allow myself a moment to breathe my confusion and frustration out through my nose. "She's talking."

This Linda woman intensifies her glare in my direction. "So she *is* here? How? She's dead."

There's an obvious answer to that. At least obvious to my mind. I mean, Bible stories and folklore aside, there is but one instance of very real people walking the streets *after* they've died. But somehow I feel like simply saying *vampire* isn't the right call here.

It's clear Rayne hasn't told anybody yet, so I'm not going to be the one to do it for her. There's no way I can make that my job.

So I keep my mouth closed.

Linda huffs once, then spins about on her heel. Only then do I notice she's wearing tall wedge-heeled shoes that are apparently responsible for at least three inches of her height. Who *is* she? And why does she look catwalk ready at stupid o'clock in the morning?

She mutters something about waiting, then glides from the room, leaving behind a cloud of whatever perfume she's wearing. No idea what it is, but it smells expensive. That's as much as I know.

This place is a whirlwind, that's for sure.

My next attempt to get out of bed is successful, and I use it to get to my clothes. They are filthy and torn. Shredded in places. What the hell did Rayne have to do to rescue me?

I manage to find my phone in the remains of one of my pockets and quickly call out.

Solo answers on the first ring. "It's half an hour until sunrise. Where are you?"

"We got in trouble. I'm down."

Surprised little huffs down the line. "Out?"

"Temporarily. Can you find us?"

He hesitates. "You don't know where you are?"

"I woke up here and haven't been outside yet." My knees wobble in warning, so I sit on the floor. "I'll need help getting back to Fiona's place too. I don't think I'll be able to walk very well."

"We leave you alone for a couple of hours—"

Damn. I feel like a scolded child. "It's not my fault, all right? Things got...complicated."

A pause as he speaks away from the phone, likely to his brother. Then to me, "If you're still in Moarwell, we'll find you in five."

"Thanks."

"It's what we're here for. Good thing, apparently. Rayne?"

"She"—I bite my lip—"is fine."

Solo grunts. "I don't need to be a Grey Tail to hear stuff, boss." He doesn't wait for an answer, simply clicks off.

I stay on the ground, the back of my wrist pressed to my forehead. What a freaking mess.

When the door next opens, Rayne is the one to step through. More red stains her cheeks, and both eyes are edged with that little rim of silver. Seems she's had a stressful time too.

Without speaking, she lifts me, effortlessly, off the ground and wraps her arms around me. The only reason I'm not dangling from her grip is because I'm so much taller. I melt into her hug, allow her to squeeze it out until my lungs can no longer take it.

"Rayne...?"

She lets go long enough to shift her grip, then carries me back to the bed. "You shouldn't be moving," she murmurs.

"Are you okay?"

"I don't want to talk about it."

"But—"

"Yet. I will, but not now."

Guess I'll have to accept that. "We need to get back to Fiona's."

A soft shake of the head. "I'm going to stay here. Bubi...Bruce has good enough facilities to house me safely, and I don't want to be too far from you."

"I can't stay here." The thought fills me with dread. What am I going to say to these people? Sure it would have been easy if we'd arranged to meet with them. If we were open and clear. But now, in these circumstances, I don't know that anybody will have anything kind to say to me.

"You need to. Just until tonight so he can monitor you. Please trust me. We don't know what else the poison might do to you along with everything else."

She's right. Of course she's right, but nerves turn my stomach like a cement mixer.

"Where's Norma?"

Rayne pulls the smallest of smiles. "Downstairs. She came back with us when I carried you out of the cave. The only reason she's not here now is because Bruce distracted her with a chit-chit pillar."

"A what?"

"Oh, there's a proper name, but I always called it that as a child." She frowns. "Think of it like catnip but for chittarik, all wrapped around a tall post they can roost on."

That's all well and good, but far more important is what she said before that. About carrying me out of the cave. My heart sings as I think about what she must have done. "So you *did* save me."

She stares at me.

I chuckle. "Of course you did. I'm an idiot. Who else would have? But what happened?"

Rayne studies the back of her hand. For the first time I notice the thin white bandages wrapped around her wrist. Vaguely I remember the blurry sight of three darts sticking out of her skin.

"They attacked us. No warning, no sound, nothing. Just little darts flying out of the darkness. I caught a few but there were so many. Then two of them hit you and you were—" That silver flash intensifies in her eyes before dying down. "You were not okay. I was so scared. No bleeding, no marks, but your entire body got so hot. You were delirious. Sweat poured off you, and there was foam coming out of your mouth. It got worse as I carried you back."

A shudder ripples through me. "I don't remember any of this."

"You weren't really there. I put you on my back and ran as fast as I could. The gate is mangled, but it would have taken too long to jump it safely, so I kicked it down. Norma followed us all the way back, panicking and yelling. I can't imagine how much of the village knows something happened."

"You carried me all that way?"

Another of those pointed looks. "I'd carry you to the moon and back if I had to, Danika."

Warmth fires through my body from my chest out. Even my face is hot, I can feel it. Damn it, I love when she talks like that. I fold my hands in my lap to give them something to do and concentrate on keeping my expression straight.

Not that it matters. She knows full well what her words have done.

"The whole time I had you on my back, you were muttering, whispering. You were frightened. But I couldn't do anything, I couldn't help. I just knew I had to get you somewhere quickly, and the only place"—she lifts her hands helplessly—"was here."

"And *here* is…?"

"This is Bub—I mean, Bruce's Rancher office." She gnaws her bottom lip. "Since he was out earlier, I knew he'd be here, and I knew the *only* chance of helping you, short of going to Clear Blood, was here. You were lucky. He's dealt with those sprites before. If he hadn't…" More redness fills her eyes. "If he didn't have an antidote, I don't think I could have—"

"Rayne." I put my hand over hers. "It's okay."

"It's not." Crying openly now, she grips my hand in both of hers. "In a couple of minutes I'll be dead to the world and I won't know if you're all right until I wake up again. How can I protect you if I can't be awake in the day?"

I don't know what to say to that.

"Promise me," she whispers, crawling up onto the bed with me to closer stare into my eyes. "Don't leave here today, Danika. Please. Stay here and let Bruce watch over you. Let him make sure there aren't any more ill effects."

"I—"

"No. No excuses. Forget Shakka for now, forget the Blade, forget the sprites. Get better first. Please?"

More tears slide down her cheeks. The blood is thick and ever so slightly gooey, meaning she must be ready for another feed. Given that she fed barely forty-eight hours ago, I know she must have expended a lot of energy to get me back here safely. Moving that fast, with additional weight on her back? She's strong, of course she is, but that must have cost her.

"Danika?"

I wipe the tears away with the pad of my thumb. "I'll stay with Bruce."

"Your word," she insists. "Promise me. Right now."

With the index finger of my free hand, I draw an *X* over my chest, then make snipping motions towards my hair. "On my locs and hope to trim."

Tension and fear flow out of Rayne like water. I see every part of her relax instantly, and she smiles the sweetest of smiles at me.

"Thank you. Now I have to go. I'll see you tonight."

She bends in for a kiss. I give it to her.

Her skin is cold and clammy, her lips and cheeks damp, but I don't care. I kiss her back with everything I have, using the small gesture to say all the words we don't have time for right now.

With a last look at my face, she darts away, a quick flash of speed that leaves the door creaking in her wake.

I'm alone again.

# CHAPTER SIXTEEN

I use the time to eat. Or try to, anyway. My throat feels scratchy and sore, almost narrow. I assume it's a side effect of the poison and realise then why Bruce asked that I eat as much as I could. The fluids are easyish, as is the soup, but that chocolate hurts on the way down.

Though I know the healing benefits of chocolate, there is only so much of it I can handle before my throat insists on a break. But that's something now, which is better than before.

I'm just thumbing a few melted pieces into my mouth when I hear a commotion beyond the closed door, several voices raised in question and cries of alarm.

Oh, balls.

I stand and this time find the motion much easier, easy enough that I'm able to wrap the bed sheet around me, tuck it in tight, and waddle my way over to the door.

Yup. The boys have arrived.

I push the door open to meet a short landing area with a staircase that curves. The guard rail is open, so as I walk down, I can see into the living space beneath, wide and orderly with several sofas against the walls and a TV in one corner. This looks much more like a home than a Rancher's anything.

In the middle of it Duo and Solo stand side by side, their orange and red hair bright and obnoxious among all the muted colours of this space. Bruce stands well back from them, speaking with his hands slightly raised while, at his side, Viola considers the scene with interest. I can't see Linda anywhere, but that's not a problem for me. I already intensely dislike the woman.

Both wolves visibly straighten when I reach the last few steps and relax after a quick sniff of the air.

It takes Bruce a moment longer to spot me, and his voice rings with alarm. "What are you doing out of bed?"

"I heard you guys fighting. I thought I should mediate."

Solo glares at me. "I wasn't fighting."

Duo snorts. "I was."

"Guys"—I shake my head at them—"this is Bruce Dixon. He's a Rancher here and he treated me."

"Is that why you smell like old rot and dead seaweed?" Duo ventures.

Solo quips, "And look like you swallowed a golf ball?"

I sigh. "Thanks, guys."

A shrug and a soft, choroused, "It's true."

"Mr. Dixon"—I face him—"I'm sorry. I should have mentioned I asked my colleagues to come find me. I wanted them to know I was all right after I didn't check in last night."

He eyes me coolly. "There's a lot of things you neglect to mention, Agent."

Ouch.

I pull my shoulders back a little. "Some things aren't my business to mention, sir."

He glares at me. Then nods. Some of the fight seems to ooze out of him, and he plants a gentle hand on Viola's shoulder. "Are you all right?"

She sniffs.

Now that I look closer at her, I can see she has been crying. Of course, as a human, her tears are watery and clear, but the signs on her face are just as evident. She looks at me, then breaks away from her father to stand in front of me.

Like Rayne, she is tiny, but very slight with it. More so even than Rayne. "Thank you, Agent."

I lift my eyebrows at her. "Huh?"

"You might not understand what you did, and Emily—I mean, Rayne—will never tell you, but you probably saved her life. In more ways than one."

"I—" Before I even try to get the words out, I stop. I mean, nothing I say will really match what she's giving me, so I don't even try. Instead I smile as warmly as I can manage. "I would do it again in an instant."

She nods. "Can we talk later? After you've had a rest? I have... questions."

I'm sure she does. Oh, boy.

"Um…" I try to find excuses.

She hurries and says over me, "Nothing complex or invasive, I promise. I just…Pa might be a Rancher, so I meet more than most around here, but still, there's so much I want to know. I promise I won't take too much of your time. Please?"

Fuck, she's really sweet.

"I'll do my best." It's the best I can manage.

"Thank you." She backs up. "I'm going to get a bit more sleep. I have some classes later tonight, and I don't want to be falling asleep in them. You'll rest too, though, won't you, Agent?"

Again that curious stress on my title. Both Bruce and Viola do it, though I get the feeling that it is for entirely different reasons.

"Of course. Rayne made me promise."

She winces at the name but smiles hastily to cover it. "Good. Um, goodnight, again, I guess?"

The sun has risen. It's most certainly not night any more, but I don't have the heart to fight her on it. Instead I give her the smallest wave and watch her head out the door, which appears to lead outside.

Bruce looks back to me. "Please stay here, Agent. I'm working, so I'll be down here in the office. You can call me if you need anything. There's a pulley you can use near the bed that will alert me. You boys—I assume you'll want to stay here with her?"

They nod. In unison. Of course.

"Fine. In that case, your chittarik is also down here. Should I fetch her?"

I can feel the widest of smiles stretch over my face. "Yes, please."

"Of course. I'll bring her to your room."

Ha, right. Now I see where Rayne gets it from. Orders without giving orders. Directions without giving directions.

I take the hint and gesture both Solo and Duo to follow me back up the stairs. They do so quietly, one to either side of me and slightly back like a pair of matched bodyguards.

Back in the room I use the bed while Solo positions himself near the door. Duo sits on the edge of the mattress close to my knees.

The pair are tense. Not uneasy, but certainly ready.

Can't be surprised, really.

But now I need to figure out how to explain how I got this way without explaining how I got this way.

While I think about it, Bruce arrives with Norma cradled against his chest. He has one hand on her back, maybe to soothe her, but she is the most blissed out little pest I've ever seen.

Her eyes are partially closed, her wings droopy. Her tail hangs limp behind her, occasionally twitching as she breathes little sighs of contentment. It's kinda funny, to be honest.

She sees me and straightens enough to call my name, before Bruce places her on the end of my bed.

His expression shifts from vague interest to outright shock on hearing her call, then fascination as she worms her way up the bed and into my arms.

"She imprinted on you?"

"A while ago." I smile at my daft dummy of a pet. "I pulled her out of a river, and she's barely left my side since."

Bruce assesses me again. This time he seems to be considering more than I can see. "That's rare, Agent." This time when he uses my title, there's none of that odd stress on it. Just...respect? "She must really trust you."

I shrug. "She lets me trim her claws occasionally. No one else is allowed that honour."

He nods. "I've seen a lot of chittarik in my time. They mostly make sounds, repetitive ones as I'm sure you know, but rarely names. It's very special when they connect to someone enough to use their name."

"It's annoying," I mutter. "Remember that ancient TV show kids used to watch? With all those weird animals that could only say their own names? She's like that, but more irritating."

"Perhaps. But you really should be honoured. These creatures so rarely do that. This is the first time I've ever seen it in person. I've read articles here and there, but they're just theories."

I scratch Norma under her chin, particularly under the flap of skin there. She purr-croaks at me, clearly delighted at this attention. "Just lucky, I guess."

"Yeah." He strokes the huge brush of hair that makes his beard. "Lucky." Then, to the boys, "I'm more than happy to bring up anything she needs, but please, help her keep stress to a minimum and don't let her move around too much."

"I'm right here, y'know."

"Indeed. But Rayne has already warned me of your tendency to take matters into your own hands. Please don't do that today if you can help it."

Wow, thanks, Rayne.

But I nod my agreement to him.

Bruce backs out and away, leaving the door slightly ajar.

Solo turns his head slightly to angle his ear towards the door. Only after a few seconds does he look back to me. "So, what do we need to know?"

I sigh. "It's a long story."

"Apparently we have all day." Duo helps himself to a piece of my chocolate. "Let's have it, boss. What's going on?"

And so I tell them everything.

Well…*almost* everything.

❖

The day is long and boring. I sleep, but only a little, safe in the knowledge that both Duo and Solo are with me on guard duty. An odd way to put it, and yet…?

Solo in particular is merciless in his grilling of me. He wants to know everything, and I make a point of telling him. In fact, the only thing I leave out is why we were down with the sprites in the first place. In my version, we simply happened on the cave and chose to look inside, but I'm certain neither he nor Duo are fooled.

More than once they share a glance between them, and I know full well they are conversing without me. Only fair, I suppose.

The whole time, the blissed-out Norma chills on my chest, occasionally snuggling into me, occasionally calling my name, a few *dan-dan*s here and a *son-dar* there. The night has been rough on her, that's certain. Though catnip for chittarik is not something I've come across before, I'm pleased Bruce thought to use it. I never would have thought of such a thing.

And, of course, I explain Rayne's background with these people. I don't want to, not really, but I realise quickly that keeping it secret is next to impossible. Besides, the fewer lies or lies by omission I have to remember, so much the better. But I do keep it brief, simply telling the wolves that Rayne grew up in this place and that these people are her family.

Another of those looks between them, but they seem to soften towards Bruce when they see him next.

He checks on me twice before midday, once to check on my wounds, the second time with additional food. He tells me that the horrible purple lumps appear to be going down and that I should be fine to move later on that evening.

What Bruce doesn't tell me is how many people have arrived downstairs in the time I've rested.

Not that it's a secret. With their keen hearing, the wolf twins are able to tell me much of what's going on. More than that, they take it in turns to sneak to the top of the landing and listen just before the curve of the stairs, out of sight. Perfect.

And what they find is deeply interesting. Enough to stop me tearing my hair out from boredom, anyway.

Rayne had been right.

Her flight through the village in the middle of the night was more than enough to wake several people, especially with Norma screeching the entire way.

One after the other, various members of the village drop by to check in on good ole Bruce Dixon. I don't need Duo's eye roll or Solo's scoff to know just how false those claims are.

I get the feeling that the Dixons are something of an oddity around here, and the so-called well-wishes from many of his visitors over the course of the day only highlight that more and more.

The first, an older couple, have a yapping, bratty dog. Even I can hear the high-strung terrier from up the stairs. And so does Norma, who quickly came alive to yell her displeasure towards the open door.

I nip her beak shut with my thumb and forefinger, but even I hear that the dog has settled a little. Good. I hate terriers. Are they even real dogs? Tiny and yappy, with more attitude than sense. Give me a German shepherd or a malamute any day.

The second is a young teenager with her sister. The pair claim they are doing a school project and need to investigate the duties of a local and report back. Funny that they should pick today of all days to visit the Rancher who, if I'm right, is usually shunned and distrusted by all.

Bruce handles all of it with grace and polite firmness, another trait I see in Rayne on the daily.

When his wife, Kimberly, shows up, the pair of them fight off the influx of visitors together after she gets the rundown. She even comes to see me, the same cute little woman from the news article.

Up close her greys are more visible, as are the wrinkles around her eyes and mouth. But those are clearly the product of years of smiles and hard work, and I find myself warming to her immediately.

When the wolves stand slightly to one side, she takes the trouble to approach my bed and gently hold my hands in hers. "I don't know all the details yet, but I suppose I don't have to." Her voice is soft and bright. "But Emily was always special to us. I'm sure you know we have a lot of young people pass through our home?"

"Oh, I don't really know how fostering works."

"The young people we take on are either on their way somewhere else, or too troubled for somewhere else. They come to us as a sort of pit stop. That's why our turnover is so large. But some, like Emily, stay for a long time. Until they're adults, in fact. And they build relationships here. Brothers and sisters and the like."

"She calls you Mama. And Bruce—"

"Bubi?" She grins. "The cutest nickname a young person ever picked for him. He goes by Pa and Da and Pops and all sorts, but Bubi? That's my favourite."

"Rayne—sorry. Should I say Emily while I'm here? Is that easier for you?"

Kimberly frowns. "That's sweet of you, but it's not about *me*, is it? Never has been, with any of the young people who come through my doors. I should correct *myself*. Her name is Rayne now. And that's fine. Go on."

This woman is kind, warm, and loving. The way she speaks, the way she carries herself, even the cuddly nature of her looks—I can understand why so many kids would go through her and Bruce to find themselves better lives.

I smile. "Rayne was so afraid to come here. We saw you on the news, talking about the church."

"While I assume that's not why you're here, I'm glad she was able to see it. She worked on it just as much as the rest of us. Handy with cement and a trowel, that one."

The mental image of Rayne, sweaty and hot, hefting a tray of wet cement, slips into my mind. I clear my throat.

Solo snorts from his position near the door.

Blissfully unaware—thank fuck—Kimberly continues. "If you go to the back, you'll see a tiny patch where she put her name. I remember we scolded her so firmly for that, but now, after everything that happened, I'm so glad it's there. A small reminder of her."

Damn it, I want to ask. I want to ask so very badly.

I bite my lip over the urge.

Kimberly places her hand over mine, not gripping exactly but certainly not a casual touch either. "So are you two young ladies, um…?" She lifts her eyebrows.

Another snort, this time from Duo.

I glare at the wolves. "You two want to give us some space, or what?"

That infuriating shared glance. And then, "Sure." Solo grins.

Duo ruffles his gaudy orange hair. "Gossip all you want."

The pair slip out the door and close it behind them. But I'm not an idiot. I know damn well they're still out there. They won't be listening, ear to the door, but they don't need to. Hell, they could stand downstairs if needed and still hear as much as they pleased.

"Funny pair, aren't they?" Kimberly muses.

"You've no idea. Anyway, yes. Rayne and I have been seeing each other for a few months now."

"Oh." She cocks her head at me. "Even with the…the…" Her hand waves a small circle.

"Vampire part?"

She actually looks embarrassed. "This is a small place, Agent. We see little, know less. All that stuff happening in your city is so far removed from anything around here. Brucie does let me in on small parts of his work, but not much, so I'm curious."

*Brucie?* I fight to keep my face straight. Ha ha. Good luck, since the rest of me can't manage.

"What would you like to know?"

"Is it safe?"

Oh. Not what I expected.

I study Kimberly for long moments, trying to decide exactly how much I should say. In the end, given how many lies and not-quite-truths are floating around, I opt for the truth.

"No."

She blinks at me. "No?"

"It's not safe. At all. Especially for her."

"What do you mean?"

I give her my full gaze. "Rayne is a good person. A kind person. I already know the sorts of people you and Bruce are just by knowing her. You raised her, and you raised an incredible person. But inside… there's *a thing*. A need or a hunger. And it can make her do bad things. And when you're a good person like Rayne, that can hit really hard."

"That's not what I expected you to say."

"The other stuff is still true. We have to be careful around blood, make sure she's fed regularly, keep her away from stressful stimuli, and other things, I suppose. Sunlight is a problem, obviously. That's manageable, though. But I can't say it's safe for her. She gives so much every single night. Usually for me. Usually at a risk to herself."

A slow nod. "That sounds like Emily."

I hear the slip, but I can't bring myself to correct her in this moment. She's thinking deeply, and I know my speaking would interrupt that, so I don't.

"She was fiercely protective over all her siblings. Every single one. And us—Bruce and I, I mean. It was natural for her to pursue being a police officer. And now she's a SPEAR agent?"

"One of the best."

"Protecting people every day?"

"Every *night*. The big, the small, the weak, the old, the strong, the young...everyone."

Kimberly wipes a hand across her face.

Oh, balls—she's crying.

"Mrs. Dixon—"

"Kim, if you please," she says at once. "All my young people are free to call me Kim, and you must do the same. She's safe because of you. Here because of you. You've my thanks for that."

Discomfort worms through my insides. Of course this lady will have no idea why we're really here, and I can't tell her. But the idea that's she's so grateful to *me* for anything is burning me up. I've done not a damn thing except get myself in trouble. As usual.

"Kim, then. Rayne is wonderful. My life has been nothing but joy since she entered it. I should be the one thanking you."

She flaps a hand in my direction. "Don't be silly. All we do is nurture what's there. And if that's still there despite the...the change, then that shows her strength." And with that, she hugs me. Actually leans in and treats me to the warmest hug I've ever received from a stranger.

And bizarrely it doesn't feel like a stranger's touch. It feels like home. Caring. Motherly.

The backs of my own eyes begin to sting as I realise that this small gesture has brought home to me something I've been missing for a long time now.

Kimberly doesn't notice my emotion or, like a graceful lady, chooses not to acknowledge it. But she does leave the room, quietly and softly and, just on the edges of my hearing, leaves strict instructions to both Duo and Solo to leave me alone for a few minutes longer.

I use that time to pick up my mobile phone.

"Mum," I tell the voicemail software, "it's me again. I know I said yesterday, or whenever, that I can't keep doing this, but I can't *not* do it either. I love you and I miss you. So I won't give up. Not on you, not on our family, not on any of it. You and Dad taught me that." I dash a hand across my face, wiping what must obviously be sweat away from my cheeks.

"So I'm going to keep calling. Every day if I can. And even if you don't answer, at least you'll know that I love you. I'll always love you."

The message is short, but that's all my nerves can manage. I hang up, let the phone drop into my lap, and simply hold Norma as she snoozes against my chest.

# Chapter Seventeen

Later that day, Solo is telling me a series of increasingly bad knock-knock jokes while Duo stands outside. I dutifully roll my eyes at each terrible punchline and try to think up something even half as bad to come back with. I fail. But I do spot him suddenly sit straight, head cocked to one side. His nostrils flare ever so slightly.

"What?"

"Incoming," he says simply. "Want us to stop it?"

I shrug. "Can't be that bad, right?"

Oh, how wrong I am.

The door slams open and through it stomps Linda with a bemused Duo right on her heels. Behind them both is Viola who, now dressed for the day, looks entirely different to when I saw her last.

While Linda is a supermodel—classy and expensive, Viola is a fully made-up goth with more dark makeup than I've ever seen on one face. Her shoes are massive, thigh-high monstrosities with buckles and clasps and silver studs, while her dress is a long, clinging, wispy thing with huge sleeves.

It looks fucking fantastic.

Linda pauses only an instant at the sight of Solo near my bed. A small moment, but enough for me to mentally prepare myself for anything and everything she intends to throw my way.

"What the hell did you do to my fiancée?"

Oh. Fine. Anything and everything *except* that.

"What?"

"Don't play dumb. How did it happen? When? Are you the reason she left? Why she *lied* about being dead?"

I don't intend to play dumb, but I honestly can't believe that this woman actually thinks *I* had anything to do with what happened to

Rayne. Doesn't she notice me up and sitting? Awake at four in the afternoon?

Besides, there's a far more pressing issue with what she just said.

"I—"

She snaps a hand up. "Don't you dare lie to me. Emily was a beautiful, outstanding citizen with a glorious future with me ahead of her. You snatched it all away from her. How could you?"

Viola clears her throat. "You weren't engaged any more, Linda. She dumped you, or did you forget that?"

Holy crap, so we're claws-out now?

"Shut up, you little emo bitch," Linda roars. "I didn't ask for your opinion."

Solo snarls low in the back of his throat. I doubt anybody other than Duo hears it, but I'm more than close enough. I rest a hand on the back of his wrist.

Viola shrinks back like a wilted flower, flinching even when Duo places a soft, comforting hand on her shoulder.

I spit my words through gritted teeth. "Maybe we should all calm down and—"

"Don't you dare tell me to calm down. I should call the police. I should call MI5. I should have you thrown in a jail cell. I should tell everybody in town what a menace you are, bringing all this trouble to our home."

"What trouble? I—"

"Everybody heard the screaming last night. Everybody. And that *thing*"—she jabs a perfectly manicured finger at Norma—"frightened my cats so much they refuse to leave the house. I thought you spoon people were supposed to kill the unnatural critters roaming the countryside."

Spoon?

"SPEAR?" Duo offers, his lip quirked with amusement on one side.

"Whatever you are. You don't belong here. None of you. Well, maybe you." She assesses Duo with a fresh interest in her gaze. "Speak to me later, both of you. I've a modelling contact you should meet. But *you*"—the finger snaps to me—"aren't welcome."

"Says who?" again Viola chips in. Her voice is still soft, still gentle, with a hint of a quiver, but there is defiance in her stance now. Her little hands are balled into fists. "You don't own us and you're not a part of this family. You can't tell us what to do."

"Well, someone *should* tell *you* what to do." Linda lashes right back, eyes narrowed with fury. "Look at you—dressing like a devil worshipper and shacking up to that headcase of a man-woman. I can't believe Kim allows it, much less Bruce—"

"Okay, that's enough of you." Solo is off the bed in an instant. It's not overly fast, or even aggressive, but Linda is quick to take a giant step back.

"What are you doing?"

"Escorting you out," he murmurs, "before it gets nasty."

"*More* nasty," Duo corrects, opening the door wide.

Linda plants her hands on her hips. "And who are you? Some stranger wandered into *my* village trying to give orders? How dare you? Besides, this is Bruce's place of work, and only he can—"

"They were invited to stay here, Linda. You weren't." Viola twists her hands but stands firm. "And Pa has told you time and again you can't just wander in here whenever you like."

"I am family—"

"You're a bully, and I'm glad Emily came to her senses before doing something really stupid like marrying you." More hand twisting but now a slight tilt to her chin.

"You colossal brat." Linda's voice leaps to a shrillness that hurts my ears. "You have no right to speak to me like that. You do remember who I am, don't you? The power I hold here? You can't speak to me like that and expect to get away with—"

Solo steps forward until his chest bumps Linda's arm. He doesn't touch her exactly, but he certainly does use his size and relative bulk to nudge her into moving. "Out," he asserts.

"Get away from me."

"Out," he repeats, voice dangerously low. He keeps walking forward, and she keeps giving way, still yelling past his shoulder towards Viola, who now cowers near my bed. She resembles the proverbial deer in headlights people always talk about.

Near the door Solo stops and Duo takes over, using the same herding, bumping motion to keep Linda moving.

"You answer me right now," she screeches, this time in my direction. "Who are you? Why is Emily here with you? What did you do to turn her into a demon freak?"

The smart-arse answer rides on the tip of my tongue. I long to correct her about what demons actually are and how vampires are entirely different, but instead I think of Rayne and what she would do. I keep my mouth shut.

"Answer me. I have a right to know, and I'm not leaving until I get answers. Do you know who I am? I have the power to gather the whole village behind me, and together we'll run you out. Your kind doesn't belong here, troublemakers and devil-worshippers and unnatural freaks of nature."

"Come on, miss." Duo's voice is low, but with none of the steel of his brother's. He actually sounds calm and concerned as he gently nudges Linda one last time.

Which is probably why every one of us is stunned into silence when she swings around and slaps him hard across the face. The loud crack seems to echo off the walls and floor. "Don't you dare touch me," she roars.

Duo, though unharmed, is clearly shocked to the point of speechlessness.

Solo experiences no such issue. Snarling, fingernails flashing with inky blackness, he grabs Linda by the waist and hurls her onto his shoulder. "You're lucky you're small and squishy," he growls, carrying her out of the room. "The last person to touch my brother like that lost seven fingers."

Linda screams, a cacophony of rage-dripping insults and threats, with the odd shriek of *fire* and *help* thrown in.

I leap off the bed, leaving the sheet this time, and hurry after Solo in just my underwear.

"Solo—"

"I won't hurt her," he calls back at me, still not stopping. "But if she lays another hand on my brother, I'll rip out her throat."

He says it coolly, calmly, as if he were describing his intent to buy flour and eggs.

Maybe it's the threat itself. Perhaps it's the delivery. Whatever it is, Linda at last seems to realise that she might be in danger, and her screams begin anew. She begins to kick and punch, landing blows against any part of Solo she can reach. He winces once or twice but otherwise keeps walking, an easy, resolute march along the landing and down the stairs.

As we reach the bottom, Bruce darts into view from a side room. One hand loosely grips a pen, while the other is wet and dripping, stained with a thick, blue-green fluid full of lumps and flakes of scales.

"What is going on here? Linda? When did you arrive?"

Well, if I needed any more confirmation that this woman is full of bullshit, there it is.

"Don't mind me, sir." Solo one-hands the front door with ease. "Putting the rubbish out."

Bruce gives a little cry of alarm and begins to wipe his dripping hand down his shirt. "But I—"

"Bruce? Help me." Linda continues her harpy-like screeching. "Help me—no, no, you animal—put me down. Right now. Assault. Assault. He's assaulting me. Bruce, do something."

Bruce manages half a step. "I—"

Loud clomping footfalls preview Viola's arrival at the top of the stairs. "She slapped him, Pa. No, the other one. The orange hair. She slapped him."

"I defended myself—"

"You acted like a self-important bitch." Solo cuts her off. "And now you can fucking leave. Piss off." With that he plonks her down on the far side of the door frame and slams the door. In her face.

At once, hammering, knocking, even kicking—if I recognise the sounds correctly. Pretty sure I do. I've kicked down many a door in my time.

Bruce finishes wiping his hand off on his shirt. The weird goo clings like slime, and his skin is faintly stained with it, but he makes no move to clean it. Instead he stares at the door. "What on earth...?"

Solo shakes himself off and glances at his hands. He sighs, no doubt frustrated at the sprouting of fur down the backs of his wrists and fingers. Each of his fingernails is tinged black and significantly longer than they had been minutes earlier. "I didn't need this," he murmurs.

"Take a breath," I warn.

"Yeah, yeah, I know." He closes his eyes and breathes deep, a noisy inhalation that ends with an exhale more resembling a grunt than a sigh. "People like her just piss me off."

"I'm sorry—"

He flaps a hand at me. "One of my xiblings is trans. They get enough of this stuff on the daily that I just..." He growls.

I widen my eyes. "You're not a twin?"

"Oh, I am. Only Duo and I are blood related, but I do have pack xiblings where the mental bond is as strong."

"Really? How many are you?"

He glances briefly at the door, still shuddering against its hinges in the wake of Linda's enraged onslaught. "Six."

Wow. I try to imagine sharing my brain with five other people. Of having their thoughts so close to mine that I can read them at will. The thought is not attractive in the slightest. And that's just the closest bond. The rest of the pack, of course, are right there too.

I shake my head. "No wonder you two are a bit nuts."

A smile. "No, no, that's the drugs." He laughs at his own quip, then turns again to Bruce, who is still staring at the door as though it might fall in at any moment.

"You said no stress, right? I assure you, we found her to be incredibly stressful."

Bruce looks pale. Though he hides it well, I spot the occasional shifty glance at Solo's hands and the claws half grown there. "Th-that's fine."

"Should I go back up? Or would you like me to stay here in case she comes back?"

"Um…" he sputters.

"Head back up," I say quickly. "I need a few words myself if you don't mind."

A smile. The last traces of black fade from his shortening fingernails as he gathers his temper under control.

As if on cue the hammering at the door also stops.

Blissful silence.

"Sure, boss." Solo crooks a finger at Viola as he goes. "So, Danika said you had some questions about SPEAR? My brother and I are agents too, maybe we can help you out."

"Brother? I knew it." Viola and her excited responses fade out of sight and hearing as she and Solo make their way back across the landing.

I look at Bruce. "I'm so sorry."

"No, I am. I had no idea she was in here. She must have used the back door. I would never have asked her to come here, much less visit you after such a hard night."

"I'm fine."

"Maybe, but you need to rest. You go back upstairs and do that. I'll go talk to her."

I lift my hand. "Actually, she mentioned something I thought I'd ask you about."

Bruce is quick to back up. "She and Rayne were engaged, there's no secret there. The rest you'll have to ask her about—I'm sorry, but I really can't go through it with you. It feels wrong somehow."

I understand, though it frustrates me no end.

As if Rayne isn't having a hard enough time right now, when she wakes, the house will be in chaos and she'll be facing family drama the likes of which even the most convoluted TV show couldn't script.

As I make my way back to the stairs, I hear Bruce inhale sharply.

"Agent?"

I give him curious eyes.

"What on earth is that on your back? Is it a tattoo?"

I hesitate. "You didn't see it before?"

"Of course not. Kimberly was the one to undress you, with Rayne's help of course. I wasn't in the room until after you were beneath the sheets. What is it?"

"I…I don't know."

He strokes the sides of his mouth. His nose wrinkles, and he stares at his hand, seeming to remember only a short while ago it was covered in blue-green slime. A grimace, and then, "That's a scar or a brand. Where did it come from?"

Lie? Don't lie? Half truth?

I don't even know any more, and I'm more tired than I should be for making decisions like this.

"Something back home did it to me. A creature."

"What kind of creature?"

"We're not sure."

He shifts uncomfortably. "I've never seen anything like it. And those symbols are very unusual."

No need to tell _me_ that. I've seen more of my body in angles never intended to last me a lifetime. But in so doing I've been able to get a good look at the wreckage of sore, marked skin left by the yellow-eyed black creature.

"We're working on it."

A pause, then a slow nod as though he has caught up to something. "There's a woman here by the name of Fiona Bristow. She's a psychic, and while I know SPEAR doesn't put much faith in the practise, she's very skilled. I think you should visit her."

I can't help but smile. "Maybe we will. Thanks."

I walk back up the stairs, now fighting the urge to roll my shoulders against the prickling intensity of Bruce's gaze as I leave him behind.

Humph. At least _I'm_ not the one covered in fae-ring slime.

❖

My body feels better. Not great, but certainly an improvement on early this morning when even the smallest movement sent jolts of pain through every limb and joint. I sit up in the bed, the sheets tucked around me, listening to the wolf twins chatter with Viola.

The three of them seem fascinated with each other.

Viola in particular seems to have forgotten me entirely, instead focused on the boys with dozens of quick-fire questions about how they change, why they change, when they change. Her curiosity speaks to me of a future in some form of *edane* study, which doesn't surprise me much since her father is a Rancher.

Surely some of Bruce's studies and warding duties rubbed off on her.

Then, on preparing to leave, Viola explains that her interest in *edanes* is only partly to do with her future plans. As she readies herself for her classes, she grins at my cocked head and raised brows.

"I'm studying biomedical engineering." She smooths down the wispy, lacy folds of her black dress and checks each of her glossy, black fingernails. "Sometimes I think that *edanes* are the future of human health, but then I feel really creepy and gross about it." Apologetic glances at both Solo and Duo. "So instead, I figured I'd find other ways to help with the future of healthcare."

Duo smiles gently. "That's noble of you. You're a good soul."

She ducks her head with an embarrassed but obviously pleased smile.

"How did you come out of a place like this?" Solo quips.

"I lived south of Angbec before coming here. I never actually lived there, but I heard stuff. And, I guess, I read a lot of fantasy books as a kid." She laughs. We all do.

So nice to have a moment of lightness after the weirdness of the day. And somehow, we've managed to talk about anything and everything except Rayne. I don't quite know if we all made the unconscious decision as one, but I'm pleased about it. The more I learn about this place and the people in it, the more I want to bail and never come back.

I think briefly of Shakka and the tone that almost reached respect when he last spoke to me. Hmm. If anything comes of this entire shitshow, at least he might be nicer to me from now on.

Viola leaves, and Duo watches her go with more than polite interest. "I wonder—"

"She's engaged," I tell him quickly. "Consider her off-limits."

"Fuck, not again." He sighs.

Solo roars with laughter. "How many is that now?"

"I don't want to talk about it."

"Danika, he has the worst luck." Solo glances my way. "The last five people he showed any interest in were either married or dating already. I think he just attracts these people."

I offer Duo a sympathetic smile. "Don't worry. You'll find someone."

He gruffs softly under his breath. "Finding someone isn't the issue—it's finding someone available. Is everybody in Angbec taken or in their sixties?"

I shrug.

Solo laughs harder. "The last man he dated was nineteen."

A glare. "He told me he was twenty-five."

"And before that, remember the girl with the blue pigtails?"

Duo huffs and turns his back.

So again, Solo turns to me. "She was twenty-two."

I frown. "But that's not a problem, is it? Nineteen, maybe not, but twenty-two? Surely you guys aren't much older than that?"

"If we're dating humans, pack rules state they can't be younger than us. No idea why, but that's it. So yeah, it was a problem. We're twenty-six." He adds that last part when he notices my silent question.

"What about within the pack?"

Duo shudders. "I don't want to date someone who can read my thoughts, thanks. It's hard enough with *him* in my head all the time." He glares at his brother, who smirks into the back of his hand. A moment later he aims a quick punch at him. "Shut up."

"He didn't say—oh. Never mind." I let them bicker. It's no different to being in the car with them, to be honest, but this close without the buffer of Rayne or even the front seats, it's a little more intense.

They won't hurt each other, of course not, but I've seen these two play-fight before.

Recovered from her earlier high on chittarik-nip—I really must learn the correct name for that stuff so I can get some into the house—Norma sits on the floor near my clothes. She has been walking back and forth through the small space, inspecting furniture, sniffing at corners, scratching at the carpet.

She's still mellow but somehow restless with it at the same time. I hold out a spoon with the remains of my soup, and she sticks her beak into it, lapping with her stubby little tongue. It helps a little, but I know she must be hungry.

Just as I make the decision to ask Bruce for something she can nibble on, both Solo and Duo leap to their feet. It is a boneless, slick move, so sharp and sudden that I shrink back.

"What the hell?"

They don't bother looking at each other, just move—Duo straight to my bed, Solo out the door.

"Guys?"

Duo looks me over. "You need clothes." Then he's gone too.

What the hell?

I crawl out of bed, leaving Norma with the spoon, and make my way out onto the landing. I can't see anything yet but hear the vague murmur of urgent voices downstairs. Then Duo slips out of a room on the right with a bundle of cloth in his hands.

"They won't fit, but they're better than nothing. Put them on."

"What's happening?"

"Incoming," he murmurs, eyes narrowed.

Great. Just great.

I hurry back into the room and shake out the bundle of clothes. An enormous pair of trousers with pockets on the thighs and a checkered shirt with what might be claw marks down one sleeve.

No matter. Shirt first, rolling up the sleeves and knotting the hem so it doesn't flap too much. Then the trousers. Yup, far too large, but Duo quickly follows with a belt that I use to keep the damn things from slipping off. It takes belting the things right up beneath my breasts, but at least they won't slide down to my ankles.

He thrusts a pair of boots at me, then beckons to the landing.

By the time I manage to follow, still hopping to secure the second boot, he is already downstairs, talking urgently with Solo and Bruce.

Bruce has cleaned up now, no more blue-green goo all over him, just a new, ratty shirt, open over a vest dotted with dark smudges. He glances up at me as I approach. "These boys tell me there are people heading this way."

"A mob," Solo clarifies. "Unless you're expecting"—brief pause—"about twelve guests?"

"Twelve?" Bruce scratches the back of his neck. "That's a good ear—or nose?—you have. So that fur I saw on the back of your hands earlier…I didn't know SPEAR employed *edane* field agents."

"We're new," Duo murmurs. He crosses to a window and shifts the nets just enough to peer out. His upper lip curls back in a snarl. "I don't think our little friend liked being kicked out, bro."

He shrugs. "Well, I don't like her."

"Linda? What?" Bruce immediately throws open the door and steps outside.

The weak afternoon sun throws long shadows across the ground, and with the light comes a cool breeze. After the closed-off nature of the house and the lack of windows, the wash of freshness feels good. I follow it and, on seeing out there, immediately wish I hadn't.

## Chapter Eighteen

Duo is right.

Twelve people, at least, none of them looking happy. Right at their head comes Linda, with a smug, triumphant look on her face. While the crowd behind her stops a little way back, she comes forward.

For the first time I manage to look at where the Ranch is situated against the rest of the village. We're on a corner, on a large stretch of land surrounded by openness, fenced into sections. Given the sun's position, I guess that we're on the far side of the village to the caves, meaning Rayne really did have to travel all the way through to get here.

Beyond the crowd I see a tiny slip of road curving away into the distance and the faintest glint of silver that might be sunlight on water. So we've crossed the river too.

"Linda, good afternoon." Though wary, Bruce is friendly and polite. He stops a short distance away from the door, within what appears to be the immediate boundary of the property, which is surrounded by a low, prickly hedge. "I'm sorry about earlier, but you really should arrange a time if you need to visit me. You know I'm busy."

She tosses her oddly shiny golden hair with a regal flick of the head. "And *you* know I've nothing but your best interests at heart. I don't blame you, though. I'm sure Emily coming back after all this time must have left you emotional and confused."

I clench my fists. Oh, she's smart. I can see the verbal trap, all but smell it in the air, but I don't have a chance to speak before Bruce answers.

"I...no," he murmurs. "Well, a little, but—"

"Don't worry. I forgive you." Linda looks back at her crowd of onlookers, speaking up to be sure they can hear just how graceful she's being.

Ugh. Gag me with a spoon.

"But now we really must deal with the danger you've unwittingly let into your Ranch." She looks beyond Bruce to me and then further back to where Duo and Solo are standing.

Oh, so *that's* her play.

Linda smiles sweetly, her hands clasped before her. "I took it upon myself to meet with the rest of the Moarwell Neighbourhood Council to discuss the distressing disturbances we experienced last night."

I hang back, aware that Bruce lives here, and I don't.

He positions himself to stand directly in the pathway through the hedge, effectively blocking anybody trying to walk through. "But I'd already discussed that with you this morning. And everybody else. What more is there to say? An emergency situation arose that required my Ranching skills. I dealt with it. As ever I do."

"But do these...situations...usually involve yelling and screaming and crying in the streets? And in the middle of the night. Even you must admit your *visitors* have not exactly been best behaved."

"When Class A minibeasts involved, one must expect some noise." Bruce cocks his head at Linda. "What is this about? You were there when I explained all this. And why have you brought all these people with you?"

Linda glances over her shoulder. "These people? You mean your friends and neighbours who are nothing but concerned for you? Well, if I can't bring a handful of well-wishers and concerned citizens then I'm more worried than when I arrived."

"I assure you, there's nothing to worry about. Though I do apologise for the noise. That must have been distressing to some of you in the middle of the night."

"Hmm." The expression on Linda's face speaks volumes to her mood. She once more spares a glance for the gathering behind her. This time she flourishes a piece of paper, handed to her by a middle-aged woman with washed-out purple hair and a bit of a limp.

I feel a gentle hand against my wrist. It's Duo. Though he doesn't look at me, he does gently pull, tugging me slightly towards the building. I let him, but not so far that I can't hear.

With a flourish, Linda smooths the paper across her palms. "As president of the council it is my responsibility to inform you of our formal eviction notice. Your *guests* are required to leave as soon as possible. Preferably within the next three hours."

Duo's grip tightens on my wrist.

I resist. "Now, reel it back a second, you crazy—"

The fury in Linda's eyes as she whips her head my way is intense and rather frightening. "That includes you, Agent." The word is oozing with scorn. "Whatever power or control you have in that awful city down south doesn't extend to Moarwell. You and your demon freaks are not welcome here."

A little murmur from the crowd. They're restless now, shifting and eyeing us over the little hedge. And are they closer?

Duo gives me a yank this time. "Danika."

"But she—"

"Stop it. Come inside."

"Bruce," Linda calls right over me, "we appreciate you have a job to do, and we thank you for it. But it has never been secret how the council feels about your little *side hobby*. We've tolerated it for years, but now there is an active danger to our community, and we have no choice but to take action. These unnaturals are dangerous."

Another murmur from the crowd.

She goes on. "One furry animal, another likely just as bad. Then *her*"—she glares at me—"marked with devil signs and symbols all over her body. Surely even you see the risk, Bruce?"

Wait, what signs? Does she mean what the yellow-eyed creature did to my back?

Shit. She must have seen them when Solo kicked her out. I had been running about in my underwear, after all. But *all over my body* is a bit of a stretch. Not like I'm sporting full-on body art.

Bruce lifts both massive hands in a placating gesture. "But there *is* no risk. These are employees of SPEAR."

A haughty chuckle. "Oh yes, SPEAR, the oh-so-grand *agency*"—wow, those air quotes are really audible—"filled with guns, failed police officers, and wannabe cowboys. But who are they, Bruce? Do you even know? No one does. Not really. Well, they can do whatever they want as far as I'm concerned, but well away from here. We don't want guns here, we don't want monsters here, we certainly don't want freaks and devils around our elderly and our children."

I open my mouth again, but this time Duo simply drags me away. He herds me through the front door and into Solo, who takes over holding me while his brother shuts the door.

The pair of them stare at me, not so much bodyguards this time as prison officers.

"What?"

Solo shakes his head at me. "You're an idiot."

"What did I do?"

"We need to leave," Duo adds. "The way we came was quiet. Maybe we can use that to sneak back."

"We can't." I clutch at the slipping waistband of my too-large trousers. "What about Bruce?"

The pair share a look.

"Stop that." I don't quite stamp my foot, but I'm close. "What do you two know that I don't? Why can't we talk some sense into these people?"

A small sigh from Solo. "Can't talk sense into folk who don't want it."

"That blond nightmare has already whipped them up, and she seems to be the one in charge. Do you really want to cause any more trouble for Bruce and his family?"

Though he doesn't say it, I know that family also includes Rayne. I fight with myself but eventually shake it off. "Of course I don't."

"Then we go back to Fiona's and wait there until this shit-storm blows over. Pretty sure Bruce can handle it."

Duo nods his agreement. "I get the feeling he's had to do this more than once."

"So we just leave him here?"

"They're not going to hurt him. It's *us* they want gone." Solo flexes his fingers. "I should have held my temper earlier. She would never have known."

Maybe, but no point worrying about it now. Though something tells me that Linda would have found any way possible to get us out of the way. She hasn't even seen Rayne yet, but the possessive ownership vibes panning off her are strong enough for even me to catch.

"It's not your fault," I murmur.

Duo moves through the small space to the arch beneath the stairs. He peers through, then beckons us over. "We'll go this way. If everybody is at the front, then now is a good time to leave."

I back up. "No. I can't."

"Of course you can—"

"We can't just leave Bruce."

"They won't bother him if we're gone." Solo joins his bother in the arch. "Let's go. Whistle down Norma, so we can get out of here."

No. I can't.

One hand shifts slightly towards the ends of my locs. "I can't. I promised Rayne I wouldn't leave. I gave her my word. I'm supposed to be here when she wakes up."

"I think she'll understand."

Oh, she will. Of course she will. Rayne is probably one of the most understanding people I have ever met, but it's much more than that now.

We've been through so much together over the last few months, so many difficulties and tests and struggles. The last thing I want to do is give her any reason to doubt my word. She needs a constant right now. We all do.

On my locs and hope to trim.

And I meant it.

"I'll leave when she wakes up."

"Danika."

"Don't make me leave without her."

A loud shout comes from outside. A moment later, Bruce hurries back into the house and slams the door. He leans against it and wipes a film of sweat off his forehead.

"What on earth?" he mumbles. "This is crazy. I've never seen them like this before."

I step towards him. "What are they doing?"

Bruce gazes at me, wide-eyed and confused. "Oliver brought his shotgun. Why would he do that? He wasn't hunting—why did he bring his gun?"

Clearly the twins know something I don't because they don't appear the least bit surprised by this news. I, on the other hand, am stunned and let them all know it.

"What does he even have a gun for? This isn't the Wild West."

"He's a farmer, Agent. Needs to have something to frighten off predators and catch pheasants every now and then." Bruce rubs the sides of his mouth. "But that aside, I've never seen him carry it outside the fields. In fact, I've never seen him act like this before. Not any of them."

A sudden loud bang on the door. It shudders beneath Bruce's back.

"You need to sneak out." Bruce points towards the arch. "Use the back way."

"But—"

"I'm scared for you," he cries. "Never, in all my years, have I seen my friends and neighbours act like this. No reason, no sense, just anger. I have no idea why they're like this, but I don't want you caught in it. Sneak out the back."

His fear is catching. My stomach twists with a flood of anxiety, and I whistle sharply for Norma. "But Rayne—"

"They won't come near her. She's safe in the cellar, but you three? Linda has them baying for your insides."

Another slam against the door.

Bruce leans harder against it.

Norma appears at the head of the stairs to chitter and cackle her way to me. She walks instead of flying, her little tail bobbing for balance as she hop-jumps her way down each step. At my feet, she digs her claws into the baggy, sagging fabric of my borrowed trousers and begins to climb.

"I promised her—"

"You have to leave, Danika."

That stops me in my tracks. I think that might be the first time Bruce has ever used my name, rather than my title. It's jarring on the ear, frightening somehow, but clearly it's enough for the twins.

Solo and Duo grab an arm of mine each and frogmarch me through the arch.

This is clearly a study—two desks, each piled with tottering stacks of books or papers at least a foot high. Several small cages, most of them empty, though one of them seems to hold a stiff pool of that same blue-green slime from earlier. The space has a strange, musty smell, rather like a pet shop, and in one corner a skull mounted on a plain wooden board hangs above a wall clock.

It's nearly sundown.

Norma finishes her climb up my body and drags herself over my shoulder. The boys continue to pull me on, and I allow them to cart me towards the door.

"Will *you* be okay?" I call back towards Bruce.

Yet another loud slam against the front door. "They won't hurt me," he says, though the little quiver in his voice suggests he isn't sure.

Fuck. I want to stay. I want to protect him. I'm a SPEAR, after all, that's my job. These idiots outside won't stand a chance against me, let alone me and two werewolves. But somehow the thought of starting a fight in Rayne's old home hits me differently.

Maybe if I hang back out of sight? Maybe that way, if I'm needed, I can still be close enough to help, instead of on the other side of the village…

"No." Solo's hand tightens on my shoulder. "Don't even think about it. We're leaving. We're grateful, but we can't stay. Rayne will be fine. Move."

And so I do. Not that they give me much choice—through the office space and out into a kitchen with another door that leads outside. The wolves lead me through it without a single word and sneak through in the green space beyond.

Small, but cute. As we pass a small pond, I see dozens upon dozens of frog spawn wedged into a crack to the side of a small water feature.

Butterflies and bees flit their way through the wild space, which is full to brimming with untamed grass and wildflowers.

I have just the time to appreciate how a garden *should* look before we reach the back gate.

Not locked, just bolted. The three of us, Norma in tow, slip out the back and off the properly of the Ranch into the village itself.

# CHAPTER NINETEEN

The boys don't release me all the way back to Fiona's B & B. That does require some awkward running and some even more difficult traversal of garden fences, but I trust them and their superior senses to get squishy human me to safety.

I don't say anything, just keep my shoulder steady so Norma can keep her place and fight with the guilt that follows me with every step.

I told Rayne I would stay.

After Shakka's jibe so recently, the idea that I've broken my word is tearing up my insides. I hate it.

Solo releases me only long enough to drop down a steep slope, riding the pebbly surface like a surfer. At the bottom he lifts his hands and grins when Duo simply shoves me after him. Sure my balance is reasonable, but I don't expect it, and unlike his brother's graceful journey down, mine is a stumbling, windmilling shambles. It takes all my effort not to yell out in surprise.

The stupid, too-large boots resemble boats around my feet, and one of them is still at the top of the small hill by the time I'm done.

I land half in, half on Solo's arms and catch him myself to regain my balance.

"You're dicks," I murmur to the pair of them.

"Just checking if you've still got it," he says with a chuckle.

Eye roll. "So now I need to watch out for you two as well as Noel. Great."

At the slope's base I finally recognise where we are. A huge tree stump forms a glossy surface, clearly buffed and polished over the years. All around it are little stones in a narrow circle. Beyond that is a woodpile, lots of wild grass, and then a fence I've not yet seen from this side. Behind that and to the left is the B & B.

Despite my grumbling, the boys' playfulness does help to ease some of the tension riding my shoulders. I walk ahead of them, gnawing on my bottom lip, trying to calculate how long before sunset. A glance at my watch indicates only ten minutes, maybe twenty at most, so I know I have all that time to think about how Rayne might feel when she wakes and I'm not where I'm supposed to be.

Fuck's sake, Linda. What the hell is her problem anyway?

I twitch and roll my shoulders against a horrible prickle of discomfort down my back. Is this really all because of what happened last night? Or is something else going on? Even the fact that we've taken an instant dislike to each other doesn't seem to justify her level of anger with me.

Fiona meets us at the back door. Clearly this is an off-duty day because she wears none of the gaudy charms and jewellery of the night before. Instead she wears comfortable mum jeans and a baggy shirt covered in paint stains. Her hair is still crazy, though—long, braided, and dotted with all those little charms. Guess they must be a pain to take off.

"Bruce Dixon called," she says as soon as we're in earshot. "I thought this visit of yours was supposed to be secret. Why would you go to the one man in the entire village that might recognise what you are?"

Both Solo and Duo look at me.

Thanks, boys.

I tug on the side of my borrowed shirt to show the lump to the side of my neck. "There was an…incident. We needed professional help."

Fiona's eyes widen. "What were you doing down in the caves? Those sprites have been very agitated lately."

"So I keep hearing. You know about them?"

"Who do you think helped Bruce make that vaccine?" She waves us in. "You really should sit down. Too much exertion in the first twenty-four hours will likely make you feel sick and weak."

She's not wrong, either. I thought I was feeling guilt over breaking my promise, but as soon as the words leave her mouth, I recognise nausea bubbling through my gut.

But something about her words gives me pause.

"Vaccine?"

A curt nod. "Bruce had to investigate down there several times while the church was worked on. So we developed an antidote that also gave him immunity. Very useful."

"For sure." My vision swims. "*Can* I sit down?"

She leads us all downstairs this time. I can sense the awe and quiet impressed looks from the boys, but I've already seen it. All I want right now is to flop face down onto the bed and rest some more.

I do just that, though I do need to wait for Fiona to produce the spare keys for the workroom.

The space is just as Rayne and I left it, plain but for the meagre furniture and our belongings. I collapse onto the bed, fighting the crawling sensations powering through my midsection.

"Did Linda Halidon really bring the whole neighbourhood council out to the Ranch?"

I nod, though I can't really see her. My face is jammed into the pillows right now since I'd rather not puke down here.

"Fucking bitch," Fiona mutters.

That jerks my head up. I stare at her, but she keeps talking as though she hasn't said anything out of the ordinary. Maybe she hasn't.

"As if it's any of her business what I do in my own home. Trying to get me arrested like that. And succeeding too because she bullied the council into turning me in. She's lucky I only got nine months. No. She's lucky I was able to turn things around for myself. That woman needs to learn about not putting her nose in places it shouldn't fit."

As if I needed more confirmation that Linda's attitude is a pattern.

Okay. Fine. In that case… "Fiona, can you think of anywhere safe to stash a van?"

She pauses mid-rant to glance at me.

"If Linda has a history of snooping or putting herself where she shouldn't, then we can't let her know that we're staying here. She'll only come after you if she does, and I guess she's done that before."

"Nine months," Fiona rages. Quietly, but yeah, for sure angry. "Nine months. But that doesn't stop her floating in here all nice-nice and sweet as you please when she wants her fortune read. Tall, dark stranger—yes, perhaps, but that's not hard around here, is it? Never before lived in such a blond, white town."

I catch myself giggling.

Yeah, I like Fiona.

The moment my watch beeps to mark sunset, I turn over in the bed and try to stay calm. How long will it take Rayne to realise what has happened? Five minutes? Ten? What will Bruce tell her? Will Linda and her little crowd of council members still be at the Ranch? Will Rayne be able to get away?

Norma stays close to me while I ponder it all. It seems the effects of her nip experience are fully gone now, and she's more like herself.

While occasionally leaving my side to study the room, she still refuses to allow me out of her direct eyeline.

In the adjoining room, Solo, Fiona, and Duo talk quietly together, no doubt planning what to do about the van.

I would join them, but my insistence on gazing at my watch probably wouldn't be helpful.

I hear a few murmurs and a grunt that might signal approval, then soft footsteps heading up the stairs.

Duo puts his head through the doorway. "Hey, Fiona is going to move the van. She knows a place where it should be safe and reasonably hidden. You'll stay here?" He phrases it as a question even though I know damn well he's aware of the answer.

"I'm not going anywhere until Rayne arrives."

A nod. "Good. Last thing we need is you running lose in this stupid spit of a village. We won't be long." Off he goes, and a moment later, Solo takes his place.

The older of the twins leans in the doorway casually, but as much a guard on duty as ever I've seen.

"How are you feeling?" he mutters.

"Sick."

"You smell better."

I think that's supposed to be comforting. "Thanks, I guess."

"No, I mean that whatever was wrong with your leg and neck has eased. The other thing is still there, though."

"The stain?"

He nods. "What if Fiona can't do anything? What if no one can?"

I shrug. Not only have I asked myself that question over and over, but I, like everyone else, have no answers.

Outwardly I seem fine. Without any knowledge of the skin on my back, anybody might expect me to be entirely normal and going about my life. But at night, or in moments of stillness, those eyes continue to haunt me. Those horrible yellow eyes and a thin gash of a mouth between them that spews fear and choking black smoke in equal measure.

"Do werewolves have nightmares?" I whisper.

Solo eyes me. "Just like any human, sure. Or like any other living creature that sleeps. I used to dream about Duo all the time. When we were younger, I was always scared he'd do something stupid and I wouldn't be able to protect him."

"And now?"

"Now I dream he *has* done something stupid and that I *have* to save him. Same shit, different night, Danika." He grins and I take the hint and join him.

His look becomes thoughtful. Gentle. "Do *you* have dreams you want to talk about?"

I feel a prickle down my back. "Not right now. Thanks, though."

He sighs. "We don't know each other very well. I know we're on a team and we work together, but that's not the same as *knowing* a person, right?"

"Where are you going with this?"

"I'm on your side," he says simply. "Me and Duo. You're not just the boss, you know? You're not just our team leader, you're our friend. You know that, right?"

I'm touched. Incredibly so.

Though Kappa does work very well as one unit, there has always been a little bit of distance between me and the rest. Or so I felt. Not Rayne, of course, but maybe even *because* of her, my relationships with the others have often felt not quite whole. Maybe because they're all *edane* and I'm not. Perhaps because I'm in charge. Possibly even just that I'm a woman in a position of power, though that seems the least likely.

"Thank you," I say at last. "That means a lot."

He nods. After a quick glance over his shoulder, he returns his attention to me. "I know it got really shitty a few weeks back. I also know that you went through the wringer over everything that happened with the Dire Wolves."

I wince, yet I'm grateful that he managed to phrase my fuck-ups so gently.

"We don't blame you."

I freeze, grimace locked to my face. "What?"

"None of us blame you." He talks faster now, as though aware that if he doesn't get the words out quickly, I might not be in a space to hear them. "Wensleydale Gordan was a good, noble alpha, and he served his pack well. You did the best you could with what you thought was right. Nobody can ask more than that."

"I—"

"You made mistakes. You're human. It's allowed." Another glance over his shoulder, then he steps to the side. "Don't let guilt close you off to us. We can't help you if you don't let us. And I'm not just talking about me and Duo."

The question is on the tip of my tongue, but I realise quickly why he has stepped aside.

Rayne dashes into the room in a blur of motion and colour and slams herself onto the bed beside me.

She wears exactly what she had when we parted ways this morning, right down to mud, rips, tears, and grass stains. A few spindly twigs cling to her hair as well as a tiny spider, frantically leg-waving from a slender silk strand near her ear.

"Did you claw through jungle to reach me?"

Smiling, she cups her hand to my cheek. "Bubi said you were doing better, but I couldn't relax until I saw for myself. You seem fine to me."

"I haven't tried to wear any clothes that fit yet."

Her lips quirk at the corners, but that's all the amusement Rayne allows herself. Instead she hurls her arms around me and crushes me to her in a bone-crunching hug. "Bubi told me what happened. I'm sorry I couldn't be there."

"And I'm sorry I had to leave. I wanted to stay—I tried to, but—"

"If you had, I'd be far more upset. You did the right thing."

"By breaking my word?"

"By taking care of my family."

In the doorway, Solo gives the smallest of nods before walking away. He doesn't go far, only to the other side of Fiona's tourist-trap working space, but the illusion of privacy is kind of him.

Rayne and I cuddle together with Norma, each drawing comfort from the presence of the other as the seconds tick slowly into minutes.

# CHAPTER TWENTY

By the time Fiona and Duo arrive back into the house and come downstairs, I've had time to change out of the uncomfortable borrowed clothes and gingerly climb into my own. I've folded down the ankle on one of my boots, but at least I can get the damn thing on my foot.

Fiona walks straight through to the workspace and stands to the side of the bed. Her face is drawn and wrinkled with worry, her lips a thin, tight slash. "What did you do out there?"

I shrug. "It doesn't take much."

"I'm serious, child. I've never seen the people like this before. Linda Halidon is raging like I've never seen. There's talk of a citizen's arrest for Bruce Dixon."

Rayne stiffens.

I place a hand on her knee—not that such a motion will stop her if she decides to move. "Do people actually do that?"

"She says he's wilfully endangering the community and plans to get county police involved." Fiona begins to pace. "The whole village feels hot and scratchy on my skin. I've never experienced anything like this."

She doesn't say it, but I know what she's thinking. I twitch my shoulders against a sudden discomfort across the skin of my back.

"Is it me?" I say at last. "Did I bring it here?"

"It's very possible. Whatever you're carrying is like nothing I've ever felt before."

Rayne sniffs. "So how long do you need to protect yourself before we begin?"

Fiona looks at each of us in turn. Her gaze is deep and piercing, with an edge of something I've not yet seen in her before now. Determination.

"There's no time. Child, if you're willing, I'd like to see what I can see now."

I shrink back. "But you said—"

"If you're forced to leave before I can help, then all of this is for nothing. I'll be fine." She waves a hand to encompass the room. "This is my space. I've cleansed it. I've worked here for years and years. There's no safer space for me, and something tells me the longer we leave this… thing, the worse it will become."

"I don't know about this." The objections rest on the end of my tongue, but Rayne is faster.

She takes my hands in hers and gently strokes the backs of my fingers with her thumb. "She knows what she's doing, Danika. We have to trust her. After coming all this way, with everything already spinning out of control around us, do we really want to wait? We *have* to know."

"And if it doesn't work?"

"Then at least we'll know, and we'll move on to plan B."

My answering sigh is long and heavy. "More like plan Q."

"Do you want us to do anything?" Solo is grim and serious, his hands balled into fists. Not sure that he even realises he's done so.

"Take the little dragon lizard with you, please." Fiona begins pulling off her gloves. "In fact, if all of you could go and give us some space, that would be splendid."

Rayne plants her feet more firmly. "I'll be staying, thank you."

"Rayne—"

"I'm staying." No raised voice, no menace, just calm statement of fact.

Whatever. I'm not going to fight her at a time like this. I don't even want to be doing this.

Something about this plan feels rushed, even to me, and I don't know what to do about it.

I want to know what Fiona can find out. I *need* to know. But is this the wisest way? Everybody is so high-strung right now, I don't know that we're making the best decisions. And I've enough experience of what can happen if people make decisions in less than their ideal state of mind.

"Lie down, child. On your front, please. Lift the shirt." Fiona folds her long gloves and places them into her pocket. Her hands are wrinkled and thin, with long, plain fingernails rounded to smooth points. No rings, no bracelets or even a watch, just plain and unfurnished.

While I obey, Rayne carefully plucks Norma off the bed and

hands her off to Duo. Neither of them look happy about it, but Rayne is quick to shut the door and any potential complaints out of view and hearing.

She returns to the bed and helps me lie down, fluffing up pillows around me.

The room is warm, thankfully, but lying there on my front reminds me of those hours upon hours at Clear Blood. Hopefully there will be far fewer needles, cauterising tools, and scalpels in this procedure.

I fold my hands beneath my chin to hold my head up and try to relax.

Nope. Not happening.

To the side of the bed, Fiona moves around me, muttering to herself. I can't catch all the words, but I'm pretty sure not all of them are English ones. There might be some Latin in there, as well as some Cold Blood Tongue, which I don't expect.

Rayne kneels beside the bed, as close as she can get, her gaze pinned on me. "How do you feel?"

"Cold," I mutter with a dry smile.

"This isn't the time for joking around."

"I'm not. I'm actually cold."

Fiona stops muttering to add, "Sorry, child, that would be me. Just a few words to secure the space and prepare for whatever I might see. My hands will be cold too, so sorry."

"I'm used to it. Are you sure about this?"

She inhales deeply. "No. But then, who is ever sure about anything? Just try to be very still. Any movement might disrupt me."

Well, the only way I have even the smallest hope of that is closing my eyes, so I do.

Behind the curtain of my own eyelids, in the darkness, I hope there will be no gleam or glint of yellow.

Without my sight, I depend on my hearing to tell me what's happening. Rayne hasn't moved, though now her hand rests lightly on the pillow against my cheek. Fiona is close enough that I can feel the brush of her clothing against my ribs. Then a little whisper of air as she moves closer.

"Let us see now…"

Then, silence.

I lie there. Waiting. Listening. Feeling.

But there's nothing to hear or feel.

Nobody is moving.

Why is nobody moving?

Barely, I can hear the gentle gust of Fiona's breath as she leans over me. Nothing from Rayne, of course, and now barely even her hand, as her skin warms to match my own temperature.

A little murmur of confusion. Fiona's hands finally touch the small of my back. "Now then, what is this?"

Cool fingers, gentle but firm, walk their way up my spine.

At this point I know roughly where all the curves and swirls are on my skin. I've seen enough photos of them. I can feel her reaching the bottom of the horrendous mark, not quite touching the rough, raised skin, but the area immediately around it. Probing, poking, resting, testing.

"Normal. All this feels as it should. You have a strong inner fire, child. It burns so brightly it could almost fight against the darkness. But this—whatever it is—is stronger than you. It is taking you over slowly, a piece at a time."

"What do you mean?"

"Shh," she hisses. "Don't interrupt."

Again her fingers move, this time along the sides of my ribs where the marks curve in wide arcs towards my front. They never quite cross the invisible line left by my arm, but they come close. Still she doesn't touch the carved marks themselves.

"It's sticky." Fiona seems to struggle for the word she wants. "It clings to you like honey, but thicker. It is *on* you, but also *part* of you. It pulses."

I have no idea where she's getting all this. No one at Clear Blood has been able to describe the markings in any way other than *strange* or *unusual* or *black* or even *disgusting*. The fact that Fiona is able to give them recognisable characteristics is progress at least.

"There's a residue near them, but not quite. And it's weaker. Like something is leaking off your body."

I can't help myself. "Leaking?"

Fiona tuts impatiently. And then, "I don't know, child. Like a fish food pellet in a tank. It slowly releases food throughout the days an owner might be away. Do you know the ones? Always there, but gradually giving off its contents as the hours pass. I don't know how else to describe this."

"But what's leaking out of it?" Rayne's voice makes me jump. She is so still and silent, as ever, that it is so easy to forget she is even there.

"Evil," Fiona says. "Rage. Fear. Anger. Distress. Shame, hatred, anguish…hunger. So much hunger. But this isn't food, like the fish pellet, but emotions. And it isn't feeding anything so much as calling something to it. This mark is a beacon or a signpost."

My stomach knots up. I fight to keep calm, but everything—from the dreams, to the waking nightmares, to the supposed *stain*—it's all adding up. I want to scream. I want to lash out and punch things, kick things. That helps, right? Punching shit. Or shooting it. That's always helped me in the past, so why can't I do that now? Surely that will work. It *has* to work.

Fiona shifts again. She's muttering again, coaching herself.

"Wait, what are you going to d—"

Her hands touch directly against the mark.

She's in no way rough or cruel about it, but her skin against those sensitive areas of mine sends a crawling sensation through my entire body like nothing I've ever felt before.

I can feel her. Not just her fingers against my back, but *her*. I feel the very essence of her against my skin like her soul brushing up against mine. It's hot, then cold. Prickly, then smooth. It's bright, then dark, then all of them at once at the same time, over and over again.

There's a sound like a whine. It's shrill and keen, growing louder and louder in my ears.

Precious seconds pass before I realise it's Fiona.

She's screaming. Actually screaming.

My eyes pop open, and I can see her, still on the side of the bed, but now her hands are locked to my spine, her arms and wrists stiff like claws. Her eyes are wide, so very wide, and the sound pouring from her mouth is one of pure, unfiltered terror.

"Rayne—"

She's already there, grabbing Fiona by the waist to heave her away. But she can't move her.

I see the effort, even spy muscles Rayne probably hasn't used in over a year bulging as she strains to pull Fiona away from me. But the older woman is locked to me as if by glue, her fingers and palm pressed tight to my back and fused there.

The door crashes open. Norma is first through it, followed by Solo and Duo who stop dead at the sight before them.

"Do something," I yell.

Darkness swirls across my vision. Not a fog, but more like a grainy mist filled with glittering sparkles of gold. No, not gold. Yellow. It's that thing. It's here. It's coming for me.

Breath locks in my throat. I'm scrambling now, struggling to stand, to kneel—hell, to move at all—but I can't. My limbs are locked in place just as surely as Fiona is locked to me, the pair of us bound in some horrible waking nightmare.

Flashes of colour. Little snippets of vision. Voices.

People are yelling. Panicking. Shouting orders. Crying out. Screeching.

Then there's a young woman with long hair. Very long hair. She wears a flowing summer dress and peers down into a pool of water beneath a young oak tree in a bright, sunny field. Her smile is wide and cheerful, one finger dabbling in the water where small sparkles of silver light spring up beneath her digits.

But the scene shifts. Clouds roll across the sky and with them loud booms of thunder.

Rain slashes down upon the water, dashing the sparkles away into pinprick points of blinding, garish yellow.

The clouds grow dark and in them forms the shape of a thin, lipless mouth and two yawning sockets into which the yellow sparkles gather to form cruel eyes with slitted pupils.

My scream boils at the back of my throat. I let it go with a roar that strains and tears but carries with it the last notes of defiance I have left to me.

"Get the fuck away from her."

The vision shatters like glass, sending shards of memory spinning away into the ether.

With a colossal wrench, I throw myself to the side and down, off the end of the bed, and to the floor.

A wet tearing sound accompanies fresh screams, though these are now pain rather than fear.

My body slams the rug with a thud that sends the last puffs of air right out of my lungs. But I'm free. I can feel it.

Fiona isn't touching me any more. In fact, nobody is. I'm lying on my face, on the ground on the far side of the bed, and a second later the soft kiss of blankets falls down around me.

Norma lands beside my face and forces her way beneath the blankets. The soft fabric catches on her barbs as she crawls inward to reach me. She rubs her beak against my cheek. "Dan dan?"

"I'm okay." A lie. "I'm fine." Still lying. "Come here." I scoop the little pet to me and hold her shuddering body.

The screaming stops. Pain-wracked whimpers take their place.

As I fight free of the blanket, I spot Fiona, kneeling on the far side of the bed, her hands held trembling before her.

"Oh, sweet fuck…"

Her hands are shredded. Huge sloughs of skin hang loose from her palms and fingers, which are raw and bloody underneath. Black ooze slides down the backs of her hands and hits the floor with soft, pitiful slaps.

"Fiona—"

She shrieks, a wordless cry of fear and agony. She scrambles back on her arse, using her hands to help. Fuck, it must hurt, but clearly not so much that it eclipses her panic, which I see shining bright in her eyes.

"Stay back," she hisses. "Stay away from me. Don't come near."

"But—"

"No!" No anger but terror, real unfiltered terror. She keeps scuttling backward until her back hits the wall, never once taking her gaze off mine.

"Your hands—"

"Don't touch me," she screeches. "Never again. Never touch me again, never ever. What are you, child? What is *in* you? Are you even human?"

Her words double me over, far more than any punch to the gut might have. "I—"

Rayne grabs me. Her firm hands close around my shoulders and steer me to the side, well away from Fiona, who looks like she wants to crawl into the wall and vanish forever.

"Come on," she murmurs.

"But—"

Fiona's bellow fills the room. "Get out. You have to get out. Get out."

My legs move, but I'm not really controlling them. In fact, it takes strong focus just to hold on to Norma. Rayne steers me firmly and easily out of the room, giving as wide a berth to Fiona as she can manage.

Near the wall, Solo and Duo crouch beside Fiona, inspecting her mangled hands.

She's crying now, gut-wrenching, heart-crushing sobs with no words. Just sounds. Howls.

The twins stay close without touching, doing more of that speaking-without-speaking as they inspect her palms.

I hesitate. "Fiona—"

"Get out," she roars.

Solo stands. "We've got her. You two go." He digs into his pocket and pulls out a set of keys, which he tosses to Rayne.

She catches them without breaking stride, steering me through the room filled with faux-magical packets, powders, and talismans.

I stumble, and Norma frees my hands by fluttering up to my head. Her little claws dig into my scalp, but at least I can use my arms now, something extra to fight the little pulses of dizziness that sweep over and past me like waves.

"Far side of the village, near the church," Solo calls. "Hidden in a ditch and covered up with branches and grass clippings."

I think he's talking about the van.

Rayne must know, because she nods and just keeps walking, her firm hands guiding me up the stairs and out the back door. Her mouth is tight and thin, her eyes dangerously narrowed.

"Rayne—"

"Keep walking," she says. "Don't stop."

So I do, the growing chill of the night air barely touching the blistering heat of the marks down my back.

❖

Though we make it to the van, its not without being noticed. In a village this small, with residents already on edge, there seem to be more people around. I see the woman with the limp, making her slow way across the low bridge that crosses the river. She pauses on spotting us and stares intently.

I fight the desire to yell back at her, an urge helped by Norma, who begins crooning softly.

Another figure, one with a shotgun resting on their shoulder, marches away from us towards the entry of the village and the colourful welcome sign. They stop, peer into the gloom of deepening shadow, but seem satisfied that there is nothing to see.

Even Norma seems to sense that this is a moment for quiet because aside from her crooning, she doesn't say a word.

At one point even Linda crosses our path, but Rayne uses shadow and stillness to keep us both out of sight.

Though I can't hear all the details, I do catch that Linda is on the phone to *someone*, complaining thoroughly about SPEAR and *danger* and *freaks* and *monsters*.

Rayne takes care to wait until each person is well out of sight before moving us again.

At a slower pace now, I can keep up and wrestle my top back into place so my back is no longer exposed. "Rayne?"

Her head whips towards me.

I hesitate. "Do you think Fiona will be okay?"

"Solo and Duo will look after her."

That's not what I asked, but maybe she doesn't have an answer. Fair, because I certainly don't.

# CHAPTER TWENTY-ONE

As promised, the van is off-road, down a little slip of hill, and wedged between two trees with low branches. We have to use the rear doors to enter and then climb through in order to reach the front seats. Rayne takes the driver's side. I take passenger and coax Norma down into my lap.

"She looked burned," I murmur.

"Son-dar? Kar, kar?" Norma considers me with one beady eye.

Rayne grips the steering wheel. "I've never seen anything like that before. She was fused to you. I couldn't lift her away. Nothing I did could move her. I felt like something was holding her there. Something stronger than me."

"I thought it was just a scar, but this? She asked what was *in me*. Like I'm carrying something."

My back feels normal now. Or at least as normal as ever it has over the last few weeks. With my shirt back in place, I'm able to use the backrest of the seat and not feel a thing. Maybe an itch or a twinge, but no pain. And certainly no traces of the strips of skin Fiona lost.

"We need to leave," she says at last. "Moarwell isn't equipped to deal with whatever this is. We need to get back to Clear Blood or at least SPEAR, so we can tell them what we know."

"But we don't know anything."

She tenses. "We know that something on or in you is calling out to someone or some*thing* else. We know that our being here gives Linda permission to harass Bubi. We know that Fiona is terrified of you, and we know that the sprites in those caves are hostile. That's enough."

"But the Blade—"

"It has to wait."

"For what?" I face her. "What, exactly? None of this is going to get any better. Since we're here, shouldn't we do everything we can now?"

Rayne gazes out the front window. "I think we should leave. We should regroup and find a better plan."

"You want us to *come back* here? Isn't that worse?"

"It might give the council members time to cool off."

I can't help but stare at her. This is nuts, she must know that. "And in the meantime? We let Linda bully us out of doing our jobs and leave without what we came for?"

"I came for you."

"Well, I came for Shakka. That creep isn't going to let me off so lightly. Remember *he's* the one that fixed things so we could get here. I can't leave without that spearhead."

At last, Rayne looks at me. Her eyes have the tiniest silver sparkle in them, which is the only sign she offers of her fraying temper. "Those sprites nearly killed you."

"So we go in more carefully this time. Maybe there's another way."

"There isn't."

"Perhaps we can dig in?"

"And disrupt their home even further? You heard Fiona, and Bubi for that matter. Those sprites have been agitated for a while, probably because of excavation work to gather stone for the church. They want to be left alone."

Norma gives a little squeak in my lap. It's a sign that I'm holding her too tightly, so I let go entirely and watch her crawl her way to the back of the van.

As ever, she barely takes her eyes off me as she goes, and when she does lie down, she does so in her customary ball, with her tail wrapped around her body like a spiky scarf. Still, she stares at me.

Whatever. I need Rayne to understand that we can't leave yet.

"We might not get another chance. Who says the sprites won't move the Blade? Or that all the excavation you mentioned doesn't cause a cave-in?"

Her eyes widen. Clearly she hadn't thought of that. "You're not endearing the idea to me."

"All I'm saying is that if we leave now to come back later, we're making it harder on ourselves. Let's just get it done and then we can leave everyone alone. Nobody will have any need to see us ever again."

Rayne looks down at her hands. Her shoulders sag.

Well, shit. Way to put your foot in it, Danika.

I touch her wrist. "That's not what I meant. Now that the Dixons know you're alive, of course you can come back. You're quick on your feet and sneaky—there's no need for anybody to know you're here."

"There's so much that can go wrong."

"Isn't there always?"

She nods slowly.

"I wouldn't press this normally, but...Okay, fine, maybe I would." I backtrack as she eyes me dubiously. "I totally would, but think about it. Linda wants us gone. So why don't we just do what we came for and leave?"

"And Fiona?"

I consider that. "If she'll let us, maybe we could take her to Clear Blood. They might be able to help with her..."

Another nod. "I never really believed in psychics before, but I think it's safe to say we found a real one this time."

"Yup. Remember Master Milvision III? At least this time all we had to do was facilitate a plea deal."

At last a small smile from Rayne.

The last psychic hired by SPEAR was a young man, barely twenty, with wild choppy hair coloured grey and wrinkles forced into his skin with layers of make-up and skilful contouring. He hadn't fooled anybody for an instant—except perhaps Maury?—and spent four painful hours waving his hands over my back, chanting nonsense—probably pig Latin or Klingon—while waving incense sticks around the room.

The last time I saw someone quite that high, I had been roped into searching for a teenager supposedly abducted by sirens. No. Not a siren in sight, just a young girl and her boyfriend smoking so much weed that their eyes had crossed long ago.

Of course Master Milvision III had been sent packing, though not without his fee, which, if Maury's frustration was to be believed, had reached four figures. Oh, well. At least the lad would be able to finance his tools and peripherals for many more scams.

"If we go back"—Rayne lifts a hand at my excited shifting in my seat—"*if*, Danika, if we go back, we need to be more prepared this time."

"Of course."

"We need to be able to negotiate with the sprites, so they don't fire more darts at you."

"I'd rather not go flying on another trip to space, thanks." The words are barely free of my mouth before I remember Fiona's words. "Wait, wait, wait a second. I'm fine."

Rayne snorts. "No matter how much you believe yourself to be Superman, you're still human."

"Okay, ouch. But I mean, Fiona said the antidote was a vaccine. I'm immune now."

Her eyes widen. "Really?"

"She and Bruce developed it because he had to keep going into the caves. I bet that's why he knew exactly what I needed and how to treat it all."

"So they can't hurt you again?"

I'm so ready to say yes. But the hopeful look in her eyes is just too much. I can't lie to her. "I want to believe that. I don't know. Fiona didn't say anything about how long the immunity lasts or how much additional poison it can take, but it's better than nothing, right? And it certainly won't be there if we wait much longer."

A soft sigh. "You didn't see yourself, Danika. You were gone. Your eyes were open, but you weren't in them any more. You spoke to me, but nothing you said made sense, and I was so, so scared for you."

"I'm sorry."

"It's not your fault. But I think I understand how you felt those times you caught me in mania."

With that comparison I finally understand how Rayne must have felt. Watching her become someone else, some*thing* else, is one of the most painful things I've ever had to see.

"I'll protect you," she says at last. "I'll be faster. Stronger. I'll—"

"No. No way. Don't do that, Rayne." I talk straight over her. "I'm not a child, and I'm not an idiot. You're not my keeper. *We* will protect *each other*. That's the only way to do this. You can't take all that on to yourself."

"But you—"

"Are squishy, a squishy human, yes, I know. But I'm still a SPEAR agent. I know how to do my job. I'll be careful, I promise. Will you trust me?"

"You promise? Your word on it?"

I hesitate. "That doesn't seem to mean much right now."

"It does to me." She stares at me then, her eyes darker still in the gloom of the van. The silver is gone, and I know that just the brown remains, that swirling amalgamation of autumn colours I love so very much. I can't see it clearly, but knowing it's there has always warmed me.

"On my locs and hope to trim," I tell her.

"Fine. Let's go." She moves as if to open the door to the van, but I stop her with a smile.

I pull out my phone. "You said be careful, have a plan. I have one."

Rayne widens her eyes at me.

"The reason Shakka even knew about these caves was because a sprite made it into SPEAR custody. I wonder if we can offer the sprites their mate back in exchange for the Blade."

"That could work. No harm in trying."

"And even if it doesn't"—I scroll through my contacts to find Shakka's name—"at least we'll be able to get that sprite out of SPEAR's holding cells. They don't belong there."

Shakka answers after the second ring. As ever he is rude and grumpy, but as soon as he hears about the hostility of the sprites, his rage is palpable down the phone line. But my plan? Oh, my plan gets him moving.

I can hear him pushing buttons and flicking switches as he yells down to the sprite.

Very faintly I hear a call of, "Release, please?" before he claps back.

"I'll get it to you. Be ready."

That's not quite what I expected. "What do you mean?"

He chuckles. "Karson, you have no idea the reach and pull I have around here. The amount of people who owe me. That sprite will be with you before midnight. Just wait."

"How?"

His amusement feels sinister. "Air delivery. Keep an eye on the sky." And he hangs up.

Rayne leans back in her seat. "Remind me, if I ever ask that goblin for a favour, that it's a terrible idea."

"Once is bad enough, but I'm pretty sure I owe him another one after this."

She winces. "Not smart."

"Don't rub it in."

"So we wait for an air delivery?"

I shrug. "Whatever that means."

Rayne turns and climbs back through the van. "Fine. Wait here."

"What?"

"I want to check on Fiona. You should stay away from her for now."

She's right. But I don't like it. Her face as she screamed at me still haunts me even now. Wild eyes, slack mouth, and fear. So much fear. Pain too.

To think *I* caused that in someone turns my stomach.

"Tell her…" I wave my hand around. Tell her what exactly? What could she possibly say to convey my guilt and sorrow for her?

"Don't worry, I will."

Yeah. I've no idea what she plans to say, but I do trust her, so I leave her to go.

Alone, I decide to move to the back of the van with Norma. My little chittarik still watches me, though now that I'm closer, she moves into my arms to lie there instead.

I take the time to cuddle her, stroke her, appreciate her.

Sure, she's a pest. Yes, she often gets on my nerves and gets into places she absolutely shouldn't be, but she's *my* pest. And she's a pest who refuses to abandon me even when dozens upon others might.

"You're a sweet little thing," I tell her, scratching beneath her chin. "Even though I must be radiating evil, you're still right here. It's almost like you don't know any better."

"Nika son," she murmurs sleepily.

I hold tighter. She squeaks. I let go.

The back of the van is cold without the engine running. And without the banter from the boys up front, or the gentle touch of Rayne's fingers against mine, it is a dim, barren sort of place. Once or twice I do get up and leave the van long enough to walk around it and stretch my legs, but never for too long.

Can't help but be wary that the van isn't quite as hidden as it might otherwise be, and too much movement in this area might bring me attention that I don't want or need.

But no one sees me, no one bothers me, and I use the time to think.

I ponder what exactly this new understanding of my marked back actually means. I certainly have some information to give to Clear Blood now, but what will they do with it? Unless they can get in contact with some similarly powerful psychics, there's little to be done. And even if they do, how do they get rid of it?

The mark is *calling out*. To what? And why?

The questions swirl through me over and over, and none of the answers are particularly attractive. Hell, most of them are horror stories dredged from the depths of my most morbid imagination, which seem to often include that spindly legged black creature crawling out of my body like it did Liddell's.

I wish I could have spoken to him. Or at least learned something about how he came into contact with the creature before it took him over. Perhaps he could have given some insight. But he's dead. Very, very dead. And the thought that keeps returning, now matter how I spin it, is that the only way to escape is to be the same.

Norma nips my finger, gently but firmly. "Dar," she snaps. "Ka ka dan son."

I've no idea what she's saying, of course, but I imagine it to be a weary instruction not to let my imagination run wild.

"I'm trying," I tell her. "But I have a bad feeling about this."

"Son, son. Ka nika."

"We'll see."

A gentle tap on the window startles me out of my one-sided confab.

Rayne is back, and she gestures me back to give her space.

"You were quick."

She eyes me closely. "I've been gone two hours."

A glance at my watch. "Fuck."

"Are you losing time? Did you sleep? Did you pass out? Have you—"

"I'm fine." I lift my hand to cut her off. "I was just thinking."

"So much that you lost time?"

I sigh. "How is Fiona?"

A clumsy attempt to change the subject, but Rayne takes it, though not without a knowing glance at me.

"She'll be fine. Solo bandaged her up while Duo helped her upstairs. She's resting now and refuses the hospital, even though we all said that would be best."

"Well, how would she explain it?"

"True. But when we offered SPEAR, she didn't want to go there either. She said she can't travel."

"Maury did mention that. Otherwise he would never have let me come here in the first place."

Rayne sighs. "She also said that she wants to try again."

Now *that* I didn't expect. I stare at Rayne, checking for signs of a joke, but she's not. No, she actually means it.

Wow.

"But her hands—"

"Now that she's calmer and had time to go through it, she thinks it might be possible to protect herself better from whatever is in you."

"So there *is* something in me?"

A shrug. "Fiona is certain that her touching you disturbed whatever is there."

"But plenty of people have touched the mark. Hell, you've touched it."

She nods slowly. "But nobody with an actual gift or skill has touched it yet. Nobody able to feel or see things the way Fiona does. Which means nobody will be able to discover anything about it but her."

I shake my head. Hard. "No. No way. This thing already destroyed her hands—there has to be another way."

"Like what?"

"I don't know." I don't mean to raise my voice, but even Norma winces in my arms at the sudden shout. "I don't know. I don't know anything. I don't know what this thing is, why it's even in me, or what it's trying to do. I don't know anything. But I *do* know that before now it hasn't hurt anybody. And I can't let it hurt anybody else."

"Fiona wants to help." Rayne's voice becomes gentle, a direct counter to my heat. "What other option do you have?"

"It maimed her."

"She knows the risks."

"She has second degree burns. At least."

"Danika?" The way she says my name…Can't help it, my mouth snaps closed. She's not angry with me or even admonishing me, not really. She just wants my attention.

I look over to her, watch her face in the semi-gloom. Fuck, she's beautiful. How? How on earth did I somehow find the luck to have this woman look at me with that expression? I don't deserve it.

"Danika, stop. Let us help you."

Ouch. Okay. I guess, but—

"Stop it."

Is this woman in my head?

"Whatever you're thinking, just stop it," she says.

"I'm sorry."

"Don't be sorry, be you." She touches my shoulder. "I know you're shaken. So am I. But now is the time for you to be Danika Karson. Do you understand?"

I find myself smiling. It seems to come from deep inside of me, but that level of faith is just what I needed. The little boost to keep me moving.

Deep breath in. Deeper one out.

"Fine. Let's head back to the caves. Not to go in," I add, at her curious look, "just to scope it out a bit better. Maybe we can learn more from the outside rather than just going straight in."

A nod. "And Shakka's air delivery?"

"I'm sure we'll find out soon enough."

Somehow having a plan makes me feel better. Being in motion, acting, moving forward. All of these things prevent me dwelling on that glimpse of Fiona's hands, or the horrendous screams as she scrambled backward to escape me.

At this point, I'll take it. Anything to get it all out of my mind and allow me to keep moving.

"Norma, you stay."

"Son dar?" She stands, ready to take her usual place on my head or shoulder.

I back up, hands raised. "No. This time, you stay." I don't like the idea of leaving her, but I like the idea of her being poisoned even less. What if one of those darts had hit her last time? As an *edane* creature would she have the same protections as Rayne? There's no way to know.

"Nika son-son. Dar, dar ka—"

"No, baby. You have to stay. Protect the van for us. We don't want any nasty people coming to take it away."

She eyes me, hard. Her little brain must be working overtime, either to understand my words or decide if she plans to obey regardless of what she understands.

When I climb out of the back of the van, she follows as far as the rear doors.

"Norma…"

She lashes her tail at me, head up high. "Da." Her little limbs are tense and trembling, and I know what's coming.

"Don't you do it…"

"Nika nika nika nika nika nika nika n—"

I grab her and stuff her bodily into the top of my shirt. "Damn it, fine, you freaking pest."

"Dan, dan."

"Whatever. Just be quiet."

Rayne sighs. "We should have left her at home."

"You really think she would have let us?"

"Son, son?"

"Shut up," I grumble, shoving her head deeper down into my top. "Just be quiet, so we can go."

"You're sure?"

"No. But would you rather leave her here yelling the place down? She made enough noise last night."

I'm right. Of course I am, but I can tell Rayne is unhappy. I'm not thrilled about it either, but the bed is made now, time to lie in it. Or however the phrase goes.

So Rayne leads me back to the caves.

We leave the van and go a different way this time, skirting areas we know people frequent before reaching the narrow little paths Rayne used in her youth.

This time we're slower and more cautious, eyes and ears peeled for anybody watching or listening.

There's nothing, though more than once Rayne stops me to listen more carefully to the still night air.

Somehow, Norma seems to recognise that this is quiet time too. Maybe because I've pinned her inside my clothing rather than letting her go free. Or maybe she just reads tension and unease better than I thought. Whatever the case, she twists her hard, scaly body to keep her head poked out my neckline but remains silent the entire way.

Despite my worry, I have to admit it's nice to have her there. Her warm, prickly presence is a constant these days, and with everything else being so weird and all over the place, it's something I need.

As we reach the last path and start making our way down, my phone begins to buzz against my thigh.

"Karson," I mutter into it.

"Good. Where are you?" Shakka's voice is quick and clipped, like usual, though there is a hint of excitement in it that doesn't usually show.

I fight the urge to be literal—and annoying—with my answer. "Heading back to the caves."

"Good. Are they easy to see from the air?"

I look at Rayne.

She takes the phone and presses it to her ear. "Yes. No. Outside. South. Large pond, plenty of trees. Should be."

Without her hearing, I can't catch Shakka's part of the conversation, but when she's done, there is a strange glint in her eye.

"Shakka…?"

"He's already gone." Rayne steers me towards the edge of the trees on the nearest side of the pond and drops into a waiting crouch. "Shouldn't be long now."

"What?"

She grins. Then points.

I follow her finger and feel my mouth drop open. "How? How does that greasy little goblin have so many favours just waiting to be called in?"

Rayne joins me in watching the sky. "No idea. But I think this means we should all be careful in future when it comes to assuming what we know about people. Even people like him."

"No shit."

Our *air delivery* swoops out of the darkness, banking into loose spirals down, down towards the ground.

I don't recognise this gargoyle.

She is young, perhaps barely even sixty, with blue-green skin, a thick middle, and short, spiky hair dyed red. Huffing, puffing, grumbling, she lands on the grass beside us with a heavy thud. From her back comes a frightened yell and a string of what I assume to be cursing. I've never known this branch of sprite language.

The gargoyle courier drops to one knee and allows a sprite, that same cave sprite, to slide down to the ground.

The little creature is all sharp-toothed grins and thanks, with the occasional little shriek of pleasure as they look around. They hop from foot to foot in obvious excitement, and with each little step, the soft clink of chains is audible in the air.

"Release?" comes the hopeful request.

"Not yet, you little shit. Give it a rest." Grunting, still huffing, the gargoyle flexes her wings, then stretches her arms. The small gesture briefly makes her take up three times as much room. Then she looks to us. "Which one of you is the vampire?"

Rayne tilts her head. "Me."

"This is yours, then." She tugs a small envelope from a pocket on her shorts and tosses it over. "That's the key for the cuffs. Apparently you're to let her go only when you have what you came for, whatever the hell that means."

"Wait, you—"

"Elder," she cuts over me. "My name is Elder, and I'm done. This is far beyond what I ever imagined when I agreed to help that creep."

"Shakka?"

She grimaces. "Over one hundred miles for that cretin. I can't remember the last time I flew so far in one go. And that was taking shortcuts."

I stare at her. Can't help it. "You flew all that way? Just now? Carrying the sprite?"

"Hooman? Release now? Release?" The sprite shuffles closer, chains and all, and peers up at me hopefully. But I don't have the key, and now I understand why.

Elder yawns widely and loudly. "Is this everything? Do I need to stay here any longer?"

"Unless there was anything else to say…?"

"Good." She gives her hair a little flick. "As for you, you little shit"—she bends to address the sprite—"next time use your own damn wings."

"Release?"

"And learn to hold a conversation. Damn. Boring as all hell, and for what? No sword is worth this amount of flying."

I'm taken aback at the idea that Shakka might have shared his intent with anybody.

"What did you want with a sword?" Rayne asks, clearly smarter than me.

Slight caginess fills Elder's eyes. "I just think they're cool. Those SPEAR weirdos get to play about with weapons, so why can't I? Just because I'm not a soldier or whatever. But it isn't cool enough to be flying to the ass-end of nowhere with cargo." Another stretch. "But I'm done now. Thank fuck. What did you poor sods do to get roped into this mess?"

"I—"

Rayne interrupts with, "Our favours are private, I'm afraid."

Another hair flick. "Well, you're no damn fun. Look, enjoy your party or whatever. I need to go home."

I step forward. "Don't you want to rest? We have a van you could—"

"I'm not a freaking sparrow," Elder snaps. "Besides, this place looks like a right dive. No way I'm staying here longer than I need to. No, thanks. You've got your sprite, you've got the stupid keys, and my debt is paid. I'm off." And with that, she beats her wings twice and vaults into the air.

After spiralling once to get her bearings, Elder throws out her arms and glides away into the night.

I look down to the sprite still standing uncomfortably close to my leg.

"Release?"

"Yeah, I guess." I look at Rayne. "Want to use that key?"

But Rayne is opening the envelope inside which is not just a key but also a little slip of paper. She scans it quickly, eyes popping as she takes it in.

"He says we don't let them go until we have the Blade."

"No. He can't—"

Rayne lifts the paper and reads aloud. "*I most certainly can do that, Karson. So don't argue. Either do it my way, or consider your debt unfilled. I want my Blade.*"

I snatch at the paper. "No way he actually said that." But as I skim my own gaze over the thick, chunky writing, it becomes plain that yes, yes, he did. Not only that, but he expects that the sprite work on his behalf to get the Blade back because without doing so we aren't to release them.

The pair of us look down at the sprite. Unblinking black eyes consider us both in turn. "Release?" With each word, the tiny needles of the sprite's teeth become visible against the pale interior of their mouth. Even Norma seems to be staring, curious and cautious inside my clothing.

"Can you speak English?" I ask.

"Hooman talk, no."

Wow. The first words out of this sprite that haven't been requests to leave. I've no idea if they truly understand me or not, but at least we know they can speak a few other words.

I bend to eye level. "We're taking you back to your friends, but you just need to wait a moment longer."

The sprite says...*something*. I'm sure it's supposed to be speech from tone and facial expression, but there are no words I can pick out, just sounds.

I glance at Rayne, bemused.

She shrugs. "Guess these sprites have their own language."

"The screeching? So what are we going to do?"

"Our best." She shoves the envelope into her pocket and holds out the key for all the see. "This will release you," she says, slowly and clearly. "Will you help us?"

The sprite considers. "Release home?"

"Yes."

More murmuring that produces shrill little noises in equal parts with clicking and squawks. If I didn't know better, I could almost assume she was talking to Norma.

"Inside." The sprite points.

I grin. This, at least, is progress.

# CHAPTER TWENTY-TWO

Inside the cave, I decide to call the sprite Squeaky. Though the little creature has been able to replicate that sound more than once, the answering utterances thrown my way are simply not ones I can reproduce. I've no idea how these creatures speak, but if they do it with vocal chords similar to mine, then they shouldn't be able to make those sounds.

Rayne tries too with next to no luck, though she does eventually settle on *Xenet*, or at least something that sounds like that.

Squeaky—or Xenet—seems satisfied and begins to lead the way into the cave.

They don't go too far ahead of us, though they do walk with an assuredness that neither of us have.

I find myself watching the walls and ceiling, clutching Norma inside my clothing in case she decides to do a runner. Behind me, watching our backs, Rayne walks with an air of readiness about her slightly bent knees and loose arms.

Neither of us speaks.

Our steps, though soft, do echo on the stony ground, and each sound is thrown back to us hundreds of times by the bare, craggy walls.

After a short distance we're forced to use torches again. Well, I am, anyway. The sprite seems to have no such issue, carefully picking their way along the narrowing, shortening path.

Before too much longer, I have to duck my head into my shoulders a little, bending my legs rather like Rayne to avoid cracking my skull. She's probably fine for a short while longer, given the height I have on her, but neither of us is comfortable. That much is plain.

Another couple of minutes and we're far deeper than before. Deep enough that no sounds from above remain. The air is cool and damp, and the walls glisten in the light thrown by our torches.

Rayne is right at my back. She touches my hip gently. "I've never been this far before. I'm not sure when, but we've passed the point where the passage used to be blocked. I don't know if the sprites cleared it or excavation work did, but this is new. Those little holes and openings in the walls are coming more often too."

Great. Just great. So plenty of spots through which we might be ambushed.

I keep walking, but with every step, my unease grows. Tension crawls across my back and shoulders until every muscle there aches. I can taste my pulse. No amount of swallowing seems to tamp it down.

"How much further?" I ask.

Xenet stops and glances back. In the narrow shaft of light, their eyes are huge reflective pools, like a cat at night. I see them raise their skinny little arms. "Release?"

"Not yet."

More of those strange sounds. I think they indicate annoyance, but I can't be sure.

Rayne growls low at the back of her throat. In the time it takes me to turn, she has slipped around me and blocked two flying darts with the back of her wrist. Her eyes blaze with silver, and she shoves me back against the wall, pressing her back against me to keep me protected.

My torch goes flying, spinning through the darkness to throw broken shards of light up, down, and all over the place.

Norma bellows her annoyance with a roaring chorus of *dan dan dan*s, and the narrow space echoes with her sudden yelling.

I pinch at her beak, just so I can hear myself speak or even think. "Rayne—"

"There's at least three of them," she hisses. "But I don't know where. They keep moving. How are they moving through the walls?"

My torch beam lifts and aims directly at my eyes. It takes a moment too long to recognize that Xenet has picked it up and is playing with it. More of those odd sounds slide from parted lips, and they play the beam up and down the walls.

Again Rayne's hands dart out.

"Please," I call out, "we're not here to hurt you."

The next dart I hear crack against the wall near my face.

"Xenet, tell them. Release, remember? Home?"

Again the torchlight lands on my face. I squint into it, hoping, begging, praying this strange little creature will understand.

More squawks that might be words. The light dances over the tunnel walls, showing off tiny nooks and crevices where danger might be lurking.

Rayne hisses again. "They're moving away."

I dare to hope that Xenet has understood. Or at least if they haven't, they'd prefer not to get caught in friendly fire. Either is good. It will have to do.

When agreeing to this mad adventure, I hadn't anticipated not being able to speak with the sprites or even understand them fully. Most *edanes* I've come across have spoken English very well or at least used a language that I can understand. How the hell are we going to do this?

At last Rayne lets me off the wall and yanks the darts out of her wrist…and arm…and shoulder…and cheek.

At least one of us can see in the dark. I didn't even see them land, much less know they were coming.

She turns and checks me over, running her hands over my arms, shoulders, stomach, chest, legs.

"I'm fine," I tell her.

"Hush." And she continues to check. At any other time it might have felt nice to be the subject of such thorough attention, but the grim twist to her mouth and silver glint to her eyes makes clear this is not fun time. She even checks Norma, lifting my chittarik out of my clothing to inspect her front and back.

Calmer now, Norma shoots back a soft, "Kaaaaar son da?" before wriggling free and to the ground. I catch sight of her sniffing around at the dropped darts and recoiling from each with a little cackle of disgust.

"You're fine," Rayne says at last. "Both of you."

"Like I said—"

She glares at me. "You nearly weren't. Those first two were aimed at your face. Let me protect you. Let me look after you. Please."

"I—fine. Okay."

"Keep going."

Now there's an order, not a request.

Xenet, having been watching us curiously, again holds up their bound hands. Then, of course, "Release?"

I sigh. Maybe they have a point.

I glance back at Rayne. "Can I get that key?"

She looks the question at me.

"We already have a language barrier—maybe walking into *their* territory with one of their number bound like this isn't sending the best message. Besides, are we really going to keep them if we don't get the Blade?"

Her lips tighten, just for a moment. "But if it means the rest of them won't hurt you…"

"They can't hurt me. You won't let them."

Her upper lip curls. "If they fire again—"

I take the keys before she can finish the thought. Her desire to protect me is strong—hell, I've seen it in action several times—but I don't really want to see what she's capable of in this moment. Especially against a bunch of cave sprites. She could smear them into the ground without breaking a sweat, blindfolded and with one hand tied behind her back. Both, even. In fact, likely we both could. It's not like cave sprites are particularly strong, but both of us have arrived with a unspoken but very clear intent that nobody be hurt. That's not our way, and that's not our job.

A quick survey of the keys shows that there are only two—one for the tiny chains binding Xenet's wings down to their arms and another used to hobble the skinny little ankles. I unlock both, careful to maintain eye contact with every motion.

"Release," I say softly.

The sharp, pointed teeth are all the more frightening when exposed in what I hope is a smile. Xenet extends a thin, tiny hand and pats the side of my cheek. "Thank."

Progress. I hope.

I leave the chains on the floor of the cave. They should make a nice marker for when we start to head back.

Norma stays out of my clothing now, apparently too agitated to keep still. She moves lightly, that curious bobbing motion so like a cat. Her tail stays up, her attention fully forward, both wings arced tight over her back.

I know these motions. She's prowling. Hunting.

Great.

I've no idea how she would fare against a cave sprite, but seeing her size against Xenet, I begin to think it might actually be a reasonably matched fight. Norma is a tough little pest, that's for sure.

Another few minutes—I think—and the ceiling dips again. Now I'm bent and hunched to keep going, and progress is far slower. I use my hands to steady myself and spy tiny glints of moisture beneath my hands.

Wait...*is* it moisture?

I catch more of the glints in the walls and floor until, abruptly, it becomes plain that they aren't moisture at all, but some kind of mineral.

"Are the walls glittering?"

Rayne pauses before answering. "Mica, probably. It would match the geology of the area."

I have to trust her word on that. I've no idea.

"Does that mean we're getting close?"

She shakes her head. "The mica has nothing to do with it. But I'd say that the smoothness of the ground is a decent sign."

And she's right. Where before the tunnel path had been rough, pitted, and crumbling, now it is level, hard-packed, and seems formed far more of earth than stone.

Even Xenet's stride has changed, a slightly faster pace with more of a spring in it. Clearly they know where they are.

For the first time too, with the change in the walls and floor, I realise that the tunnel has been curving, slightly enough so as not to be obvious, but now as I glance back, I can see the turn before the rest of our path is blocked from sight. Perhaps we're not as far away from the entrance as I fear we may be.

That's when Rayne stops dead in her tracks. Her torch beam stops bouncing, and her footfalls fall silent. She gives a little hiss, and I stop too, joining her in listening, though I've no idea what for.

Xenet doesn't stop, just happily skips along ahead of us, now speaking in that screeching, squawking manner that seems to form their own language. I liken it to a flock of sparrows coughing after smoking six packs of cigarettes a day. But that flock of sparrows is arguing with a bunch of human children who haven't yet found their words, so they converse in gurgles, squeals, shrieks, and yelps.

It's…odd.

Then I hear the response. More voices, just like Xenet's, coming from somewhere on the right, in the direction of the tunnel's curve.

We found them.

Once more I try to swallow down my pulse. It doesn't work.

My heart feels about ready to burst from my chest.

What if they do fire those darts again? Will the antidote-vaccine work if more than one of them decide to attack?

Xenet abruptly vanishes.

I blink at the space they just left, trying to figure out if they are somehow suddenly invisible, before realising that the ground has dropped down and away.

The caves are now truly caves, an open space, perhaps as wide as a large office room, filled with at least two dozen cave sprites. Their eyes shine in the torchlight like a bunch of little rodents, and the sudden chatter as we step into view increases exponentially.

Each of them holds a little tube in tiny hands, tools I can only assume to be blowdarts.

Rayne quickly pushes me back to stand behind her.

I tense, and this time I even hear the little clicks as darts miss their mark and hit the wall behind.

Norma screeches in fury and dives down into the fray. Her tiny form darts back and forth, claws slashing, tail lashing at anything she can reach. "Dan. Ka nika. Son da-da-ka nika nika—"

Several of the sprites lift their blow darts. I dart forward.

The only reason I'm able to do so is because Rayne has already moved. She is down in the lower section, using both hands to scoop and toss the offending sprites. The silver hue is back in her eyes again, and her grunts of exertion come from deep in her belly.

Only when I reach the ground and sprint to reach my pet do I realise why.

Mania. But not quite.

Rayne's efforts come from holding herself in check, keeping her temper. Though she's rough with the sprites, her motions are nowhere near as violent as they otherwise might be. The sprites land easily from where she has thrown them, some with graceful rolls, others landing cleanly on their feet. She isn't hurting them at all.

I have the smallest instant to feel a swell of pride for my vampire girlfriend before a little stab of pain pierces my left thigh.

Shit. Oh, shit, shit.

An involuntary cry of surprise flees my lips as I spy the dart.

Pulling it out doesn't hurt at all, but the little shaft of wood has probably left several splinters in my leg if not my clothes. I snag Norma by the tail and haul her into my arms, pinning her there while she struggles and yells.

Rayne drops to a low crouch and leg sweeps the sprites closest, bowling them over like pins. "Time to go," she cries.

"No."

"Danika—"

"I'm already hit," I yell back through the chaos of squawks and squeals. "And there's enough of them that we can't dodge them all anyway. We need to make them understand." And then, like a complete and utter moron, I dump Norma on the ground, stand still, lift my arms above my head, and wait.

And wait.

And wait some more.

The sprites have stopped moving. All of them. They're looking at each other, sharing confused stares and bemused little murmurs.

Our sprite, Xenet, stands in front of them, clearly giving sermon, chattering animatedly with those sounds that mean more to them than us.

Rayne freezes midswing and, after a moment, copies my stance, though her arms are out to the side rather than high above her head.

Fine. Whatever. So long as we're showing that we're not a threat.

Xenet seems to be having an argument. They become increasingly shrill as they gesture to me, then outward, a vague gesture that seems to indicate the outside world. Then they back up, slowly, slowly, until standing directly in front of me.

Norma growls menacingly until I hush her.

"Hooman?"

I know that word, at least. I risk bending down enough to match their eyeline.

Another of those gentle pats to my cheek. "Thank."

"You're welcome, I guess." What else am I supposed to say?

Slowly, oh so slowly, the other sprites lower their blow tubes. Or some of them do. But that's better than nothing. And now, suddenly, in this unexpected moment of still, I'm able to look around the small space.

The cave, though small, is filled with trash.

In the light thrown by our dropped torches and a small battery powered lamp in one corner, I see broken umbrellas, knives and forks, broken jewellery, pipes, shards of glass, wooden boxes and crates, old scraps of clothes, plates and bowls, an old picnic table, a mangled CD player, bicycle tires, all sorts of nonsense. It's junk, all of it, but as I gaze at the collection in the light of the torch, I recognise it all has a similar trait—it is, or was, shiny.

The clothes have gleaming brass buttons, the picnic table has protruding screws, the umbrella shafts are lightly rusted metal. Even the crockery is fancy stuff with gold inlay in places.

"Rayne…"

"I see it too." Calmer now, she looks out over the space with eyes returned to their usual warm brown. The tiniest smile tugs at the corners of her lips. "They're hoarders."

"They're something."

I risk standing straighter again, now that Xenet has the attention of the others.

"How do we tell them what we're here for?"

Slowly, Rayne risks a step forward. When several blow tubes lift in her direction, she stops. "I don't know if we can."

"So what do we do?"

Tiny claws dig into my right calf. "Son dar? Nika nika daaaan dan."

"Not helping," I tell Norma.

The slight pain reminds me of the dart to the thigh. I can't really check it now without taking off my trousers, something I'd rather not do down here in the darkness. But I don't *feel* affected by it. If anything, my own adrenaline is the problem because my pulse is back in my throat again, and my chest is tight with nerves. Or at least, I hope it's nerves.

"Glal," I say at last. Maybe a name will be more helpful than trying to converse with these little creatures using words they may or may not understand.

A murmur among the gathered sprites. Even Xenet looks at me oddly.

I position my hands to indicate how large I imagine the spearhead to be. "Glal. *Goblin.*" I use the Goblin word, rather than the English one, hoping that might be more recognizable.

More chatter. More obvious conferring.

Xenet gestures the rest of the sprites over to the pile of assorted junk and begins to dig through. They are all the same pale brown colour, with similarly coloured wings. As the other sprites join in, pushing and shoving to get closer to the pile, I realise there's no way I can tell them apart now.

I fight the urge to hold my breath. Have we done it? Have these little creatures actually understood what we want?

Rayne sidles a step closer, using their distraction to advance on the stash. I can see her scanning it quickly, gaze skimming over all the junk to hopefully land on something precious.

One of the sprites leaves the gathering and walks over to me. It's not Xenet—this one has a smaller face and a rounder chin, with a small scar down the bicep of one skinny arm.

It holds a long piece of metal with a slight bowl at one end, clearly not a spearhead, though certainly very shiny. It speaks—I think—several sounds and squawks before laying the thing very carefully in front of my boots and backing away.

I fight the sudden urge to laugh. "Did you really just give me a spoon?"

"It's progress," Rayne offers.

Yet another sprite, still not Xenet, comes forward. This one is bulkier and broader across the chest and seems to be missing a finger. Still it carries two shards of glazed pottery and lays them with the spoon, artfully arranged one on top of the other. And, just like the other, it backs off slowly.

And so begins a little line, each sprite picking something from the pile of junk to lay at my feet. Some move quickly and fearfully, others of them reluctant and slow. All of them, however, place their chosen item at my feet with all the reverence of a ceremonial offering.

Soon Norma is forced to climb up my leg and back to my head to avoid all the things being piled around her. She is quiet though does occasionally snap her little beak if one of the sprites gets closer than she's willing to allow.

I stare at the collection of trash piled up around my feet. More cutlery, a tea strainer, two light bulbs—both broken—the hands of a broken clock, a wrench, half a watch strap, two dog collars, a set of rusted car keys, the door from what might be an old birdcage, and more screws and nails than I can count.

None of it is the Blade of Glal, though.

Last comes Xenet, now recognizable because of their slightly smaller frame. "Thank, release. Hooman." And they place an old coin on the ground before me.

My eyes fly wide, I can't help it. I pick it up, twisting and turning the thin piece of metal to get a better idea of what it might be. Sure, a coin, but not in any currency we're currently using. This thing is old. Maybe even as old as an old goblin spearhead?

"Xenet"—I try again to say what I think might be their name—"do you have more like this? Where did this come from?"

The little sprite looks alarmed. Down at the pile of junk at my feet, then back to me. "Thank?"

I kick the trash aside. "No, no, this. This, like this?" I hold out the coin so they can see it better, then point back to the remaining pile. "This?"

Little murmurs come from the sprites. A moment passes before I recognize annoyance and maybe even anger.

They talk again, more words I can't possibly understand, but I can't stop now. This is the first true sign I've received since coming to Moarwell that Shakka's damn treasure might actually be here.

This coin is incredibly old. Ancient, even. At the very least it's likely older than the restored church back on the surface, and that thing was abandoned for years. If the sprites have this, that must be a good sign, right?

I flip the coin to Rayne and notice that she's even closer to the stash of trash than she had been a moment before. Still, she catches the coin and studies it close, even giving a little gasp of surprise. No doubt she can see it better than me and so may even have a better idea of what it really is.

"Danika—"

"I know."

"Do you think they realise?"

"No idea." I look again at Xenet. "More like that?" Again I gesture with my hands to indicate the spearhead. I mime a stabbing motion just for good measure.

They say something, no idea what, to the rest of the sprites. Then, as one, the small group begin grabbing armfuls of junk to dump in front of me.

Bicycle handlebars, plug socket covers, fountain pens, split pins, broken pipe, more nails, more screws, a surprisingly sharp looking butcher knife, a crochet hook, a paintbrush…the junk begins to pile quicker than I can check it all, but still, none of it looks remotely like a spearhead.

"Bad," Xenet murmurs. "Release, thank. Hooman bad." They pick up an old, twisted fork, turn, and hurl it at me with all their might.

Lucky for me, their might is not so mighty, because the tool barely reaches me across the small space. It lands on the ground at least a foot away, but that small act is enough to teach the others what to do.

The offerings suddenly become projectiles, and I find all manner of shiny, metallic junk hurtling towards me.

Norma beats her wings defiantly and starts yelling her annoyance but doesn't leave my head. Thank goodness, because the barrage is getting intense and I don't know how much longer I want to stand in it.

Then from the corner of my eye, I see Rayne finally end her subtle sideways shuffle to reach the piles of rubbish. I watch her scan the pile, occasionally moving a piece here and there with her foot.

Then a claw hammer comes flying at my face.

That clearly took more than one of the sprites to move because it has decent velocity and speed as it hurtles past me.

Yup. They're clearly pissed now.

"If you can, Rayne"—I dodge a hurled CD—"you might want to hurry it up. A spearhead. Old as heck, but goblin made, so probably still really shiny."

"I'm trying," she calls. Now she gives up on any sort of subtlety and begins to dig through the trash pile with both hands. Stuff begins to totter and fall from uneven and wobbly pillars and stacks, crashing down to the ground around her.

Assaulted on two fronts now, the sprites become frantic. Most peel away from me to reach Rayne, lifting their blowdarts again. The rest stay focused on me.

I snatch an old road sign from the crap on the floor and hold it in front of me like a shield. Several darts slap against its surface.

"Norma, go."

Her claws tighten ever so slightly on my scalp. I had thought she intended to jump clear, but no, she's digging in for the long haul, along for whatever the ride happens to be.

More projectiles, including a old clothes hanger, bounce off my makeshift shield.

"Rayne?"

"I'm trying," she calls back.

All the sprites are yelling now, some with sounds that are almost recognisable words. I continue to back up, the road sign held high to protect my face and Norma. I feel the little sting of darts as they strike my legs and hips and find myself thinking of Bruce.

I hope he's right. I so, so hope he's right.

My back butts up against the wall. Above me is that little lip that leads back into the tunnel we entered through.

"Rayne?"

"Go."

I grit my teeth. "Not a chance. They're only sprites. We could lay them out in a heartbeat." The second the words are out of my mouth, I want them back.

Where the fuck did *that* come from?

Since when did I walk over and through people to get what I wanted? Even annoyances like these.

Sure, we *could* deal with the sprites easily, but that was never what this was about. Never during this trip did I intend to hurt anybody. Did I?

I shake my head hard, as if to force the awful thoughts out of my head. It doesn't work. Instead I find myself mulling how easy it would be to simply pull a gun and shoot these little annoyances to find what I'm looking for.

Ugh. I don't like that at all. No, in fact, I *hate* that. What's wrong with me?

Norma chitters and cackles at me, yanking at my locs as if she might be able to lift me back onto the little platform.

So I climb, a quick hop and a flex of my arms to scoot me upward and then a little two-step against the sheer surface to get me the rest of the way up.

Below, Rayne has given up on the pile of rubbish and is now hurrying over. I blink and she is beside me, one of those little bursts of speed I'm so used to *not* seeing. She gives me a shove towards the exit.

"Let's go."

So we do, Norma bounding off my head and down to lead the way. This time we don't bother with the torches, having left them behind in the cave. Instead I scoot my way forward in the dark, hands outstretched to the sides and slightly up, to feel the walls and ceiling.

Behind, Rayne follows with one hand on my hip, nudging or pulling me left or right when she notices the danger of my path.

Somehow, the way back is much faster than the way in. Or maybe fleeing from danger just gives the tunnel a sense of shortness. Before many minutes have passed, we're back at the mangled gate and springing out into the cool night air.

A light drizzle falls, and after the close dry air of the cave, I'm relieved to see stars, feel air, and taste moisture on my lips.

We don't stop until far from the cave's entrance, and my own breath is hissing through my mouth. I bend over my knees and suck in air.

The world is spinning ever so slightly, and despite the rain, my skin feels hot and prickly.

Rayne looks me over again, wordlessly inspecting every inch of my body she can reach. A growl of anger rumbles at the back of her throat when she pulls two more darts out of my leg.

"How do you feel?"

"Like I'm going to vomit, actually. Thanks for asking." I flop to the ground and lie on my back. It's cold, it's wet, it's uncomfortable, but I don't care.

I screwed up. Again.

Not only do we not have the Blade, but we've now given up our bargaining chip such as Xenet was. We know where the sprites are, but we also know that they really, *really* don't like visitors. Is there much point in going back?

Something small and hard drops against my stomach.

I flinch, expecting to feel Norma, but she is sitting in the grass close to my head, tail gently tangling in my hair. Instead, when I feel around for it, I find the hard round edges of that coin.

Rayne smiles at me. "I wonder what era it's from."

In the slightly improved light I look again. The markings on it are worn and faded, but I can just feel the edges of what might be a cross or an X with my fingertips.

A shrug. "Not Glal's, so who cares?"

I sigh and reach over to scoop Norma to me. As if sensing my weariness, she cuddles in close, nuzzling her face against my cheek.

"Oh?" There is a definite smile in Rayne's voice now. "What about this, then?" She drops something else on my stomach.

This is heavier, thicker, and gleams wetly as I pick it up.

Twinned serrated edges curve in a broad leaf shape to a wicked point, and at the base, a long horizontal bar tops the narrower tube presumably designed to fit onto a wooden shaft. The metal is cold and shiny, etched with partially faded symbols that I vaguely recognise to be words. It also strongly resembles the sketches in Shakka's notes.

I stare at Rayne, mouth open, mindless of the rain dropping into it. "How?"

She grins. "It was right there. On the floor. I don't think they had any idea what they were holding on to, but it was certainly the prettiest thing in that cave."

I turn the spearhead over and over in my hands. She's not wrong. The thing is deadly but strangely beautiful, with only the smallest hints of dirt or grime caught in the etchings. From tip to base the thing measures roughly the length of my forearm.

"You think this is it?"

"If it isn't, I don't know what else it might be."

For the first time in hours I smile a real smile. Hell, I laugh. I toss my head back and laugh up at the sky while Norma dances and cavorts around me. To my side, Rayne heaves a relieved sigh and flops down into the grass to sit beside me.

Finally, something is going our way.

# CHAPTER TWENTY-THREE

Back at the van I can barely contain my excitement. There is a spring in my step and joy in my voice as I gleefully remind Rayne that it's now over. We've achieved our main mission. She smiles and hugs me and kisses the top of my head as I sigh out my relief and bury my face in her shoulder.

Perhaps that's why neither of us notices Duo leaning quietly against the door of the van until he steps out of the shadows with his arms folded, his bright orange hair flapping gently in the breeze. His eyes are narrowed, his mouth twisted up, nose wrinkled in distaste.

"So you've been off again?"

Norma gives a cackle of alarm. Clearly she didn't notice him either.

I stop dead, my fingers loose on the spearhead. "What are you doing here?"

He snarls. "Fiona wanted to see you, and neither of you were answering your phones, so I came out to find you. No you, though, just an empty van, no sign, no note, no warning, just gone. I was preparing to follow you."

Rayne looks at me.

I hesitate. "I—"

"I thought we were a team." Rather than angry, Duo sounds hurt. "We're friends, aren't we? You're our boss, sure, but we're a team. Friends."

"We are, but—"

"Then where have you been?"

The simple question slaps so hard I almost stumble at it. "I…" Again, I look at Rayne.

Duo bristles. "Stop trying to figure out the lie—you know I can just check. All I need to do is follow your scent, so you might as well tell me. Where did you go?"

Slowly, I hold up the shiny, ancient spearhead. "We had to collect this."

He eyes it coolly. "Nice trinket. But why do you smell like a vintage auction? You're covered in the scent of old stuff. And you're wet. *And* you're sick again."

That catches my attention. "What?"

"Whatever laid you out yesterday, you've done it again. The scent of it is all over you. If you were going into danger, why didn't you tell us? Why wouldn't you let us help?"

I press my hand to my thigh. So the darts *are* affecting me. But at least I'm not flying through space and seeing stars again. Thank you, Bruce Dixon.

"It was supposed to be secret."

"You told Rayne." Duo thrusts an accusing finger in her direction.

"That's different, she—"

"She's your girlfriend?" If possible, Duo's voice becomes cooler still. "Or she's a vampire? She's a woman? You're boning her? Come on, which is it that makes her more trustworthy than me and Solo?"

Wow, oh wow. His hurt is palpable now.

On the ground, curious and concerned, Norma shares her gaze between us. She looks like a viewer at a tennis match, but her throaty little croaks tell the story of her distress.

"It's not like that. Duo, I'm sorry. It was a special mission and—"

"SPEAR sanctioned this?" His orange eyebrows lift quizzically. "Then why would it be secret from us? We're agents too."

I tuck the spear into my waistband to free my hands. "Not from SPEAR."

The hurt morphs into disdain. "Work on the side, Danika? Have you forgotten what happened last time you did that?"

Okay, double ouch.

"I'm fulfilling a favour," I shoot back as my own temper begins to rise. "You know, just because we're a team doesn't mean you have the right to know every small detail of my life."

A low snarl. "No, just the details required to keep us on hand like good little guard dogs." Duo backs off and starts walking away. "Like I said, Fiona wants you. Come or don't, I don't care."

I take a step after him. "Duo, please—"

He lifts a hand, displaying the back of his middle finger.

Rayne catches my arm. "Let him go."

So I do. I watch him walk slowly up the little slope and out of sight around the little cluster of trees that form a partial wall against intruding eyes.

"Fuck."

So much for the feel-good of the last half hour or so.

"He'll be fine."

I nod, but I'm not so sure. Duo is a sensitive kind of guy, with such a strong sense of loyalty and honour. I know some of that comes from his pack, but the rest is rooted simply in the sort of man he is. His hurt and confusion over his omission comes from a genuine desire to do right by those he cares for.

I should be lucky to count myself as one of those people.

"What am I going to do?"

"Visit Fiona," Rayne says. "It must be important if she wants to see you after…earlier. Duo will come round."

I nod. Maybe he will, but he has a twin brother.

Solo is far harder and harsher than Duo. His loyalty sometimes manifests in violence to protect those he cares for and a strong outburst towards those who do him wrong. I realise abruptly that while Duo might forgive me, Solo will be the hard one to convince.

"What are you going to do with that?" She points to the spearhead tucked into my waist.

"I'm not taking my eyes off this thing even for a second. It was hard enough to get—I want to know where it is at all times."

We walk back together, Rayne quiet and pensive, me distressed and distracted from our victory. Close by, clearly picking up my mood, Norma climbs up my body to rest on my shoulder. She seems to prefer my shoulder when I'm upset, the better to be closer to my face.

I'm grateful for it.

One hand gently stroking her back, I chew my lip as I go, wondering what Duo has said to his brother and how they'll react once we're all in the same spot. In truth, I'm distracted enough that I barely notice how out in the open we are until Rayne's grip tightens on my other hand.

When I follow her gaze, I notice a small face in the window of one of the houses, peering out at us.

"Is that…?"

Rayne grips tighter on my hand. "She's watching us."

I fight the urge to make daft faces at the small sliver of Linda's face just visible behind her curtains.

"Screw her. We're nearly done here, anyway. There's nothing more she can do."

"Don't assume that. She's…resourceful."

I try to assess what she means by that. "You never told me you were engaged, by the way."

The grip on my hand slackens, then drops away entirely. "It was a long time ago."

"She's still not over it."

Rayne stops walking. She looks down at the ground. "I...we..." Her expression is so pained, her voice so small.

I want to know. Fuck, I really, really want to know but not if it's going to make her look like this.

"Don't worry about it." I wave my hand to dismiss the answer. "Now isn't the time, and you don't have to tell me anything you don't want to."

"I don't like keeping secrets from you."

"It's not a secret. You can tell me another time."

She nibbles her bottom lip. "I asked her to marry me just as we finished school. She was so refined and beautiful and perfect, and I was a short wastrel of an orphan with no prospects. She said yes straight away."

My mouth opens automatically, but I snap it shut again just as fast. This isn't the time to interrupt.

"We had only been dating a month or two, but I was so, so in love with her. Or I thought I was." Rayne's pace slows ever so slightly. "She did a good job of convincing me we were in love. But what *she* loved was the idea of rescuing me and making me better. I was a project to her, something fun and interesting to poke at during the weekends when she was bored. I realised it was far more about what she could change in me than what she liked. And what I could give her."

Another pause. This time the fight to stay silent causes me to bite my own lip.

"She thought that being with me would give her access to Mama and Bubi since they were so well known and respected, particularly for their foster work. She planned to use them to advance her position in the village council and maybe leapfrog out into something bigger. But they knew what she was like long before I did, and her plans fell through. So, to get back at them for destroying her dreams, she turned the council against them by stirring fear and distrust about Bubi's Ranching duties." A soft sigh. "I broke it off, but it was too late by then. She hated them and me. And then, of course, I left."

"But why is she so caught up on you now?" I lose the fight with myself and glare briefly at the window as I walk. "It's been long enough—surely she's moved on. Does she still want you?" The words feel slick on my tongue, but I *have* to ask. I have to know.

She considers. "Before me, I don't think anybody ever said no to her. I think, at this point, she is more caught up on the *idea* of me than me myself, since I represent a very real, and rather public, rejection. And certainly, I always remember her getting exactly what she wanted, whenever she wanted it. Linda isn't spoilt but—"

"Spoilt," I cut in. "And then along you come to show her that the world doesn't, in fact, revolve around her. No wonder she can't let go." Silly, but abruptly, I feel better.

There isn't some big, hidden secret between Linda and Rayne. There's nothing between them at all, just another woman so beside her own self-importance that the very idea of rejection is foreign to them. I've met her type before. Those types of people…I know how to handle them.

"Perhaps. But I also think the prestige of being connected to anything from The Big City is very real. It makes one appear important and gives an air of authority and power, whether it's deserved or not."

I roll my eyes. "Small-town folk are weird."

"No weirder than you or me."

I nod. "Perhaps, though I do question your taste."

She chuckles. At least that joke still lands well.

We ignore Linda and keep walking. Somehow, the fact that we have our prize makes us significantly less careful and we arrive at the Kidson Bed and Breakfast via the front. After following the little track round to the back, Rayne is first to tap gently on the back door.

Solo yanks it open before Rayne's knuckles have fully left the wood. His hands and neck are hairy, his fingernails tinged black.

Oh, boy.

"Tell me," he snaps. "Right now."

"Can we at least come in?"

"Start. Talking."

So I stand outside in the cold and the drizzle, and I talk. "Shakka called in a favour."

That immediately frays Solo's temper further. "What the fuck does that little shit stain want with you?"

With a sigh, I pull the Blade from my waistband and show it off.

His nose wrinkles. "A big silver knife. Big whoop."

"It's a spearhead. An old one. Shakka's ancestors made it, and when he discovered where it was, he asked me to get it back."

"And I assume they didn't want to give it to you?" He gives a mirthless bark of laughter at my confused stare. "You were *attacked*. The poison? That goblin bastard sent you into danger and didn't even have the good grace to include the rest of us so we could help you. Worse than that, you didn't *let* us help."

My own heat begins to rise. "It was a favour. *My* favour. I don't understand why you're so upset. Aren't there things *you* need to do on your own?"

"Not that need me to lie about them. I hate liars, Karson."

Oof. Like a punch to the gut. He's never, ever referred to me so coldly.

"I—"

"You stole the truth from us. You brought us out here on some fake mission, and now an innocent woman is hurt. I hope you're pleased with yourself."

That's a little too close to my guilt over all of this. "Coming here to see Fiona *was* a real mission. Maury arranged for it so I could get help for whatever is on my back. This"—I wave the spearhead at him—"is nothing to do with that. We're just lucky the locations clashed."

"And the gargoyle that flew overhead a few hours ago?"

I blink at him. "You saw her?"

"She's not subtle. Let's just say that." Solo sucks in a deep breath, then snorts it out through both nostrils. "Fiona wants to see you. No idea why, but there you go. Duo and I are going out."

"But—"

"I'm hungry, and I know he is too. This is the countryside—there's plenty of game we can chase without hurting anybody."

I reach out, but he jerks away. "Solo, please. Stay. We can talk it through."

"Maybe later. Right now, if I do, I'm going to say something I don't mean." Finally he moves away from the doorway, but outward instead of in. He shoves by me and towards the fence separating off the garden area, shucking clothes as he goes. By the time he reaches the gate, his form begins to twist and writhe, and a soft growl of pain floats back on the night air.

His change, though clearly painful, is smooth and seamless, and he leaps over the fence in his pure wolf form.

As a wolf, his hair dye is a distant memory. Instead Solo is a small, lithe, grey wolf with a white crest along the back.

Already out in the darkness an identical wolf waits for him, though the white colouring is along the chest rather than the back. Duo.

The pair of them pause long enough to look back at me before diving off into the darkness.

"Damn it."

The last thing I want is two pissed-off wolves roaming the countryside. I've already seen one farmer with a gun—what if there are more? Sure, they would likely easily survive a traditional shotgun blast, but do we really want to spook the locals more than we already have?

Rayne rests a gentle hand on my shoulder. "You speak to Fiona. I'll go. I can keep up, and I might be able to convince them to come back."

"Be careful."

She grins in answer, then jogs away.

I look back at the quaint little house and feel a small quiver of fear pulse through me.

What could Fiona possibly want with me after her last disastrous attempt? Well. Only one way to find out, right?

I treat myself to another pat of Norma's back—more for my comfort than hers—then head inside.

Fiona is waiting in the kitchen. Her back is to me, but I can already see her bandaged hands resting lightly on the table in front of her. Her hair is down and messy and, when I walk round to see her face, I can see the faint rings of fatigue around her lower eyelids.

She gestures to the chair across from her, which I take without speaking.

Norma I lift off my shoulder and place on the floor. The little creature eyes me coolly before helping herself up onto one of the countertops where she sits and watches and waits.

For long seconds we sit in silence.

"Those boys are quite upset," Fiona says at last.

I wince. "I played it badly."

A soft hum of assent. "You're guilty. And angry."

"You don't need to be a psychic to tell that."

"Perhaps not, but you reek of it, child. Are you all right?"

I glare at her. "Me? Me, all right? No, frankly, but thanks for asking. I've got you sitting in front of me, bandaged and maimed. I have two of my friends rightly furious with me, and a girlfriend trying to keep it all together on my behalf. I don't deserve her."

"You don't think so?"

A sigh. "What did you need, Fiona? I don't think I should be here as it is, especially after what I did to you before, but if you have something to say?"

She reaches beneath the table. Her moves are slow and so, so careful, but she holds up an old book. Or I assume it's a book. The cover is leather or something close and inside are plenty of pieces of paper, though the pages don't seem to be bound. They are also handwritten.

I shrug.

"My great-aunt was a psychic, rather like me. Or rather, I'm like her. She was very powerful, able to see things in people and objects that no one else ever could. And her grandmother was also like us. Down the line of females in my family, regularly skipping generations, would be those of us who could *see*."

It's a nice story, but I really can't see how it helps me. But I know she's trying, so I bite my tongue over the urge to complain. Instead, I wait.

"Many of them kept diaries, or at least notes of things they saw. And each time a member of the family was found to have the ability, we would pass this to them." She waves the book.

Still I wait.

She sighs. "After I...touched you, I knew there was no way I'd be able to identify your taint on my own. There's something there, I know that for sure, but I don't know what it is. I wondered if maybe my relatives did." Slowly, still carefully, she opens the leather cover.

The pages inside are a mix of different types of paper, plain cards, and even parchment. Some of them are so old that the edges are yellow and crumbling. Each sheet is covered in tiny, precise handwriting, all in different styles and weights. The words of dozens upon dozens of women are in these pages. Along with the papers are other little trinkets, like dried leaves, sprigs of herbs wrapped in string, the occasional small bone or twig.

Fiona spreads it all out on the table in front of her, making little groupings of the papers and oddments.

Rather like my first sight of her real workspace down below, now I get the true sense of who this woman is and how she works. She is the real deal, no matter what facade she puts on for the outside world.

Eventually she brings a single sheet of parchment to the top and smooths it out in front of her. The words are faded and scrawling, the language something I barely recognise as English, though it is much easier to read the right way up.

*O'er time immortal liveth t creature*
*'Pon hapless souls t sups to gréatan*
*Fear and rage maketh the meat*

I shrug. "I've no idea what that means."

A steady stare from Fiona. Wordlessly, she points further down the page.

*Mark'd corpse shall embody t*
*Thus cometh that most pure an fell evel*
*Minions bruise the path*
*Bold an fast in that most gold'n eyed hue*
*Like to sunflowers, yet nay so faire*
*"Mast'r" crieth they and lo, t comes*
*And our earth tun ceald lyk death*

My back itches—in response, in fear, in discomfort, I don't know. But I do know that as I read, the words abruptly ring closer to home than I want them to.

"I don't know what happened to you when the creature marked you, child, but I know what I saw when I touched you. Darkness. Yellow eyes."

"Like sunflowers," I mutter.

She nods. "This thing, whatever it is, is known."

"But what does the passage mean?"

When Fiona next meets my gaze it's with pity in her eyes. She moves that sheet to the side and picks out another. This is a different hand, and the paper is slightly less fragile but still old. The corners are torn in places, and a large rusty stain down one edge reminds me far too much of blood.

Still, I read.

*Mark'd, that hapless gent doth weep by the moon*
*Not a one by his side for fear*
*Evel swells lyk fog 'bout him*
*Anger a dark shadow on our kin*
*We might not but slay him an in so fierce a task*
*Free him from the burden*

"Fiona…"

She pushes one last piece of paper in my direction. This one is the smallest of them all, but the writing is bold and clear, as though someone pressed hard with their scribing implement.

*Slain*
*As lyfe did leave that mangled frame*

*So too the mark did pass*
*Skies above split with godly fyre*
*An gentle rain wash'd clean*
*Saved by sacrifice*
*Evel be held at bay*

Ice seems to replace my blood. I shake my head once, then again. And again. Suddenly I'm standing, I'm slapping at the table, sending papers and knick-knacks flying in every direction.

Norma cries out in alarm, flapping her way around the kitchen with her customary cries.

But I don't care. I can't stop. Again I slam the table, and it shudders beneath the blow. Again. Again. Again.

"Danika—"

"No," I cry out, slapping my hands on the now empty table. "No. No way. There has to be another way."

The whole time, Fiona doesn't move. She allows me to toss her belongings all over the kitchen, merely watching as I rage. Maybe she's scared, maybe she's not, but she is definitely pitying now, and that irks me all the more.

"Say something," I demand. "You have to say something. Surely this isn't it? Isn't there more?"

"I did look," she says at last. "Of course I did, child. But this is all I have to go on. A few notes here, a scrap of text there. They don't even have a name for the creature doing this to you."

"But they do suggest killing me?"

At the word *kill*, Norma drops down onto the table. She hops back and forth to catch my gaze, making careful eye contact as soon as I allow it.

"Dan ka? Ika ni?"

Those new words again. Or at least to my ear they seem new. But my pet is distressed and doing her best to comfort me in mine. I lift her to me for a brief nuzzle against her beak. She croons, but I can't hold on to her, my hands are too itchy, too twitchy. I plop her on the table again and fight to control myself.

Fiona lifts one maimed hand. "I don't think that's their suggestion, child, no. Or rather, they say only that that was the choice *they* made. We don't have to make the same choice."

"And if we don't? If this mark stays on me and we can't get rid of it, then what?" I scan the floor for the paper and give up almost at once. "Then the minions call down their master and…everybody dies?"

"We don't—"

"Cold like death, it said. If this *thing*, whatever it is, comes into my body, it destroys the world." She winces, but I press on. "Yeah, it sounds dramatic, but I don't know how else to read all that."

"Child—"

"Fiona." I lean low over the table to see clearly into her eyes. "Are these old diary entries suggesting the only way to get rid of this thing, before it gets worse, is to kill me?"

She meets my gaze firmly and clearly. With a long deep breath she nods. "Yes. That appears to be the message."

I sit down. It's that or fall.

"Dan dan?" Norma whispers. Her voice is low and hollow, so unlike her that when she crawls into my lap, I don't have the heart to fend her off.

I hold her, she holds me, and together we listen to Fiona speak.

"This thing is so old it doesn't have a name. If the writings are to be believed, it feeds off anger and fear, all those things I felt in you when we touched." Fiona lifts her hands slightly. "I told you I felt hunger. And now, I believe that's what this is. The creature hungers for all those negative emotions and puts out a call to bring it in. Worse still, the mark on your back is a beacon or sign to this creature, from a minion, that you are suitable for purpose. I would say, with a human body to use, this master entity would have a much easier job of feeding on the emotions it craves."

"But all those people, all those women. One of them must have seen something or found something to get rid of the mark. Right? Surely they didn't just murder everyone they found with these marks on their skin?"

A single tear slides down Fiona's cheek. "Child, I'm sorry. I'm so, so sorry. But there's nothing more. I searched and searched. I even called out at this unseemly hour, asking my peers what they knew."

"And?" My voice is reaching dangerously high levels.

"One psychic in Brazil told me of a child in the nineteen sixties who appeared one day with marks on his arms. He had been playing in the woods when a creature with yellow eyes touched him. The next day the child fell into the sea on a fishing trip and drowned. So she told me."

Her hidden meaning is clear. "A kid? They drowned a kid?"

"This entity brings fear with it. Any and everybody I've found who came across it has decided it couldn't be worth the unknown fate to leave the host alive. They sacrificed anybody they found for the greater good."

"Host?" I screech. "So this thing is a freaking parasite?"

"In a manner."

I grab great fistfuls of my locs and pull. The pain is sharp but steadying, and I use that moment of clarity to try to think. Think, think, think. There has to be something, anything at all.

"I've not finished reaching out," Fiona assures me. "So long as we have time, I believe we can find a way to get rid of the mark. A cleansing ritual or an exorcism, something like that."

"I don't think there is time." After the pain, some of the fight seems to leak out of me. I think back over the past few days—the creature in my dreams, the yellow eyes springing up out of nowhere, increasingly frequent and more intense each time, along with memories of my past that do nothing but dredge up fear and guilt.

Seems to match up perfectly.

"I've been dreaming of that yellow-eyed thing for ages. And every time it gets worse. What if that's what it means? What if all those dreams are just me getting closer to the master-thing coming to take me over?"

No response.

Then again, what can she say, really?

A sudden shout breaks me out of my thoughts. It comes from the rear door, which, as I look, slowly swings shut.

Fuck.

Was it open the whole time? Was someone out there?

I dash around the table, dislodging a screeching Norma, and hurl myself through the door, out in the night.

The rain has stopped, but the ground is wet and on it, tangled together, are Rayne and Linda.

Linda is screaming and kicking, fighting and punching, while Rayne holds her calmly by locking her arms through Linda's to pin them in place.

The blond woman rages impotently, her eyes narrowed in fury.

"What did you hear?" I snap.

She spits in my face. "I knew you were evil. I just knew it. You're going to kill us all with your demon master, I just knew it."

Rayne jerks her tighter, not to harm her but in an effort to stop her raging. "I got back and found her listening at the door. She jumped like a rabbit when she saw me and tried to run. I only wanted to talk."

"I don't want to talk to you," Linda yells. "I'll never talk to you again. Let go of me. Right now, you unholy monster. Get off, let go, let me go."

The noise is immense. Someone will be out to see what's going on if we don't shut her up.

Rayne releases Linda from her police officer's hold and steps back. "If you'll just stay calm and tell me—"

"Calm? Didn't you hear? That bitch has a demon inside her, and it's going to kill us all. You need to get out of here. You need to go back to that awful city filled with monsters and demons and keep it all away from us, do you understand me?" She continues backing off. "You're evil. All of you. And if we let you, you'll murder us all. I knew it. And Bruce...I told him, and he let you stay anyway."

"Leave him out of this." A coolness fills Rayne's voice.

"Oh, we'll see." Linda backs off still further, never once taking her eyes off us. "By morning you'll be gone, do you hear me? Gone or we'll deal with you ourselves. We have children here. If you have even the smallest shred of decency left, you'll be gone before morning."

With that, she turns and darts away, pointy heels sinking into the soft, wet road as she goes.

Rayne turns back to me, her face a picture of confusion and worry. "What on earth did I come back to?"

I sigh. How the fuck am I going to tell her? How do I even begin to explain what Fiona has found?

I swallow the sudden spiky lump seeming to fill the back of my throat. "You'd better come inside."

❖

Rayne stares down at her hands without speaking. She is statue still in that way I bounce between admiring and fearing. Red stains smear her cheeks from all the tears, and her hands still bear the marks of her fingernails from where she pressed them deeply into her palms.

I sit with my head bowed, my hands laced in my lap. If I don't hold on to them, and myself for that matter, I'll end up running screaming through the streets.

Beyond the kitchen, in her lower space, Fiona is still making phone calls. I can't hear her whispered conversations, just the low murmur of urgency in her voice.

"Rayne..."

She lifts her head, a sudden snap of motion. "We can't tell anyone."

"What?"

"We can't tell anyone. Nobody. We need time. We need to give Fiona time to find more help."

I lift my hands helplessly. "But I have to let SPEAR know. Maury sent us out here for answers, and finally we have some. I can't keep it to myself."

A little furrow forms in her forehead. "And what do you think they'll do with those answers if you hand them over now?"

I gape at her. She can't be serious. Can she? Does she really believe they would kill me over some words scrawled on paper hundreds of years old?

"We can't tell anyone yet." Her eyes are glistening again. "Please."

"Then what do we do?"

She stands, another burst of motion. "We leave. Immediately. I don't think we'll reach Angbec before sunrise, but I'll sleep in the travel pod. At the very least we need to get away from here before Linda makes good on her threat."

I snort. "What can she really do?"

"Plenty." A quick scoot around the table. Now she's wiping tears from her face, trying to clean herself up. "Start packing. I'll find the boys and bring them back."

"You didn't find them before?"

"No, I found them. But they weren't doing any harm, so I decided to come back. I'm glad I did."

Me too, though really, what can Linda do? Sure she might be president of the Moarwell council, but they have no power over us, not really. The most they can do is tell us to leave, and that's exactly what we plan to do.

I do feel vague worry over Bruce and Kimberly Dixon, but surely Linda will have no reason to bother them if we're gone. Things can go back to what they were, right?

I gather Norma with me and head downstairs first.

As I pass Fiona, she gives me a faint nod, then turns her back. I leave her to the illusion of privacy and enter the room with the bed.

To think, only the night before I had worried about having to spend days down here.

I shake the thought aside, gather up our few belongings, and cart them back upstairs. Norma follows behind, carrying a couple of straps in her beak. She isn't doing much, but her desire to help is welcome, and I don't try to stop her. Instead I beckon her to follow up the stairs and across the landing to what I assume is the room the boys were sharing.

Upstairs is as cute and quaint as one might expect a countryside B & B to be. Framed landscape photos or paintings, weird farmyard trinkets, and tools in corners or hanging on walls. The room at the end is closed, but when I open it I find a view through the window down onto the rear car park. It is the right room.

The boys have already packed. Or maybe they didn't unpack. I've no idea, but it is easy to grab their bags too and haul them down with me.

Norma follows, dragging a baseball cap behind her. I think it's Duo's. Well, I hope it's his, because as she comes, Norma gnaws hard on the rim, ruining the fabric and stitching.

I'm only waiting a couple of minutes before Rayne comes jogging back with a wolf in tow. She looks like something out of a fantasy novel—small, lithe, and gorgeous with her loyal animal companion bringing up the rear. As she comes, she scoops clothing off the ground, folding it neatly across her arm to hand over.

Behind, with a soft growl, Solo's form ripples into being out of the smaller, shorter wolf shape. He's naked and sweaty, covered in mud, sticks, and leaves. His red hair fires up in all directions.

He takes the clothes Rayne offers and pulls them on without a word, mindless of the grime on them and himself.

"I'm still pissed," he mutters, "but apparently we've got bigger problems."

"Thank you." I don't know if it's enough, or even if he cares for my gratitude, but I have to say something. "I brought your stuff down."

Silence. Awkward, thick, and stuffy.

Rayne clears her throat.

I kick at a loose clot of earth.

Solo turns his head a little, his nostrils flaring. "Come on, the van is out front."

Ah, so that's where Duo is.

All of us grab some bags and walk around the building, splashing through the few shallow puddles left behind by the drizzle. Norma bounds along after us, darting ahead with her tail bobbing. She pulls up short at the edge of the house and spreads her wings with a gleeful murmur of, "Kar dan dan," before scurrying forward.

There is Bruce Dixon, seemingly surprised and pleased to catch the chittarik as she hurls herself at him. He croons to her, patting her gently, stroking her back with large firm hands. She wriggles deeper into him.

Guess he must be a good guy after all. Norma isn't known for her love of men.

Rayne hurries forward. "Bubi? What's going on?"

He reaches out to one-handed hug her. "Fiona called me. She said you were leaving and that I should say goodbye."

"It's the middle of the night."

"Perfectly reasonable time for you." He smiles. "Besides, I was already up. Linda also called, yelling some nonsense about demons and curses. I've no idea why she's so upset, but I wanted to check on you. She said you were here, so…" He trails off and lifts a hand in a *well, here I am* sort of gesture.

"Fiona is right, sir." I look past him towards the van parked up at the door. Duo is inside, hopping out to start gathering bags. "To say we've overstayed our welcome is…well, yeah. We need to go."

Bruce turns to me, still holding Rayne around the shoulders. "Did you get what you came for?"

I hesitate. The words teeter on the end of my tongue. "Yes. I guess I did."

"Good. I'm glad you got answers or whatever it is you wanted." His warm smile breaks something inside me. "I hope that helps you."

"It will." My voice cracks, but I don't let myself stop.

Instead of handing my things to Duo, I take them to the back of the van myself, leaving Rayne to have a private moment with her father.

# CHAPTER TWENTY-FOUR

I sit in the back of the van, hands trembling, head bowed, Norma in my lap. That racing feeling is in my chest again, but this time it's much more than adrenaline. This is fear. This is pure, unfiltered, unmatched fear.

I cling to my pet, and she rubs herself against me, pressing in as if fighting to get inside my skin. Her warmth and her stiff scales are a strange comfort to me now, familiar.

"Nika son?"

I sniff hard against the feeling of tears at the back of my throat. "Yeah. I guess so, baby. Home now."

She wraps her tail around my wrist and settles in more comfortably, her eyes drifting closed moments later.

Oh, I wish I could settle so easily. But right now, I doubt I'll ever sleep again, much less rest comfortably.

A moment later the front doors open, and both wolf twins help themselves in. There's no playful game of rock-paper-scissors this time, no light-hearted banter or chatter. The pair of them are stiff and uneasy, sharing more conversation between them with meaningful looks and facial expressions.

I can't begrudge them their secrecy. Not right now. Not after what I've done.

Was I wrong to keep them out of Shakka's mission? Sure, he didn't want anybody to know, but I didn't have to give them details. I could have given them the basics, a retrieval mission as a favour to a fellow SPEAR operative. They didn't even need to know who it was, much less the history of the spearhead now wrapped in newspaper and carefully stowed in my bag.

In fact, all I needed to tell them was that I needed help. That would have been enough.

I sigh.

Norma snores.

We wait.

Several minutes later, Rayne climbs into the back of the van with me. She has clearly been crying. More redness brightens her pale cheeks, which she tries, without success, to wipe away.

"Are you going to be okay?"

She stares down at her hands. "I don't know."

At least she's honest. I want to touch her, comfort her, something, but I can't bear to let my skin touch hers. Not my awful, marked, tainted skin. Instead I smile as warm a smile as I can manage and use my foot to nudge one of the bags closest to her.

"Your pod is in there. If we don't make it, I'll help you get inside."

The engine starts with a soft purr. Duo looks back over the front seats to pin us both with a steely stare. "Oh, we'll make it," he mutters.

Ominous as fuck.

But he pulls away from the building with smooth easy grace, and soon we're heading back through the village towards the tiny B-road we used to make our way in.

The view of Moarwell slides past my view, odd shadows and shapes thrown by the glare of our glass windows. I spy the welcome sign, now from the rear, telling us to *drive safely* and *thank you for visiting*.

As Moarwell drops away behind us, I hope that the idyllic little village can remain as calm, peaceful, and beautiful as ever it has been, if not for the sake of the inhabitants, then for Rayne, who watches her one-time home vanish from sight with her bottom lip drawn up between her fangs.

❖

We've been travelling perhaps an hour when my phone rings. It is the familiar hip-hop sounds of some early aughties artist who speaks faster than most people can think. I use it for acquaintances and businesses, the people I don't mind leaving unanswered, as I listen to the catchy tune.

But I do answer this time, because the name on the display makes me run cold all over.

"What's up, Maury?"

"Danika, what have you done?"

I blink owlishly at the phone. For a moment I feel like I'm talking to Quinn, listening to her berate me over some stupid stunt or another that got the job done but failed to follow the rules. It's a curious little flashback that I'm not ready for.

"Well, good evening to you too, dick nugget."

He sighs. "Pack it in. I need to know what you've been doing. Are you okay out there?"

I glance at Rayne. She shakes her head furiously at me, but I shrug. What am I supposed to say? "We're fine. In fact, we're done. We're coming home."

"Good," he snaps. "I have a ream of complaints here from some little village up north. I thought it was just some civvies complaining about a raid a few weeks back, but no, they're from Moarwell. All of them."

"What?"

"All eight of them." I can hear him fanning papers around. "Civilian complaints raised with Delta team about some agents running rogue."

Shit. Shit, double shit.

Fucking Linda, what the hell did she do?

I clear my throat. "We haven't done anything that—"

"Multiple complaints, Karson." Maury rides right over me. "Something about wilfully endangering the lives of children and the elderly. You only went there to talk to a psychic."

"I know."

"It's been barely forty-eight hours."

"I know."

Rayne puts a hand on my knee. I'm glad of it because I can all but feel my blood beginning to stir.

"They cite you specifically too. By name. They accuse you of"— more paper shuffling—"bullying, brandishing a deadly weapon, stirring up local *edane* wildlife, discourteous conduct and"—a snort—"foul-mouthed arrogance, to name a few."

Good grief. Linda really does have it in for me. Who the hell else would it be?

"Maury, I promise you, we've done nothing except what we came here for, and we did so in the best, most streamlined way."

"Is that why this woman is also complaining about a"—he clears his throat—"vicious dragon-monster who attacked their cats in the middle of the night?" A weary sigh. "Why on earth would you take the chittarik pest with you? Are you really this mad?"

I pull Norma closer to me. "Her anxiety, she wouldn't let me leave without her. You know she imprinted on me."

The signal dips in and out briefly. Probably a good thing because I can tell Maury is still raging at me.

"Say again," I mutter, hoping that he doesn't.

"Just get here as soon as you can. Don't bother going home—we need you for debrief. All four of you, in fact." Pause. "And the chittarik, I guess."

"Her name is Norma."

"I don't care. Just get here as soon as you can, and don't loiter. Don't speak to anyone, don't mess with anyone, just please stop giving people a reason to get angry with you, and come home in one piece. I also need you to let me know—"

But I lose the rest of his words under the soft beeping coming from the handset. I move it from my ear to better see the screen and notice with a jolt that now Pippa is calling me.

Even Rayne raises an eyebrow at that.

"Maury"—I interrupt whatever he's saying next—"I'll be there. We all will. Just give us time to drive back. We're already on the move, okay? Just chill."

"Chill," he murmurs, with a mirthless laugh. "I'll give you chill. I think I'm beginning to understand just why Francine had so much to say about you."

I grit my teeth and cut him off in favour of the next call.

Pippa's voice immediately takes over. "Dani? Are you okay?" And at once I know she's upset.

Another pointed look from Rayne.

"Yeah, why?"

She sniffs loudly. "Something weird is happening. All research has been put on standby, and we've been ordered to prepare a holding cell for a new subject."

I stroke gently at Norma who, despite loud mentions of her name, hasn't budged from my lap. "So? What's the problem?"

"The subject is coming from Moarwell. Isn't that where you are?"

My hand freezes on the phone. Hell, everything freezes, from my body to my thoughts. For long agonising seconds I can't do anything, can't even think, just hold the phone like a broken robot while Rayne pats and taps at my thigh.

"Dani? Danika!"

"Yeah, yeah, I'm here." The freeze breaks abruptly, and I suck in a huge breath. "And yes, that's where we are. Were. That's where we were."

"What do you mean?"

"We left an hour ago."

My sister lets out a little squeak of alarm. "What did you find out there? Are you bringing something with you? What happened with Shakka and his Blade thingy?"

I risk a glance at the twins.

They aren't looking my way, both of them with their eyes focused on the road, but I know damn well that they're listening.

Great. Now I'll have to explain that she was someone else who knew, over them.

"We have that. It's fine. The debt is paid as soon as I get the damn thing into his stubby little hands. But what do you mean, subject? There's no one here, just us."

She tuts at me. "That's what I'm trying to say. If it's only you guys then…" She trails off with another sniff. Fuck, she seems on the verge of tears. "They want us to make a high-risk containment cell. No one in or out without an airlock. Sensory deprived and apart from the rest of the staff. They want it monitored with cameras and audio and they want…emergency measures."

"What do you mean?"

"Electric floor. Holy-water sprinkler. Gas input. The works. Dani…" Another sniff. "Dani, is it for you?"

I laugh. "What? No way. Why would it be for me?"

"Your back. The thing, whatever it is, is it doing something to you? Did you find some information? Please, please tell me. Please."

"Hey, calm down." I raise my hands to placate her, even if she can't see them. "Just take a breath for me."

"Very funny," she snaps back. "But this isn't the time for jokes. Please just tell me, are you coming home to go into a cell?"

"No." I speak clearly and firmly. "I just spoke with Maury, he wants me at HQ for debrief, nothing about a holding cell. I have a lot to tell him about what we found, so I want to see him too. It's fine."

Pippa sighs softly. "Then what is it?"

"No idea. But it can't be me, right? I've been free since Liddell marked me in the first place, and nobody has ever put me in containment before. It has to be something else."

"Okay." She says it, though she doesn't seem sure. "Do you want me to do anything or bring anything?"

"No. It will be nearly sunrise by the time we arrive anyway. Just get yourself home and safe so you can rest."

"I…" Another sniff. "Okay. I will. Tell me you're okay, Danika. Tell me nothing's wrong."

I hesitate. "I'll talk to you later on."

"What? No, Dani, don't. Don't you dare hang up on me, Danika—"

I cut her off.

Silence in the van.

Finally, Solo speaks up from the front of the vehicle. "So, hands up, who thinks the boss is going to get banged up like some ole captured gribbly." He raises his hand. So does Duo.

Even Rayne looks at me with her eyes wide and frightened. "Linda didn't just complain about your behaviour," she whispers in a low, hollow voice. "She told them what Fiona said. She told them about the mark and what it really means."

I think back to Fiona's kitchen. I remember the door swinging open, a sign that someone just moments before had been stood there, listening in. Easier to recall is the conversation—me raging about old diary entries and Fiona confirming that her ancestors would have murdered me at a moment's notice.

Fuck. Oh, fucking fuck.

"No." I put my foot down decisively. Or try to, at least—a little difficult inside the van.

Since ending the call with Pippa, Rayne as well as the wolf twins have been trying to talk me into hiding. Rayne in particular all but begs me to join her somewhere else, far away from SPEAR, so we can figure out what we're going to do. Her fear is fierce and fiery, and nothing I can do seems to soothe her. Even Duo, usually so calm and mellow, seems to be having a hard time.

Of course I tell them everything. After keeping the Blade silent, the thought of doing anything less makes me feel physically ill. So I tell them. All of them. I talk about the dreams, my sleepless nights, the waking visions of yellow eyes that catch me in unaware moments.

Rayne listens quietly with her hands folded in her lap. Though she's outwardly calm, I can see the thin trails of blood oozing from the cracks in her clenched fist.

Even Solo is silent, such a change from his usual brusque self.

By the time I'm done, we've left the motorway for smaller A-roads that will take us properly into Angbec from the outer districts. The sky is slowly beginning to grow pale, and I know that soon Rayne will have no choice but to climb into the travel pod.

I'd prefer not, but short of breaking every speed limit out there, we won't make it safely back to SPEAR in time. Or anywhere else for that matter.

"Normally I'm all for rules, boss. Well, the ones that aren't stupid." Solo speaks quietly and thoughtfully. "But this time, I don't know. I think you should listen to Rayne."

"Maury already knows we're coming back. Besides that, you think there isn't some sort of tracker on this car? He'll know. And then what? You guys *need* to stop worrying—no one is going to hurt me."

Duo sighs. "I think this is one of those times you being human is working against you, Danika."

I stiffen. "And what the hell is that supposed to mean?"

"Don't get upset, I'm just..."

"Just what?"

"Bro, help me out."

Swivelling in his seat, Solo faces me properly. "You're human. You've always been human. So you've never been on the receiving end of a human's fear for anything they don't understand."

I snort loudly. "Please, did you even hear me tell you about Linda? The woman is unhinged. That's plenty of fear right there if you ask me."

Rayne abruptly shifts in her seat. She flexes her hands, watching as the crescent-shaped cuts in her palms close up without a trace. "I was human once," she murmurs. "Not too long ago. I remember the way people used to look at me. They way they would trust me without question. Even out of my uniform, I was a person they could trust." Her gaze flicks to mine, hot, hard, and intense. "Now, when people learn I'm a vampire, there's a door that shutters them off from me. Police officer, SPEAR agent, none of it matters. All humans see now is a vampire. A creature that sucks blood and kills."

I shake my head. "But vampires don't kill—"

"You know that. We know that. They don't."

"They who?"

"Humans." An edge of impatience fills her voice. "Do you really think the average civilian knows anything about what we're actually like? How Clear Blood has secured our food supply? Do you think they understand that we're still the same, just with different urges and needs?"

I hesitate. It wasn't all that long ago that even I had clear and damning opinions about *edanes*, vampires in particular. I'm still unlearning some of those prejudices and behaviours, even after all my years as a SPEAR agent.

"But—"

"Danika"—she grasps my hands—"you're not like them any more. No matter what you *were*, in their eyes you're now tainted. Both more and less than human. And they'll treat you that way."

No. That can't be right. She must be worried over nothing,

stressed over the ordeal with the sprites and now the journey home. Surely she can't think that my colleagues would treat me as anything other than that.

But then Duo pipes up to add, "Even Linda was pleasant to us until she realised we're not human. Everybody—no, every *human*—has that in them, whether you want to believe it or not. No matter what the laws say, no matter how many *edane* bars, massage parlours, restaurants, and nightclubs they visit, we're always going to be different. Other. Less than. And now that includes you."

Again I shake my head. This can't be right. They can't mean it, surely. "But I *am* human. Nothing about me has changed. It's just a horrible scar or brand. Like burning yourself on an iron."

"An iron we know now is a minion for some other, bigger malevolent force." Rayne presses my hands to her chest. "I know it's hard, truly, but you have to accept it. We can't help you unless you do. SPEAR doesn't consider you human any more. They consider you an *edane* threat."

I jerk my hands away and retreat as far as I can to the other side of the van. I don't want to hear it. I can't. Instead I pick up Norma and hold her to me, trying to soothe my racing thoughts.

From the corner of my eye, I catch my companions share knowing glances among themselves, but I don't care. They can't mean that. There's no way. Surely Maury would never let that happen?

I'm a SPEAR agent. One of the best in the city. How could any of them know me and my history and believe that I'm anything other than what I've always been—dedicated, loyal, and a bit of a bitch with an authority issue?

More and more the sky lightens, and at last Rayne has no choice but to admit she needs the pod.

With deft hands she opens the miniature tent and flicks it open. A long zip down the centre allows her entry, and the inside is lined with soft blackout material. There's even a raised area near the head, which supposedly serves as a pillow. At least it's a comfortable body bag, right?

She climbs in and pulls the zipper up as far as her hips.

"Danika." Her voice is soft. "I'm not going to tell you what to do. I don't think you'd listen anyway. But please, please, think about what I said. Think about what we've learned, and think about what Phillipa told you. Don't go to SPEAR. Go to Noel's, or Jadz's, or even Shakka's lock-up, but please, don't go to headquarters."

"I—"

"Please." She stares, begging with her eyes. Then, with a gasp, her eyes roll back in her head, and she slumps down boneless and lifeless against the bag.

Well, that's the end of that, I suppose.

I zip her into it as carefully as I can manage, wary of the sharp zipper teeth catching her face or hair. When that's done, I pull the additional flap from its pocket and fold it out over the entire bag, covering the zip and blocking it off from the light.

Norma watches me move, her head cocked to one side with curiosity and interest. "Nika?" she murmurs, talons extended to rest gently on the bag.

"Rayne is inside. We'll see her later."

"Dan-dan."

The van stops at last, the first set of real traffic lights we've found in a while. Through the windows I can see the familiar large houses, which make up the outskirts of Angbec. I know Noel lives in this area with Jadz, and I also know they would take me in instantly. They wouldn't even ask why.

Hell, I've spent more time there than in my own home for the past few weeks.

But I can't. I just can't.

"I'm still human," I murmur softly.

Solo gives a little mumble of assent. "You know that. We know that. But will everyone else?"

I gaze down at Rayne's travelling pod. Ha. Pod. It's a body bag. We all know it. Having failed to come up with anything else lightweight and compact for missions, all vampires on field teams are required to have one to hand.

A frown teases my brow as I try to imagine what it might be like to know that my job requires that I sleep in a body bag day after day.

It's so inhumane.

But then, isn't that always the way? Isn't that how we've always treated *edanes*?

I think about Clear Blood and Rayne's Foundation ID in the form of a microchip they implanted under her skin. Even then I compared the practise to tagging animals.

Then my mind takes me to Wendy, Spannah, and Jadz in lock-up. I remember the jet-injector used to force sedatives into their captured bodies close to the night of the full moon. Even that didn't feel right at the time. And the experimental drug used on Wendy back then may well have contributed to his death.

The more I think about it, the more I find examples of the way *edane* citizens are treated like humans, but not quite. Never in a million years could I imagine a law requiring that any human on earth be required to wear an ID chip. In fact there is only one instance in history that I can recall in which something similar happened, and that was in the middle of a world war.

A shudder of discomfort ripples through me.

But the van keeps moving and I say nothing.

A few more streets and the sun is fully risen. I can feel the warmth through the front window, and the light inside the van is a welcome change after hours of gloom.

I stretch into it, glancing sideways at my phone when it rings again, that same hip-hop tune.

Solo growls.

Duo stiffens.

"Guys, chill." I answer. "Hey, Maury, we're nearly back and—"

"Change of plan, Danika." His voice is sharp and brisk. "Can you meet me at Clear Blood instead? I'm already there, and rather than waiting we might as well debrief here. Your route will pass here before headquarters, right?"

"Oh, shit," Duo murmurs.

I ignore him. Try to. "Um, I..."

"I think one of the researchers here has a few questions for you as well. Just come over here, and I'll meet you. Come to the back entrance. The ones vampires use for feeding."

You mean the one where no one can see who leaves or enters?

I keep the thought to myself and lick my lips to moisten them. It doesn't work because my tongue is suddenly desert dry. "I...yeah. Okay. We won't be long."

A pause. "Is Rayne down?"

"She's in the travelling pod."

"Oh, good." Is that a hint of relief in his voice? "I wouldn't want her caught out by the change of plan."

"No, I've got her. It's fine. Duo and Solo can stay with her or transfer her after we debrief."

Maury continues breezily, "Oh, they can take her immediately, all they need to do is drop you off. I'll speak with them once I'm done with you."

Alarms. Red flags. Panic. Warning bells. Danger.

"So just me?"

"Yep." His cheerful nonchalance feels forced now. "No need to pile everyone in here all at once, right?"

"Right." I fight the urge to poke holes in this nonsense plan.

After all, if we're going to Clear Blood, isn't that the perfect place to take Rayne to rest up during the day? There are plenty of vampire safe spaces there that could be used for her, and it would take only one of the twins to carry her tiny form that distance.

And why wouldn't we debrief together? As far as Maury knows, we're all on the same mission.

Red flag. Warning. Danger. Alarm.

"So we'll see you shortly?"

"Yeah," I tell him.

"Good. Hurry along now." And with that he's gone.

I drop the phone. It lands next to Norma who inspects it carefully before crawling back into my lap to nuzzle.

Duo stops the van.

We're nowhere near Clear Blood or headquarters, just some quiet back street somewhere in the suburbs.

I swallow down the little knot of fear at the back of my throat.

"Last chance, boss." He turns to look at me, eyes solemn and intense. So strange under all that orange dye, but his expression is enough to make it serious. "Where do you want to go?"

It's a coincidence. It has to be. There's no way the room Pippa mentioned is for me. I'm not a threat, I'm not a danger, I'm just me. We know what to do now. If I can explain to Maury what Fiona said about a banishing or an exorcism, they'll know there's nothing to worry about.

We don't even know for sure that Linda really did tell them what she heard. That's speculation without proof. We can't do anything without proof.

I blow a slow breath through pursed lips. "It's okay, guys. Take me to Clear Blood."

The twins share a last knowing look, then return their attention to the road.

Duo starts the van and begins driving again, though not without a subtle shake of the head and some agitated muttering that I can't quite hear.

It's fine, I tell myself over and over again. It's fine. It has to be.

I'm just overreacting.

Everything is going to be fine.

# CHAPTER TWENTY-FIVE

Maury meets us at the underground car park entrance. He smiles broadly at the sight of us and waves us through, following after as we aim for a parking spot.

"No need for that," he calls from outside. "Danika, just hop out. You two can drop Rayne off at SPEAR."

Solo rolls down his window to lean out of it. "Wouldn't it make more sense to stop here? This place has vampire safe rooms, right?"

A pause. I can see Maury's eyes dart left and right. He licks his lips. Fuck. He really is trying to separate us.

I tighten my grip on Norma, resolving then that she at least will be at my side for as long as possible.

"Yeah." Duo stops the van and hops out at once. He doesn't even wait for whatever response Maury might come up with, simply walks to the back and heaves Rayne's travel pod onto his shoulders. "I'll bring her in. I know where the vampire safe areas are." And he walks on, looking back just long enough to give me the smallest wink.

Maury splutters wordless objections as Duo breezes past him. "Well, you at least can take the van back—"

"Nope." Solo also climbs down and shuts the door with a bump of his hip. "He took the keys. May as well just come through."

More spluttering and I find a moment to enjoy the swelling rush of gratitude for these two werewolves. No matter their irritation with me, they still have my back. More than ever, I'm sorry I didn't tell them what was really going on.

I rest a hand on Solo's shoulder, silent thanks for his support.

He looks at me as though I've grown a second head but jerks his chin in acknowledgement before walking on.

I guess he has a point, though. Did I really expect any different?

With his plan thwarted and no good way to stop it, Maury returns a wide, sunny smile to me. "This way, then. We've a room we can use to debrief. I want to know everything that happened while you were up there. And you can tell me about these complaints. There were enough of them that we have to take it seriously."

"Sure, whatever." I bump Norma up to my head.

Even she hunkers down, her tail tangling in my hair, her talons firm but gentle.

Maury eyes her warily. "I can't believe you took that thing with you."

"Try making her do something she doesn't want to do. She's worse than I've ever been, trust me on that."

This entrance into Clear Blood is small and subtle, a simple door almost hidden among the walls of the car park. Vampires registered with a FID will use this way to enter the building and get their blood supply as regulated by use of the Life Blood Serum. Once again I find myself grateful that one blunder in the lab, followed by some specific research, allowed blood donations to be given a longer shelf life. Without it, well…

The ground floor of Clear Blood is public facing and, therefore, gleaming, shiny, clean, and well decorated. After all this time I still think private doctor's surgery rather than huge pharmaceutical giant—fancy wallpaper, lush carpets, paintings, and posters.

But we don't go that way. Instead we use the bright but narrow corridor that leads to the rear. This part is still clean, still white, still gleaming, but my practised eye can see the points in the walls where security gates slide out. And the sprinklers in the ceiling that I know are linked to a blessed-water supply. We pass a set of double doors that lead to the large room commonly referred to as the cafeteria and instead take the single door that leads to the emergency stairwell.

Up, up, and up we go.

Maury doesn't speak, though he does, more than once, look back to ensure we're following. Solo has put himself right beside me, close enough that his arm occasionally brushes mine. It's a silent show of support that I might otherwise miss if not familiar with how werewolves work. Physical contact, even in small ways, has a lot of meaning.

On the third flight of steps, Maury turns off the stairwell and through a door on the left. So we're not going all the way to the top. He leads us down a corridor lined with offices that eventually takes us to the front of the building where some of the first set of labs are.

A loose set of swinging double doors reveals an open-plan office with another large room on the far side. A room with observation glass taking the place of its fourth wall.

Solo nudges me. I nod.

No denying it now. Without looking I can tell that Maury is winding his way through the desks to reach the door to that room. And yeah, it might look like a cosy waiting area—there are sofas in there, a desk, a mini-fridge, even a magnetic dart board on the left wall. But I see no windows besides the observation glass. There is only one door. The ceiling is high with recessed lights and a faint curl to the carpet inside shows the edges of a reinforced floor.

I'd be willing to bet cold, hard cash that the glass is reinforced too.

I follow him through the desks, some empty, some seating researchers tapping away at their keyboards while staring hard at computer screens. Some wear lab coats, others wear casual clothing, none of them seem at all surprised to see me.

Is this normal for them? Someone quietly being led through to a holding cell right under their noses?

Still smiling, Maury opens the door to the side of the room. "Shall we?"

I stop, several feet away. "You think I'm an idiot," I murmur.

He blinks innocently at me. "What was that?"

"I'm not a child, Maurice, and I'm not stupid. If you're going to lock me up, at least have the good grace to tell me."

The mask drops away instantly. He sighs and rubs a hand across his shiny bald head. "How did you know?"

I lift a hand to gesture about me. "You're not exactly subtle."

"I tried. Please believe me, I don't want this."

"Then why are you doing it?"

He gives me the full weight of his gaze. "This is bigger than both of us. Those complaints and…other stuff—they went above me. They went above this leg of SPEAR."

I wait.

Maury shifts uncomfortably from foot to foot.

Fuck him. I'm not going to make it easy for him. No way. If he's really going to do this, he could tell me to my face.

"We need you contained."

Still I wait, arms folded. To my side, Solo mimics my motions, still with his elbow lightly brushing against mine.

"You are…This thing, it's dangerous."

"And it wasn't before?"

"We have new intelligence now. We're SPEARs—we learn and adapt."

So Linda *did* tell them what she heard. Great. But why then am I being detained on the word of a civilian before they even speak to me?

"Please go inside, Danika."

"No."

"It's comfortable. You can rest. You can talk to us, you're not being detained, it's just quarantine."

"Bullshit," I snap back. "You're the one who sent me out there. If I'm so dangerous now, what the hell was I doing out there in the first place? There's nothing wrong with me."

"Then you shouldn't mind going in there until we can prove that."

I stand my ground.

He sighs again. "Don't make this harder than it has to be. Please. Just go inside. You can even take Norma with you if you have to."

Wow. He really must be desperate if he remembers her name.

I pat gently at my pet, wary of her shifting weight. She can feel my unease too because instead of sitting comfortably, she's standing, worming her way down to my shoulders for a better grip. I can hear her low growl rumbling in the back of her throat.

"At least tell me what she said."

"She?" Maury narrows his eyes at me.

"Are you really going to pretend you haven't spoken to her? I know she called in. I know who spoke to Delta team. At least tell me what has you so spooked."

Silence.

In fact, too much silence. The gentle murmur of voices and people working behind me, even that has stopped. Not only that, but Solo has also turned to look back over his shoulder. He is growling too, low and soft under his breath.

I follow his gaze.

Well, shit.

The researchers at their desks are standing. Every one of them has a gun. Each of those guns is trained on me.

"Welcome to the club, boss." Solo speaks softly but clearly enough that I can hear both that and the resignation in his voice. "You're one of us now."

Decision time. Do I go in? Do I run?

There are several gun wielders, I assume agents, waiting for me to make a single wrong move. I count seven. I'm quick and agile—I might be able to get by them. If Solo decides to help, I may only take one shot.

But what then? Surely this isn't the only security they have.

And do I really want to get shot for this?

I assume they're loaded with tranquilising ammunition, but after everything I've seen and heard this morning, that's not the smartest assumption to make. Hell, I probably shouldn't assume anything at all.

Maury gestures through the door. "Your choice. Please, there's no need for this to get messy."

Screw it, then.

Head high, shoulders back, I offer Solo one last pat on the arm before walking into the holding cell.

Nobody follows.

The door shuts behind me with a firm click, followed by several others as a hidden locking mechanism fires bolts from every side.

The room is nice, in fairness to him. From the inside I can see that every effort has been made to keep the space comfortable. One of the sofas is actually a futon, and there's even a portioned-off section, which I quickly see homes a small toilet and sink. No door, just an extra subtle wall that extends far enough to shield the user from casual view of the office space. A desk, no pens or paper, and a chair. Even a small digital radio hanging above a clock on the near wall. No television, though.

But that is where the hotel-style furnishings stop to become more sinister.

The recessed lights make no attempt to hide the little gas outputs poorly hidden in the ceiling tiles. Nor do they hide the sprinklers. What I originally thought to be designs in the wall paint now show themselves to be small hinged hatches. I've no idea what will be flying through those openings, but I'm willing to bet they would be sharp and pointy.

Norma hops off my shoulder and begins a quiet sniff around, inspecting the furniture piece by piece. She's agitated, with her tail up and her wings quivering, but at least she isn't yelling.

The air too has a curious scent, something like lavender but not quite. Some distant part of me wonders if the intent is to fill the room with soothing, calming smells to improve my mood, and though it feels ridiculous, is it really such a crazy thing for my colleagues to try at this point?

On the other side of the glass, Maury and Solo stand toe to toe. Both are tense and heated, the one gesturing while the other stands stoic and stony-faced.

And I can't hear a single word.

Great. Soundproofed too?

I place two fingers in my mouth and whistle, hard, sharp, and fast. The sound brings Norma to my side at once, but neither Solo nor Maury even look my way.

Yup. Soundproofed.

Though there *is* something. The little device bolted to the wall that I assumed to be a radio. It crackles once with static then bursts into sound, a clear, authoritative voice that I've never heard before.

"Yes, Agent Karson, the room is clean. We can hear you, though you'll not hear us unless you use the button on the wall device, or if we open communication channels."

I turn, looking for the camera. There must be one.

"You won't find them," says the voice, as though reading my mind. "Though, consider it a challenge for you, should you become bored. There are twelve cameras secreted about this space, all of them able to see you clearly."

I smile. "Perverts. If you wanted to see someone on the toilet, there are websites for that."

The voice stutters. "I…You…We don't—"

"Most of them are free too. And if you look especially carefully, I'm sure there are live feeds."

"That isn't our aim, Agent. You'll have all due privacy when you require use of the facilities. You're still human, after all."

Interesting.

I frown, turning slowly to give the cameras every opportunity to catch my displeasure. "*Edanes* have rights to privacy too. Or is that something they give up on entering Clear Blood?"

A cleared throat. Maybe the shuffling of papers. "You will be monitored from this point forward, so if there's anything you need, please ask. The mini-fridge contains four full chilled meals and a selection of drinks and snacks."

"Such service," I shoot back. "Cheese sandwiches? Those are my favourite."

"Ham. Possibly chicken."

I chuckle. "Is there a feedback form? I need to give you guys a review."

A little click and the room falls silent again. Clearly they don't appreciate my joke.

Sighing, I allow myself to flop down onto the sofa. It is soft and pleasantly squishy, so at least I'm going to be comfortable. After her circuit of the room, Norma joins me, parting her beak to gently drop a small round black thing into my lap.

"Nika dan?"

I pick it up. Inspect it. Laugh out loud. "Hey, that's eleven cameras now," I call out to the empty room. "I hope the others are better hidden."

Another crackle from the radio. "Please refrain from damaging our cameras. They are very expensive. Thank you."

More silence.

Great. Just great. This is going to be boring as all hell.

# CHAPTER TWENTY-SIX

I'm. So. Bored.

There is nothing to do in here, nothing to see.

Even beyond the reinforced glass—which I did test—the open-plan office is empty. I had thought that the real researchers would come back to continue work, but there is no one. The room is empty, with not even a passing member of staff to watch.

I have the room and the inside of my own eyelids to keep me company. And Norma, of course. She inspects the room a few more times, sniffing into corners, scratching at the carpet. Each time she performs a circuit, I make note of the areas she pays the most attention, realising that these are probably the sites of various security measures.

We've already found all the cameras by this point. By looking carefully, I've been able to stop Norma from destroying the rest, though one, hidden inside the rim of the clock, now has a scratched-up lens. Oh, well.

The one thing I do discover is that the toilet area is not, in fact, free of coverage by the cameras. Now that I know where the little machines are, it's plain that the camera looking down on that area would have to be manually shut off in order to protect one's modesty.

A little jolt of anger fizzes through me at the thought. Not that I care. Hell, I'd strip off and have a shower if they gave me the chance, but the fact that they would lie is even worse. Do they really not care?

Is this how *edanes* are treated?

I don't know. I can't know. But Solo's words come back to haunt me as I sprawl across that damn sofa, trying to occupy myself.

*Welcome to the club*, he'd said.

I don't know that I want to be part of this club.

It's around midday before something happens. It's Maury, back again and standing on the other side of the glass. He stands close, close enough that I might be fooled into believing we were face to face. If I could be bothered to get off the sofa.

He clicks a button on the little remote-like device in his hand, and the speaker crackles with his voice.

"How are you doing?"

"Sandwiches are dry. Drinks are boring. No salt and vinegar crisps and only dry roasted peanuts. Gross, by the way. And what do I have to do to get some coffee around here?"

"You're not funny."

"You sure?" I cock my head at him. "Mama always said I was a real hoot."

"Karson—"

I sit up, swing my legs back down to the ground, and clasp my hands between my knees. "What do you want, Maury?"

He lowers his gaze. "This isn't what I wanted. I need you to know that."

"So you said before. But if that's the case, why do it?"

"Higher orders than me."

I raise my hands. "From who? Short of the general there's no one who outranks you in this city."

Did he just flinch?

Stunned, I stand. "Maury?" When he refuses to answer, I move closer to the glass, to slap it with one hand. "Maury. Who outranks you? Hey!"

At last he looks at me. If possible, he looks to have aged several years in the past couple of hours. Even his shoulders are hunched up, making him look old and bent. "If you go to the door, I'll be putting some handcuffs through the chute. You're to put them on."

I gape back at him.

"Hands behind you, please. Then you're to sit down and stay sitting until told otherwise."

"And if I don't?"

"Please. Danika."

I slap at the glass again, and yes, this time he really does flinch. I don't care. "Why won't you tell me anything? What's happening? Who have you been talking to?"

"Put the cuffs on, and I'll tell you."

"Tell me, and I'll put the cuffs on."

"For crying out loud, you're not helping yourself. Just do as I ask." His voice cracks ever so slightly. "Do you want them to bring the security team back?"

I watch him closely. Still he won't look at me, actively avoiding my gaze to stare at my shoulder or my shoes or my chin. The more I try to catch his gaze, the more he avoids it, though I do see the smallest hints of something in his eyes.

Is that worry? Is it fear? Could it be sadness?

I'm not sure, but none of it makes me feel any better.

Wordlessly, I take myself to the door.

It opens as I approach, but not all the way, just a little lift from the ground by about three inches. Very fancy.

In the exposed strip of air, Maury places a pair of handcuffs, which I take with me back to the sofa.

These don't even feel like metal. Or rather, they do, but they're heavier than the traditional cuffs I might carry day by day.

What the hell are these?"

"You know I'm not going to hurt anybody, right?" I hold the cuffs open, the first bracelet not quite shut on my wrist. "Why would I? I don't want to injure anybody."

He waits.

"If I put these on…what happens then?"

The speakers crackle. "Then we continue with our meeting. Danika Karson, please stop stalling and do as you have been instructed." It's that other voice. I don't know it. I've never heard it before in my life, but I do recognise the authority and command of a voice used to being obeyed. "The sooner you do, the sooner we can get started. Failing that, we will send someone to sedate you."

"Just you try it." I ball my hands into fists. "I'm not an animal."

"Then act rationally and put the cuffs on."

I think about Wendy. I think about him standing in SPEAR headquarters in the centre of a circle of armed agents. I remember his anger and disdain for the instructions.

Is this how he felt back then?

Slowly, I tighten the first bracelet shut on my wrist. It closes tightly, and metal is warm, rather than cold as I might expect. This is more than steel. What do these people think I am?

"And the other."

I twist my arms behind me and fumble for the second bracelet. With some effort and shoulder-aching twisting, I get it in place and twist it shut. The final click as the lock activates is loud and final in my ears.

Through the glass, I see Maury sigh before he lifts the remote again.

"Thank you. Now sit."

I do, glaring, leaning slightly forward to prevent squishing my arms.

This sucks. All of it. Bullshit to a degree I've never before seen, and there will be hell to pay once I'm done.

The double doors at the back of the office swing open. For the first time I understand that this whole section is part of the containment cell. The desks with all their computers were never part of an active workspace. This area is designed to lull someone into a false sense of security, to draw them into this overcomfortable cell and lock them in.

I might have fallen for it utterly if not for Solo because how would I have known? Well, aside from Maury being a terrible, terrible liar. I hope no one ever has to depend on his subtlety in the field.

Through the doors come a small cluster of people—some I recognise, some I don't.

First is Fiona with a helper at her side, carefully guiding her through the maze of desks and chairs. When she sees me, her eyes grow wide and round, and she snaps a startled look back over her shoulder. Her hands are still bandaged, though these are smaller and neater. Apparently someone with more medical know-how has taken a look. That's good, at least.

But I follow her gaze to the next person and feel heat rise in my belly. Linda Halidon.

She's dressed as smart and glitzy as ever, with perfect make-up and clothing. Only this time her hair is caught in a neat, no-nonsense bun at the back of her neck, and her eyes are partially hidden behind thin, trendy glasses. With her is a man I don't recognise, though he has the tailored suit and highbrow haircut of some sort of law official. A solicitor maybe? He carries a briefcase and ticks all the boxes I'd associate with the type, from the sneering lift to the corner of his mouth to the expensive shiny shoes.

Behind them is another woman. She is small and timid and looks younger than me, with baggy tights that gather at her ankles. She holds a little machine covered in buttons, and several pens, as well as what looks like a voice recorder, though I can't be sure from this distance. With her is another man, tall and slender, with a notepad and about six pencils jammed into his messy man-bun. The two seem to be a pair and move to the right while everybody else moves to the left.

The doors swing again and a new person steps through, alone.

They walk fast and purposefully with all the confidence of a being entirely at home with their surroundings. I might almost mistake them for a vampire, but the time of day is wrong. Still, they have a smoothness to their motions that makes me think of an *edane*.

But if they are, they would be the only one present.

I can't help but notice that all these people have arranged themselves to look in on me but maintain such a distance that even if I were skilled at reading lips, I wouldn't be able to.

The last person speaks quietly to all those gathered beyond the glass, then signals to the pair on the right.

The woman immediately sits and lays out her voice recorder on which she immediately presses a button. Then she sets down the little button machine and curves her fingers over it.

It must be one of those shorthand machines, a stenotype or something like that. Seems a bit excessive for taking notes, though.

Beside her, the man plucks a pencil from his hair and examines it briefly before selecting another. Once satisfied, he too sits and begins to draw.

Why does this feel like some sort of court case or something?

I stand, meaning to get closer to the glass, but the moment I do the little radio speaker snaps into life. "Remain seated, please. Final warning."

Warning?

With a grunt, I plant my arse back down and instead lean forward to better see, for all the good it does—they're too far away, and I can't see more than their lips moving.

That single person, the almost *edane*, is speaking, clearly giving out information to those gathered. I'd give a lot to hear what they were saying right now.

Maury looks my way. His face is drawn and tired, his shoulders sagging, but he still holds the remote he used to communicate with me.

I jerk my head, shift my gaze back and forth, anything to catch his understanding without the use of my hands. What a pain that I'm bound right now, just when he was learning Sprite Sign.

His eyebrows twitch. Just slightly. Then I see his hands drop and move round to rest behind him, effectively hiding his motions from view.

An instant later, I hear voices.

Thank you, Maury. Thank you so much.

"—called in today to confirm the identity of Agent Danika Karson.

We've reason to believe we have apprehended the rogue entity and have her safely ensconced in SPEAR custody." It's that last person, the one with the serious expression and hard face.

I have no idea who they are, but their power here is so very clear. Every other person on the far side of the glass defers to them without question. There is quiet respect and perhaps even awe from Maury who can barely take his eyes off them.

Who the hell is this person?

I can't even tell if they're male or female. Possibly both, maybe neither because their clothes give nothing away either, just neat red trousers beneath a matching waistcoat over a plain white shirt and tie. Even their hair—short, curly, and choppy on top and buzzed around the back and sides—is entirely androgynous.

"We have one last person to arrive and then we can begin."

Linda tuts from behind a raised hand. "I don't see why we need to wait. That's her. That's the one I've been telling you about. She's been taken over by demons and—"

"Thank you, Ms. Halidon." Red Suit speaks quietly but firmly, again with their air of expectation when it comes to obedience. "We will wait."

The reprimand is subtle, but even Linda catches it. It doesn't stop her, though. "But it's her. I know it, you know it. Fiona, you were right there. You were the one who saw it all—tell them. Tell them that's the demon woman."

My fingers prickle with the desire to wrap them around Linda's perfect skinny neck.

By contrast, Fiona has her head down and her eyes still lower. She refuses to look at anybody and looks horribly out of place among all this tech and modern machinery, with her long hair and beads and feathers.

Finally the double doors swing open one last time. Moving fast, tucking a mobile phone into his pocket, sweeps Jackson Cobé, mayor of Angbec and, by this point, personal friend. He looks alarmed at the sight before him and glances back over his shoulder as if to check he's in the right place. Then he spies me through the glass, and his expression hardens.

His gaze sweeps over those gathered in front of him and finally on Red Suit. "I didn't realise you were coming all this way, General."

"Given the circumstances I didn't really have much choice. Please, sit." They gesture to a chair near Maury.

Jack obeys and begins a hurried conversation with Maury under his breath, but I don't even try to hear it. Instead I stare at the figure in the red suit and feel a lead weight of dread drop into the pit of my stomach.

General. *The* general? General director and leader of SPEAR? Well, shit.

# CHAPTER TWENTY-SEVEN

Silence fills the room. I can feel it, actually feel the tension in my bones. I want to twitch and shift and scratch my face, but I can't even lift my hands. Instead, I've no choice but to sit and watch and wait and think.

And boy, do I think. My mind races several hundred miles a minute as I fight to keep track of what this all means.

The general has always been a distant fairy tale sort of figure among myself and colleagues. Of course we know that the structure of our organisation extends beyond what we do in our own building and even in our city, but the distant higher-ups beyond our level seven alpha grades are exactly that, distant and intangible. I, at least, know very little about the upper structure of command and have never worried about it before this point. I haven't needed to.

But I do know, just like everyone else, that the general is an authority point.

When the British Army stepped in during the werewolf wars, Colonel Addington had made a specific point to scoff at the idea of a general. He said back then that he outranked anybody we might dare to bring forward, and that's how he and the Extra Mundane Control Unit had grounded every *edane* agent and sent drones darting through the city, spewing weaponized gas.

But the fact remains that within SPEAR there *is* a structure and a chain of command. And that the general is near the top if not *the* top. Not quite like a general in the army but more like a CEO. If they are here now, then...

I glance at Maury again. I want to feel sorry for him. I understand now that this really has progressed far beyond anything he might have a say in, but he's not the one sitting in a sterile room with his hands cuffed behind his back.

Still, at least I know this isn't all his doing.

"My name is Amery Warner." Red Suit takes the time to look into each face in turn, studying them, giving them time to look back. Every face but mine. "I am Chief Directorial Agent of SPEAR in the United Kingdom and would like to thank you for joining me here this afternoon. Some of you may have heard of me, others not, so I'll take a brief moment to explain my role here and the powers I hold before we get down to business.

"SPEAR was founded in a tiny shed in the rear garden of a run-down terraced house in the north end of Angbec almost one hundred and twenty years ago. Then, our organisation was nothing like it is now and operated for the most part in secret. No funding, no structure, no tools, no aid or even a name, only knowledge passed by word of mouth and the dedication of those few rogues who saw the dangers in the world and took it upon themselves to correct them for the betterment of others."

I find myself leaning forward. Sure I know this story, or at least bits of it, but somehow to hear Amery tell it is an entirely different experience.

"We knew so little then, compared to what we know now. Not only that, but the world has changed. Extra mundane creatures are now known, and largely accepted. They are a useful part of society and serve a number of fascinating purposes that our predecessors might never have anticipated."

Norma clambers up onto the sofa beside me. She sniffs at the cuffs, chitters at them, and precedes to gnaw on the chain linking to the two bracelets.

"No, baby—"

"Da-da-dan. Son." She continues chewing, and I hear the metal grind and warp beneath her powerful beak.

I can't even twist away, so I leave her to it.

"But something our predecessors did anticipate is danger. They knew, even back then, that there are some dangers that cannot be fought with guns or knives or anything else we might be able to fashion as a weapon. And they also knew that there are some creatures in the world we are not supposed to fight. They understood that we either bow before them or flee."

Linda tuts loudly. "So even then they knew that demons were in the world? Why did they do nothing, then? Why wait for us to have to deal with it?"

Amery's eyes narrow to frightening little slits. "Remind me, who are you?"

A little gasp of surprise. "Me? I'm Linda Halidon. I'm the one responsible for bringing that monster to your attention and I—"

"So yours were the complaints?" Amery looks Linda up and down. I've no idea what they are thinking, but from that expression I would guess that it isn't pleasant. "I see."

"Complaints? I made reports. I passed on information to protect me, my people, and my home." She yanks her arm free of the solicitor at her side, who seems frantic to shut her up. "No, you don't seem to understand. I did what no one else has done. Certainly nobody here, if rumours are to be believed. SPEAR or whatever you call yourselves have known about this threat for weeks. Weeks! And not only did you do nothing, but you sent it to Moarwell. And if you, Chief Directorial Agent Warner, are so much in charge, then you're responsible for any harm that comes to my community. Harm already done."

"And what harm is that?"

Linda jabs a trembling finger over at Fiona, who immediately shrinks back into her seat, as if trying to melt into it.

"There. You see that? See her hands? Your monster freak did that. And who knows what other damage she did while prancing around my village. What are you going to do about it? How are you going to protect us? How are you going to fix what you've done?"

From my vantage point, it looks as though Linda has talked her way all the way up to a frenzied point and now has run out of steam. She stands, leaning slightly forward, eyes blazing, hands balled into fists, little tendrils of hair tumbling from the neatness of her bun. She looks...mad.

Amery nods slowly. "How indeed." And with that, they turn away from Linda and continue to address everyone. Everyone but me.

"In those days, before the time of advanced technology, communication and resources, the choices were somewhat limited. Flee before danger or delay it for a time. Now, as our organisation has grown and expanded, we are able to make cleaner, more informed choices to do our duty as set out by the founders all those years ago. I believe some of you know the words?"

I certainly do. More than that, I see those words every single time I walk into SPEAR headquarters, both on the wall and on the ground, picked out in gold across the crest of our organisation. I have lived by those words for the last eight years.

Protect and serve. Learn and understand. Hunt and exterminate.

Again Amery continues. "Our mission has always been to protect and serve the human species from any and all dangers. We seek to learn and understand all enemies, the better to combat them and see everybody safe. But most importantly, our job has always been to hunt down threats and exterminate them with the utmost prejudice."

Funny, but that's not quite how I understood those words. I always felt that protecting and serving as a SPEAR referred to any and all under our care, not just humans. Isn't that also part of the Supernatural Creatures Act? Don't *edanes* have as much right to safety and protection as any other being we share the earth with?

I find myself studying them with fresh eyes, wondering what else they and I may think differently on.

"In recent years those mission statements have always been to the forefront of every decision we make, both on the ground and in the office. They have also been my guiding force since I took up the position of CDA. Therefore it is with the safety of the wider populace in mind that I take the decision I have today."

And then they look at me. It's an instant, just a fraction of a second, but it's enough.

I recoil as though slapped.

Their eyes are purple.

I stand. Can't help it.

Norma, disrupted from her gnawing and chewing of my cuffs, screeches unhappily, but I leave her behind on the sofa. Fighting to catch my balance, I dart over to the glass and press myself against it, struggling to see all the way through.

I was right. Fuck, I was right. Amery Warner is an *edane* and an older powerful one at that. Vampire. Easily more than one hundred years old, as one must be to get eyes that colour. And in the middle of the day—yes, this is an old, old, powerful vampire. I've only met one other who didn't immediately succumb to the sun-induced death experienced by every vampire I've ever known. She's dead, though.

The speaker crackles. "Agent Karson, sit down."

"Amery is a vampire," I blurt out, unable to keep it in. "Did you know?"

"Sit down. Final warning."

I twist and writhe against the handcuffs. "The general is a vampire, what's wrong with you? Are you listening to me?"

There's a blur in front of me, a dark streak of colour slashed with deep, deep red.

Amery stands in front of the glass, hair waving gently from the speed of their motion. The room behind is still staring where they once were and several seconds pass before they realise what has happened. In those seconds Amery stares at me, cool, calm, and curious.

"Agent Karson, sit down. We won't hesitate to compel you to—"

"Don't worry." Amery smiles in at me. "She can't hurt us. She may stand if she wants to."

Good. Because I've no intention of sitting down now. I need to see. I need to be close. I need to understand what the fuck is happening outside my little cell.

I stare back, captured by that deep purple gaze, while cold seeps through me.

It's like staring at death personified.

The smile widens. "Can you hear me?"

I find myself nodding. I can't help it.

"Then you know who I am?"

"You're a vampire. How can the general of SPEAR be a vampire?"

A slow, almost sad smile. "Because a vampire was the one to found SPEAR all those years ago."

Those gathered in the room behind finally realise that Amery has moved. Linda looks confused, Fiona concerned. Maury has his mouth open, and Jack rubs lightly at the back of his neck. I know, though no one else might, that that particular area on his neck is his preferred site for vampire bites when he donates blood.

Did he know? Does Maury know?

The woman taking notes on the stenotype actually stops moving. Her fingers freeze in place over the keys as she looks left, right, and back again. The court artist, because that's who he must be, pauses with his pencil hovering over his pad of paper.

"Bullshit," I snap back. "Absolute bullshit."

"Is it, though?"

"Of course it is." I lean even closer to the glass. "A vampire pulling together a bunch of humans to fight against *edane* threats? I've never heard of anything so stupid."

"I wasn't always a vampire, Danika."

Ugh, the sound of my name in that voice makes my skin crawl. Any and all awe I felt is now gone, replaced by confusion and a not insignificant measure of revulsion.

"You've been a vampire long enough to be standing here right now. How? How did you do this?"

"I told you—in the shed of a small terraced house years and years ago, I decided that the extra mundane forces of the world were too dangerous to be left unchecked. I was old enough even then to understand my power, and had seen first-hand the damage I and my kind could do. So I strengthened my solo efforts by pooling some loyal followers to hunt and exterminate."

This is too much. This is stupid. This just can't be true. This...
this...it just can't.

"But—"

"Before I became a vampire, I was human. Back then, the battles
between this landmass and what is now the United States of America
allowed for significant travel back and forth between nations. Further,
it allowed this country to greet all manner of new peoples. Peoples who
were dangerous. I lost my family in 1776 and my own life in 1789."

"You can't—"

Again they ride over me. "I saw first-hand the violence and death
various non-human creatures could bring and spent many, many years
coming to terms with my own urges. My own truth. My own violence.
It wasn't until I reached this country that I realised there was something
I could do. My knowledge, my learnings, my experience could help
protect the humans I had once called my kind, even if I could no longer
count myself among them. So I fought. I found danger and eradicated
it. I learned as much as I could about the various threats to humanity
and used that knowledge to protect them. I protected those unable to
protect themselves from dangers they were too innocent to see. And I
did it alone."

Amery is very close to the glass. So close, in fact, that I can see
clearly that with each word, there is no puff of condensation against it,
nor gathering of moist air. I see no traces of a pulse in their neck or any
other sign I might normally look for on a human.

Beyond the looming image of Amery's face I can see the rest of the
room. Their expressions range from confused to bored to straight-up
annoyed, but it soon becomes plain that none of them can hear what
I can hear. Amery is speaking softly, so close to the glass that I am the
only one who can catch those words.

"But eventually I couldn't do it alone. I was but one and the dangers
too many. So I found help. Help that over the years has grown and
flourished and organised and strengthened and expanded to become
what we know today. SPEAR is my brainchild, and you, believe it or
not, work for me."

I stumble back. Lack of my arms further robs me of my balance,
and once again I struggle to keep myself standing. I spread my feet on
the carpet and straighten my back, the better to give this...this *thing*
my full attention.

"What are you going to do to me?"

The smile actually becomes a little sad. "My job. As I promised
more than three hundred years ago, to serve and protect humans is my

purpose. I strive to learn and understand the threats to them from all corners. And, once I've done so, I hunt and exterminate that threat."

And with that, they whirl away from the glass, back to the centre of the room.

Maury looks at me, hands fidgeting on the little remote in his hands. There is a question in his eyes but not much I can do about it. In fact, all I can do is watch as Amery addresses themself once more to the larger room.

The woman at the stenotype begins clicking at the keys again.

"Miss Halidon, do you confirm that the woman you see in quarantine before you is Agent Danika Karson?"

Linda rolls her eyes. "Yes, finally. Yes, I do. She's the one with the demon inside her, the one carrying evil and all sorts of—"

"Thank you." Amery doesn't wait for the rest. "And you, Mayor Cobé, do you confirm that the woman you see in quarantine before you is Agent Danika Karson?"

"I do." He tugs at the collar of his shirt. "But shouldn't we talk about this a little more and—"

"Thank you." Again, no waiting. "Maurice Cruush, Alpha Agent Level Seven and leader of Angbec's SPEAR division, do you confirm that the woman you see in quarantine before you is Agent Danika Karson?"

Maury looks horrified. He looks at me, then Amery, then back again. "I do, but—"

"And do you also confirm that you sent her to the village of Moarwell to meet with a psychic by the name of Fiona Bristow."

"Yes, but I really think—"

"And you"—Amery whirls round—"Mrs. Fiona Bristow. Do you confirm yourself to be the same psychic who examined Agent Danika Karson and found her to be contaminated?"

Fiona winces at the description. She stares down at her mangled hands, as if searching for answers in the clean white bandages protecting the remains of her skin from fingertip to elbow. "Y-yes." She swallows hard.

"Please confirm for the record and for the benefit of those gathered here what it was your examination found."

She sniffs. "Evil. I don't have another word for it other than evil."

"And what else did you discover?"

More sniffing. I think she's crying. "My old relatives—my ancestors—talked about an evil that couldn't be changed or removed or fixed. The old writings say that a person, when marked by this evil, is like a conduit, calling down a larger, more malevolent entity to inhabit them, rather as a host. But they aren't doing it on purpose." She hurries to add that last part, as though knowing the involuntary nature of my involvement in all this might help matters. "The child isn't doing it herself—it is the mark on her back."

"And what does this mark do?"

"It calls down a greater force. Like offering the person with the mark as a body for the larger evil to inhabit."

"Hmm." Amery briefly studies their fingernails. "And, in your opinion, if that is allowed to happen, what might we expect?"

Silence. Long, stretched, and damning.

"Death," Fiona murmurs, staring down at her hands. "This thing, whatever it is, feeds on negative emotions like food. It sends out minions to cause as much trouble as possible, fights, wars, that sort of thing. And when there's enough, it feeds through the host."

Still wringing her hands, Fiona looks at me now. She looks mortified and offers so much apology with her eyes that I can't quite bring myself to be angry with her. She tried. She really did try.

"A decision like the one I have made is not to be taken lightly." Amery stands a little straighter. "I might be CDA, but I'm not fool enough to think I could make a decision like this on my own. The Crown Court of Supernatural Justice met this morning for lengthy discussion, and several high level agents were given an opportunity to vote anonymously on the course of action we should take. The information they had to form their decision was a copy of a statement made by Fiona Bristow and an explanation that the host in question is a fellow agent. No names, locations, dates, or times were given to ensure their voting was as unbiased as possible."

Maury raises his hand. "But what was the vote on?" His voice is smaller than I've ever heard it, hollow and tinged with fear.

"On whether we should act as brave souls have in the past and take pre-emptive steps to stop this evil force. Or if we should wait and find alternative means to correct it."

I feel cold. I feel sick.

My skin crawls all over with tiny pinprick spines while my stomach turns and flops like a grounded fish. I can't breathe. I can't think. I can barely even see.

Jack heaves a deep breath. "And what was the result of the vote?"

"A perfectly even split," Amery says softly. "Half voted to exterminate the host, while the rest voted to find alternative means. Which means the final say rests with me."

With that, Amery turns to once more look me dead in the eye. "And my final decision is that we exterminate the host for the betterment and protection of the wider populace."

# CHAPTER TWENTY-EIGHT

It's a blur. I'm sure somewhere in there, Maury is yelling. I might even be confident in saying that Jack is up in arms and doing his best to be heard over the sudden riot of sound, but it is a blur.

My legs are jelly. Eventually I sit because there's not much choice, and Norma crawls all over me. I can feel her spiny little body across my lap, near my hip, at my back where my hands are. She's talking too, but I can't hear it. Not really.

Someone bangs on the glass. I can see Jack peering down at me, his eyes wide and frightened. Beyond him, Linda has a look of shock painted on her perfectly made-up face, and Fiona is openly weeping.

I put my back to them and gaze instead at the one camera closest, hidden in the arm of the sofa. I stare directly into the lens. Just stare.

There's nothing to say, so I don't bother.

Or maybe I can't?

My brain is locked, my lips are screwed to one position, and my tongue falls limp and dry within the cavern of my mouth.

"Dan? Son kar-ka?"

Something in my shoulders gives, and my arms suddenly flop forward.

Norma, my beautiful, resilient, crazy little pet has gnawed through the chain holding the cuff bracelets together, and now my hands are free. I have twinned jewellery to show for it, but I can move again.

I gather her to me and crush my face into her back.

She squirms for all of a second, before nuzzling back, crooning at the back of her throat.

Exterminate.

They're going to kill me?

My head snaps up so hard I fear whiplash.

"Fuck…"

Who the hell is going to tell Rayne?

❖

Things seem to be moving much faster now. When I eventually manage to stand and look back through the glass, the office space is empty. Everyone has vanished, and the space stays empty for a long while after that.

In the meantime, several voices speak to me over the little radio against the wall.

"Danika? Danika, can you hear me? Hello?"

"What, Jack?"

"Are you okay?"

I look up briefly from my sprawl on the sofa. Norma is tucked up against my chin, her tail curving to gently cup my throat. "Do I need to answer that?"

A sigh. "No. Sorry, that was dumb. Listen, this isn't going to happen, okay? No way. We don't do that here. Just sit tight, I've got you."

"Yeah, yeah, sure." I wave my hand, but I've no idea if he can see me or not.

"Karson?" This time, it's Maury.

"Yo."

A long, very awkward pause. "How are you feeling?"

"Horny."

"What? Are you serious?"

Eye roll. "No, I'm not fucking serious. What do you want?"

"I—I'm sorry."

"You and me both, Maury."

"Do you want me to do anything? Talk to anyone…?"

I gaze up at the ceiling. Now there's a question.

My fate hasn't quite sunk in yet. I don't really understand what's happening in my mind, but everything is kinda numb. Should I be angry? Should I be scared? Perhaps I should be raging and kicking and screaming. Maybe I should be tearing up furniture, banging at the glass, scratching at the walls. Or would it be better to simply curl up in a corner and wait for the end to come?

"I don't know," I tell him at last.

"I'm going to send some things through to you. You'll find them at the door. Also, if you want anything, need anything at all, just ask.

I've asked the team to leave the monitors on for good now. You can just speak, and they'll hear you."

Yay.

"Also…"

"What, Maury?"

"Agent Warner said you have twenty-four hours. They're sourcing the most humane way to do this, but the decision seems to be lethal injection."

"Goody. At least that's luckier than the last humans executed here."

"What?"

I wave my hands. "Two guys robbed and murdered a friend of theirs. Not a big deal at the time, but they were the last people legally executed in this country. Until we discovered *edanes*, I suppose. Those two were hanged, by the way. Frankly, I'm pretty sure that would screw up my hair, so injection sounds good."

"Karson, please—"

"Please, what? Please don't joke about it? Please don't be so bleak? Please make it easier for you? What do you want me to do?"

"I'm sorry, I—"

"Anything else?"

Another longer pause. "I'll be back later in case there are any messages you want me to send out."

Then perhaps an hour later, another voice. "Hey, Dee-Dee? Speak to me? Hello?"

That one makes me sit up. "Noel?"

"Sí, is me. You're in trouble again, I see?"

"Fuck you, dude." But I'm chuckling. This *is* Noel, after all. He has seen me get into more trouble than maybe anybody else on the planet.

He laughs too. "Finally? The time has come? I must be very special if I am to be your last."

"Shut up."

"I'm sorry." His laughter fades into nothing. "I heard from Erkyan. This is bullshit. All of it. Who decided this is the way?"

Wait, Erkyan? How the hell did she know?

Though, as I ponder it, I find it hard to believe that Maury would be able to keep my fate away from the ears of my team. Good luck to him when the sun dips below the horizon and Rayne learns about it.

I sigh. "The general decided. They were here."

Stunned silence.

In it, I try to decide if I should tell my friend what I know. Amery was cautious in saying as much as they did, and by turning to exclude the rest of the room. Even the woman on the stenotype had been unable to record what they were saying to me.

So perhaps it isn't common knowledge?

But then, what would Noel stand to gain from knowing the truth? Regardless of how SPEAR began, we do good work and protect the people that need to be protected. We are smart, widespread, powerful, and noble—most of us—and revealing what I know could put everything at risk. Imagine if the general public found out they were being protected, all this time, by a vampire.

"You met the general?" Noel's voice is filled with enough awe to make the decision for me.

"Yeah, they're a butthead for sure, but…but they're doing their job."

Noel curses long and flowing in his native Spanish. "Their job is to protect, not to murder. I will fight this for you, Dee-Dee. We all will. We won't stand for it."

"Thank you, I—" But before I can finish the thought, a new one comes to mind. "Don't."

"What?"

"Don't fight this."

"Dee-Dee…"

I clutch Norma a little tighter. "This thing, whatever it is, has turned up time and time again. I don't think it can ever be truly defeated. But if history is anything to go by, getting rid of the host has always been able to put it off for a few years. Maybe…maybe by putting it off one more time we can learn how to get it gone for good."

A soft whimper over the speakers. Fuck, is that a sob? "No. No, Dee-Dee, don't say this. Please, we find a way."

"Noel—"

"You are my friend. We find a way."

He makes a few more promises, claims of research and time and powerful friends, but I've already tuned out well before he eventually leaves.

The more I think about it, the more I realise that Amery is right. The older generations of Fiona's family were right.

Now, even now, we don't know what this thing is. But we do know what the minions are capable of. I think again of Amelia Smythe and her plans as Vixen to reclaim Angbec for vampires across the country. Even then, at the core of that attempt, the tall black creature with the yellow eyes worked their deadly magic from the background.

Then, more directly, the yellow-eyed minion began actively recruiting followers by taking over Flint Liddell and drawing an entire werewolf pack under their control. That thing indirectly caused a small war that ripped the city to shreds and still saw repair efforts taking place weeks later.

Imagine if the master got loose.

Through me.

No. No way. The idea that *I* might be in any way connected to events worse than those of a few weeks back makes my skin crawl. I can't be a part of something that would potentially put so many people in danger. I won't.

Grim determination curls through my gut, an angry sort of fire.

"How dare you?" I mutter.

"Son? Da-dar? Ika?" Norma looks up from her cosy spot around my neck.

"How fucking dare you?" I close my eyes, and as if in answer, twin points of garish, gleaming yellow fill my vision beneath my eyelids. "You come to *my* city, claim *my* body, and try to force *me* to do your dirty work? No. No!" I sit up, glaring at those eyes and the entity behind them. "You think you can come into my body and use me to feed your master? Screw you. Screw you to Uranus and back again, you disgusting fuck. You can't have me, you hear me? You don't get me, you don't get my family, you don't get my friends, you don't get my city. Get it? You're done. You're over. You're fucked, you're—"

"Karson."

My eyes snap open. The room remains empty but for Norma and myself of course, but this new voice comes through the radio clear as day.

"Karson, you lazy bitch, are you asleep?"

"Shakka?"

"Good." I hear shuffling, then a squeal that might be a metal chair dragging over a hard floor. "Did you get it?"

I laugh. Can't help it. I flop back on the sofa, roll my head back, and laugh, and laugh, and laugh.

"This isn't a joke."

"No, it isn't, I suppose. At least in all of this you're consistent, Shakka. How did you get in here, by the way?"

"Did. You. Get. It?"

Still chuckling, I wipe moisture from beneath my eyes. "Yeah, it's in the van. Ask Solo or Duo where they parked, and they can hand you my bag." Pause. "You're welcome, by the way."

"You had it? You touched it?"

I frown. "Oh, I'm sorry I didn't have a chance to wash it after my grubby human hands touched the most sacred of sacred artifacts."

"No, I…" He sounds…surprised. "That's not what I meant. You held it in your hands? You've truly seen it and held it? It's real?"

A little fissure of irritation runs through me. Real? Damn right it's real, and I got poisoned for it. Twice. Did he doubt the stupid relic was even there?

I bite back the angry retort. Instead I say, "Like I said, in the van with the rest of my shit. I doubt anybody knows what it is, so it should still be there."

Shakka sniffs. It's soft and subtle, but if I were anyone else I might have sworn he's a little teary. But I'm not. I'm me. And there's no way that grumpy goblin has any other emotional settings beyond rage and disdain.

"I'll get it," he says at last. "You've done me a bigger service than you'll ever know."

I shrug. "I owed you a favour. At least I'm paid up now."

A sigh. "I'll see what I can do about all this and…never mind."

There's no strength in me to press on whatever he intended to say. Probably some snide comment about having the thing deep cleaned.

Silence. More silence.

And then, "My history is a strange thing. It spans hundreds upon hundreds of years. Thousands. And the points at which it crosses into human knowledge are small. But whenever it does, those moments are important ones. This is one of those."

I wave a hand breezily at the ceiling. "Momentous moments." The alliteration makes me smile.

Another sniff from Shakka. "I'll retrieve the blade and check it, but I don't doubt you. I know you did what you agreed, and regardless of if it's the real deal or not, I owe you."

*He* owes *me*? Holy hell.

I sit straight. "Shakka—"

"Goodbye, Karson."

And he's gone. Just like that.

Now there's a favour I'll be thrilled to call in. Oh. Wait…

❖

I wake to the sound of splintering glass.

"Get her legs—"

"I'm trying—"

"We need more agents in here."

"How is she so strong?"

"As if we don't have enough to deal with—"

"Pin her arms—"

I look up and there, fending off the grip of six agents, is Rayne.

Norma leaps off my chest and goes spiralling around the room, yelling over and over like a mad thing.

More cracking sounds, then shouts become audible even through the sealed-up room.

"Get her on the ground."

"Should I tranq her?"

Rayne's eyes blaze with silver, and her fangs gleam long and sharp between her widely parted lips. She throws up her arms, and two of the agents scrambling to hold her fly away across the office like rag dolls. The remaining four cling for dear life as she pounds again on the glass.

For the first time I realise that she's calling me.

"I'm here," I yell, scrambling up to get to the glass. "Rayne, I'm here. Calm down. I'm here, can you hear me?"

The moment I'm standing, the moment she sees me clearly, she stills. Her arms stop flailing, her legs stop kicking. She presses herself to the glass and lays one hand against the huge cracks she's somehow been able to put into it. Long lines of red streak her cheeks.

The agents struggling to hold her stumble and fall at the abrupt shift in momentum and force.

"I thought they did it already." Her voice is a rush, high and panicked. "I thought you were gone—you were lying there so still. No one would talk to me—I thought—I thought—"

"I'm fine." I put my own hand against the glass to match hers. "I was sleeping. See? Look at me. I'm standing, I'm here, I'm fine."

She stares deep into my eyes for long, painful seconds, then slumps to her knees in front of me. The fangs recede. The silver fades away.

The gathered agents, bemused, stand around her looking lost.

I wave them away.

Only two of them move. The remainder pull guns and train them on Rayne, though she barely spares them a glance at this point. Her attention is all on me.

"Danika, this can't be happening. This isn't fair. You don't get a trial or a period of quarantine or anything? They simply kill you?"

Before now I've been calm. Up to this point I've been able to come at this whole mad situation with a touch of dry, dark humour, the same kind I use to get me through my day. But now, seeing Rayne on the ground, her face smeared with bloodied tears, I don't quite have it in me.

Norma finally stills her frantic screeching enough to land beside me. She sniffs at the remainders of the cuffs still about my wrists, then sits to face the glass. "Dan, dan?"

"There was a vote," I murmur. "The general put a vote to a number of agents, and they ended up being the tiebreaker."

"The general." That silver flare briefly lights up Rayne's eyes before vanishing again. "How dare *they* decide what happens to your human life when they get to live forever?"

"You've met them?"

"Briefly, when I woke tonight. They're older than Vixen ever was." I nod. "By a significant amount, I'd say."

Rayne wipes at her eyes. Only then does she spare a glance for the agents still gathered around her.

At far ends of the office, the two she tossed manage to pull themselves free of mangled computer parts and broken chairs.

"I'm sorry," she murmurs. "I don't know what came over me."

One of the agents shakes his head. "What the hell we're doing with vampires on staff I'll never know."

The woman beside him speaks briefly into a walkie-talkie clipped to her shoulder. "Outside? What? Right now? I thought they were at headquarters?"

I pay them no attention. Instead I tap the glass to bring Rayne's gaze back to me. "Are you okay?"

A pained look. "They're going to execute you. So no, Danika, I'm not okay. I'm angry, I'm confused, I'm scared. You're human. If they would do this to you, then what might they do to the rest of us?"

I lift an eyebrow at her.

"*Edanes.* Solo and Duo are right—they consider you one of us now. And if they're willing to execute you, of all people, what's going to happen the next time it's more convenient to get rid of a problem rather than fixing it?"

"I don't think I *can* be fixed."

She grits her teeth. "Don't do that. Don't you dare. Don't give up."

Is that what this is, though? Is it giving up or is it accepting an inevitable truth?

I've always known dying on the job was a risk. It is one of the reasons my mother hates the job so much, never knowing if I would return from one mission or another. I always told her that it was a risk I am willing to take and one I step out every single day knowing may well come to pass.

This is that day.

Sure it's a little more premeditated than I might have imagined, but the result is the same, isn't it? Dying for my job. Dying to see safe those I swore to protect. Doing my duty right down to the last breath.

When put that way, it seems kinda noble, but as I look into Rayne's pale, tear-stained face, I feel it at last.

Fear.

What will it be like to die?

Will there be pain?

Will I know it's happening, or will they put me to sleep?

How long will it take?

The questions swirl in my mind round and round without answers, and a tight band seems to spread across my chest.

"I'm not giving up," I say at last. "This is my job. I swore to do this. We all did."

"We swore to protect and serve, not to roll onto our backs, bellies exposed, at the first sign of danger. Please, Danika, help me here. Surely you haven't accepted this?"

I give her my calm, steady gaze. "What if this is the only way?"

"It isn't—"

"But if it is? What if it's the only way to protect Angbec and everyone else from whatever else might be coming? What if it's the only way to save Mum? And Pippa? What if it's the only way to save Jack, Noel, Erkyan, Hawk, Solo, Duo, Willow, Jadz." I touch the glass again. "What if it's the only way to save you?"

She straightens. "There is another way."

Behind her, the agents gathered are sharing urgent, whispered conversation. I can't hear a word, but I see that Rayne has cocked her head and has placed a single finger to her lips. She's listening, that's for sure.

A moment later, five of the six agents sprint out of the room, leaving one behind with his gun trained on Rayne.

I look the question at her.

She tuts. "Some sort of protest outside. I've no idea what's going on, but apparently people are getting rowdy."

"Protest for what?"

"I've no idea. Does it matter? I'm far more concerned about you. Can we focus on that?"

"But why are people protesting—"

"Danika."

I snap my mouth closed.

"Don't give up. Don't you dare. We haven't come this far and seen this much for things to end now. No way. It's barely sunset—we have plenty of time. Just…don't lose hope." She stands.

So do I. Suddenly I don't want her to leave.

I know this is the end, I know it's over, so I want her to stay and spend those hours with me. Everything else can wait, nothing else matters, but if Maury is right and I have twenty-four hours—less now—then this is the last time I'll ever see her face because they'll execute me before she wakes tomorrow night.

"Rayne—"

"Do everything they tell you," she murmurs, brushing herself down. "Don't make a fuss, don't say anything weird—in fact, no, make a fuss, say weird things. Just be you. That's what they'll be expecting. Don't do anything different."

"What are you talking about? What are you going to do?"

She looks back at me, expression grim, eyes gleaming briefly with silver. "My job," she mutters.

And with that, Rayne turns on her heel and walks away.

I watch her go, pained and lonely, wishing I could touch her face one last time.

# CHAPTER TWENTY-NINE

In the time Rayne's gone, I finally inspect the items Maury said he was going to push through the opening in the cell door. There is an odd assortment of junk there, including several pads of paper, pens, envelopes, a voice recorder, and even a small video recorder. Among them is a bar of chocolate, a pack of crisps—salt and vinegar—as well as a bottle of something called a cold brew caramel macchiato.

I carry the whole lot over to the little desk near the radio and spread it all out, the better to see.

The intent is clear. All those writing tools—I'm supposed to pen my final goodbyes. Maybe even record some video if the mood takes me.

Seems a bit archaic and even a little Path of the Damned, but there's little else for me to do.

With Norma draped over my shoulder, crooning against my cheek, I take up a pen, slide some paper towards me, and begin to write.

First, to my mother.

The pen stops almost immediately.

What the hell am I supposed to say to her? She hasn't talked to me in weeks. She refuses to see me or take my calls, or even listen to my messages, as far as I know. As far as she's concerned, I may well already be dead. What is the point in spending any of my last precious minutes writing to someone who doesn't want to know?

And yet my pen hovers over the page.

At last, I write. Only a few words, but they'll have to do.

*Mum. I don't know if you'll ever read this, but at least I've said it to you. I know the last few months have been hard and that losing Pippa and me after what happened to Dad is probably the last straw. But you never really lost us. We were always there, and now Pippa will always be there.*

*Give her the chance, Mum. Let her know you. Learn to know her again.*
*I won't get that chance, but the two of you deserve that at least.*
*I love you.*
*Danika*

After that, the tears in my eyes are a little too much to see through, so I pause to sip that bizarre coffee monstrosity.

It's good. Sweet, cold, and thick on the tongue, it more resembles a thin milkshake than anything truly like coffee. But if it's to be one of the last things I drink, I'm happy with it. Still, I'd give a lot for some of my mother's home-brewed sorrel right now.

Next I write my sister's name at the top of a fresh piece of paper.

Again my pen hovers.

She will no doubt live years and years after this. If Angbec continues to trendset and grow the way I've experienced over the last eight years, there's no reason at all why Pippa, and Rayne for that matter, shouldn't live for hundreds of years.

I try to think of what life will be like then.

*Edanes* and humans living in harmony? *Edanes* taking over with their growing numbers and obvious strengths? Humans fighting back with superior numbers and beating *edanes* back into lives of secrecy, obscurity, and fear?

Guess I'll never know.

In the end, I reach to the back of my neck and pull one of my locs down over my shoulder.

This one is slightly longer than the rest and always manages to stick out the bottom when I lift my hair into a high pony. My original plan, way, way back, had been to have a rat-tail like I'd seen so many cool kids do when I was a pre-teen. Mum hated that idea, but I allowed that one little section of hair to grow and grow, and then kept growing it when I decided to loc the rest.

And so that one loc has significant length to the rest of my hair.

I twirl it now between my fingers, feeling out the smoothness of the carefully styled and groomed hair.

"Norma?"

She shifts slightly. "Kar dan?"

"Can I borrow your tail?"

Her bright eyes consider me for long moments before she stands and flicks her wings up, exposing her tail on the side.

I take it gently and turn the tip so the barbs are exposed.

Slowly, so as not to hurt her, I use the sharp edges to saw through that one long loc at the root. It takes time and pulls—a lot—but eventually the loc is free of my scalp and resting in my hands.

Years and years of my life are represented in that one piece of hair. It means so much, both to my personal hair journey and the memories I hold of my father.

With careful hands, I fold it up, place it inside an envelope. With it I put a single note.

*On my locs and hope to trim.*
*I'm so sorry I couldn't keep my promise to you, sis.*
*But you're big, bad, and strong now. I know you can take care of yourself.*
*Dani*

Done. I seal the envelope, write Pippa's name on the front, then put it to one side along with the short, spidery scrawl addressed to my mother.

Next.

I sit like that for at least an hour, writing note after note, letter after letter.

Frankly there's not much else to do, but the idea of leaving one last message to my friends and family is appealing to me.

I thank Maury for putting up with my inescapable bullshit. I thank Noel for being good, just, and loyal. I congratulate Erkyan on her service to her Enk'mal. I tell Jadz that I want my damn matchsticks back. I apologise to both Solo and Duo for lying and leaving them out of the mission to collect Shakka's Blade. Oh, and I tell Shakka he's an annoying, grumpy fuck who I've actually been pretty lucky to know over the years. I tell Jack that even though I'd never date him, he's been a pretty good friend and that he'd better make sure Rayne and Pippa can keep our house. I share a personal anecdote with Willow about how beautiful I find her tree and that willows have always been a source of comfort for me. I tell Hawk he looks cool in his glasses. I remind Link that he'll never find another human more capable with a sword or a battleaxe than me. I even tell Quinn, on the off-chance that a letter might reach her, that I still hate her, but I understand why she acted as she did because I was and will now always be a known pain in the backside.

The hardest to say goodbye to is Rayne.

I sit at that stupid bolted-down table with the video recorder in my hands and stare into the damn lens.

What am I supposed to say? What *can* I say?

How can I possibly put into words the maelstrom of feelings and thoughts twirling through my mind like stars and comets through space?

I'll never have enough time to say it all. Any memory card this recorder holds won't have the capacity.

I lick my lips. "Rayne—"

A soft sound behind me cuts off my train of thought.

For a moment I think I must be dreaming. I grind my knuckles against my eyes like a child and look back again, but yes, sure enough, I saw right the first time.

Rayne. She's standing there. Right behind me.

❖

The door to the cell is wide open, and Noel stands in the middle of it, a rifle clutched tight to his chest. Just beyond him, the one guard left to watch over me sits cross-legged on the ground with a bloodied nose and both hands tied behind his back.

I leap to my feet. "Rayne—"

She kisses me. I don't even see her move. One moment she's ahead of me, the next she's all over me, mouth slanting open over mine, hands tangled in my locs, hips and stomach pressed tight against me.

I melt into her touch, weaving my arms around her tiny waist, pulling her in, feeling her surprising warmth.

The faintest metallic taste lingers on her tongue.

Oh. Oh fuck.

From the door Noel gently clears his throat. "Beautiful reunion," he says brightly, "but time is against us. We go quickly, if you please, ladies."

I touch her cheek, her lips, her hair. "What are you doing?"

"Serving and protecting," she mutters.

"But—"

"There's no time. The protests are a good distraction, but soon someone will come to check why that agent isn't responding." She hooks a thumb back at the tied agent on the ground. "So let's go."

"But I—"

She grabs my hands and pulls.

I stumble along with her, away from the desk, past the sofa, out the door, and free of that awful, awful room. Even the air is different out here, fresher somehow, and lighter against my skin. For the first time in hours I hear the hum of all the electrical machinery and the more subtle sounds of chanting voices somewhere in the distance.

Noel grins and claps my shoulder as I pass him. "You didn't think we would leave you, Dee-Dee? Ah, maybe you are a fool after all."

Just enough presence of mind remains to let out a quick whistle.

With a cackle, Norma shoots out of the cell and flies after me. She doesn't land on or near me this time, instead choosing to stop on top of one of the few computers still intact after Rayne's earlier rage. Her wings are up, her tail out straight, her head held high on her neck and ready. She knows what's up.

"What's all that noise?"

Rayne still doesn't release my hand. "There are protests outside."

I remember the other agents talking about that earlier. But no more information has been forthcoming.

She actually grins at me. "It seems Linda Halidon has made a vital error."

Noel snorts as he lifts the single agent by his collar and shoves him into the cell. He shuts the door with a flourish then turns to us. "The blond woman with the bad make-up? Sí, she fucked up." He walks back over to us, rifle now over his shoulder. "On the news, so proud and smug. *I saved us all*, she says." He mimics her voice with startling accuracy. "Yes, yes, she *saved* us from an unknown danger, but she also made enemies of every friend of Danika Karson." Noel smiles at me.

That tells me nothing, but thankfully Rayne steps in.

"She went to the local news, telling them that she was responsible for saving everyone from the danger you posed. But she made the mistake of naming you. The second she did that, the city has been plastered with coverage from the Werewolf Wars, and now both Clear Blood and SPEAR headquarters are surrounded by protesters furious that you're going to be executed." Her eyes sparkle now, not with angry silver, but with pride and pleasure. "There are picket lines, signs, chants, and sit-downs. People are blocking SPEAR facilities, and there are news reporters everywhere."

"The blond viper fucked up," says Noel simply.

My chest swells with *something*. "But who would be out there? There aren't enough people who give a shit about me to make any sort of protest."

Rayne actually looks surprised. "You think so?" She strokes my cheek with the backs of her fingers. "From the splinter group of the Dire Wolves, to every single member of the Loup Garou, you think any of them would let this go without a fight?"

"But a couple of werewolves won't make much of a difference."

Noel counts on his fingers. "The red and orange boys of your team, they did call in the Fire Fangs. Jadz, my love, she called the Grey

Tails. One of the civilian police officers heard your name and called her colleagues to move too. Tina, I think is her name."

Wow. I remember her. She helped us find Vixen's hideout when we were searching for her so many months ago.

"And Phillipa, do you think she would let you go without a fight?" Rayne begins tugging me towards the swinging double doors. "She helped us find you in this cell in the first place and arranged for a fire drill to empty the building. Many of her teammates have cleared a path for us to get down to the car park, but only if we hurry."

I try to speak, but I can't.

That *something* in my chest swells even larger, and a strange warmth seems to fill my body.

The backs of my eyes prickle.

Yet again, Noel slaps me on the shoulder, matching it now with a hearty smack behind the shoulder blades. "Come now, Dee-Dee, no tears. We have work to do, sí?"

"Oh, fuck you," I manage, through a throat all but clogged with emotion.

He smiles. "You keep offering, one day I will hold you to it."

And I hug him. I can't help it.

He hugs back, arms curled gently around me, breathing hot and gentle against my ear.

Getting down to the car park is surprisingly easy. Whatever Pippa has done, it is deeply effective in clearing the way. With Rayne in front listening and watching for trouble and Noel in the back bringing up the rear, we make our way down with no trouble at all.

From here the calls and yells of those outside the building are obvious even to me.

I stop briefly to listen, despite Rayne's little huffs of impatience.

One voice: "We don't exchange one life for another. Our agents are children, sisters, mothers."

And then another: "Protect and serve is not reserved for humans." That one is especially catchy and the loudest of them all, which seems to suggest to me that despite the huge numbers outside, not everybody knows the specifics of why they are there. Not that it matters, though— their voices are loud and passionate, raised high enough that even below ground they are clear to my ears.

Noel leads us to a car I don't recognise and offers me a jacket with a large, loose hood. I put it on and cover my head, much to Norma's annoyance, who then insists on sliding into the back of it and hiding near my neck.

He and Rayne take the front while I sit in the back seat, ready to duck down should the need arise.

But no one cares or even seems to notice us leave.

As the car pulls out of the underground areas, I see a crowd outside the main public-facing doors of the Clear Blood Foundation. It isn't a huge crowd, probably no more than a hundred, but that's still a mad amount of people. So many? For me?

There are a couple of signs and a portable amp. Someone I can't see is screaming into a microphone, repeating that second chant over and over. "Protect and serve is not reserved for humans. Protect and serve is not reserved for humans."

I spy a news crew near the doors. Two reporters are there, microphones in hand, talking animatedly with, if the uniform speaks right, members of the Clear Blood security team. They aren't SPEAR agents, but they are professional and seem to be practising their de-escalation training.

Not that it's working.

Noel drives slowly so as not to draw attention.

Closer now, I see a couple of furry shapes among all the humanoid ones, some wolves, others in half form. They don't leap around or make a fuss, probably wary of the effect their presence may have. But they are there, they are visible, and they are watching.

I've no idea who any of these people are. Maybe it doesn't matter. Perhaps all that matters is that these citizens of Angbec have left their homes to protest the idea of an execution. Some of them may simply recognise the positive influence SPEAR has on such a city as ours and value the agents that protect it. It may even be that folk have arrived simply to be a part of the noise due to a fear of missing out.

But does it matter? Really? They are here, and as I look, there are more coming, and soon the street will be full of more voices and noise than anyone has heard in one area for a long time.

Someone calls out my name. I've no idea who, but quickly someone else takes up the call. Then another. And another. Within ten seconds I can hear my name clearly through the press of sound, floating up to join that powerful chant still repeating over and over.

*Protect and serve is not reserved for humans. Protect and serve is not reserved for humans.*

Leaving the streets near Clear Blood behind takes us to quieter areas. Rayne carefully climbs between the seats to get back to me and gathers my hands into hers.

"How are you feeling?"

I shake my head. It's all I can manage.

She squeezes my fingers. "Fiona has been in tears for hours. She called me, so full of guilt. She said she never meant for anybody to know what she said, only that we would have the full information. She didn't want you to die."

"It's not her fault," I croak out.

"No, but she feels responsible. So she intensified her search for a cleansing ritual."

A flare of hope fires through my chest, then dies immediately. "Come on, cleansing? This thing is more powerful than that. It won't work."

"You don't know that."

"It never has before."

She squeezes my fingers even tighter. "No one has tried before."

I can't bring myself to hope. "And if it doesn't work? What then? Do I run away and take this thing, whatever it is, with me?" I fight back the urge to cry. "I won't do that. It's dangerous. *I'm* dangerous. I won't put other people in danger because I'm a coward."

"Hey." Rayne grabs my chin with her free hand and jerks me round to face her. "Never say that again. You're not a coward. You're the most courageous person I've ever met."

"I'm an idiot."

"The pair aren't mutually exclusive."

I frown, trying to figure out if I've been insulted or not, but she's too quick for me.

Still holding my chin, she presses on. "You're kind, noble, and dedicated. Anybody who tells you otherwise doesn't know you. You've given eight years of your life to protecting others, and now it's our turn to protect you."

"And when it doesn't work?"

"If."

"When, Rayne. I have to accept that possibility. When it doesn't work, and it becomes clear this thing isn't going anywhere, do I go back to Clear Blood?"

She presses her lips ever so gently to mine. "If—and only if—*I* decide it can't be done, I'll do whatever you want. Whatever you decide, I'll make it happen."

"Rayne—"

"I need you to trust me now. Let me help you. Let us try. You never know, Fiona might be able to make something work. Imagine if we could do something that no one else has ever done before."

"How often does that happen?"

She smiles the smallest of half smiles. "I can control my blood mania. How many vampires have done that before me?"

"I—" But she's right. I can't think of a single example before now of a vampire successfully pulling themselves back from the brink of an anger induced rage without blood to soothe them.

Maybe…just maybe.

No. I shake my head. I can't allow myself to hope like that. I can't face that level of disappointment. No. I won't.

But for her…

I touch her cheek. "When this doesn't work—"

"If," she insists.

Eye roll. "*If* this doesn't work, I want you to do it. I want you to end it."

Her eyes widen slightly. "Danika—"

"You agree to this right now, or I'm not doing it. I'll jump from this car and run back to Clear Blood myself. When…*if* this doesn't work, I want you to be the one to finish me off." My voice drops to a low whisper. "If anybody is going to save the world, I want it to be you. Not SPEAR, not Clear Blood, not the fucking general. I want *you* to get the credit. No one else, understand?"

Long, tense silence.

Eventually, she holds up her hand, fingers all folded down but for the pinkie, which she extends towards me.

I mirror the gesture and link my pinkie finger through hers.

"On my word or meet the sunlight," she murmurs.

Hmm. Not quite as good as my locs one, but it will do.

# CHAPTER THIRTY

I have no idea where we're going. What I do know is that changing cars has me dizzy and disoriented. We have changed directions so many times that I barely know which way is north. More than that, this is our third car. Noel insists on changing vehicles in case we're being followed, and no matter how often I ask who they belong to, he simply taps the side of his nose.

The last car is a tiny, scrappy little thing, blue where it isn't covered in rust, with next to no suspension and certainly no sign of smart brakes.

Rayne sits in the back with me, one arm across my chest as if to keep me from flying out of my seat. It is such a small but motherly gesture that I find that warm feeling swelling through my chest again. It almost hurts, but in a good way.

At the last stop a motorcycle parked up alongside us seats a figure dressed entirely in leather. Their huge helmet covers their face and head so I can see nothing but a reflection as I glance at them. But they raise a gloved thumb to us and pull away slowly, allowing us to follow.

"Who is that?"

Rayne shrugs.

And follow we do. The bike winds through streets popping out of Angbec on the side opposite to our arrival from Moarwell the night before.

We're south now and heading further in that direction, towards areas of countryside walks, hiking, and woodland conservation.

Not too far, though, and once we change to the last car, the drive is a mere fifteen minutes more. The bike stops outside a gated track at the end of a narrow slip off the main road. The sign there reads *Wild Dyke Campsite*.

Never heard of the place, but beyond the gate I can see a small cluster of wooden structures along with a huge sloping thing that might be a tent. Or a wigwam. Or a yurt. Who even knows?

The rider dismounts and yanks off their gloves, teasing the fingers one by one to make it easier. Then they lift the helmet off their head.

"Hi, Karson."

I throw open the car's creaking passenger door and dart out on the dirt road. "Maury?"

He grins. "Sorry to keep you." His shiny bald head gleams in the moonlight. "I just wanted to be sure there was no one following us. And to give the others time to set up."

"Since when were you cool enough to ride a motorcycle?"

"Ha. There's a lot about me you don't know. Let's leave it at that."

"But what the hell are you doing?"

He gestures to the gate, which he opens with a key from the bunch on his bike. "My cousin runs this campsite for Scout holidays. Sometimes the local druids meet here for the solstices too. Mostly it's just a place where people gather around a fire and use the tents, but apparently, it's an area of power."

"What does that mean?"

Shrug. "No idea, but I'm not going to question the people who know better than me. You need to get inside so I can lock the gate. We don't want to be disturbed."

"But the general. How did you—"

"Screw them." His expression darkens. "I get it, really I do, but you're one of mine, and I'm not letting you go without a fight. Hell, if you aren't enough of a pain in my backside, I want all that stress and agony to be worth it. You've got years left in you yet."

I smile. Can't help it.

Rayne beckons me back to the car. "Nobody is ready to give up on you yet, Danika."

I nod and climb back in.

Maury opens the gate, swings it wide enough to pass through, and Noel does just that. Through the back window, I catch site of Maury closing the gate before a turn in the road hides him from sight.

The road slants slightly upward, winding through tall deciduous trees towards a ridge just visible as a dark line against the sky. Along it, more trees, and the road continues to the right and curves down again in a shallow arc towards those structures I saw from the gates.

Definitely tents or yurts or something along those lines. I can see how they would be useful for Scout and Girl Guide trips, or cheap trips away.

But in the middle of them all is a wide clear space where several people have already gathered. They are milling around, talking softly, though one seems to be walking in a circle flinging something into the air with every step.

Noel stops the car, and we climb out together, leaving the vehicle parked on the slope to meet the gathering between the semi-permanent tents. The way down is well-lit with lamps, designed to look like fiery torches or old-fashioned oil lamps, but clearly lit with electricity. There are more of them down below, and each of the structures has a light to the front, to illuminate the scene below.

I gasp.

My entire team is there, the whole of Kappa, talking quietly amongst themselves. Not only are they present, but so too are other people I recognise, from Jadz to Spannah and Chalks. I see Tina Marks of the Angbec police force and Delta members of SPEAR who usually sit at desks. I see the grumpy nurse who cared for me after Vixen tried to drain me dry, and a short, bored looking man who, after some study, I recognise to be a detective sergeant, again from the police force. Hozier, was it?

Looking closer, I spy Link, our chief agent in charge of combat training. He stands head and shoulders above the rest with his impressive wings capped over his shoulders to share space. Close by, looking still shorter by comparison, is Shakka, who holds animated conversation with Erkyan.

I see Gina, Ingrid, and Opal of the Loup Garou, along with several others, close to Solo and Duo with their wildly coloured hair. In fact, I see one figure with yellow hair, another with green, a third with blue, and a fourth with purple. A literal rainbow of colours.

The figure with purple hair is the first among them to face me, and she does so with a smile and a limp as she walks towards me. Limp?

"I know you," I find myself saying as we meet on the path. "What are you doing here? Don't you live in Moarwell?"

"I wondered if you'd remember me or if you even noticed me." Where before this woman was crouched and timid, she is now tall and straight backed. Sure, her limp is still there, but in the context of the others around her, I can't believe I didn't earlier notice the *edane* ease and smoothness to her movements.

"You're a werewolf?"

"Fire Fang," she says softly. "And yes, I live in Moarwell. It isn't a problem, usually, unless someone comes and stirs things up. I live there quite peacefully, keeping an eye on the residents, minding my own business."

I nod, quietly impressed. "I had no idea."

"Good. You weren't supposed to."

"But what are you doing here?"

A soft, gentle smile in my direction. "My brothers called me for help, and I answered. More than that, though, I happened to be positioned to bring along some other people who wanted to help."

She points, but before I can see where her finger aims, Solo bounds over and flings an arm around the woman's shoulders. "Don't be modest, Sess, you're a lifesaver over there. Those idiots in that village don't know the guardian angel they have in you." He grins, flashing sharp, white teeth.

"I brought more able bodies," she says, utterly ignoring him. "When they realised what Linda had done and where I would be going, they wanted to lend their support."

At last I can see who she means. Bruce and Kimberly Dixon stand near one of the yurts, talking softly with Viola. There is someone else with them who I don't know, though they wear plenty of leather and chains and boast several piercings. Viola's paramour, maybe?

I snap a glance at Rayne.

She sighs. "It didn't take long for them to realise what Linda did. She went back to Moarwell boasting about it. They got on the train at once and made their way to Fiona."

It's hard to believe. These people I met barely forty-eight hours before, acting so kindly and selflessly to help me.

Do they know what they're doing? Do they understand what they're getting into? Are they even aware of the risks?

I tug Rayne slightly aside. "You shouldn't have let them come."

Her look back at me is quiet but defiant. "Would *you* have stopped them? Besides, this isn't for you—they're doing it for me. They know what you mean to me."

I don't know how to argue with that. I don't know if I *can* argue with that, but still it rubs me the wrong way.

"I didn't force them to be here. They chose to come, same as everybody else on this campsite." She lifts a hand to gesture around her. "Fiona has told them what we're up against. She explained that nobody really knows what we're doing. But they're here anyway. Why can't you accept that?"

Because why the ever-loving hell would all these people endanger themselves for me?

But I don't say that. Instead I turn to the purple-haired woman. "We didn't get a chance to speak before. Hi, and thanks for coming down, I guess."

"My name is Sestina," she says with a little flick of that purple hair.

She tries to work herself free of Solo's grip and gives up when he grips all the harder. "And I'm sorry it's come to this. I did my best to talk Linda down, but she never listens to the likes of me. Sure, I could have given her reason to, but"—she gives an apologetic half smile—"I prefer to keep my little secret."

"Uh, don't worry about it," I stutter, watching her and Solo move together.

They have an easy grace about them, a beauty and economy of movement alongside each other that speaks of long practise or—I gasp. "Are you related as well?"

Sestina roars with laughter. "To this idiot? No. Well, yes and no. We're of a pack, yes, but we're also xiblings."

I remember that word. It's how the twins described the other pack members who share a close mental bond with them. With that I look again at the small cluster of people with brightly coloured hair and realise what I must be looking at.

"You're all xiblings?"

Duo joins us, ruffling his own orange hair with one hand while dragging the yellow-haired woman along with him. Well, more blond than yellow. She might have the most normal hair colour of the lot of them. "Yup. All of us." He smiles. "Solo and I, then Trioka"—he gestures to the yellow-haired woman—"then Tetrad, Quintain"—green and blue, both male—"and lastly, resident grumpy pants, Sestina."

At my side, Rayne hides a giggle behind the back of her hand.

Noel is nowhere near as subtle. "You all have number names, sí? Why? You are like little pins lined up in a row; one, two, three, four, five, and six."

Solo gives a bark of laughter. "Those aren't our real names, dumbass, those are titles. You really think I go through my actual life called *Solo*?"

Actually I did, but I decide not to tell him that.

He shakes his head. "Anyway, that's what we call each other, and that's what we use in the pack. Just makes things easier when we're thinking about power and strength."

"And mating lines," Duo adds with a grin.

Sestina rolls her eyes. "Gross."

"But true," Quintain adds. His blue hair is waist length and captured at the back of his neck with a single simple ribbon. "I don't know why I'm so far down the line…"

"Because finding a match for you is like looking for candy at a salad bar. You're impossible to please." This from Trioka who is soft-spoken yet shaped like a bodybuilder.

"And everybody knows that I'll find a mate before you do, so it makes sense for me to go ahead of you." Tetrad gives a wicked grin. He has several missing teeth and a bold tattoo running up the side of his neck that flexes as he talks.

"Bullshit you'll go ahead of me—"

"Now, now, boys, calm down—"

"He started it—"

"Well, you should end it—"

And with that, the six of them fall to bickering amongst themselves. I remember, then, the journey to Moarwell in the van. Well, if this is what life is like with all six of them together, I'm glad that I've only ever been exposed to two of them at once.

Rayne tugs me on and away from the twittering xiblings and draws me towards that figure still throwing things into the air.

It's Fiona. She wears a long white robe like a nightgown and has her masses of long hair gathered up into a messy pile on the top of her head. She carries a huge tin in one hand and occasionally dips into it to toss handfuls of the contents into the air or to scatter them onto the ground.

When she sees me, she slams the tin onto the floor and rushes up to me. This close I can see that her hands are still bandaged, but that doesn't stop her from carefully drawing me into an enthusiastic hug.

"Child, I am so very sorry." Her face sparkles with sweat and possibly tears. "I had no idea. I didn't know. I will never forgive myself for what I've put you through over the last few hours."

"It's not your fault," I murmur.

"I shouldn't have said anything. I should've waited until I knew more. I could have kept the knowledge in my own mind until I knew better what to do. Instead I opened my mouth and out comes your undoing. Will you ever forgive me?"

I touch her bandaged hands. "I should be the sorry one. Look what this thing did to you."

"Ah, it is a risk of the job, child. I wouldn't be a psychic if everything I did was easy. Besides, I've learned more from you in that one simple touch than I have in doing anything else. You led me to look at texts I never before considered, researching and learning of all manner of banishment and cleansing rituals."

That spark of hope ignites in my chest again.

I slam it down without mercy.

This isn't going to work. I can't let myself believe for even an instant that it will.

"You're a witch?" I ask.

Fiona places a hand on her chest. If I didn't know any better, I would say she was deeply flattered. "Me? Oh no, no. I don't have that sort of power. But I have borrowed the mind and teachings of one, if that's all right." She gestures past me to a little dark-haired figure chatting with Hozier.

Wait, really?

As if sensing the attention on her, Tina Marks turns to face me. I remember her, first for being one of the few civilian police officers willing to help me find Vixen, again for somehow always being the officer on call when I contact the Angbec police force. I also remember her handing me a chocolate bar and a sandwich through the bars of a holding cell in the bottom of the police station.

She grins and scuffs her foot along the ground, even looking a little bashful. "Hello."

"You're a witch?"

A shrug. "I would have told you, but it never really came up. Besides, every time I've seen you, there's been more than enough on your plate to deal with, wouldn't you say?"

Rayne clings to my arm. "There are banishing and cleansing rituals she says might work."

This time, an enthusiastic nod. "Oh yeah. I've called up things I've never meant to in the past, so surely this can't be too much harder than that."

I grit my teeth. "But this is stronger than anything you've called before. You must know that."

"Oh, I know." Her eyes take on a steely determination. "But that's why there's so many of us. If this thing is so powerful, then we'll just need more of us to draw from. Are you ready?"

No. No, I'm not.

This whole thing is insane and now dozens more people are going to be in danger because of me.

Without warning I turn to the side, breaking away from Rayne to vomit hard against the stony earth.

# CHAPTER THIRTY-ONE

My back prickles as if in warning, and a horrible cold sensation seems to seep through my bones.

I hate this. This is dumb. It can't work. It won't work.

Disturbed by the unusual motion, Norma crawls her way out from inside the back of my hood. She grumbles softly, that throaty growl at the back of her throat, before hopping down to the ground.

She sniffs at the puddle, then stalks away, making her way to Hawk, who greets her with smiles, pets, and cuddles beneath his own large wings.

Meanwhile, Rayne is at my side, gently pulling my hair away from my dripping mouth. "You're going to be fine," she murmurs. "We'll protect you, just this once. Will you let us?"

One more horrible heave and I'm able to stand.

Gasping, I wipe my mouth on the back of my hand and look at the people gathered before me. Werewolves, vampires, goblins, humans, and gargoyles. Well it's certainly a powerful bunch of people.

All that *edane* energy in the air is enough to allow even me to feel it.

And there's a witch, to boot.

Maybe, just maybe…

No. I stamp it down again. Hope is dangerous. I can't allow it.

But as Rayne stares deep into my face, her eyes swimming with emotion, I don't have the heart to deny her.

"Tell me what to do," I murmur.

And so she does.

Quickly, Rayne takes me through the open space, explaining, with help from Fiona, what they intend to do.

I learn that Fiona has been cleansing the ground and the air as much as possible with a fine mix of clove, sage, rosemary, and cedar all ground into powder. Quite unlike her fake mixtures back in Moarwell, the stuff mixed into her tin smells wonderful and brings a strange stillness and ethereal quality to the air. Next, she sets out little pots of the stuff to burn in a loose, lopsided circle around us. The gentle curls of smoke drifting into the air are like white snakes winding towards the clouds.

Fiona shows me the space at the centre of the circle in which she intends to sit with me.

"It should be fairly simple," she says, though her voice hitches just a little. "Tina will cast the circle and mark out the five points to evoke the elements. That should help to protect people on the outside. You and I will sit in the centre and, under the protection of those gathered, draw out the entity."

"Is that it?"

She shrugs. "I don't know how much more you want. There won't be flashing lights, bangs, crashes, and an air full of sparkles if that's what you mean. But I'm sure you'll feel something."

"Like what?"

Her hands tremble slightly. "Perhaps some pain, physical and emotional. This thing, after all, has quite a grip on you, child. Maybe you'll feel nothing."

"How will we know if it works?"

"Your mark will be gone, I assume."

Despite myself, I find my hands reaching towards my back. "But it's *in* my skin—how will it disappear? It's like a tattoo or a brand or a burn."

"But it isn't a true part of you. The creature that put it there intended it as a marker. If we remove the marker, the master will have nowhere to go, so it makes sense to me that the marks will be gone."

I lower my face to my hands. "You don't actually know, do you?"

"I have no idea." Her admission seems hard-pressed. "I've read a lot over the last day or so, and nothing there indicates that anyone has attempted something like this. The decision was always to sacrifice the infected person and leave the overall problem to the next psychic to come along. If I can help it, I intend to solve the problem, so no one else need make such a horrible choice."

Fine. The quicker we do all this, the quicker it's over and we realise there's nothing more to be done. The one saving grace to all this is that I'll get to spend my last night with Rayne.

She tucks her hand into mine, as if to think of her is to call her to me. Her body is tight to mine, a cool presence I want to fall into and hold on to forever.

"I'll sit in the circle with you. You won't be alone."

"No." Fiona cuts across that thought immediately. "You'll need to be on the outside of the circle where it is safest."

A frown. "I thought—"

"No. Only she and I will be in the circle."

Rayne is ready to fight—I can see it in her eyes. "How can I help from out there? What if the creature comes in? What if it attacks? What if Danika needs to be restrained?"

"And what if I turn around and attack people?" I shoot back. "This is hard enough as is, and we don't know what we're doing. Can we at least follow the few rules we have?"

Her complaints are cut off by a roar from up the hill. It's Maury, revving his motorcycle as he makes his way down, cutting a smooth curve in the gravel and dirt by slamming the brakes. He spies me but doesn't stop, instead crossing the crowded space to make his way to Noel. I have no idea what the pair are saying, but the sight of him does give me pause to stop and look around.

Kappa. Many werewolves from various packs. Civvie bashers, SPEAR agents, and new acquaintances from Moarwell. But there are two obvious faces I can't yet see.

"Rayne, where is Pip?"

She glances away, up the hill, before answering. "On her way. She and Jackson needed to make one last stop before coming out."

"Are we going to wait for her?"

Fiona stalks by me then, carrying a bundle of candles and a small knife with a black handle.

Rayne sighs. "I don't think we have time. As it is, we don't know how long this will take, and at the least I'll need to be under cover before sunrise."

Well. If there is any risk at all that she will be stuck out here without shelter when this pointless task flops, I won't stand for it. I make my way to the centre of the circle at once and face Fiona. "What do you want me to do?"

"Take your shirt off," she says without looking at me. "I need to be able to see your back."

Oh. Yay. So I'm going to be sitting in the middle of a circle of my co-workers and various allies showing off my bra, am I? Great. Just great.

The air isn't as cold as I expected it to be. Maybe it's the season, or maybe it's the fact that I'm in the middle of a circle full of so many warm bodies. Werewolves run hot as a matter of course, but everybody else seems to be a normal level of warm. Except for Rayne, of course.

She stands in an area of the circle that allows me to see her, her arms slightly spread to touch her fingers to those on either side—Noel and Maury.

Around me is everybody else, all the werewolves, my Kappa team, the small cluster of friendly faces from Moarwell, other members of SPEAR, Shakka too. The circle they form is tight and wonky but clearly a ring around me and Fiona, who sits in front of me with her legs lightly crossed.

I join her, my back itching with cold.

I can't see the mark, of course, but now, more than ever before, I imagine I can feel it brushing against the straps of the bra Fiona mercifully allowed me to keep on.

Not that some of these people wouldn't enjoy the show.

High above, clouds scudding across the moon occasionally change the light from a bright silver glow to the warmer, more orange tones of the electric lamps posing as flaming torches. Somewhere an owl hoots, and I catch sight of several bats winging through the darkness.

On any other day, at any other time, this might have been calm and peaceful. I imagine campfires built where I'm sitting right now and cheerful faces gathered around the flickering light to sing camp songs and roast marshmallows.

Pacing out her steps, Tina walks around me, shoving candles into the earth. More than once they fall, and she is forced to jam them in harder, packing the dirt around them with her feet and hands. Five in total, evenly spaced.

Then, knife in hand, she paces over to the inner edge of the circle and holds the blade high towards the sky.

"Is everyone ready?"

No. I want to yell it, scream it, but the determined looks from those gathered around me keep my lips pressed tightly closed.

Tina begins to walk clockwise around the inside of the circle. Not slow or even rushed, just at a casual walking pace as she gestures with the blade.

"A circle of protection," she calls, "is a simple thing. We draw on our own energies to make a safe space into which we pour our intent. So that is what we're going to do. I'll mark the circle with my athame"— she gestures with the knife—"and all you need do is direct your intent to our safety and protection. Whatever we call out of Agent Karson tonight stays within that circle. And whatever interference may come from our side? Well, that stays out."

Oh. I never considered that someone from the outside might

cause problems. But then who? Surely there's no one out there who even knows where we are, much less would come with intent to disturb us. Right?

There are some nods and murmurs of assent from those gathered around us.

"The rest of our intent"—she makes more patterns with the knife—"is to be focused on expelling negative energies."

I hear a scoff from somewhere on my right. That might be from Shakka.

Tina rides right over him, though not without a stern look in his direction. "Whether you believe it or not, we are all powerful beings. Our will and our place in nature give us far more strength and power than any of us realise. And with enough of us gathered in one place, we have a good chance of providing enough energy to enforce our will."

A chill breeze whips through the space. I shudder into it and fight to put aside thoughts of whispering voices predicting our failure.

"Feel free to call on whatever deity or deities you feel most comfortable with. I'll be calling on the Triple Goddess."

My head reels. I've never heard of that before. Sure, despite my Christian upbringing, I know full well that there are other deities some folk would consider their one and only. Or that there are multiples that people refer to, depending on what they need that day. There are those who believe in one, all, and none, all at the same time. Faith and everything related to it is almost as complicated as my day-to-day job, but the idea that anybody can draw on any belief to help is bewildering.

In front of me, Fiona closes her eyes and begins murmuring. I've no idea who or what she's calling to, though I'm pretty sure I catch the word *ancestor* in there more than once.

Still Tina keeps walking, gesturing with the knife, which I now know is called an athame. "In the north," she calls, "I call on the Guardians who reside in earth to watch over this circle."

More breeze and I rub my hands up and down my bare arms.

"In the east, I call on the Guardians who reside in air to watch over this circle."

A faint smell fills my nostrils. I've no idea what it is or where it comes from, but it is pleasant, like flowers or candied fruit peels.

"In the south, I call on the Guardians who reside in fire to watch over this circle." Tina is moving slightly faster now, her arms making broader motions. Her forehead is creased with concentration, her free hand held before her with the palm down, like a guide. "In the west, I call on the Guardians who reside in water to watch over this circle."

The ground beneath my rear rumbles and grumbles. Something large and heavy must be passing by on the road beyond the campsite if I can feel it so easily.

But now the air is very still and very quiet. Even the owl I heard earlier is gone.

As Tina makes her way back to the empty space in the circle, her voice rises higher and louder. "And last, I call on the Guardians who reside over spirit, the powerful force nestled deep in each of us. Under the watchful eye of the Guardians and in the sight of the Triple Goddess, bless and seal this circle."

And that's it.

As Tina takes her place and faces inward with the rest of us, I see nothing. I feel nothing.

Even Rayne, standing directly ahead of me, looks confused, glancing left and right as if to find something new or out of place.

But Fiona…Fiona sits across from me with her eyes wide open, her injured hands pressed flat to the earth, her head thrown back. Her breathing is fast and shallow, and even as I watch, sweat breaks out on her brow.

"Do you feel that?" she whispers.

I look left. Then right. "Me?"

"Tell me you feel it."

I give an apologetic shrug. "Nothing. Sorry. Just cold, I suppose. But you'd expect that since I'm sitting in my underwear, right?"

She sighs. "It's so strong. You have very powerful friends, child."

"Yeah?"

"Their intent is palpable." She does that thing with her hands where she feels out the air, as though touching against something that no one else can see. "I wish you could feel what I feel. Sense what I sense."

I think back to her screams of agony and the way the marks fused her skin to my back. "Forgive me if I don't agree. I'll take my basic, normal mundane insensitivity all day, every day, thanks."

"Are you always like this?"

I laugh. Can't help it. "Actually, yes."

"Well, stop it. I need to concentrate." And with that, she begins to peel the bandages off her hands.

I open my mouth, meaning to stop her, but the look she shoots me is pure venom. It is the look of a teacher at her wits' end with the class clown. So I snap my mouth shut and watch.

When she drops the bandages and inspects her hands, I find myself wincing in sympathy. Though clearly beginning to heal, her hands are still badly injured. Angry red patches slash across her wrists and palms, and thick black scabs are forming on each of her fingertips.

She stares at her hands for long, long moments, then steels herself with visible effort. Slow and measured, she walks around within the little circle of candles to stand behind me. "Are you ready?"

The snarky answer is ready on my tongue, but then I chance a look at the circle.

My friends and colleagues, all of them putting themselves on the line to help me. So many people putting all their will and energy into creating a circle of safety so we can even attempt this crazy feat.

"I'm ready," I tell her.

"Then be still, child. Let me see what I can see." And, with one last deep breath, Fiona places her hands flat against my back.

# CHAPTER THIRTY-TWO

Darkness. Instant, black, cloaking darkness.

I worry that I've closed my eyes, but I haven't. I just can't see. There's nothing *to* see.

Then the eyes.

I suck in a breath or try to, but the air is close and thick.

My tongue forms a solid wedge of immovable muscle against the roof of my mouth.

Bright. Yellow. Eyes.

Again I try to breathe. Again my chest struggles with it.

Standing. Maybe that's better. Maybe if I stand, I can trick myself into breathing just from the shock of it.

But I can't do that either.

My legs don't work.

Hell, nothing works.

Not my eyes, my legs, my mouth, my hands.

I'm locked in place, paralysed and helpless, as the garish Day-Glo yellow seems to float closer, closer, ever closer.

Fuck. Fuck, oh fuck.

Why can't I do anything? Why can't I move?

Straining does nothing. Struggling does nothing. Pushing and pulling with every muscle in me does nothing.

And still the eyes advance.

"Little bird?"

That awful, awful voice.

I remember it now, like thousands of marbles rattling through the interiors of just as many metal pipes.

"Ah, yes," the eyes seem to say. "I remember you. I marked you. Are you enjoying my gift?"

No. Screw you. You and your gift can eat shit.

I want to say it. Hell, I want to scream it, but my mouth is still locked shut with nothing I can do to change it.

The darkness around me gathers into a shape. Not physically, but before me a void of even deeper black seems to form around the eyes to make the shape of a head. In it, the thin slit of a mouth opens to reveal still more empty nothingness. How is this creature able to work in varied shades of black?

"Didn't think I'd see you before the time, little bird. Have you come to sing for me?"

Oh no, no, no, no, I remember what that means.

It did this to me before.

Last time, on the floor of the church of the Loup Garou pack, this mad creature sent me spiralling back into my memories and made me live the most painful moments of my life over and over again.

Please no.

I don't want that again. I can't do that again. Not now. Not when there's already so much in my mind to tumble through.

It laughs. The damn thing laughs at me and extends a single clawed hand. I see long fingers with way too many knuckles, and sharp points at each tip that might be claws, might be talons, who even knows?

The hand closes over my chin, and the long fingers dive into my mouth. They force my lips apart, and between them, it flows inward.

I gag.

My throat flexes and convulses as though trying to swallow silk covered in sand.

No, no, no, please no. Please don't.

"I tried last time, little bird, do you remember? But I was too weak, and your vampire friend stopped me before I could complete my move. But where is she now? Did she abandon you? Did all of your friends abandon you? There's no one here but you and me, so this time you're all alone. Just perfect for me to feast on. This will be so, so sweet."

Before the creature moved as smoke. Now it is tangible and real with physical force and pressure. Or at least it feels that way. It slides down, down my throat, filling me slowly piece by piece, flooding my lungs with pain and suffering.

My body jerks from side to side. Tears fill my eyes.

"Alone. All alone, just you and me. The pair of us like this, wrapped together for eternity. How does it feel, little bird?"

It sucks. That's how it feels. Rage builds within me, buried deep in my gut and heavy with its own weight. It bubbles slowly, rises like boiling water, travelling up and up, higher and higher until it bursts from my mouth in a guttural roar of fury.

"Get. The hell. Off me." And I throw myself backward…

Straight into Fiona, who tumbles away from me on the stony ground. She doesn't quite fall but manages to kick a candle over as she finds her balance once again.

I stare up at the sky, aware suddenly that I can see stars and moon above me.

The moon is huge and almost full, but for a thin sliver at one edge, and glows a deep, angry red.

There are gasps outside the circle, murmurs of confusion.

Fiona hurries over to me and peers down into my face. Her expression is a soft blend of confusion and agitation. "Why did you do that?"

"I'm sorry—it wasn't you…"

"You mustn't do this. I know you're afraid, child, but you must allow me to touch you."

I frown. "What are you talking about?"

"The very moment I touched you, you threw yourself around like a mad creature. That won't do. Please let me touch you, so I can connect with the creature inside. If I can find it, perhaps I can draw it out."

I scramble up as far as my knees. "But I was gone. I was choking, and the thing was there. It was trying to crawl into me again. Into my mouth."

She grips my shoulders. It must hurt, but her eyes are wide and lively with hope, not pain. "There was more time for you?"

"At least a couple of minutes."

"Good. Good, good. Again. We must do it again. Quickly."

I have no idea why she's so worked up, but something weird has clearly happened here.

From the corner of my eye I catch Rayne looking at me. Her hands are still spread so her fingertips touch against those of Maury and Noel, but her gaze is all for me. She is leaning forward ever so slightly—even her weight is balanced for a sharp take-off if she decides to run, though she's likely to run into that weird white haze if she does.

Wait.

I squint, but no, it's really there, the faintest shimmer in the air. I might have missed it if not for paying attention to the weirdness around me. All around us and above in a tall dome, a faint shimmering of gleaming white.

"Fiona, what's that?"

She ignores me, fussing over getting me back into place. I jerk away to get her attention.

"What the hell is that in the air, Fiona? It's all around us, what is it?"

She grins. "You can see the circle." It isn't a question.

But what the hell else can it be? It is circular. It follows the path Tina walked with her athame. It has distinctly stronger shimmers in four cardinal points, which I assume to be the north, south, east, and west. In fact they must be, because the one closest to Rayne I know for a fact is west, just because of where the deeply red moon is.

"I guess so. But how did I—"

"No time. Sit back down. We're doing it again, and whatever it was you did last time, do it again. When you threw yourself backward there was a pulse of something. I don't know what, but it felt like anger and defiance."

I lick my lips in an attempt to ease the dryness. "Oh, that was me. That thing was trying to get into me."

"Good."

"What?"

"Child, if the minion is trying to enter you, that means the larger creature is not yet ready." Her excitement runs her words together. "Fight it. Chase it off and, if you can, convince it to take the mark too."

Oh, sure, yes. We'll just sit and have a little discussion over cream tea and biscuits.

I'd laugh at the ridiculous thought, but the fear is already creeping in again.

I don't want to go back, even for a second.

I can't bear it.

Back to that darkness. The all-consuming bleakness with nothing but haunting yellow eyes for company.

But Fiona is already turning me around, pressing me down to the ground. She rights the candles. She pats me gently on the shoulder. She rests her hands on my back again.

*Rayne stops in the middle of the road. Traffic is slow but enough to be dangerous, cars swerving around her in a flurry of horns, screeching tyres, and fist shakes.*

*I pull closer, flicking on my hazards and hoping that's enough. "Rayne, listen to me—"*

*"Why not drive at me, Agent? Like you did before?"*

*The car rumbles beneath me, and I consider revving it up again. Pressing my foot down like I did before, like I intended to do to the wolves.*

*My leg trembles.*

*"I can smell you," she mutters. "Your hunger, anger, and fear."*

*My gun is still on the passenger seat. I grab it and dive out of the car, free hand raised to hold aloft my SPEAR ID.*

*A single ounce of pressure, and the shot is clean. She's right there, not moving. A clear, easy target. A chest shot would end this mess in seconds.*

*My finger tightens on the trigger. The gunshot is a deafening roar in my ears, matched by the agony of my own wild screams.*

Screams that die out as the darkness returns.

The creature is in front of me again, yellow eyes blinking eerily over their slitted pupils. "I don't know that one. Recent, little bird? Or old? Not so old as last time we met?"

My breath is rasping in my throat. I'm hot, cold, and hot again all at once, but I can move. At last. In that swirling void of darkness, I can stand and speak and lift my hands. I do all three with a fire burning in me.

"That's not a true memory, you fuck. I didn't shoot her."

"You wanted to."

"I didn't shoot her. What, you're making stuff up now? Huh? Filling my head with lies isn't going to get you what you want. I know what happened. I know the truth of Rayne and me, and nothing you do will change that."

The eyes narrow, their first showing of annoyance.

Good to know I've still got it, I suppose.

"Little bird, you test me. Fine, if you want more, I'll give you more. Let's see how many precious memories I can feast on today."

It reaches for me, many-knuckled fingers clawing and grasping, but this time, I'm ready.

As aims for my chin, I duck down and dig my own fingers in, gripping the thin areas I assume to be wrists and pushing back with all my might. "No. Screw you. You can't have me…"

The wrists and fingers collapse into smoke. Grainy, gritty, choking smoke that, once again, slides into my mouth.

*From the corner of my eye I catch sight of Rayne, struggling to free herself from three sets of chains while following the scent of my blood. Her fangs are longer than I've seen them, her eyes ablaze with silver.*

*I'm not going to make it.*

*The guard is yelling, someone else is screaming, but my focus is all ahead. Down the corridor. Door on the left. Three small steps up.*

*Footsteps behind me, light and quick. Panting. My heart in my throat.*

*I'm not going to make it.*

*Another corridor. Turn right. Right again. Left. There.*

*The swing doors fronting the cafeteria hold fast as I barrel into them. The impact knocks me flat, and Rayne dives down and onto me. Her strong vampire hands push at my shoulder, my face, stretching my neck out ready for her fangs.*

*Hissing, spitting, screeching with rage and hunger, she lays fangs to my throat and bites hard.*

*Pain explodes through my body, jerking my legs, flailing my arms.*

*Rayne dumps her weight on me, forcing me flat to the ground while her lips close over my bleeding flesh.*

*I catch the silver in her eyes, the hunger oozing out as a furious growl at the back of her throat as she begins to drink me down. She sucks and moans and scratches at me, her pleasure at the feed making her messy and rough.*

*And she's too strong. I can't move her. I can't do anything.*

*Pinned as a butterfly to a board, weak and helpless as a child, I have no choice but to lie beneath her, waiting for her to kill me slowly, painfully, totally.*

*I'm screaming, I'm kicking at the air, tears are blurring my vision, but I fight because that's all I know how to do. That's all I've ever done. I bellow my impotent rage to the ceiling of the Clear Blood Foundation as the vampire I should have killed hours ago drains me slowly dry.*

I drop to my knees.

It takes far too many seconds to realise that I'm not already on the ground. That I'm not beneath Rayne's ravenous mouth. That I'm not dying.

That last one is debatable, though.

Back in the darkness again, struggling to catch my breath. One breath. Two. Three. Stand. Slowly.

The creature has a more solid form now. The darkness around us is becoming paler, almost grey. As though this thing is leeching the lack of colour from the void around us to fuel itself. That and my own torn-up emotions and memories.

But this one is a lie too.

Rayne never killed me that night because of course she didn't. She tried to—oh, she certainly tried to, since she had no control over her blood mania then. But I reached the cafeteria in time. She hadn't bitten anything except three separate blood bags, handed over by petrified members of staff, while more calm and orderly vampires watched with unabashed interest.

I smile. Can't help it. "Why do I get the feeling you're losing?"

The thing swells to larger, more impressive heights.

I don't care.

"Go on. Tell me. More fake memories? You think you can weaken me with those? You better try harder, you fuck."

"I have power unimaginable, little bird, and—"

I cut it off with a sweep of my hand. "Whatever they're doing out there is working, isn't it? This banishing? That's why you're so desperate. My friends and family are out there right now, putting everything they have into chasing you off, and you fucking know it."

The creature grins. I can tell because the area below the eyes gets briefly darker still. "Friends, yes, but family? What family? They abandoned you long ago."

My bravado stutters. "Shut up."

"Father dead at *your* hand. Sister a vampire. You failed her so completely that she isn't even human any more. And a mother. A mother so sick at the very sight of you that she couldn't even come to watch you die."

"Shut up—"

"She hates you. They all hate you, the ones who matter. And I'll show you. Drop back, little bird. Fall into those memories and sing the song of pain. Feel it. Know it. Drown. In. It."

And once more it clutches at me. I struggle. I wave my hands at the thickening form, but again it gathers around me, swirling, clawing, fighting, enveloping.

*"Good to see you, Mum." I smooth my hands over the crisp white sheets hospitals always insist on using.*

*From the doorway she simply assesses me, eyes cool and unfeeling. "Mm-hmm," is the only sounds she makes.*

*"Sorry I didn't call before. I got swept up in the case and..." Why is she staring at me like that? As if drinking me in for the final time. "Mum?"*

*Slowly, she roots through her handbag and comes out with a small plastic bag. "I came to give you this." She tosses it at the bed, still standing in the doorway.*

*Why won't she come into the room? There's no one else here. No one will bother us.*

*I use the sheets to pull the bag closer. Inside, a photo in a tarnished silver frame. Mum, Dad, Pippa, and me, standing in front of our old house back in Cipla. It's spring there. Flowers are blooming, and the sky is pale blue, streaked with soft puffs of cloud. Sparrows perch in the heavy fronds of jasmine crawling up the side of our home.*

*Wow. I remember that day.*

*We were about to go on a day trip, some beach down south. Mum hated*

*it, but Dad couldn't wait to dive into the sea and show us how to swim as he
did as a child. We came back that night exhausted but happy, covered in sand
and crusted streaks of sea salt.*

*"I have a copy"—Mum points—"and there's another one for Phillipa.
One each, so you can remember your family."*

*I pause my happy consideration of the photo. "What?"*

*Mum folds her arms. "That is what family looks like, Danika. Look at
that and remember what we used to be before you broke us."*

*The words pierce like a blunt spoon. I'm hunched over, gasping as if
punched. "I broke? Mum—"*

*"I know you let that monster bite my girl. How could you? To spite me?
To make sure I've no daughters left at all?"*

*Words stick in my throat. "No. Mum, that's not...You can't mean that."*

*"You're a sexual deviant, and Phillipa is a blood-sucking monster. I'm
all alone. First your father, now my two girls. My babies. You've left me alone."*

*I grip the photo hard enough that the frame creaks. "We're here, Mum,
nothing has changed. Pippa might be different now, but she's still our Pip. And
I'm still Danika."*

*Her gaze hardens. "Not my Danika. She and my Phillipa are gone.
Goodbye."*

*"Mum? Mum, wait. Mum!"*

She left me. As I lay in hospital, barely recovered from a very real
brush with death, my mother left me. Abandoned me. Since that day
she has refused to answer a single call, respond to a single text message,
answer her door any time I visit her home.

She hates me. Truly.

My own mother wants nothing to do with me.

A pained sob spews from my throat. I want to catch it, I want to
drag it back, but I can't.

Because this thing is right.

Everybody else came to see me. Learning of my last twenty-four
hours on this earth, most everyone came to speak with me. Hell, even
Shakka. No matter that all he wanted was his Blade.

But my mother? Nowhere.

The tears burn as they roll down my cheeks.

Fuck, it's right.

She does hate me. She doesn't want me. She blames me for taking
Pippa from her. I've failed. In every possible way, I've failed.

In that moment, I find myself thanking a God I barely believe
in that she doesn't know the truth of what happened between me and

Dad. To think just how much more she would despise me if she were to learn that I was the one to drive a wooden chair leg through my own father's chest.

Slow, confident chuckles from the creature. "Yes. You killed him. You killed your sister. And you left your mother to fend for herself in a cruel, hard world that cares nothing for her or her safety. On your locs and hope to trim? Little bird, you should have been bald *years* ago."

Tears are coursing down my cheeks.

There's nothing I can do.

My limbs are weak and lifeless, my defiance all gone.

It's over. I'm done.

I *have* failed.

All those people gathered outside the circle don't know the truth. The image they have of me is warped and tinted by rose-coloured glasses. They know nothing of the terrible person I truly am.

Dad is dead because of me. Pip is a vampire because I was too slow to stop Vixen hurting her. Noel lost huge chunks of his bowel on my watch. Wendy is dead because of me. Chalks is forever crippled because of me. Fiona's hands are maimed, possibly beyond repair. And who knows how many other poor souls have suffered because of my absolute failure to get anything right.

Pain roars across my back, and for the first time in that darkness, I spot the first few flecks of red.

The creature croons happily as it pours deeper and deeper down my throat. "Master is coming," it purrs. "At least in this you'll not be a failure, little bird. You've done everything right. Not long now. Almost there."

I lie back.

Maybe it's better this way. Maybe taking myself out of the equation will stop anybody else getting hurt. After all, if I'm not there, I can't hurt them, right? If I'm not there with my colossal cock-up of a self to—

"Danika Carmen Susan Karson, is this how you greet me after all this time?"

My eyes flash open.

# CHAPTER THIRTY-THREE

I'm back outside. I'm on my face this time, rather than staring at the sky, and dirt mixed with herbs fills my mouth in a disgusting blend. My back pulses in time with a raging heartbeat that has nothing to do with me, and my eyes burn with tears.

But I'm back.

And that voice. There's only one person on earth who addresses me with every damn one of my government names. And that usually means I'm in trouble.

I want to turn over, but it hurts too much, so instead, I push to my hands and look around me.

The shimmering white dome is still in place over me. Everybody is on the outside looking in, their faces distorted by the gleam.

But directly in front of me there's a hole.

I blink again.

No, I was right.

In the hazy dome of magick no one else can see, a large, rectangular hole shows the space beyond in all the dim, gloomy colours of nature at night.

Through it rushes Rayne, dragging behind her two figures I never, ever thought to see again.

"Pip?" Again, I push against the ground, struggling to stand. "Mum?"

All three of them dash towards me, clearing the small space in a number of steps.

Rayne is first to reach me, bodily heaving me to my feet, while somewhere behind me, Tina yells something about holding the circle steady. I see Jack has arrived, and he steps smoothly into Rayne's old space, holding out his hands to touch fingertips with Maury and Noel.

Pippa grips my left hand, squeezing it tightly. Her vampire strength crushes my fingers, but I don't care. I barely feel it, in truth. The other hand, my right, is wrapped tight and close in that of my mother.

I blink, but it's her. It's her.

She's aged years, it seems, in the weeks we've been apart. Her eyes are ringed in heavy dark circles, and her usually bright and puffy hair is limp and dry. When was the last time she treated it?

Mum holds my hand tight in hers and lifts my fingers gently to her lips.

"Danika, baby, I'm here. I'm here."

My throat ceases. Then the ugliest, most violent sob bursts out.

"Mum?"

She smiles. Touches my cheek. "I'm here and I'm sorry. I'm so sorry."

To my left, Pippa is squeezing tighter than ever. "Jack found her at the Clear Blood protests. He called me, and I knew I had to bring her."

Again I stare at my mother. This woman who barely cares about anything other than her Spanish classes, fancy restaurants, and Bible studies. What the hell was she doing at a protest?

But then I remember the chant.

*Our agents are children, sisters, mothers.*

My sister, my mother, and my girlfriend. All of them are in front of me now. Each of them is holding me. Watching me. Loving me. Supporting me.

And around them, my friends are lending their will and their intent to this circle, giving weight to my own desire to be clean again.

If only I can force the damn thing out.

For the very first time, I allow myself to hope.

I'm not a failure.

I'm not a waste of space.

I'm not a liability—well, I may be, actually, but I'm definitely not a quitter. And maybe, just maybe, everything I've been told up to this point has some real merit to it. Some truth.

I stare at them each in turn, my mother, my sister, my girlfriend. And that *something* from before swells up inside me.

Only this time, I recognise it.

Warmth. Love. Respect. Awe. All those things and more, wrapped up in one neat package in the form of all these people out in the middle of nowhere to protect me. *Me.*

Well, fuck.

Fiona gently taps my shoulder. "You were longer that time. I at least was able to help you to the ground before you threw me aside. You have to go again, child. Can you do it?"

Rayne grips my face and kisses me hard. "I'm not giving up on you," she whispers. "Never. I'll meet the sun before I do."

Never. No fucking way.

"Do it," I tell Fiona.

Once more, her hands press to the bare skin of my back.

I land in the darkness with a thump that forces me to bend my knees. I'm upright, standing and tall, while the yellow-eyed creature considers me closely.

The darkness is flecked with still more red, like little motes of blood spinning through the air.

The grim thought only makes me angry.

"You lied," I tell it.

That smile again. The one with a void of nothingness opening up in the yawning space passing for a mouth. "You told me that fake memories have no power over you, little bird, so I found a real one. Your very own mother abandoned and left you. Tell me, what about that is a lie?"

I toss my head. "My mother is holding my hand right now. So is my sister."

"No, you—"

"Can't see that, can you?" I take a step forward. "They came to support me because they give a shit. And they're there right now. And my friends are out there."

"You're in my domain now, little bi—"

I cut it off with a swipe of my hand. "My name is Danika. And I think you'll find that *you're* in *mine*. Magick circle. Surrounded by *edanes* and humans and a freaking witch with nothing better to do than to cast you the fuck out."

For the first time, the creature seems concerned.

The red flecks floating in the air grow thicker.

I bat them aside. Step forward. "Leave. There's nothing left for you now."

"But you're not finished singing for me. I love your song of pain and suffering and—"

"I'm a terrible singer." Another step forward. "Unless I'm in the shower. But even then, you're not invited."

It hesitates. Yellow eyes blink rapidly, and…is it smaller now?

One more step forward.

"Pain? I have that for days. Do you have any idea how many times I've been bitten, stabbed, cut, and even shot?" I shudder at the memory of that little mishap. Sure it was only a graze, straight through and out the meaty flesh of my arm, but yeah, that one hurt.

Still I press forward. "And suffering is listening to Maury go through yet another meeting that could and should have been an email. But they're *my* pain and suffering, understand? Not yours or anything to feed to your creepy, faceless master."

Again the creature moves in, long black arms extended.

I don't care.

This time I barrel straight into it, and as the mouth opens once more to speak, I shove my own hand in.

"How do you like it?" I yell, pushing harder and further as I rage. "You want me? Take me if you can, you fuck. But you'd better be ready because there's not yet one person on earth who can handle me."

The creature struggles. Tries to pull back.

I hold on, actually grip tighter and force the thing closer. And as I do, my hand dips deeper.

Up to my wrist. Further.

The sensation resembles dipping my fingers into thin, cloying threads of yarn.

I don't care.

More. I give it more, and with each push I pour in my anger, my frustration, my fear, and most of all my pain.

"You want this?" I yell. "Then take it. And take your poorly designed back tattoo with you. Take it and crawl back into whatever pit you oozed out of."

The creature screeches wildly. It struggles and flails and tries to fade into smoke.

But I don't let go.

And still I push.

I close my eyes, and just as Tina described, I force my will on the damn thing.

*Take it*, I chant over and over in the back of my mind. *Take it. I don't want it. Take your damn mark. Take your master. Take your own lying self and get the hell out of my body.*

My back roars with pain, white hot needles of pain slamming into my skin over and over and over.

I want to throw up.

But I can't let go.

I have to keep pushing.

It's working. I can feel it.

*Something* is moving, and whatever it is, I know it's something I don't want to hold on to.

"But you killed the werewolf, little bird—"

"Wendy made a choice," I shoot back. "It was stupid, and I didn't help matters, but he'd be pissed if I tried to take credit for something *he* decided to do. So no. Try again."

The words stutter. Struggle.

Still I push.

"Your sister is an undead monster—"

"And so is my girlfriend. Next."

"Y-you—your peers don't—"

I laugh. "My friends are outside. Want to see them? I'll show you each of their faces before I hurl you out into space."

"T-this is your purpose. Your body is perfect for my master."

One more push. My arm is deep in this creature as far as the elbow and…What's that?

I flex my fingers. Feel around.

There.

A tiny round ball. Soft. Wet, even. Slightly squishy.

All around me, the creature flexes and struggles, now clearly panicked.

A shriek, so loud it rattles my brain in my skull.

More pain.

But at this point, physical pain is nothing.

I think about losing Rayne. I think about losing Pippa. I think about never seeing my mother again. I think about failing the one thing I promised myself I would do all those years ago when I danced into that shopping centre, showing my father that brand new SPEAR ID lanyard.

*Don't hesitate*, he told me.

*Never*, I told him.

I don't think, simply squeeze.

The wet, squishy ball explodes between my fingers, flattening into a weird, sticky mush.

Another agony-laced yell comes from the creature, and I yank my hand free, bringing with it a lumpy, sticky mass of thin yellow pus.

A peeling sensation washes across my back. Fuck, like someone tearing the skin from my flesh…or an unnatural brand from my body.

With one last yell of defiance, I pull back my hand and hurl the sticky yellow mass as far from me as I can manage.

"Get lost," I bellow, "and take your master with you."

Screams fade before me. Darkness closes in. The world drops out from beneath my feet, and I fall down, down, down, down forever…

❖

Shit. Fuck. Why is the floor so cold?

I groan and spit a damp, gritty mouthful of gunk onto the floor. Yup. More dirt and that mix of sweet-smelling herbs. Yuck.

Someone is pulling at me, trying to turn me over. My limbs feel like wet cardboard, so I don't fight it. They turn me, I blink, and there is the sky again. But in front of it is my mother.

Damn. Is she crying?

"Danika? My baby, my sweet baby girl. My girl." And she's hugging me. No, she's crushing me, flinging both arms around my neck and clinging as though I might be the only thing to save her from drowning. She buries her face in the bend of my shoulder and cries and cries and cries some more.

I pat her back gently.

"Mum."

"I'm so sorry." Her voice is a low wail. "It should never have come to this. I should have been with you. What kind of mother am I?"

A tear catches in my eye. "The best one."

"No, I should never have abandoned you. I should—"

"Mum, shut up."

A hiccup of surprise, but she does, for a wonder, stop talking.

In the still I'm able to look around me.

Tina is walking around the circle, anticlockwise this time. Her voice is raised, and she seems to be thanking the Guardians for watching over us all. As she moves, the shimmering whiteness breaks in the centre and begins to drop down, like a curtain of night falling. When it reaches the ground, the edges begin to trace the path she walks, until back at her start point, the shimmer fades to nothing and is gone.

At last I can see clearly outside. Confused faces. Concerned faces. Curious faces. No one moves yet, apparently afraid to come closer, but I do notice that Fiona has slumped down to sit a little way away.

I flail a hand in her direction. It's the most I can manage with Mum still clinging to me.

She smiles. "It's gone, child."

Mum's head bobs in an enthusiastic nod. "You know how I feel about tattoos, baby, but it's gone now. Imagine, all that tribal marking all over your back. Why would you do such a thing?"

I stare at her, open-mouthed.

Just behind, I hear laughter and realise that Pippa and Rayne are right there. They're hugging each other, trying to stop the red smears of tears streaking their faces, but neither of them are having much luck. The tears are as obvious as their joy and relief, and I treasure both.

When I feel around my back, as far as my stiff arms can reach, sure enough there is nothing there. The skin is sore and tender, but the raised edges of the marks are no longer present. More than that, I feel light, as though I could leap to my feet and keep going, up and up and up some more. One bound could take me into the sky high enough to reach clouds, and I would float down slowly and gracefully like a dropped feather.

The chill of the air whirls around me, ruffling my locs, goose-pimpling my skin. I try to wrap my arms around myself, but Mum is still there, still holding, still clinging.

Instead, she runs a hand over my dirty, gritty hair. "Danika, baby, you need a steam treatment."

I laugh. Can't help it. "Says you," I shoot back. "Never seen your hair look so dry."

"Worry will do that to you." At last she lets go and allows me to stand.

My legs wobble, my knees tremble, but I'm up. One step, then two, and then I'm walking, unsteady but mobile. I make my way to Fiona, who hasn't yet moved, staring at her scarred hands with curiosity in her eyes.

"Are you okay?"

She frowns. "I think so, child. That thing, whatever it was, is gone. I can't feel it in or around you any more."

"Good. It overstayed its welcome."

"Perhaps. But it isn't dead."

It takes little effort to catch the unspoken worry. "I don't think it *can* be killed."

A nod. "I agree. But at least it no longer wants you."

"I'll take it."

"I do wonder where it went, though."

I shrug. "Wherever it hides between showings. If the writings of your family are to be believed, we may not see it again for a few hundred years."

Fiona stands. Her hair has tumbled from the pile on top of her head to billow around her in grey waves. She sighs and flexes her fingers. "Then I've a lot of writing to do. We know we can be rid of the thing. I must detail everything that happened here tonight. I never want a descendant of mine to face what I have over the past two days."

"Hey"—I touch her arm—"you didn't do anything wrong. Please believe that. And if not for you, who knows what would have happened to me."

She smiles, but the gesture is sad. "I've so much to learn about my gifts. About how to treat those who don't understand what it is to see. Child, thank you for allowing me to right my wrong."

"Thank *you* for putting yourself on the line for me. I've already cost you so much"—I eye her hands—"but you came for me anyway. And you didn't have to."

A small flap of the hand, as if to wave away my words. Then she slowly walks away, towards the edge of the circle.

Pippa is directly behind me. With a squeal she throws herself onto my back and clings. I allow her the awkward hug, then turn to embrace her properly.

"Why are you always getting into trouble, Dani?" she whispers, no longer making an effort to hide her tears.

"Pure skill," I shoot back. "You know me, right?"

A little cough of laughter. "I know you and I love you and you're an idiot and I can't believe it—"

"It's okay, Pip."

But I can't believe it either. Mere hours ago, I'd been sitting in a closed-off room, writing goodbye letters to all the people I care about—and some to those I don't. Now, I'm in a campsite, half naked, watching the stars and moon shine their brightness down on a brand-new start. A fresh beginning. A second chance.

She cups my face in her hands and I do the same with hers. We stare, for long moments, drinking each other in, reminding ourselves that we have more days ahead of us now due to the incredible kindness and strength of others.

"Talk to Mum," I tell her gently. "I'll be with you in a second."

She nods and slips away, quickly gathering our mother with her to the outer edge of the circle.

Last. Not least.

Rayne waits patiently for me. Her eyes are wide and rimmed with red, her hands fidgeting in front of her. Her mussed-up hair is ruffled gently in the low breeze as she finally takes a step towards me.

"Danika—"

But I don't need to hear anything she has to say. Right now I don't think I can stand it. So instead I rush to her, I pull her to me, and I hold her tight. She folds into my embrace, resting her head on my shoulder, pressing every part of her body as close to me as she can get.

"You never gave up on me even for a second," I murmur into her hair.

"Of course not."

"You never let me give up on myself."

"You're not a quitter," she says simply.

I squeeze tighter. She's a vampire, she can take it, I know she can, even with our distinct height differences. So I hold on for long, glorious moments, drinking her in, enjoying her smell, her touch, her taste as I press my lips to the top of her head.

Fuck. To think I almost lost this. That I almost gave up.

"Hey"—she pokes me—"stop it."

"What?"

"You're thinking something sad. I can hear your breathing. It's okay. It's over. You made it. We made it."

But as I hold her and those outside the circle finally begin to come closer, I wonder how true that is.

Everyone coos and ahs over the clearness of my back, over the spectacle of—from their perspective—watching me thrash about on the ground for a few moments before the black traces simply melted away like paint. It seems so easy and simple when put that way.

But I'm tired. I'm so, so tired.

Rayne helps me away from the centre of the circle while Tina gathers up the candles. She gives me a cheerful wave and a tilt of the head, which holds the smallest trace of I-told-you-so energy. The Fire Fang xiblings gather around me, chattering and arguing as ever they do. Even my Kappa team gather close, with Hawk daring to sweep me up into the air with his powerful arms, his wings spread wide in pleasure.

But I'm tired.

The whole time Rayne stays close, her presence a beautiful, comforting, soothing balm to my frayed nerves.

And as talk begins to gather pace on how to get everyone home, I realise that I'll be able to lie on my back without pain or discomfort for the first time in weeks. Not only that, but I may even get a full night's sleep if I don't have to worry about the yellow-eyed creature filling my dreams with nightmares.

Sounds blissful.

Why then do I feel weary? Not just sleepy-tired, but exhausted right down to my very bones.

So very, very tired.

And as Pippa grabs my hand on one side and my mother snags the other, I wonder if this is the sort of fatigue I'll actually be able to recover from.

# Chapter Thirty-four

Rayne gives me a comforting squeeze as I stand before the plain, nondescript door that marks the agent entrance for SPEAR headquarters.

My palms are slick with sweat, my forehead the same. I wipe both with my sleeves, then steel myself one more time to enter.

"Are you sure you want to do this?" Her smile is so gentle and kind. And her eyes…that colour of ripe acorns, all the most gorgeous shades of autumn gathered together and captured in her gaze. I could stare into her eyes forever.

"Never been more sure." I squeeze her hand gently. "How long can I really stay away?"

She lifts an eyebrow at me.

And she's right, of course. Maury has given me as much time off as I need. Paid too. After the ritual, before hopping onto his bike, he had hugged me—actually hugged me—and promised to see me right in the days after. And he had. True to his word, he appointed Solo my second in command and Hawk after that, allowing the Kappa team to continue functioning, though I've no idea how much work they managed to do, given how much time they spent with me.

My house has become something of a meeting hub for my closest friends, with Noel and Tina in particular barely leaving. Tina has become obsessed with the idea that I could actually see her magic circle and often casts small ones in the kitchen to see if I can repeat the trick.

I can't, of course. No doubt it was Fiona's influence that allowed me to see anything that night. She is the psychic, after all.

And Noel? Well, he and Jadz moved our poker operation right to my living room and spent hour after fun-filled hour cracking jokes, serving up spicy foods, and cheating me out of more matchsticks, though Jadz's skills as a Grey Tail have to work doubly hard whenever Rayne finds herself in our games.

But after a week, my nerves begin to itch, my boredom kicks in, and I realise that I don't have to stay home any more. Sure, Clear Blood and all the researchers are stunned at my miraculous recovery, but given that my back is as clear as ever it was, they can't quite find a reason to keep me under lock and key.

There are questions, of course. Oh, there are questions, and I know of at least three internal enquires that will put the actions of myself, Rayne, and Noel under a fine microscope. Neither of them seems worried, though. Perhaps they're too relieved to see me in one piece to recognise the potential impact their actions could have on their futures at SPEAR. Maybe they don't care. I don't know, and they won't tell me.

I put myself in front of the retinal scanner and let it collect my credentials. It beeps and blurps through reading off my ID before doing the same to Rayne. And then the upgraded checks for *edane* workers, including holy water spray, silver hand scanners, and iron plates.

The norm.

I perform each check in turn with my heart thudding somewhere near my throat.

Why am I so nervous?

Of course I've done these checks hundreds if not thousands of times over my years as a SPEAR. I know the words and the process and the timings inside out. I can even measure my steps perfectly from one end to the other, so I've no need to stop at any point.

But for some reason, stepping into the place after so long away feels…strange. Distant. Unusual.

Through the security measures, we step into the staff side of headquarters. As ever, that sci-fi novel, vintage American police station mash-up prompts a smile. A smile that wilts when a booming voice fills my ears.

"And here she is, agent of the hour, woman of the year, downright lucky bitch, and pain in my arse, Agent Danika Karson." Maury stands on a table, yelling out over the office as I walk deeper into the clear space.

What the hell?

There are cheers, loud and lively, as I walk over the middle of the floor, my booted feet scuffing against the SPEAR insignia laid out on the ground—crossed swords above a single arrow surrounded by flares of light. Our motto is underneath that, in Latin, though of course I know well the English translation.

Protect and serve. Learn and understand. Hunt and exterminate.

I stare, open-mouthed, at the gathering before me, struggling to figure out what on earth is happening.

Someone I don't know shoves a champagne glass into my startled hands and ushers me towards the centre where there is a cleared space just waiting for someone to fill it.

With most of the desks scattered out on one side, and the training booth behind Plexiglas tucked against another wall, there is plenty of space for people to gather. And gather they have. Agents from every grade and team fill the space with filled glasses of their own.

On the left there is food, laid out in a huge, wide array of snacks and finger bits, including sandwiches, biscuits, cheese, chicken wings, quiche, and some weird pink stuff that looks like a meaty, sickly jelly.

Rayne hurries to my side, looking as alarmed as I feel. "I—I didn't know about this," she murmurs. "No one told me and I—"

She breaks off as Maury leaps down from the table and hurries towards us. He still has the microphone in one hand and now a champagne flute in the other. His grin is wide and slightly mad as he rounds to address the crowd of gathered agents.

"Everyone, everyone, settle down. Come on. We have a lot to get through. Danika, this way please." He snags my arm, tugging me away from Rayne despite our twin protests. "Now then"—his smile broadens—"I know we don't normally do things like this, but I think, this once, it's worth acknowledging the occasion."

I squirm back and forth on my heels and toes.

Why has he brought me to the middle of all this? Wasn't the applause and yelling of my name enough of an embarrassment to see me through the day?

"Maury, I—"

"Danika Karson has been an agent of SPEAR for the last eight years." He speaks right over me, now into the microphone again to address the crowd. His voice seems to come from every direction all at once. "The youngest woman to ever join the regiment and, to date, the operative with the highest capture rate ever known."

Polite applause, sprinkled with whoops of pleasure or admiration.

My cheeks grow hot.

Fuck. Why do people insist on using those two facts to mark my skill? Once upon a time I was proud of them, but the last fact, which he has mercifully left off, is the one that people used to quote the most. My kill rate. Before I understood what being *edane* could truly mean. Before I knew what vampires had the capacity to be. Before I met Rayne.

She meets my eyes but says nothing, instead making *steady* gestures with her hands.

Instead of watching Maury, I keep my eyes locked on her, a source of steadiness and calm in a sea of noise, baffling movement, and intensity.

"Over the years Danika has given herself wholly to what we do here, protecting anybody and everybody who has ever needed it, serving the greater good that we do here. I know first-hand how much time and effort she has put into learning new things and understanding the differences between humans and *edanes* to bring us together. And yes, I've already mentioned her numbers. In all, Agent Karson is a prime example of exactly what it is to be an agent of SPEAR."

More applause and cheering.

I feel sick.

Once more I try to scoot away, but now Maury has his arm around my shoulders, holding me in place. The champagne glass tilts worryingly close to dousing me in alcohol, and I push gently at the rim with my fingertip to steady it.

He doesn't even notice.

"Some of you may know what happened early last week, but for those of you who don't, it's important that you understand the significance of it all."

I brace myself.

"During the Werewolf Wars, Agent Karson sustained an injury that we later came to know was truly life threatening. An unknown creature intended to use Agent Karson as a host for a larger, more cruel entity that we now know feasts on the likes of fear, anger, and general discourse, the very things produced by the Werewolf Wars. If not for her incredible efforts then and since, those few days under the command of the EMCU could have been significantly worse for us, for humans, and for everything Angbec is doing as a whole to normalise real relationships between humans and *edanes*. To say she took one for the team that night is a wild understatement."

"Maury, please—"

He grins. "Don't be modest now. We know it's true." Again to the wider room, "And in doing so she sustained the injury that left her banned from active duty for several weeks. An injury that we later learned required drastic action to prevent further loss of life. Sacrifice. A fatal sacrifice."

The heat in my cheeks intensifies.

This time when I try to squirm away, Maury actually yanks me closer to him, grinning like a madman out at the gathered agents. "When we join SPEAR, every single one of us makes a promise. An oath. We swear to do everything in our power to protect those in need and to give our lives to the cause if necessary. Agent Karson"—he smiles at me—"Danika…was willing to do that. When the difficult decision to end her life was made, she accepted it with grace and understanding until circumstances changed enough to reverse that decision."

Oh. So he's not going to tell the whole story?

On the one hand, that's great, because I don't think I could cope if my colleagues and peers knew exactly how low I had been that night. Or if they truly understood just what had been asked of me.

This vague, glossy version of my *adventures* is sanitised enough to be palatable for those who aren't in the know, and yet with so little detail that even I have questions. And I was there.

"But the fact remains that she was willing to do it. And that sacrifice is one that can't and won't be forgotten." The smile softens to something less manic. "Agent Danika Karson, you are a shining example of what it is to be a SPEAR, and nothing you've done for us will ever be forgotten. Please accept my personal thanks and those of every member of our team as we raise our glasses to you."

That's the cue.

The entire room lifts their champagne glass. Then Maury. "To Danika Karson," he murmurs.

The words are repeated all over the room, back and forth, over and over until the call of my name resembles that of the riots outside this very building as well as Clear Blood.

I swallow back the spiky lump at the back of my throat and hide the panic by taking large, gulping slugs of my own drink. Of course I start coughing immediately, at which point Maury laughs riotously and slaps me hard on the back.

It doesn't help.

I recover in time to catch the microphone as Maury slams it into my hands.

"Speech," he cries, and that call is taken up over and over and over around me.

I clutch my empty champagne glass, stare at the microphone as though it were a deadly viper.

Really? They want me to talk? Have they ever met me? Surely they understand there isn't a damn thing I can say to match a situation like this.

But the call has become a chant. A playful, lively one, like at a football match, but the desire is clear.

*Speech. Speech. Speech. Speech. Speech.*

I look to Rayne.

She gives me a comforting nod. "I believe in you," she mouths at me.

Deep breath.

Slowly I raise the microphone to my lips.

The chant gives way to raucous cheering.

I open my mouth, and just like I practised, the words simply fall out. "I quit."

The cheering takes a while to catch up. Not surprising since I'm willing to bet cold, hard cash that wasn't what anybody was expecting to hear.

When the cheers die off to be replaced by curious murmurs, I repeat myself.

"I quit, guys."

More murmurs. Some coughing.

Maury snatches for the microphone, but I angle it away from him. They wanted a speech. Fine. I can give them a speech.

"Thank you for all of this, truly. You daft idiots are as much my family as anybody related by blood, and I'm lucky to know every single one of you. We've been through a lot together as well. Werewolf Wars are one thing, but everything before that?" I smile. "The memories I'm taking away from this place will live with me forever. Chasing pixies down sewer pipes. Climbing the walls of abandoned churches to reach gargoyle nests. Hunting vampires who refuse to register for a Foundation ID. Pulling civilians out of collapsing buildings. Getting to use that amazing troll battleaxe—that thing is *so* cool. We've done so much good together in the time I've been here, but I have to be honest with you all…I'm tired."

Silence now.

Never in all my time at SPEAR have I ever heard this space so silent. Even the chittarik normally roosting in the ceiling seem to be absent today, maybe to stop the gathered agents getting pelted with falling droppings, but it gives the huge space such a strange, eerie edge.

"I'm tired, and I know better."

Maury again tries to reach for the microphone. He looks frightened, but I keep him at bay with my hand against his chest.

"Let me," I murmur.

"Can't we talk about this first? Please. You can't do this now, we need you and—"

"No. I quit. Right now, right this second. In fact…" And I start to pull off my gear. It takes a while, and Maury uses that time to finally sneak the microphone away from me, but I don't care. With so much attention focused wholly on me, I don't need it anyway.

Guns. Knives. Utility belt. Various small weapons dotted across my person. The stiletto blade I've returned to keeping in my hair. All of it goes into a pile on the nearest table. A pile that slides slowly into a plate of pineapple and cheese cubes skewered on toothpicks. On top of all of it, I place my ID badge.

"Guys, I need you to understand something." My voice is no longer amplified, but it doesn't matter. My sudden resolve lifts my voice high and strong, allow me to project it out to the far reaches of the room. "I was ready to die that night. It was an inevitability. There was a vote, and members of the Crown Court of Supernatural Justice as well as SPEARs and the general came to that conclusion. I was pissed at first, but then I remembered what I was taught. What we're all taught."

Now the words are coming, and I don't know how to stop them.

I hadn't meant to do it like this.

When agreeing to come to SPEAR this evening, my intent had been to quietly take Maury to an office room and tell him my plans. But somehow, with all my fellow agents—ex fellow agents?—gathered around me, I realise how important it is to share what I've learned.

"We are trained to die for what we do. And that's fine. I was never, ever afraid to die for the work I do here. But through that teaching, somehow we learn that we give up our lives because others are worth more. We really are just agents to protect and serve everybody else. And that's all I've known. For eight years."

The silence is so very intense.

I hate it.

I turn quickly, find Rayne and her peaceful gaze in that sea of intense, confused staring. I drink her in and use her silent support as a springboard to keep going.

I need to say this. And everybody needs to hear it.

"Unconsciously or otherwise, I've taken on the teaching that my life is worth less than those of the people we serve. And I believed it. For so long. But that night, when I knew I was going to die, it took others to remind me that that isn't okay. That my life isn't a poker chip to trade in when the betting requires it. They taught me that my life is worth something and that while I may be prepared to give it up, that shouldn't be an expectation. Nobody should be *expected* to give up their own life when things get tough, because every life is precious."

My voice hitches, and I have to swallow several times to moisten my lips. It barely works. My mouth is dry, my forehead is soaked with sweat, and my hands are shaking. But I'm nearly there. I have to get the last few words out.

"My life is precious," I whisper, "and every life deserves to be saved. Even mine." Deep breath. "But my life has become a tool for SPEAR over the last eight years. A tool that can easily be replaced with another when it breaks. My life has no value except as a means to serve others. But I realised, that night, that my life is worth so much more. I have a sister, a mother, a girlfriend, friends, colleagues—and every single one of them put their lives on the line to save mine. Not because SPEAR expected them to—fuck, SPEAR actively tried to stop them. These people did it to save *my* life, because my life is valuable."

Rayne nods. Her eyes sparkle with the redness of unshed tears.

"So in honour of them and for myself, I choose to keep my life." I sigh. "And don't get me wrong, I'll always be a SPEAR in my heart. I don't think I could just stop looking out for people, but it's time to recognise that I'm worth saving too."

Silence. Painful, uncomfortable, thick, cloying silence.

Then somewhere near the back, someone lets out a huge, bellowing whoop.

Heads turn.

I crane my neck.

Hawk springs up onto a table at the back of the room. His wings are spread and his eyes are lively and he pumps at the air with one huge fist. "Damn right you're worth something, boss. About time you saw it for yourself."

The table rocks violently as Erkyan clambers onto it.

"You're a good person. Always. Time for rest now, I say." Her voice is nowhere near as loud and booming, but somehow she makes herself heard.

Behind them a flash of red appears, joined by a similar blur of orange. Solo and Duo hop onto tables of their own and begin to clap.

They're alone until Hawk joins them, then Erkyan. Willow is soon after, sliding forward in her graceful way to gently pat her long-fingered hands together.

No one joins them.

The office space is filled with confused stares and baffled whispers, but I don't care. My own eyes fill with tears as I watch my team give me their support and love, still making noise enough to serve the place of several more agents.

Noisy fucks.

Rayne hurries to my side and pulls me into a gentle hug. She presses her lips lightly to my cheeks, then tugs me away towards the doors.

"Wait!" That's Maury, scurrying after us with my ID badge dangling from his grip. "Please rethink this. There's so much more you can do here. Why would you leave now, after everything you've been through?"

I wish I could tell him. I wish I could phrase it in a way he might be able to understand, but he's been a SPEAR longer than I have. And he's worked up the ranks, just as I did, to become leader of the alpha team. In this country, there's probably no other agent with more authority and power than him.

I pat his shoulder gently but say nothing. What more can I say?

"Danika, please."

I smile. "I'll be back in later to discuss my P45. For now, though, I want to spend some time at home."

He watches, helpless and forlorn, as I walk away to the sound of more cheers and whooping from my ex-teammates.

# CHAPTER THIRTY-FIVE

Oh. Gross. I'd forgotten about the smell.

Unlike his predecessor, Jackson Cobé, mayor of Angbec, has chosen to house his office in the building of his original job. Instead of City Hall, Jack's office is on the upper floors of the Clear Blood Foundation he helped to build with his miraculous Life Blood Serum. A chemist, first and foremost, his personal space is littered with notes, stacks of papers, old journals, and the remnants of several experiments from his past. And dozens upon dozens of little bowls or balls of potpourri.

I dunk my hand into one of the bowls and pull out a lump of dried rose petals.

"Do you really need all this?"

He sniffs from his comfortable seat behind his desk. "Do *you* understand what it's like to stink of chemicals all day?"

"You could shower."

A sigh. "Sit down, Danika."

Still fiddling with the petals, I do as I'm told.

He eyes me for several seconds.

I can't look at him. So I don't try.

Instead I watch the petals crumble into sweet-scented pink dust in my palms.

"No more SPEAR, huh?"

I shrug. "I had a good run."

"Bullshit."

That gets my attention. I do look at him now, watching his face and his expression shift as he notices my surprise.

"Come on. I might not know you well, but I know you well enough to understand that this is no small change for you. SPEAR has been your life for longer than I've known you."

"It's not like we've known each other for years and years."

"Stop deflecting," he snaps.

I bite my lip.

"I may not understand all the reasoning behind why you quit, but I get enough. Or like to think I do. It must have been a shock to realise how quickly you could be disposed of."

Another shrug. I like this man, but there's no way I'm letting him that far into my head. I don't think I have the stamina.

"But protecting people is in your blood. I know about Charles."

I frown at him without really meaning to. "My dad—"

"Was a good man, from what I've heard. But that's by the by. I just mean that he worked security to protect people. You became a SPEAR to do the same. I don't think the drive or the urge to do that will go away just because you quit your job."

"So...?"

"So I want to offer you a new one."

That sits me straight in my chair. "One what? A job?"

He nods. "It's weird around here. Clear Blood has always been the centre of this city. What we do here has allowed us to do what we do and be an example for the rest of the country. But lately there have been...problems."

"Yeah, sorry about that."

Jack winks. "Apology accepted, but you can't take on all the blame. The shifting werewolf packs, the sudden influx of unregistered vampires, and of course every other *edane* type in the country has been making their way here. We're not at saturation point, but with such an"—he waves a hand around—"eclectic mix in such a small space, there are bound to be problems."

"And that has what to do with me?"

"I want you to work for me."

I plant my hands on the arms of my chair and push to my feet. "What is it with the mayors of this city? When will you lot understand that I'm not a gun for hire, I'm a—"

"SPEAR agent?" he murmurs, with a wry lift of an eyebrow.

I freeze, halfway to straight.

He has a point.

Slowly, I plant my arse back in the chair. "Fine. Tell me."

"SPEAR has all sorts of rules they have to follow to stay in line with what the general wants. More than that, they are beholden to a specific set of guidelines and priorities that the average agent has no control over. You deserve more than that."

My fingertips prickle, a curious combination of nerves and… anticipation? "Go on."

"You'll report to me, because I'll be paying your salary, but you'll work on your own, under your own guidance, under your own direction."

"Doing what?"

He grins, and in that moment I finally recognise the excitement bubbling just beneath the surface of his calm, professional demeanour. "Research. Investigatory private detective work. Negotiations. All for Clear Blood."

"I don't understand."

Jack scrambles from his seat to reach my chair. This close I can clearly see the make-up he insists on wearing and smell the cologne he wears to combat the scent of I don't even know what. His boyish face is bright and animated with some of that rakish cheek and playfulness left over from the very first time we met.

"Essentially you'll be a SPEAR in everything but name because you'll be employed by Clear Blood. You'll be working for me." When I open my mouth, he rushes on. "There are so many different *edane* habitats and creatures we've yet to meet. In order for Clear Blood to continue doing what we do, I need to have a capable, reliable, and self-sufficient person I can send out to various places to get in contact with these people. I need someone who can chase down leads for things we're doing here that SPEAR just doesn't have time for. And more than that, I need someone who is free to work outside the city."

I sigh. He beams.

"Jack—"

"You don't have to do anything now. You don't have to say anything now. Just think about it. Please? I already have so many ideas about how you can help me, and you've got to admit, the relationships you already have with various *edanes* make you the perfect candidate for this type of work. You'll be a public relations specialist who happens to be really good with a gun."

"Or my fists," I add.

A chuckle and Jack rubs gently at the spot on his jaw where I punched him so many months ago. "Especially with your fists," he murmurs. "So. Will you think about it? I'll come up with a title later— Edane Public Relations Specialist or something like that. But tell me— would you consider it?"

"I…" My breathing catches in my throat. "Sure. I'll think about it. No promises, though."

He backs off at once, hands raised. "Of course not. And no

pressure either. But if it helps, consider this a pay hike of at least twenty percent and a personal budget to buy whatever kit you might need to keep yourself safe out there." He rubs the sides of his mouth with his fingertips. "I can't promise any battleaxes or whatever it is you like, but I can promise state of the art weaponry if you want it, complete with any modifications you could possibly want as designed by the Clear Blood tech team."

I tut softly. "You're not selling it, Jack. I really like axes."

"Fine, fine, how about we make you an axe? Would you say yes, then?"

I stand for real this time and back away from the chair and the table. "I'm thinking about it, okay? Give me some time."

He nods. "Sure. Fine. Don't worry about it. Take all the time you want…until next Thursday. I need to know if you'll be able to visit some cecaelia on the north coast who have been wrecking fishing boats."

Some *what*? I've no idea what to address first, but that entire sentence is dripping with problems.

"You know we're one of the most landlocked cities in the country, right? Why are you sending me to the coast? We don't have any real power there beyond capture or retrieve."

*They*, I remind myself. They don't have any power. I can no longer count myself among them.

"SPEAR don't yet." Jack's eyes take on an excited sparkle. "But Clear Blood does. Remember, Clear Blood provides Life Blood for blood banks up and down the country. This is our base, but we have research points in six major cities. In this role, I'll be able to send you anywhere you're needed with all the prestige and power of a SPEAR and none of the restrictions."

I nod, quietly.

Part of me recognises that I've already accepted his offer. What he describes sounds incredible, and working for him rather than the general allows me a peace I've not felt since I met the enigmatic vampire. Not that working for an *edane* is bad exactly, but a creature with such a long life is likely to have a very different outlook on life and its worth compared to a human. A truth I've already experienced first-hand.

So yes, I will take his offer.

No need to make it easy for him, though. It might be fun to see him sweat for a bit.

So I wave my goodbyes and walk out of the office. Down the corridor, into the lift, and down to the ground floor where Rayne and Pippa sit waiting for me in the casual lounge. Pippa is dressed for work, her own ID lanyard tucked into a pocket in the front of her lab coat. Rayne is also dressed for work, casually, in a high-necked top and jeans studded with pockets.

I really have had an obvious influence on her, in more ways than one.

They greet me with smiles and curiosity live and eager in their eyes.

I grin. "Jack offered me a job."

Pippa rolls her eyes, muttering something about a biochemistry degree being worth less and less as the years go on. She hugs me briefly and, satisfied that I'm not in trouble yet again, returns to her own work on the research floors.

Rayne touches my hip lightly, a small smile playing on the corners of her lips. "You say he *offered* you a job. Do you mean that you *have* a new job?"

I shrug, playful and coy, but she knows me better than that.

"What does he want you to do?"

I link my arms through hers and steer us both out of the lush, immaculately decorated public-facing waiting room to the large, sparkling exit doors.

"He wants me to be a SPEAR."

She looks the question at me.

"The real version of SPEAR. One that extends beyond the city to do work in bringing humans and *edanes* together instead of simply policing one or the other."

Slowly, thoughtfully, she nods. "Sounds fulfilling."

There. That's the word. One I might never have managed to pick up on my own. Then again, Rayne has proved time and time again that she is the smart one when it comes to articulating her thoughts.

"It should be. No matter how niche and weird being a SPEAR was, there was always a layer of red tape over everything that made it hard to do anything."

"And now?"

"It will still be there, but bullying Jack will be much easier than fighting Maury."

Rayne tosses her head back and laughs. It's such a bright and merry sound. I could listen to her laugh all day, every day for the rest of my life.

Hey, given that I suddenly have way more life than I thought I would, maybe that's a possibility now.

We make our way to the car arm in arm, she to start her next shift, me to carefully consider the words of my soon to be drafted acceptance letter.

Edane Public Relations Specialist? A bit of a mouthful, but no more than the Supernatural Prohibition Extermination and Arrest Regiment.

Yeah. I'll give it a go. After all, it can't be any worse than what I've already been through, right?

# About the Author

Ileandra Young writes urban fantasy novels, has an unhealthy obsession with vampires, and would gleefully pick a sword over any other weapon. Yes, even that one.

She spends far more time in fantasy lands than the real one, since her hobbies include LARPing, TTRPGs, and more recently, *Stardew Valley*, as well as *Minecraft* and *Tears Of The Kingdom*. If she does graciously deign to visit the real world, you'll find her sitting in a corner, crocheting something weird while scream-singing snippets from the *Hamilton* soundtrack.

What a weirdo!

Visit her website at www.ileandrayoung.co.uk.

# Books Available From Bold Strokes Books

**Blood Rage** by Illeandra Young. A stolen artifact, a family in the dark, an entire city on edge. Can SPEAR agent Danika Karson juggle all three over a weekend with the "in-laws" while an unknown, malevolent entity lies in wait upon her very skin? (978-1-63679-539-3)

**Ghost Town** by R.E. Ward. Blair Wyndon and Leif Henderson are set to prove ghosts exist when the mystery suddenly turns deadly. Someone or something else is in Masonville, and if they don't find a way to escape, they might never leave. (978-1-63679-523-2)

**Good Christian Girls** by Elizabeth Bradshaw. In this heartfelt coming of age lesbian romance, Lacey and Jo help each other untangle who they are from who everyone says they're supposed to be. (978-1-63679-555-3)

**Guide Us Home** by CF Frizzell and Jesse J. Thoma. When acquisition of an abandoned lighthouse pits ambitious competitors Nancy and Sam against each other, it takes a WWII tale of two brave women to make them see the light. (978-1-63679-533-1)

**Lost Harbor** by Kimberly Cooper Griffin. For Alice and Bridget's love to survive, they must find a way to reconcile the most important passions in their lives—devotion to the church and each other. (978-1-63679-463-1)

**Never a Bridesmaid** by Spencer Greene. As her sister's wedding gets closer, Jessica finds that her hatred for the maid of honor is a bit more complicated than she thought. Could it be something more than hatred? (978-1-63679-559-1)

**The Rewind** by Nicole Stiling. For police detective Cami Lyons and crime reporter Alicia Flynn, some choices break hearts. Others leave a body count. (978-1-63679-572-0)

**Turning Point** by Cathy Dunnell. When Asha and her former high school bully Jody struggle to deny their growing attraction, can they move forward without going back? (978-1-63679-549-2)

**When Tomorrow Comes** by D. Jackson Leigh. Teague Maxwell, convinced she will die before she turns 41, hires animal rescue owner Baye Cobb to rehome her extensive menagerie. (978-1-63679-557-7)

**You Had Me at Merlot** by Melissa Brayden. Leighton and Jamie have all the ingredients to turn their attraction into love, but it's a recipe for disaster.(978-1-63679-543-0)

**Appalachian Awakening** by Nance Sparks. The more Amber's and Leslie's paths cross, the more this hike of a lifetime begins to look like a love of a lifetime. (978-1-63679-527-0)

**Dreamer** by Kris Bryant. When life seems to be too good to be true and love is within reach, Sawyer and Macey discover the truth about the town of Ladybug Junction, and the cold light of reality tests the hearts of these dreamers. (978-1-63679-378-8)

**Eyes on Her** by Eden Darry. When increasingly violent acts of sabotage threaten to derail the opening of her glamping business, Callie Pope is sure her ex, Jules, has something to do with it. But Jules is dead…isn't she? (978-1-63679-214-9)

**Letters from Sarah** by Joy Argento. A simple mistake brought them together, but Sarah must release past love to create a future with Lindsey she never dreamed possible. (978-1-63679-509-6)

**Lost in the Wild** by Kadyan. When their plane crash-lands, Allison and Mike face hunger, cold, a terrifying encounter with a bear, and feelings for each other neither expects. (978-1-63679-545-4)

**Not Just Friends** by Jordan Meadows. A tragedy leaves Jen struggling to figure out who she is and what is important to her. (978-1-63679-517-1)

**Of Auras and Shadows** by Jennifer Karter. Eryn and Rina's unexpected love may be exactly what the Community needs to heal the rot that comes not from the fetid Dark Lands that surround the Community but from within. (978-1-63679-541-6)

**The Secret Duchess** by Jane Walsh. A determined widow defies a duke and falls in love with a fashionable spinster in a fight for her rightful home. (978-1-63679-519-5)

**Winter's Spell** by Ursula Klein. When former college roommates reunite at a wedding in Provincetown, sparks fly, but can they find true love when evil sirens and trickster mermaids get in the way? (978-1-63679-503-4)

**Coasting and Crashing** by Ana Hartnett. Life comes easy to Emma Wilson until Lake Palmer shows up at Alder University and derails her every plan. (978-1-63679-511-9)

**Every Beat of Her Heart** by KC Richardson. Piper and Gillian have their own fears about falling in love, but will they be able to overcome those feelings once they learn each other's secrets? (978-1-63679-515-7)

**Fire in the Sky** by Radclyffe and Julie Cannon. Two women from different worlds have nothing in common and every reason to wish they'd never met—except for the attraction neither can deny. (978-1-63679-561-4)

**Grave Consequences** by Sandra Barret. A decade after necromancy became licensed and legalized, can Tamar and Maddy overcome the lingering prejudice against their kind and their growing attraction to each other to uncover a plot that threatens both their lives? (978-1-63679-467-9)

**Haunted by Myth** by Barbara Ann Wright. When ghost-hunter Chloe seeks an answer to the current spectral epidemic, all clues point to one very famous face: Helen of Troy, whose motives are more complicated than history suggests and whose charms few can resist. (978-1-63679-461-7)

**Invisible** by Anna Larner. When medical school dropout Phoebe Frink falls for the shy costume shop assistant Violet Unwin, everything about their love feels certain, but can the same be said about their future? (978-1-63679-469-3)

**Like They Do in the Movies** by Nan Campbell. Celebrity gossip writer Fran Underhill becomes Chelsea Cartwright's personal assistant with the aim of taking the popular actress down, but neither of them anticipates the clash of their attraction. (978-1-63679-525-6)

**Limelight** by Gun Brooke. Liberty Bell and Palmer Elliston loathe each other. They clash every week on the hottest new TV show, until Liberty starts to sing and the impossible happens. (978-1-63679-192-0)

**The Memories of Marlie Rose** by Morgan Lee Miller. Broadway legend Marlie Rose undergoes a procedure to erase all of her unwanted memories, but as she starts regretting her decision, she discovers that the only person who could help is the love she's trying to forget. (978-1-63679-347-4)

**The Murders at Sugar Mill Farm** by Ronica Black. A serial killer is on the loose in southern Louisiana, and it's up to three women to solve the case while carefully dancing around feelings for each other. (978-1-63679-455-6)

**Playing with Matches** by Georgia Beers. To help save Cori's store and help Liz survive her ex's wedding, they strike a deal: a fake relationship, but just for one week. There's no way this will turn into the real deal. (978-1-63679-507-2)